TORN

TORN

Amber Lehman

CLOSET CASE PRESS

ISBN: 978-0-9795933-6-9
Library of Congress Control Number: 2009926727

1. Fiction 2. High School Students—Fiction

Printed in the USA
First Edition

Cover photography by DTG Photographic
Cover model: Devin Sparkes
Book design by Sun Editing & Book Design, www.suneditwrite.com

Closet Case Press
P.O. Box 12961
Newport Beach, CA 92658
www.closetcasepress.com

Acknowledgements:

To Don Gow for being my faithful first reader. To my editor Sandi Gelles-Cole who made it possible to turn my hope of this book into a reality. And to Jill Ronsley at Sun Editing & Book Design for her masterful work at typesetting, interior design, and cover design. Without your amazing help this book would have never made it to print.

To everyone who has ever doubted or questioned themselves,
this book is dedicated to you.

A NOTE FROM THE AUTHOR

My own difficult childhood made me sensitive to the stories my friends and lovers have shared with me over the years. I have never ceased to be amazed at the gentle intimacy that we humans can have for each other, and on the contrary, have never ceased to be shocked at the tendency for brutal inhumanity. While compiling the stories that over the years have stuck with me, with the dialogue shared from their own life—situations that burned into my memory and still echo years later—I realized that I did not want to document a series of case studies. What rang more true to the emotions that I experienced when hearing these stories was amalgamating the incidents into fictional characters. What were six boys became two; what were ten girls became five. By placing the characters in positions to interact with each other, it makes us care for them and for their hardships as multidimensional persons, and not just case numbers or studies.

If I have been successful in this task, I have created a place in which hearing these stories is as intimate and personal, as confusing and saddening, as the moments when these stories were first shared with me.

The world is a difficult place for children. Thank God we turn out as well as we do.

1

If Sister Augustine's fiery depiction of hell hadn't been so vivid, I swear I would prefer that to what lay ahead. It's not that I hate school or anything, at least not as much as some of my friends, but I'm not exactly excited about starting high school in the public system.

My brother Marc's always been cool but he used to be way stuffier before he moved to England to study. He's always wanted to be a pediatrician and right now he's working as an intern at Hoag hospital and staying with me and my other brother Josh while my Mom is gone for a year on a church mission. Marc and I have always been tight as peas so I'm just glad he's back.

"*Krista*—I'm not going to tell you again."

Except when it comes to getting up for school.

"*Fine* already," I say and rise to my elbow. "I'm getting up."

The only thing worse than waking up at 5:30 A.M. is walking half a mile to school in the freezing cold at 6:00 A.M. I am not looking forward to it. *Zero period should be outlawed.* Why'd I select a class that meets an hour before school normally starts? For God's sake, it's still dark outside! People always think that just because this is Southern California that every minute of the day is perfect and warm, but sometimes like this morning, the fall weather can be colder than the winter. I tried to explain that to my best friend Lindsay after my family and I moved out here from Ohio but she's not buying it. And she's convinced that everyone in California is either an actress or a model and that someday I will be too.

The idea of public school scares me. At least at Our Holy Sisters I never had to worry about kids bringing guns to school and acting like hit-men. Even though my transferring to public school was mom's idea, I'd bet every dollar in my piggy bank that Marc voiced his opinion on the matter too: I remember the day they told me.

Mom's decision is a sound one, he said. Mom approached the topic with me while I was eating a heavenly Cinnabun at the kitchen table, which now looking back at the matter was probably her way of buttering me up.

Out of nowhere she says, "Krista, you're just too sheltered at Our Holy Sisters. I think you need to experience the real world and you're just not going to be exposed to it there." This is the last thing I ever expect to hear coming from mom.

One of mom's favorite sayings is, "Never forget, the people you associate with say everything about you. Steer clear of riff-raff." From what little I've learned about him through Marc, I wish mom would've followed her own advice before she hooked up with my "dad."

I definitely remember Marc, casually leaning against the kitchen counter, adding with a smile, "Try making a few friends that are boys before you start dating . . . better that than decide that they're a foreign species altogether."

Dating . . . now there's something I don't get. Some of my smartest friends from Our Holy Sisters — they're allowed to date boys on the weekends — act like half-wits whenever they're around boys. What's *that* all about? Why do girls get *so* . . . it's as if every girl who kisses a boy loses her brain while they're kissing. Yuck! That's just . . . yuck. I don't want to be seen that way — clinging to a boy like the world will end if he excuses himself to use the restroom.

Now I have to figure out what clothes are "in." *And I thought algebra was stressful!* Last night I spent an hour trying to decide on an outfit to wear and got a zit for my troubles. Usually I don't have to worry about zits; unless I'm super nervous or something, I never get them so I don't have anything to treat them with. That's another reason I know how major today is. I usually *always* have a clear complexion so I know something is up. I run into Josh's bathroom, grab one of the

Stridex pads I always see him using, then start scrubbing my blemish. Thing is, it seems like it's only making my pimple redder.

Anyway, I did study *Seventeen* magazine but almost every page had pictures of girls wearing skin-tight tops that show their stomach. The problem is I don't have many regular clothes to choose from since I used to only need them on the weekends. Except for those velour sweat suits that came out last year which I practically live in because mom bought me one in every color. Even though Josh offered to take me shopping, I said I didn't want to buy anything yet until I can see for myself what everyone's wearing.

Boy I miss mom, but she is in Nicaragua. I talk to her all the time, but talking to her about my zits and clothes doesn't seem the same over a satellite phone.

So I finally decided that I'd go casual: jeans and a conservative white button-up shirt seemed the safest choice. Something straight out of a GAP ad.

I stare at my reflection on the closet door mirror. At least my hair is cooperating today; no static-cling in the air to make my hair dull. If I get any taller this year I might reach five-foot-five. That'd be great. I want to be tall. The taller you are the more regal you look. At least that's my opinion.

In the reflection I can also see my bedroom. This year I think it's time for a change. I've outgrown the frilly lavender bedspread, the clouds on the wallpaper and the matching clouds and rainbows decorating my room. I don't know what I want next exactly, I just know I want something different.

I wish I could say that clothing and décor are the most of my concerns but that would be a lie. Fact is, the thing about Crestmount that scares me the most is having to deal with … boys.

Boys.

Just the thought of them has my nerves in a racket. It doesn't matter that I have two half-brothers. Marc isn't exactly a boy; I still have no idea what to expect. How am I supposed to act around them and what are they going to be like? Are they bullies or will they act like the sex-crazed freaks that are always on MTV? I don't even have a girl friend to eat lunch with so I don't know how I'll spend my time.

If I could make one wish, the only thing I'd hope for is that there's at least one nice person who wants to be my friend. Even a single conversation would be an encouraging sign. I just want to feel accepted. If I don't have to spend lunchtime sitting in a corner by myself, that'll make my day.

The warning bell rang and I ran across the street. I had five minutes to locate the gym.

Few students were on campus this early. I whisked through desolate corridors in search of the dance class that was about to begin. As I turned the corner, a boy barreled into me, slamming me against the hall lockers without apology as he joked with his buddy. I glimpsed varsity jackets — just a flash before my head crashed against corrugated metal and my vision gave way to disorienting bursts of light. I pushed myself off the wall of lockers. The metallic taste of blood filled my mouth; my lower lip began to smart, and my entire head throbbed.

Breathe — don't cry. I straightened, then resumed my search for the school gym. The second bell shrilled above my ears. I was officially late to my first day of school.

The gym sat at the opposite end of campus; the smaller dance room, reserved for our class, was an adjoining room the size of a typical classroom. When I finally walked into the mirrored room where a large group of girls sat patiently on the floor, I was some five minutes late. Luckily the dance teacher was easygoing — so much so that she introduced herself as Bree — as in we were supposed to call her by her first name — how weird. "Why don't you put your bag down?" she brushed off my apology.

Silence filled the room as I quietly walked to the back and placed my dance bag in the corner.

When I turned around, she said, "Take your place behind Carrie, here in the front." She indicated the unclaimed space on the floor behind an attractive girl.

Our eyes met briefly, hers reflected indifference. The fair-haired waif was diminutive compared to the other students. She wore a black unitard accented by an exotically tasseled tangerine wrap, tied around her waist. Unlike the casual clothing worn by her peers, her mysterious style piqued my curiosity.

I wordlessly took my seat.

Class began, and each girl practiced her technique against the teacher's. They were surprisingly good—accomplished in ability, individual in style. One was exceptional: a petite brunette with Indian eyes.

Carrie came up for her turn. She flipped back her sun-gold mane, and it fell loosely around her shoulders, cascaded down her back. Her pale sapphire eyes focused on an invisible spot in the distance. It was almost disquieting, the way she danced; her slender frame seemed too fragile to execute such powerful moves with such fluid grace.

As I sat there watching, I realized that, in spite of my predawn regrets, I had made the right choice. The familiar, addictive draw of mirrored walls and expansive flooring just begging to be danced upon. A rush of excitement coursed through me, and I imagined my own music, a new beat, and exhilarating moves. Dance class would be fun.

It was almost 7:30; first period would begin soon. Everyone adjourned to the dance team locker room, a special room full of floor-length mirrors and standing lockers, reserved for the privileged few. I could definitely get used to this. The corner locker I'd been assigned was just perfect for me.

I stashed my dance bag in my locker and looked over my shoulder. Carrie was three lockers away.

She pressed a towel to her hairline, curtailing beads of perspiration. She looked over at me, acknowledging me with a single raised brow. "You look like a sacrifice. Upperclassmen are gonna have a field day with you."

Is this California's equivalent of a greeting? "Thanks for sharing," I said, my tone flat. "I don't suppose you'd have any useful advice?"

She eyed me skeptically, taking her time. "You new to this district?"

"I'm from Ohio."

"I guess that'd explain the Plain Jane look you've got goin' on."

I turned my back to her, slammed my locker shut, and tried to ignore the nagging ache in my throat as tears threatened.

When I turned back, she had moved to the locker beside me. "You're lucky you're in the dance program. You just saved yourself from being a social outcast."

"The first blessing of the day."

"Gotta do something about your wardrobe, though. You can't pull that off for long."

"If I make any friends, I'll be sure to ask for their advice."

Her eyes narrowed, scrutinized me; then she hesitated as if making a life-altering decision. She lowered her towel, and extended her other hand toward me. "Carrie Stevens."

I accepted her handshake tentatively at first, then relaxed when she finally smiled.

"Krista McKinley."

"I usually don't befriend newcomers, but..." She shrugged. "If you stick with me and my friends, you're as good as in."

2

The corridors of Crestmount are so confusing! Seriously, it's ridiculous. I have to check my class schedule for like the fiftieth time because I have to know where I'm going before I even *attempt* to squeeze through the mass of students roaming the campus. The bell shrills above me warning that there's only five minutes left before next class starts. I head that way, past the sounds of lockers slamming and clips of conversations from the confusion of voices around me.

A couple of students stand by the lockers on the other side of the court. Carrie is one of them. She's talking to a boy who looks at least a foot taller than her. He must be her boyfriend. What's strange is that he looks more preppie than the boys from Ohio prep school. I can't imagine what they'd have in common. They're laughing now and he gives her a hug—not a polite hug but a lingering, *full body* contact kind of hug. I can feel myself staring as he kisses her. This isn't just some peck on the lips; it's totally blatant and lingers as long as their hug. But what *really* gets me flustered is this: this guy, still kissing Carrie—I kid you not—looks right at me while they kiss then actually squeezes her butt. He pulls back from Carrie, licks his lips at me as if she's not even there.

3

It's the first day of actual practice and I'm still not sure what to expect. Bree hadn't been too specific when telling us what to wear. I decide to wear my dance clothes under my regular clothes. That way I won't be so nervous and I can kinda get an idea of what's to come next. How everyone interacts, what they're wearing. In Ohio everyone had to wear white tights and black leotards so the teacher could see the lines of our bodies and correct our posture, so that's what I'm wearing today. I imagine Bree has to correct us too; how else will we get better? The strange thing is, I've just learned that our dance group is more of a mix of dance and cheerleading. Nothing like we had at my old school because this squad includes *boys,* as I've just discovered today. This throws me off a little since they weren't at our earlier practice and I'm not used to working with boys in such close proximity. I'm not exactly happy. Right now everyone is gathered outside of the dance room.

The excitable one—a thin boy with short, spiky hair bleached nearly white—was surrounded by a group of girls, engaged in a conversation about hair dying. He was distressed by his black roots, which were already showing after only a week.

Hmm...

I decided to forgo that circle for the moment, and joined a different group of girls.

Was that Carrie?

She noticed me approaching and smiled wryly. "Welcome aboard."

Carrie introduced me to the other girls, including her two best friends, Chloe and Joy.

But it was another boy who truly held my interest. He seemed strangely out of place as he sat in solitude on the edge of the school's field. He seemed unusually withdrawn, which made it hard to believe that he would be involved in the sport at all. The sunlight accentuated his coloring, turned his mocha hair and toffee-colored skin to a flattering golden-bronze. A single dandelion held his attention, and he plucked it, twirling the stem between his finger and thumb.

"Oh, that's Nick," Carrie said. "Come on, I'll introduce you to him."

When he saw us approaching, he self-consciously dropped the flower behind him and stood. He had engaging green eyes—eyes the cloudy color of green tea ice cream, soft and unassuming. He had exceptionally high cheekbones, and a pair of the fullest, poutiest lips I'd ever seen.

"Hi, I'm Nick."

"Krista's new here. I'm taking her under my wing," Carrie said.

He nodded. "Great. Glad to have you on the team."

I smiled, relieved by their acceptance, but feeling awkward nonetheless.

"Did Aeleise bring you to school today?" Carrie asked him.

He nodded, his gaze diverting to something behind us.

"How is the happy couple, anyway?" she asked.

Nick looked as if he'd been catapulted back into reality. He blinked. "Oh—Aeleise. We're fine…everything's great." He smiled, lips together.

Carrie turned to me. "Aeleise is a sophomore on JV cheer; Nick likes his women older."

Nick's cheeks flushed at her comment.

She looked at him again. "How long have the two of you been together now?"

"Uh…I don't know."

He began chewing on his thumbnail.

They're totally making out again; kissing six inches in front of me, making these sounds that make my stomach drop because I can tell they wish they were doing more. I swear, if you've never had this happen in front of you before, it's *worse* than embarrassing.

He has her back pressed against the lockers; his hands are on either side of her.

I slam my locker shut and turn to leave. Carrie's boyfriend says, "Hey—"

The last thing I want to do right now is to look at either of them, but I make myself turn around.

"Do you have any idea where I could find a backpack like yours?" he says. All nonchalant like, as if two seconds ago they weren't trying to make babies between layers of clothes. "We were hoping they'd have them in black or burgundy instead of sparkling bubblegum pink with faux angora."

"Well, I don't know if—"

"Forget the bag for now," he says and peels his body off Carrie's. "Carrie tells me you're in her dance class; you're not half bad either. I'm Brandon," he says and then lifts my hand until the back of it brushes his lips. I freeze, then pull my hand back.

"Actually he's more like Lucifer in the Flesh," Carrie says.

Brandon ignores her. "You're not from around here, are you?"

I open my mouth to speak but Brandon says, "My eyes are up here."

I don't even know him, but I hate Brandon right now; hate how he makes his voice sound like he's naked or something when my cheeks are already burning. I meet his gaze; he's got the most amazing amber eyes. "Ohio originally," I manage to say.

Brandon's smile is more like a smirk. "So what's with the K-mart Jaclyn Smith collection?"

"I'm sorry?"

"Brandon's always teasing," Carrie says.

Brandon reaches out and runs his fingers through my hair. "Is it naturally straight?" he says.

Carrie swats his chest. "Lighten up, Brandon. You want to scare her away already?"

"*Heavens*, no. So what's your story?" Brandon asks, his eyes still focused on me.

"I don't think I have one."

"We'll change that," he says. "We'll get together tomorrow. Show you around."

Finally. Someone to talk to. Even if Brandon and Carrie *do* seem a little off I'm not about to be picky. Anything is better than hanging out alone.

Brandon looks at his watch. "I've gotta split if I'm gonna catch the swell." He looks at Carrie. "Call you tonight?"

"Yep."

He kisses her cheek then turns to me. He puts his hand on my shoulder then slides it down my arm to my elbow. I freeze. He's smiling like he knows a secret I don't. "Krista...a pleasure."

I'm just standing here, stunned. He vanishes into the crowd. I hear Carrie behind me say, "Sorry...sometimes he comes on kinda strong."

Kind of? Why does she let her boyfriend get away with that? I want to tell her to make him keep his paws to himself, or at least not let them stray beyond her. Instead I say, "Is he always like that?"

"Only if he likes you. Brandon won't give the time of day to most people. But he's a total flirt otherwise. You'll get used to it."

I turn to face her. "Isn't flirting something reserved for times when you're single?"

"Depends on who you are." Carrie's busy studying her hair for split-ends. "I thought you were really good at technique today," she says.

"Thanks."

She stops fussing with her hair and looks at me. "So tomorrow. Let's meet at these lockers come lunchtime."

"Uh, sure," I say.

Carrie turns away, starts walking toward the field. "See ya, manana," she says.

"So, what are you?" Carrie says.

What are you? I hate that question. I squirm in my skin, actually itch. I can never find an answer I'm comfortable with. I'm a doll, I'm a mouse, I'm an orangutan, I'm a bunny hopping away, I'm a kid being dragged here on a slave ship, I'm human but I sometimes feel less-than, and I'm the misfit girl sitting across from you. My name is Krista McKinley and I *hate* it when you ask me that. I can already hear the progression of questions, the never-ending tape recording that plays in my head: Who's black—your mom or your dad? What do they do? Where is he? Have you ever met him? Do you want to?...and so on and so forth. It gets old. Really, *really* old.

"You've got this exotic look happening...sorta Mariah Carry-ish," Brandon says. I open my mouth to speak but Brandon adds, "She's part black, I believe."

At least he saved me from saying it. I hold up my finger and sing, "*Ding, ding, ding.*"

"*Really?*" Carrie says.

"Guilty as charged."

Actually, the truth is a little more profound. My father did not marry my mother. Marc and Josh are sons of my mother's husband Phillip. After she divorced him she hung out with my father. He disappeared, the usual. Phillip still shows up to see Marc and Josh but I have only Mom and Mom has a thing about God and the church.

"There are better things to talk about," I say.

"Suggest one," Brandon says.

"No offense, but you two make an odd couple."

Brandon laughs. "Did we ever tell you we were a couple?"

"It's pretty obvious."

"Wow—I owe you five bucks, Carrie."

She grins. "Cash only, please."

"Did I miss something?"

"I suppose saying yes is a credit to us," Brandon says. "Ball's in your court, Carrie."

"I'm trying to decide whether to tell her," she says.

"If it's something about dating, don't worry," I said. "I have brothers. Anything you tell me, I won't be shocked."

"Brandon's gay."

Except that.

Gay? "He's ... *gay?* What do you mean *gay?* As in homo*sexual gay?*"

"Is there any other kind?"

"But you two were just all *over* each other—he practically made you swallow his *tongue!* That didn't look very *gay* to me."

Carrie's laughing, first time I've seen her smile. Maybe this is her way of telling me she thinks I'm stupid, that I'm gullible down to the last.

"What are you talking about? He had his tongue down your throat."

"Boy, you have a lot to learn. What do they do to you in Catholic School, sew it up?"

"What's so funny?" I say. I could've choked on the intensity of Brandon's presence—*nowhere* in his masculinity did I pick up any hint that he was gay.

"Should I have kept my mouth shut?"

"I don't know yet," I say. "It's still soaking in. You're telling me that he's not interested in girls *at all?*"

"Sure he is ... as friends."

Unbelievable!

I'm searching for something to say. Something that's not too offensive but doesn't say much. Right now the best I can come up with is, "Interesting ... Wow. That's like ... interesting." So I could've chosen better words ... I'll have time to work on that. I shake my head. "I never would have thought ..."

"Most people don't."

Brandon's leaning casually against the hall lockers, hands hidden inside his pant pockets, one leg crossed in front of the other.

"*Hey,*" Carrie says, "You told me I could tell her." She's touching up her face with the assistance of her mirrored compact.

Brandon gives me this lingering look, almost like he's sizing me up. My heart skips a beat.

"And yes ..." he says, and then his arrogance melts into something silky and toying, "I've had sex with girls. Why?" I can't believe his lazy smile, or how his voice and eyes charm like the snake's in Eden. "Do you want to come home with me—play doctor in my bedroom?"

Talk about *direct*. My gaze drops and my cheeks respond in rose. "No—I mean … that's not what—"

He crackles with laughter. "She falters. *Relax*—I'm just giving you shit." He softens his manner some. "Really, you shouldn't let me get away with that. Carrie will tell you. She hassles me all the time."

"It's true," Carrie says.

Brandon pushes away from the lockers. "So our charade is finie. Well done, Carrie."

At this point, there's only one thing I want to know. "Does this mean the make out sessions come to an end?"

"Disappointed?" he says and smiles.

"*Relieved.*"

"I gotta go," he says, "I'm meeting up with Ryan."

"Say 'hey' to him for me," Carrie says.

"Done." Brandon starts walking away without as much as a goodbye.

On the way home all the queasy spots disappear in my stomach and I realize I have met two people who make me feel comfortable. How can that be? "What are you?' the question everyone asked. So maybe it was good to be around other people who were a little hard to pin down.

4

Kristaaatcrestmountblogspot.com. Met a bunch of awesome people over the last three weeks and already have a girlfriend though not as cool as Lindsay. I am adding these people, Carrie, Brandon, Ryan, and the others to myspace. Basically Brandon and Ryan are the hottest guys in school. I never thought I would think about guys that way but something weird is happening to me (those with password click here).

OK so public school wasn't as bad as I thought. I had friends. The classes were as good as those at Our Holy Sisters. And I had dance.

One Friday evening Carrie phoned with news that Brandon had called for a lunchtime meeting the following day. We were all to meet at the designated spot in the afternoon. By this time I was used to Brandon's way of pretending he was prince of Crestmount High or something, but underneath he was so kind that we all let him get away with it. Underneath everything there was something so sad about him.

Carrie and I found Aeleise, Nick, and Ryan, Brandon's best friend, all waiting for us beneath the specified oak tree, and we joined their circle. Brandon was standing, pacing, not his usual mellow self and I could see he was impatient to get whatever this was over with.

Carrie's eyes went to Brandon. "What's this all about?" she asked as she settled Indian-style onto the grass. I sat down next to her.

"I'll tell you in a minute—after I make something clear. I need all of you to understand what's going on so this won't accidentally backfire on me. I don't want anyone saying the wrong thing, assuming they're helping me."

"What are you talking about?" Carrie asked.

Brandon turned to Ryan. "Ryan, I need your help with something."

"Sure. Tell me what to do."

Brandon looked at him with affectionate pride. "I knew I could count on you." He smiled. "The Homecoming ballots. My name doesn't make the list this year."

Ryan whistled, and leaned back on his hands. "Tall order. You couldn't have asked me to stop the predicted rain showers instead?" He looked at Brandon seriously. "Why not?"

"Because … it's the same thing every year, since junior high. I don't need the added attention, and I'm tired of being crowned as some imaginary ideal." He shook his head. "Until the committee announces their decision, I'll walk around campus under the scrutiny of every student for the next four weeks. Once I'm chosen, the interested stares will drag on for at least another two weeks. I'm not into it." He pulled on the cuff of his shirt until it was perfectly symmetrical with the other. "Besides, it's about time some other chump gets the chance to play prince. I don't need another year of false ego gratification from the students of Crestmount."

"Is it really that horrible?" Nick's voice, meek and bewildered. He was so quiet that it was easy to forget he was there. "I mean, it's supposed to be an honor, isn't it?"

Brandon smiled carefully at Nick. "I suppose it is, but I'm not playing that role anymore." Nick still looked baffled. "Chances for *princess* come down to Jessa or Milla. I'm not spending my evening playing the pretty for either of them. I'm doing what I want to this year. And I'm not getting sucked into that damn Homecoming court again. I'm not pretending to be their prince."

Ryan's eyebrows rose. "I think you're nuts."

"I think you're straight."

Ryan laughed, shaking his head. "I won't argue that."

Nick's eyes had gone wide at Brandon's comeback. Apparently Aeleise hadn't clued him in. "You're *not?*" he blurted.

Brandon's smile was in place, but the stare he directed at Nick would've made a snake slink out of its skin. "My, he's quick, Aeleise," he said, eyes intense on Nick. "Give the boy a star."

Brandon shifted his attention to Ryan. "Just make sure my name is off the ballot."

"Aye-aye captain. I've got my orders."

———

It was a rare moment when I crossed paths with Josh on campus. For some reason he was near the freshman court and by himself; he appeared distracted by his thoughts. Carrie and I were just getting ready to part ways when I stopped him.

"Josh, wait," I said, when he almost passed me by. "I want to introduce you to Carrie." He stopped and turned around, his hands stuffed deep inside his jacket pockets. He freed one hand to shake hers. "Hi How's it goin'?"

She just smiled politely and accepted the handshake.

Josh was pretty popular at Crestmount, not least of all because he was on the football team. My brother was also very attractive to women, though I failed to see why. Of course they never saw him hanging out in his dirty socks and smelly jerseys or had to see him with his zit cream on.

Not ten seconds had passed before a girl materialized who could've passed for Miss Teen USA, with her feminine appeal and action-figure body. She approached with a smooth, gliding walk. Her blunt-cut hair was waist-length, and remarkably thick for being bone straight; she wore it unadorned. I envied her beguiling hazel eyes. She was taller than I was and had legs long enough to earn top scores in swimsuit competitions. She wore white cigarette pants and a tight white angora sweater that made her look like an ice princess. Her pink Kate Spade bag was the only color to her—well, that and her matching shade of lipstick.

She stopped between Carrie and Josh.

"Carrie, aren't you going to introduce me to your friend?" she asked with a sweetness I didn't trust.

"Considering I just met him five seconds ago, I'll allow, you to do that yourself."

The blond looked annoyed, but extended the back of her hand to Josh, like some fifties movie star. "I'm Jessa. Pleased to meet you."

"Josh," was all he said. He looked at me. "Kris, I gotta go." He gave a brief nod of acknowledgement to Carrie. "Nice meeting you."

He left, just like that.

His rebuff startled Jessa, but she was poised enough to glide through it. She turned to me. "I don't believe we've met."

I was relieved she didn't offer her hand to me. I wasn't about to bestow kisses, regardless of how charming she pretended to be.

Carrie said, "This is Krista. I believe I mentioned her to you."

"Ahh, yes. That's right. You came to us from Ohio, correct?"

"Yes."

"How . . . quaint." She smiled disingenuously and I had to control my urge to knock it off her face. "How do you know . . . Josh, was it?"

I looked at her pointedly. "He's my brother."

"Your brother; how wonderful. Has Carrie introduced you to many people so far?"

"We seem to be doing fine," I said.

"I'd like to introduce you to a few of my friends. I think you'd benefit from meeting Adara and Milla, wouldn't you agree Carrie?"

"If you say so," she said.

"We'll have to be sure to get together soon—all three of us. I'd love to get to know you better. Why don't we do that sometime later this week?" She looked at her watch, which I had thought was a silver bracelet. "I need to be going; we'll talk later, hmm?" She smiled at the both of us, and then sashayed away.

I turned to Carrie, almost bemused. "Is she for *real*? What *was* that?"

"That was one hundred percent Jessa Simonson. I'd say you're as good as in with her; she obviously found your brother exciting enough to make an effort. That happens about as often as you'll find all the planets in alignment."

"Well, she'd better come up with a different approach if she wants to make headway with Josh. He's repelled by anything that pretentious."

"You don't think he'd overlook that because she's so attractive? Most guys do."

I shook my head. "I could always be wrong, but if I know Josh, there's no way he'd play along with that."

She laughed. "If your brother can refuse her, then he deserves a gold medal. I haven't seen anyone deny her yet."

"Well, let's just keep our fingers crossed," I said, and smiled. "I've got to get to class; you'd better hurry or you'll be late to yours."

"Oh God," she said when she realized the time. She turned and started running toward the classrooms at the opposite end of the campus, calling, "I'll talk to you later, Kris."

Kris. Hmm ... we had moved on to nicknames. I smiled as I entered my classroom and took my seat.

———

The final bell for the day had sounded, and I was running behind in biology. Our first lab hadn't been the greatest—I had dropped the frog on the floor—poor, rubbery sacrifice—but not on purpose; I couldn't help that the smell of formaldehyde sent me running to the door, desperate to steal a breath of tree-clean air.

Yes ... I was off to a brilliant start. I cleaned up the entire mess as quickly as I could and made my way to practice.

"Krista!"

My name sailed through the hot, dry air as I was about to enter the locker room. Only a few minutes remained before cheer practice began and I still had to change clothes. I looked over my shoulder to see Brandon standing in the sophomore quad by his locker. He motioned me to come over.

He called from where he stood, "I need to ask you a question about today's Latin assignment. I missed third period."

I sighed. Of course he missed it. He'd been surfing. I ran over to give him a brief recap, praying I wouldn't be late for practice. I was out of breath by the time I reached him. He stood casually beside his locker, watching as I worked to catch my breath; there was no urgency in his manner. Great for him, but I didn't have time to dawdle.

"Our homework assignment is to complete pages thirty-seven through forty from our textbooks; she wants them written out completely, both questions and answers—"

"I don't take Latin, Kris."

I gave him questioning and impatient eyes. "What?"

"I said, I don't take Latin. Would you like to be my date for Homecoming?"

I stared at him—just stared.

"Kris?" A thread of concern in the utterance of my name. He looked at me closer.

"I'm sorry." I realized how diminutive my voice sounded and took a few even breaths, trying for composure. "Could you please repeat yourself? I want to be sure I heard you correctly."

He smiled at my uncertainty. "Will you be my date for Homecoming?"

I *had* heard correctly—but I never *imagined*... "*Me?*"

"I don't see anyone else standing beside you." He looked left, then right. "Not anyone within the length of a football field, anyway. Yes, it's safe to assume my question was directed at you."

I absorbed the shock, finally allowing myself to smile.

"You can think about it, if you'd prefer... take some time to consider. No pressure," he said.

I shook my head. "No—I mean... I don't need time to consider. I would love to go with you to Homecoming."

He smiled at that. "Great. We can go over things later. You'd better get moving for practice... sorry I pulled you away at the last minute."

I could only smile. "That's okay." He had just made my day—no, my week. I was so excited—suddenly Homecoming seemed like a wonderful thing!

"Okay," he said. "I'll talk to you later. Go easy on those back handsprings." He grinned, then headed for his car.

I sprinted to the locker room, bursting with joy. Carrie had already changed but was waiting for me in the locker room.

She grinned when she saw my expression. "Someone looks happy."

"Tell me truthfully," I said through a suspecting smile, "did you have any hand in this at all?"

"In what?"

"Brandon just asked me to Homecoming," I said, still marveling at the fact.

She jumped from the bench with an excited squeal and gave me a quick, crushing hug. I'm not sure which of us was more delighted.

"Did you set this up?"

"No—I swear, Kris. I just had this feeling that he would ask you." She sat down facing me, straddling the bench.

"Well, I can't say I'm disappointed," I confessed.

"This is *so* perfect. Ryan asked me to go with him."

"Yeah?" I smiled at the news.

She nodded, matching my smile. "We should all go together." Her eyes had taken on a dreamy stare. "I'm so happy, Kris."

I pulled her to her feet. "Come on, let's go. Miss Delaney doesn't care how happy we are."

I didn't hear from Brandon until he called at 8:00 Saturday morning, suggesting we begin our quest for Homecoming attire. Carrie and I agreed, and by 10:00 the three of us were cruising the shopping center.

Brandon was in rare form, definitely out to make an impression. I mentally dubbed him Venus Mantrap, taking in the flattering fit of his black slacks and a body-contouring burgundy shirt. It should've been illegal for him to look that good.

We made it to the third shop before someone caught his eye. I caught the slick shift of his attention—only a glance, but enough to make his assessment—toward a boy our age who was window shopping outside the boutique door. His prey spotted, Brandon cased the situation carefully, and then prepared to slide in for the kill—he was just that smooth. His eyes, as cunning as his intentions, stayed fixed on the boy as he addressed us.

"Excuse me, ladies. I have an acquaintance to make." He was off.

Carrie laughed. "Well, there goes our one male opinion." She shook her head as she filtered through the racks of dresses. "Brandon—on the prowl again."

"He does this a lot?" I asked as my gaze trailed Brandon to his meeting with the boy with candy-kissed looks. His hair was the color of iced lemons, his skin fair enough to be the blush of a peach. He reminded me of a sweet Dutch boy. Within moments, Brandon had him laughing.

Her brows arched. "Just wait—you haven't seen Brandon at his finest yet. He gets guys we could only dream about. He has a talent for persuasion." She shook her head. "I don't know how he does it."

"And he's not dating anyone?"

Her bright laugh was as animated as it was knowing. "*Brandon?* Oh, he's dating *everyone.* Brandon bores easily. He collects phone numbers—kind of like stamps; it's mostly for sport. He doesn't call half of them, just likes having them. His conquests, I guess. He keeps them in a fishbowl under his bed."

We broke into laughter. Brandon's fishbowl of opportunities.

We found a shop that sold formal wear exclusively. We walked into a world of designer dresses in every color—gowns for pageants, cocktails, formals, and weddings.

Fifteen minutes later, Brandon appeared as if he had never been gone.

"So, did you get his number?" Carrie asked expectantly.

"You doubt me?" he said, sounding almost offended.

"Well? What's the story, then?"

"Don't know yet. If I care to find out, I'll call." He held up as evidence a folded piece of paper with a phone number penned in blue ink across it. He tucked it back into his pocket. I just looked at him. "Any luck so far?" he asked, looking at the gowns in our arms.

Carrie said, "Maybe. We need your opinion."

"Well, that's what I'm here for."

"You *do* remember!" she chided him.

"All right, already—do I get a fashion show, or what?"

"Okay, we're changing." She grabbed my arm and pulled me toward the dressing rooms.

After trying on a few selections, I emerged in a strapless dress made from pale lilac taffeta. The full-length gown was form fitting, and flared delicately at the bottom, reminding me of a mermaid's tail. The bodice was intricately beaded with dainty gems in varying shades of cream and frosted lilac.

Brandon circled me, eyeing me up and down slowly. He cocked his head, his expression sliding into a confused frown. "Why I like this dress is beyond me," he said. "It's very…innocent." He scratched his head as he studied me from all angles. "I'm so accustomed to those racy numbers I always see…but…for some reason, I find this remarkably fetching on you. I actually like it. It suits you well."

"Better than the last one?" I asked.

He nodded. "Definitely. I think this is the one."

I looked at my reflection in the three-way mirror. He held up a pair of white gloves against my dress, tilting his head in consideration. "These." He handed them to me and I slid them on.

"Do *you* like it?" he asked.

"Yeah." I decided I did.

"That's all that matters."

Carrie emerged from the fitting room in a black, silk chiffon gown that held to her body like a whisper. It hung from a single strap around her neck, the front draping like an expensive silk veil in the shape of a crescent at her breasts. It was extremely elegant and complimented her delicate figure beautifully.

Brandon's eyes twinkled and he smiled fiendishly. "I would expect nothing less. Carrie, you look marvelous. Don't bother with anything else. This gown makes you look stunning."

Her smile was bright, yet worried. "Do you think Ryan will like it?"

"Will Ryan *like* it?" He chuckled. "Once he remembers that it's impolite to stare with his mouth open, I'd say yes. Ryan will most certainly appreciate the dress."

Carrie looked at me. "Let's put these on hold, Kris. We can come back tomorrow and pick them up."

"Nonsense," Brandon said. "We'll be taking them home today."

Carrie said, "We only planned on looking today."

"Get changed and bring me the dresses," he said.

"You're not buying our dresses," Carrie said.

"Yes I am. Carrie, don't squabble over something so petty."

I joined Carrie. "Brandon, I can't let you pay for my dress."

"Yes, you can—and you will." He sounded exasperated. "Pets, please don't be difficult. I *want* to do this—I can *afford* to do this. Your resistance is counter-productive. Let's all see something besides a mall tomorrow. When I'm strapped for cash, I'll let you know." Brandon beckoned me with a quick flit of his hand. "Let me unzip you."

I went to him and turned around; he carefully released the zipper.

Carrie said, "If you insist they leave the store with us now, then we'll pay you for them when we get home."

He shook his head. "You'll accept them as a gift."

Carrie took a stance. "*No.* Brandon, you're not even my date."

"Yes, I know. Yours is off battling flying pucks at the moment. And as far as Ryan goes, I'm picking up his attire with mine. Fashion with him is risky at best, and I'm not feeling confident enough to gamble on Homecoming. I won't allow your escort to be an eyesore, and I can't trust that he won't show up in Nikes and a tie. Take a hint from Ryan. I assure you, he'll be overjoyed that he's been spared the chore."

"Are you financing Homecoming night for the entire school?" she asked saucily.

"Carrie," he said in warning. "Bring me the dress."

Carrie turned to me. "Come on, Krista. Let's change and give them to the saleslady."

Brandon sighed. "Wait." He walked up to Carrie, gently put his hand on her arm. "Carrie," he said in an appeasing tone. "I hate arguing with you over such silly things. I didn't mean to get you all worked up. Hug?"

Carrie's frustration seemed to ease away, the tension slowly leaving her shoulders as she hugged Brandon, still wearing something close to a pout. He hugged her, and whatever he was quietly saying to her, I couldn't hear. His whispered words disappeared behind her ear in something close to a nuzzle. Her smile broke into a faint giggle, and I noticed he was running his hands gently up and down her back. I squinted, trying unsuccessfully to get a better look at what he was doing.

He gave her a quick kiss on the cheek. "I'll be waiting for you out here," he said.

Brandon gave me a gentle smile, but he looked almost weary.

I shrugged it off and walked into the changing room.

When we left the dressing room. Brandon wasn't anywhere in sight.

"Great," Carrie said. "We've been abandoned again for the next hot guy that passed by the window."

The woman behind the register called out to us, "*There* you are." Her perky disposition shone through from twenty feet away. She left her station to meet us, and took the dresses.

Carrie said, "We'd like to put these on hold until tomorrow."

The woman smiled vibrantly. "You already own the dresses, dear. I was just going to wrap them up for you."

"I'm sorry...?" Carrie said, her forehead creased.

"Well, that nice, handsome boy you came in with has already paid for them. He told me to let you know he'd be waiting at Starbucks downstairs. Very charming boy," she added.

Carrie laughed. "Yes, he's always surprising us," she said. "How much were the dresses?"

The woman shook her head with a teasing smile and wagged her finger at Carrie. "He warned me about you. I had specific instructions not to tell. What were his words again?" Her face brightened. "Oh, yes — 'You may tell them how lovely they look, give them their gowns, and tell them where they can find me,'" she repeated, "'nothing more.'"

Carrie supplied a phony, fluttering laugh, and allowed the woman to wrap our dresses. Still smiling, she muttered, "That clever, conniving *shit!*"

That a woman of her maturity had taken directions so expressly from a sixteen-year-old, allowing him to dictate her behavior down to the last detail, amazed me. We collected our packages, thanked the sales clerk, and made for the coffee shop.

"What now?" I asked Carrie.

"We say thank you. Kris—we'll never win. It's useless to challenge Brandon. You'll lose every time."

We found him entertaining a stranger over a cup of latte. This boy had short, almost black hair, and looked Brandon's age, if not older. Brandon was studying him the way one would a museum curiosity. He nodded now and again, seemingly interested in what he was saying, occasionally offering an expressive facial gesture for the other boy's benefit. Brandon relaxed in his chair, sipping at his beverage, his casual, laid-back manner matching his posture, while the other boy leaned forward, eagerly involved in this one-to-one.

"Hey, Casanova," Carrie called.

Brandon looked over as we walked through the door. He brightened and stood immediately, excusing himself to come greet us. "May I get you two something to drink?" he asked.

"I think you've gotten us enough," she said. "You're absolutely impossible, you know that?" she said.

He smiled. "That's what I live for."

She sighed. "Thank you, Brandon. But you really shouldn't have."

"You're most welcome. Come," he said with an elfin grin, "meet my new friend."

5

The lunchtime bell rang, and I joined the stampede to the hallways, eager to get to my locker. I gathered my books and my purse, and headed for what was by now my usual meeting spot.

Chloe called out to me just as I reached the door, "Don't forget, there's no practice after school today."

I turned around, books pressed against my chest, still managing a slow retreat as I spoke. "I remember. Nothing until tomorrow, right?"

"Right."

"See you then." I took a springing step backward. I smacked straight into someone and fell hard, flat on my butt on the dirty concrete. My books flew from my arms. Students stepped over and on them, bumping into me in a mad rush to their next class. I quickly recovered and retrieved a stray sheet of paper—the homework I'd completed for fifth period—now bearing a brown shoe print in a questionable size five. Great. As I reached for my first notebook, someone grabbed me firmly by the arm and hoisted me to my feet. I looked up into deep, cocoa-brown eyes I'd never seen before.

"Sorry about that. You okay?" he asked.

I nodded, unable to speak; was it the lingering shock of the fall, or the fresh shock of seeing this Adonis-like figure now clutching my arm? The Adonis stopped by my side. "Are you okay?"

"I'm fine," I said, regaining my composure, straightening my clothes, and dusting myself off. "Thank you."

"You sure?"

I nodded and the man with the cocoa brown eyes walked away.

"Nice spill," a male voice said behind me. I looked coolly over my shoulder. Brandon rested indolently against the hall lockers, not three feet away. "Pity we can't have an instant replay."

"Have you been standing there this entire time?"

"No. Just long enough to catch the show." He languidly pushed away from the lockers. "You look a little rattled. May I help you with your books?"

"I'm fine, thank you."

He shrugged, slow and indifferent. "Suit yourself. I was just on my way out. I'm taking lunch off campus."

"I thought this was a closed campus."

"Your point being?"

"Can't you get suspended for that?"

"Only if you're caught."

Surprised by his casual disregard for authority, I asked, "The thought of suspension doesn't bother you?"

"Not particularly. Actually, I find their flawed methods of recourse humorous." His shrug was slow and arrogant, and he slipped his hands inside his trouser pockets. "But if they insist I don't attend school as punishment for my actions, who am I to argue?" He smiled, lazy and mischievous. "I'll be free to surf the entire day without interruption."

I shook my head. "What about your parents? Wouldn't they be mad?"

His brow arched. "My parents are the least of my concerns. They'll be about as moved by school policies as I am." He sounded bored by the topic.

"Sure you don't care to join me?" he asked.

"I'm afraid I'm not as fortunate as you. My brother isn't that lenient."

He smiled softly. "Another time, then." He made the slightest bow and said, "Adieu," then turned in the other direction.

They issued the ballots right before break.

We had succeeded in our mission: Brandon's name wasn't on the ballot. Not only did people notice, they demanded to know why. Someone not so quietly asked, "Where the hell is Brandon's name?" The boy with fair strawberry hair and even fairer freckles was generally quiet, which added to my surprise at his outburst. He was one of six sophomores in my class.

"Nicely said," another student observed.

I returned my attention to the list of candidates. I was happy to see that Ryan's name made the ballot—that was the easiest selection to make. I decided to give my vote to Milla for sophomore Princess—at least she wasn't as obnoxious as Jessa.

I passed my folded ballot forward.

In the hallway, I ran into Ryan. Ryan had huge blue eyes and when he was upset, like now, he looked like a picture in a cat calendar.

"Ryan—what's wrong?"

He shook his head. "This wasn't supposed to happen. My name wasn't supposed to be on the ballot."

"Why not? I voted for you," I said with a smile.

"I wish you hadn't."

My smile dropped.

"*Shit*—how lame does it look, after I practically had to *beg* Darian to keep Brandon from being a nominee, to now find myself in his place? That wasn't what this was about—I wasn't trying to petition myself in."

"So don't worry about it. No one's going to think anything of it."

"I'm not popular enough to make the ballot, Kris. I wouldn't even flatter myself."

"Ryan—" I looked at his distress, noting that his striking crystal blue eyes had deepened a shade. "You don't give yourself enough credit. You're on the ballot because you're meant to be."

"You don't understand—you haven't been with my class year after year. Brandon's going to think I'm a joke. I'm not ready to have him laugh in my face."

Someone stopped behind Ryan, clapped both hands on his shoulders. I was as startled as he was. Brandon leaned closer, his face beside Ryan's.

"Now why would I do a cruel thing like that?"

"Brandon—"

"You didn't answer my question, friend." He tightened his grip on Ryan. His eyes flicked to me. "Hi, Kris."

"Hi."

Ryan said, "Because you'd think it's funny. And...because you could."

Brandon let go. Ryan spun to face him.

"You disappoint me, Ryan. We're friends." He waited for Ryan to reply, but he was silent. "My sincere thanks for keeping my name off the ballot. I now have one less headache." He slipped his hands into his trouser pockets and smiled. "You did well—I told you that you were capable. You had my vote long ago."

Ryan, still looking unsettled, backed away. "I've gotta go. I'll see you guys later."

Ryan walked away.

Turning to Brandon, I said, "I was excited for him. I thought he'd be excited, too."

"Ryan's...a tricky one. I'm afraid his pride bruises easily. I tried to warn him."

"You *knew* about it?"

He nodded.

The jarring sound of the warning bell brought our conversation to a halt.

"Education calls," he said dryly.

"I'll see you later," I said.

He nodded and took off in the other direction.

———

Carrie and I sat side by side in the freshman section as people continued to pour through the gym doors. The assembly was scheduled to start at 2:15. We spotted Brandon and Ryan sitting next to each other across the gym, and waved. Ryan nudged Brandon to get his attention—which currently was focused on Aiden, accompanied by a nefarious grin—and he turned and waved back. Directly behind him, a varsity cheerleader ran her hand through Brandon's hair as she passed. He looked back to see who it was, and smiled back, flirtatious.

Carrie tensed. "*God...* I *hate* it when girls act so stupid around him. It makes me sick."

I wanted to add *and irritated*, but didn't. For a guy who wasn't into girls, Brandon sure got their attention. It made me remember all that stupid advice I'd read about not letting your crush on anyone overtake your other interests. Probably Brandon was so popular with the girls because he radiated disinterest. Hmmm. Good lesson to learn. I was glad to note the space on the other side of Brandon was taken; he and Ryan were surrounded by a posse of male friends.

The Homecoming assembly opened with the parading of the varsity football team. Josh emerged fifth in the lineup, and I waved; he didn't see me. Shelley, our school mascot, droned on and on about school spirit, and our sure victory at the Homecoming game. Fifteen minutes later, we'd progressed to the Homecoming court nominees. It was time to reveal the winners for each class.

Starting with the freshmen, we learned that our Prince was Trey Valley and our Princess, Chloe Steele. Although I really didn't know Trey, I liked Chloe and was excited for her.

"And now for this year's sophomore Prince and Princess..."

I became more excited. I was excited for Ryan—for the possibility, no matter how small. Around me, minor hell broke out. Despite his not being a candidate, someone yelled out Brandon's name, and a series of lewd, encouraging female catcalls quickly followed. This only encouraged his flock of buddies to begin their own show of allegiance with loud whoops, atta-boy slaps, and go-get-em punches, all of which Brandon received in fine style.

Taking a saucy stance, one hand on hip, the other clutching the microphone, Shelley smiled and waited for the ruckus to die down. "*Okay* people, can we get back on track here?"

Attention returned to her. She carefully tore the envelope, grinned and looked toward the area she'd just finished shushing. "This year's sophomore Prince is ... Ryan Evans!"

Carrie and I jumped up, cheering and shouting, but at Ryan's reaction, I quieted and bit my lip. Ryan's face was a deep shade of red as he pushed away from his seat beside Brandon and walked to center stage, his eyes on the floor. Ryan thrived in team sports and among the company of football mates, not as solo star. But I had a feeling his embarrassment went deeper than that. Any happiness he could have felt from his victory was completely overshadowed by the knowledge that the title would've belonged to Brandon, had the system not been toyed with.

I don't think any of us were expecting it — not even Brandon. The surprise on his face was too raw to be something put-on. I knew that Brandon was genuinely happy for Ryan, but after speaking with such disdain about being Class Prince, I wondered how he would congratulate Ryan on something he had derided so thoroughly.

Ryan stood onstage beside the freshman Prince, and they draped him in a robe and crown. He looked far from thrilled.

They moved on to reveal the sophomore Princess.

Jessa's name was called, and that broke through my direct focus on Ryan. I looked up to see her face glowing as she made her way to the stage.

The assembly continued, moving on to the junior Prince and Princess, and finally the King and Queen for the senior class. When the rally wrapped up, students tumbled down the bleachers, flooding the floor before racing for the doors. We pushed our way through the unruly crowd toward the stage, to greet Ryan.

Carrie reached him first; she bounded up to him and gave him a tight hug. "I can't think of anyone I'd rather see win," she said.

He didn't hug her back, just steadied her, putting his hands on her waist. "Really," he said flatly. "You're quick to forget."

I noticed he had already ditched the class crown; he held it in his hand.

"I mean as Brandon's successor," she said. "I mean —"

I said, "Quit while you're ahead, Carrie."

"Where's your crown?" she asked.

"I'm not wearing no fucking crown," he growled.

"I guess now would be a poor time to give you a hug and offer my congratulations," I said.

"I won't refuse a hug—you can hold off on anything else."

I moved in to give him a squeeze and he squeezed me back.

Behind me, Brandon said, "You don't look happy."

I broke away to see him looking at Ryan.

Ryan looked at him contemptuously. "What's not to be happy about? I just rode your coattails to popularity. It's every person's dream."

"This is *your* victory—not mine."

"This has *jack* to do with me, and you know it!"

Brandon paused, not knowing what to say to abate Ryan's anger. Very calmly, he said, "I think it's great, Ryan."

"Yeah—so great you didn't want to have anything to do with it. Do me a favor, Brandon—save your bullshit for someone who will buy it."

Brandon sighed in frustration. "Ryan, the title—and everything that goes along with it—belongs to you. You do it justice. I wasn't comfortable standing where you are; I felt like I was tiptoeing on half-truths. I don't want to get caught up or lost in anything other than what I can count on—what's real to me."

Ryan silently stewed in frustration. His jaw twitched.

"Let's be honest; how many of the people who voted for me would still elect me, if they knew the truth?" He looked at Ryan with a sincerity and openness I'd never seen before. "Don't walk away on account of resentment. I assure you, the title is rightfully yours."

Ryan considered Brandon's words. Their pacifying effect was apparently welcome; he seemed mollified. Like Ryan, I had expected Brandon to hide behind carefully chosen words, but the truth had worked beautifully and, well, it was the truth. I was impressed.

"Come on, I'll give you a lift home." He turned to Carrie and me. "Are you waiting for a formal invitation, or are the Rah-Rahs coming?"

Carrie and I looked at one another and nodded. "We're coming," she said.

We stepped to either side of Ryan and linked our arms through his. His cheeks flushed at our attentiveness, and he focused on the floor as we followed Brandon to the car.

⎯⎯

Marc and his girlfriend Kaelie were in the kitchen when I arrived home. I saw her in profile, leaning against the counter, and headed quickly for my room, trying to bypass them.

"Kris?" Marc said as I whisked by the breakfast bar, my eyes to the floor.

I had to turn around. "Yes?"

"Where are you going so fast?"

"I need to put my books away."

"Well, can you wait a second? I'd like to introduce you to someone."

I hadn't made eye contact with her yet. "Sure." I turned back toward the kitchen.

They approached me as one. "This is Kaelie," he said. "She's been waiting to meet you."

From her black, yoga-style pants to her tight, white, spaghetti-strap top, she looked like a spokesperson for Victoria's Secret fitness wear. Felicity-like curls fell past her shoulders, blond ringlets sweetened by a strawberry sheen. Her eyes weren't green — they were teal; a shade meant for coloring books, a shade perfect for filling in mermaids' tails.

Even her casual look was something primped up. I didn't know many people who did yoga in full evening makeup. There was a cherub-like cuteness to her face, which exuded innocence despite the cosmetics; it also made it difficult to guess her age. She stood no taller than 5'7" in her jogging shoes, and from what I could see, her body had generous curves in all the appropriate places. Still... since when had Marc developed a taste for pumped-up sorority-girl looks?

I could see the damage she might cause, the potential to upset the harmony in our system.

Marc smiled at me as he stood behind Kaelie. "Kaelie, this is Krista."

She extended her hand. Taking my time with the moment, I decided to accept the gesture.

"Nice to finally meet you," she said with a sincere smile. "Marc's told me all about you."

I dropped her hand, cocked my head coolly. "Has he."

Marc said, "Kaelie's only seen the flat I used to rent in London. I wanted to show her the house before she leaves for the weekend."

Well thank goodness she was leaving. I knew Kaelie lived somewhere on the West Coast and they met in England while she was traveling for her job.

"And how do you like it?" I concentrated on being ultra polite.

"It's beautiful—your house, and the area. Laguna's always been one of my favorite places."

"But you *do* have your own home?"

"Oh, yeah—"

"Where?"

"San Marino. But I'm rarely there; I travel a lot."

Marc lightly kneaded her shoulders. "Kaelie's job takes her all over the world."

"So you won't be around much," I said, nodding.

She seemed puzzled.

"What is it you do?"

"I'm currently working as a model."

"Reeeally. Where?"

"Well, I just returned from Japan." She smiled, bringing her hand to meet Marc's as he continued to gently massage her shoulders. "I've been anxious get to home. I've missed Marc so much." She looked up at him adoringly.

Nauseating.

"Japan . . . I hear that's where everyone goes who can't make it as a model in Europe or America. Isn't that right?"

Marc gave me a firm stare, but my attention was all for Kaelie.

"Well... it's true that many models start out by going to Japan. They have a broader market and their height requirements aren't as strict."

"Yeah, I was going to say you look too short to be a model."

Marc's eyes were intense. "And Krista's forgotten her manners."

I gave him doe eyes. "I wasn't trying to be rude, Marc. It was just an observation." I returned my attention to Kaelie. "You just don't look anything like what I'd imagined."

She smiled lightly. "I don't?"

I shook my head. "Most of Marc's girlfriends have been the scholarly type—extremely bright. They liked to exercise their minds, not their looks." I pretended to consider. "Like Cara... remember her? She was fantastic—by far my favorite. You were so in love with her, Marc. Whatever happened to Cara?"

His glare was scalding. "All right, Kris, you can go back to what you were doing."

"But I'd love to stay and visit."

"And I'd love if you didn't."

I sighed. "I guess I *should* start on my homework."

"Good idea."

I gave Kaelie a honey-bear smile. "Nice meeting you." I headed for my room. Before I opened my door, I called down the hall, "Marc."

"*What.*"

"I forgot to tell you, some girl called late last night looking for you... Jessica or Erika—something like that. Just wanted to tell you before I forgot." I closed the door behind me before he could respond.

———

Marc leaned in my doorway, looking like he just ate a sour pickle.

I met his glance for a fleeting moment before returning to organizing my desk drawer. "What? Did Goddess Girl finally leave?"

He shook his head. "I don't know why I bother."

"So don't."

"Where do you get off, acting like that? I've never seen you behave so abhorrently!"

I shrugged. "I was just being myself."

"That wasn't being yourself—and if it was, then I don't like the new you."

I shot him a glare.

"I just spent the last *few* moments I've had with Kaelie today, discussing Cara—since you dredged up the topic—and making up excuses for your uncalled-for candor, explaining that you didn't mean her any offense. That's time I could've spent catching up with Kaelie, Kris. I haven't seen her in ages, and I won't get to that often."

"If you have to explain yourself to her, maybe she's not the girl for you, Marc. And you shouldn't be lying for me, either."

"How could you be so rude to her? After all the wonderful things I've told her about you … she must think I'm *nuts!*" He shook his head. "You acted like Krista's evil twin. What happened?"

"Is that what you came to say?"

"No, actually it's not. She asked me to give you a message—but I don't know; you've been so foul to her, I don't see why I should."

"And what message was that?"

"She offered to do your makeup and hair for Homecoming. I'm still trying to figure out why."

"Who said I wanted her help?"

"You're right. You don't deserve it."

I took a deep breath, and let it out. I looked at him. "Fine; she can do my makeup."

6

Kaelie was applying the final coat of hairspray to my coif when from behind me, Marc said, "Brandon's here."

My heart picked up a beat—even though by now my heart should know better when it came to Brandon—but I sat still while she sprayed. "Tell him I'll be there in a minute. I just have to put on my dress."

"He's waiting in the living room. How much longer are you two going to be?"

"We're finished," Kaelie said. "I'm just waiting for Kris's approval. She hasn't seen herself yet." Kaelie handed me a large hand mirror. "What do you think?"

I lifted the mirror.

It was the first time I'd ever experienced a communication struggle between my eyes and my brain. I couldn't believe it.

My reflection was foreign, a complete transformation. Kaelie had used her makeup brush like a wand, leaving me to absorb the results in a state of wonder. *Was* that me? I leaned into the mirror, close enough for my breath to cloud it.

"I can change anything you don't like," she reassured me when I said nothing.

"No...I...I'll get used it," I said, still mystified. I sat up straight again. "I just can't believe it." I shook my head. "You've just shown me a miracle."

"I don't know that I'd go that far—"

"I would."

Marc said, "Well, turn around—the suspense is killing me."

I turned to look at him over my shoulder. His head jutted back in a quirky way. He was quiet, taking just as long to process the makeover as I had. He finally shook his head.

I asked, tone slightly defiant, "What's wrong?"

"Nothing." He turned to Kaelie. "Well, is the fairy godmother done? I'm sure Brandon would like to get to the dance tonight."

"I'm done if she's satisfied," she said, turning to me.

In the midst of this, I'd forgotten I was supposed to dislike Kaelie, and my promise to be nice to her suddenly wasn't a chore. "Thank you, Kaelie. I can't thank you enough." I began to feel bad, regretting that I'd been so unkind to her.

"My pleasure. When there's time, I'll teach you how to do your makeup yourself."

"Or not," Marc said. "This is a special occasion; let's not get carried away."

Kaelie and I exchanged looks. "He'll get over it," she said wryly.

He turned to her, one surprised brow reaching for his hairline. "Will I?"

She was already laughing. I hopped down from the makeup chair I'd sat in for the past two hours and left them to their playful squabble. I took my dress through Marc's bathroom and into his walk-in closet. There I carefully slipped into the gown, and then returned to have her fasten me up.

When I entered the living room, Brandon was waiting on the couch. He turned when he heard the click of my heels. His eyes went as wide as I'd ever seen them. I think he was as surprised as I was at Kaelie's handiwork. He stood up and walked toward me, a peculiar look on his face. He stopped directly in front of me, "My..."

I waited for him to finish his thought, but when he didn't, I became anxious. I was apparently as alien to him as I'd been to myself. That wasn't necessarily a good thing. Brandon was opinionated. *Way* opinionated.

"Is it okay?" I asked tentatively. "I'm not used to seeing myself in makeup. Is it too much?"

He finally allowed the corner of his mouth to give up a smile. "Remarkable." Politely, he surveyed me once from head to toe. "And I thought Ryan would be the one stricken." He shook his head. "You look untouchable." But then he took my hand in his, giving it a squeeze.

Marc and Kaelie emerged from the hallway. "You guys all set?" Marc asked.

Brandon looked at me. "I believe we are."

"You both look amazing," Kaelie said. "I'm sure you'll have a great time."

Marc said, "Do I get a hug, or is that off limits?"

I gave him a big smile and went to give him a hug.

"Have fun," he said.

"I will—and thanks." I gave him a timid kiss on the cheek, leaving behind only a trace of the pound of lip-gloss Kaelie had so meticulously applied.

I returned to Brandon and he offered me his arm. Marc opened the door for us and Brandon assisted me through. I'd never been escorted this way; it didn't compare to clinging to Marc's arm while navigating a tricky set of steps, or being steered clear of a puddle. This was a moment of its own . . . and I was sad mom was missing it. I pushed the thought aside and concentrated on the present. Brandon bid them farewell and gave his reassurances, and then . . . we were out beneath the cool night sky.

Once the door shut behind us, it fully hit me—in thirty minutes or thereabouts, I was going to walk into a room on *Brandon's* arm. I was more than excited—I was nervous. I tried to bottle my mixed feelings so my uneasiness wouldn't show. Suddenly my stomach was as unsteady as I felt in my heels, and I worked to suppress the silly smile that ached to escape.

"What's wrong?" he asked.

It was pointless to conceal it any longer—it wasn't working anyway. I smiled, and it felt impossibly wide. "Absolutely nothing."

The chauffeur waiting at the sleek black limo assisted me in, and I had my first taste of luxury. I'd never been inside a limo. Outside,

Brandon gave directions to the driver; we'd pick up Carrie and Ryan. Brandon slid into the seat next to me.

I settled comfortably against the couch and looked at Brandon as the limo slowly pulled onto the street. He was lounging attractively as usual, one leg crossing the other. He was just so unaffected by everything, it blew me away. "I take it you've done this before," I said, teasing.

"Too many times to count."

"But this is only your sophomore year."

"So count seventh grade till now, then add to that every other school's dance I've attended with someone."

"Are they all the same?"

"Pretty much." A sudden look of dread crossed his face; he pressed his fists to his forehead. "Shit."

"What?" I said, worried something was terribly wrong.

"Your corsage—I left it at your house. I completely spaced."

I started to laugh. "Now that you mention it, I left your boutonniere in the refrigerator."

Slowly, his smile resurfaced. "We're off to a good start. I'm sorry."

"Don't be," I said. "Now I'll have flowers to enjoy tomorrow."

He gave me a small smile. "So you will."

Carrie and Ryan were ready when we arrived. I wasn't the only person who'd undergone a transformation; I was agog at the sight of Ryan—he'd cleaned up stunningly. He was always handsome, but Brandon's selection made him look sharp. He seemed comfortable with himself, and genuinely happy; with Carrie on his arm, how couldn't he be? They made an attractive couple. I was pleased to see that his spirits were up, any previous insecurities from his victory forgotten.

We had one final stop before the dance. Aeleise had called me earlier in the evening seeking to borrow an evening bag. The limo pulled up in front of her house and I carefully lifted the sides of my dress so I could move without restriction as the chauffeur assisted me out of the car. While the others waited in the limo, I scuttled to her front door and rang the bell. The door opened on an unexpected vision. I recognized the same rich, raven-colored hair as Aeleise's, only worn in a shorter, chin-length style. A generous portion of it covered his face. When he ran his hand back through his hair to reveal clearly the person behind it, I could only stare.

Hypnotic.

He had the arresting eyes of a snake charmer. They were a haunting shade, nearly midnight black, and gleamed like mercury. His face was so flawlessly sculpted, it was as if he were a piece of fine artwork—timeless, classic, with an androgyny that made him uncommonly beguiling. He bore a close resemblance to Aeleise, but in truth, I found the features far more flattering on him. It was hard to pull my gaze from the pale, blood-like color of his lips; lips that looked as tasty as cinnamon sticks and soft as marshmallows. I could only assume this was her older sibling.

It took a moment to remember my reason for being there. "Hi," I said after a noticeable delay. "Is Aeleise here? I brought my handbag for her."

"You must be Krista," he said with a disarming smile. "Hi, I'm Daemon. Aeleise is still getting ready. Would you like to come in?" He had a captivating voice that matched his incredible looks, and I found myself focusing on every word.

"No, thank you. Everyone is waiting for me in the limo. Can you just make sure that she gets this?"

"Sure." He opened the screen door that separated us, and I handed him the purse.

I'd remembered mom's request to send photos, and I had my digital camera in the limo. I quickly debated whether I should ask him to take a few shots. I felt hesitant because I had just met him, but in a moment I made my decision. "Daemon, would you mind taking a few pictures of all of us by the limo before we go?"

"Sure, no problem." He opened the screen door, and followed me to the limo.

Opening the door, I peeked inside. "Daemon's going to take a couple pictures for us. Brandon, can you grab my camera, please?"

He handed me my camera, but made no effort to exit the limo.

"He's not taking them inside the car, you guys. Get out."

Reluctantly, everyone emerged from the limo and I introduced Daemon to Brandon and Ryan; Carrie already knew him. We assembled outside the door. Brandon stood behind me, arms wrapped around my waist. Ryan followed Brandon's cue and stood behind Carrie, beside me. We gave the camera the customary smiles, and Daemon stood back and played photographer. I decided four photos were sufficient. Aeleise's brother or not, I already felt strange asking a virtual stranger for a favor so quickly.

"Okay. That should do it," I said abruptly. "Thank you."

"You're welcome." He handed me my camera and I accepted it with a small smile.

Carrie, Brandon, and Ryan piled back into the car. I stood outside a moment longer to say a proper goodbye.

As he watched them disappear into the limo, he asked, "Those young men are your and Carrie's boyfriends?"

"No, they're just good friends."

He nodded. "Well, have a good time. I'll give Aeleise the bag."

"It was nice meeting you," I said.

"Likewise." Smiling, he extended his hand. The moment we touched, an exhilarating chill ran through me. I climbed into the limo and took my seat beside Brandon. Daemon closed the door. He watched as we pulled away, and then turned toward his house.

"I take it that was your first encounter with Daemon," Brandon said.

"Yeah. Have you met him before?"

"No, but I recognize him. He used to drop Aeleise off at school before she got her license."

My brows pinched. "They look a lot alike. The resemblance is uncanny."

"Yes, they do—to a certain extent." Brandon gave me the slightest grin. "Although I've never seen you get so nervous around Aeleise. Somehow, I suspect you find those similar features far more favorable on Daemon.

At a loss for a comeback, I turned my attention elsewhere. I could still feel Brandon's amused grin behind me.

"Let's put on some music, Krista," Carrie suggested.

I needed a distraction and was happy to oblige. I fiddled with and poked the bevy of colored buttons on the panel above my head, changing tunes until I found something that we all agreed upon. I leaned back against the soft black leather seats. The few miles we had yet to travel seemed to stretch on interminably. I was relieved when I spotted the school through the darkly tinted window. I was ready for a change in scenery.

We pulled up outside our high school gym, where the dance was being held. The ASB had worked all day decorating it to our theme, which was "A Night to Remember." I hoped it would be. It was eight o'clock when we arrived, and a few couples still lingered outside the gym door, waiting for friends to show. The chauffeur walked around the car and opened the door. As we exited the limo, Brandon told the chauffeur we'd be out around 10:00 P.M. Both Brandon and Ryan were complete gentlemen and offered their arm to escort us to the door.

It had cost $125.00 per couple for Homecoming tickets, which seemed ridiculous to me—in Ohio, Josh had never paid anything. Neither Brandon nor Ryan flinched at the price though, and they refused when Carrie and I offered to pay for our half.

"We asked you, didn't we?" Brandon had said. "Don't be ridiculous. Do either of us seem concerned with the price of a ticket?" He adjusted the band on his Rolex and smiled at me.

"If you insist," I said finally.

Brandon had given me the tickets to hold. Now I withdrew them from my purse and handed them to Mrs. Cassock, one of the school administrators, who searched the list for our names and stamped our hands.

Inside, it was still obvious we'd entered a gym, but the ASB had done a good job of camouflaging its many faults with black, silver, and white balloons, and streamers and special lighting—it almost seemed romantic. Tables surrounding the dance floor were draped with white tablecloths, adorned with balloon centerpieces, showered with confetti.

It was packed inside. People had already gathered in their cliques and claimed their tables. Brandon saw an empty table near the center of the room and steered me in that direction. As Carrie and I took seats, we eyed our surroundings, hoping to spot some of our other friends from the squad.

"What would you like to drink?"

I brought my attention back from a perusal of the room. "I'm fine. Thanks, Brandon."

"Carrie?" Ryan asked.

"Diet Coke, please."

"You got it. Be right back." Ryan took off in the direction of the makeshift bar.

"I'm feeling a bit parched myself. Will you excuse me for a moment?" Brandon asked.

"Of course," I said.

Carrie turned to me in a buzz of excitement. She took my hand and squeezed it, letting out a small squeal of delight. Her face was radiant. "I'm so glad they asked us. Isn't this the best?" She made it seem as if there was no other answer than yes, and I found myself nodding with a broad smile; I was excited to be here too.

"Is your brother going to be here?" she asked.

"Last I heard. I don't know who his date is, though."

Carrie nodded and we both scanned the room, suddenly curious to see if Josh had arrived. I wondered who he would be bringing. I knew many girls hoped to be his choice. He wasn't here yet.

Brandon and Ryan returned with drinks. Brandon nudged his drink toward me, and I took a sip at his urging.

"Krista." Carrie nodded toward the entrance. "Aeleise is here."

Aeleise waved to us from across the dance floor. She and Nick had just arrived. She looked stunning. Her look was classic. The dress she had chosen was simple and elegant — cream-colored silk in a modest cut, with spaghetti straps. Her hair was gracefully swept up and arranged high above her head in a style that revealed the delicate outline of her shoulders and the back of her neck. It framed her face in tiny ebony ringlets.

Nick's eyes followed the direction of her wave and his eyes widened at the sight of us. I believe he even flinched.

"That was odd," I said, my gaze still fixed upon them as they neared. "What's with Nick?"

By Brandon's tone, I didn't need to turn around to see the slight smile that colored his expression. "I'm sure he wasn't expecting me to show up at the dance with you."

I turned then to look at him. His eyes remained on Nick. I frowned. Apparently, I had missed something.

Carrie and Ryan ran up to greet them on their way to our table. Carrie gave them overzealous hugs, and the boys said hello. Carrie and Ryan wandered off in the other direction, and Aeleise approached our table with Nick trailing not far behind. Brandon was still smirking, so I gave him a quick nudge.

I greeted her with a hug. "You look amazing!"

"Thanks," she said, smiling excitedly. "So do you. Thanks for loaning me your purse."

"I'm glad it worked out for you."

"Hi Brandon," she said, her eyes bright.

"You look incredible, Aeleise." He smiled sincerely, and with his highbrow etiquette, gave her a European kiss. He pointedly locked eyes with Nick. "Hi Nick," he said.

"Hey. What's up?" Nick was trying to sound relaxed, but the rigidity in his body said he was anything but. I could not believe that I was witnessing Brandon trying to hook up with Aeleise's date at a high school prom. I suppose I should have been shocked or something but the thing was it didn't seem all that odd. The only bad part was that Aeleise was obviously crazy about Nick and clueless about what was going on.

"Been here long?" Nick asked him.

"About fifteen minutes."

Nick shifted his weight, leaning closer to Aeleise.

"Where'd Carrie and Ryan take off to in such a hurry?" Aeleise wanted to know.

"They're probably making the rounds—wandering about the room somewhere. They'll be back soon. Here," I motioned to the empty chairs next to us, "we saved you both a spot."

Aeleise took a seat. "*Wow*—they really did a nice job fixing up the place," she said as she scanned the room. Nick took a seat beside her. Brandon remained standing, chewing noisily on a piece of ice.

"Yeah," I said. "You could almost forget it was the gym."

"Almost," Brandon said, unimpressed, and finally took a seat next to me. He leaned comfortably back in his chair, his ankle resting on his knee, his arm casually draped on the back of my chair. He watched with interest as Nick shifted about in his seat, trying to find a comfortable position. I was aware, nervous over Nick's obvious discomfort.

Nick looked at Aeleise. "Can I get you a drink?"

"No, thank you." She smiled warmly at him.

His opportunity shot down, he looked anxious to leave.

Brandon smiled lightly. "Perhaps you could use a *real* drink, Nick?"

"Yeah," Nick said, but he didn't look up.

"That could be arranged. The limo has a bar," Brandon offered easily.

Nick looked up suddenly, as if he intended to accept the offer, but something in Brandon's relaxed and amused expression made him change his mind. "Thanks, I'm good." He scanned the room, then touched Aeleise's arm. "Isn't that Carrie over there in line? If you still want pictures with her, we might as well do it now."

Aeleise spotted Carrie and Ryan chatting among friends as they waited. "Good idea. We'd better hurry." She grabbed her purse. "Krista, you guys coming?"

"We'll be right behind you; you two go ahead."

Nick was already standing, ready to leave. Aeleise, oblivious to his discomfort, followed him toward Carrie and Ryan.

Brandon laughed aloud once they'd moved out of earshot. "Well, that was interesting."

"I'll say. What's with him?" Although Nick was quiet by nature, his behavior had never been so driving for an exit.

"You'd think I was going to address his invitation right here before Aeleise, by the way he was acting."

I looked at Brandon, who happily crunched down on another piece of ice. "What invitation?"

He turned to face me, smiling as he swallowed the few remaining fragments. "He invited me over to check out his 'new computer.' *Please*," he said dryly. "We rarely, if ever, exchange words in Aeleise's company, and suddenly that springs out of nowhere? I don't think so."

It didn't seem that peculiar to me. "What did you say?"

"No." Brandon's voice was flat, uninterested "I don't waste time on preliminaries or veiled excuses. This is who I am."

"What exactly are you implying?" I asked.

His direct and wordless stare made the clarification.

Quickly jumping to Nick's defense I said, "He *is* dating Aeleise. You can't seriously think that's what's going on."

He arched an eyebrow at me. "How can you possibly be surprised? He's cheering on the same squad you are."

I hadn't given it much thought previously, but I pointed out that there could be two sides to that coin. "You know, maybe *he's* the one getting the last laugh. I mean, seriously—I'm surprised more guys aren't going out for cheer, if you consider it objectively. I'm sure some might view certain aspects of the sport as a perk. Besides, what's wrong with male cheerleaders? They work hard, Brandon—*really* hard."

Brandon shook his head with a knowing smile. "Sweetie, I'm not doubting their dedication to their chosen activity; I'm simply calling attention to the fact that it's an atypical choice for most guys. I'm not blind, neither are you; you just need to pay attention. I'm calling this card—Nick is the clearest closet case I've seen in a while. It doesn't get any easier to spot than that. And I guess it bothers me when people stay closeted and then expect me to drag them out."

I could only hope that he was wrong, for Aeleise's sake.

We made our way over to the area designated for photographs. We were ushered onto a seamless paper background painted a faux starry night, and stood and smiled as directed. We had a group picture taken to commemorate the evening, and then each couple posed together separately. It felt like a cattle drive.

Pictures taken care of, Brandon and I headed back and reclaimed our seats at the table; the others made their way to the dance floor. My mind was chewing on Brandon's strange hypothesis.

We danced a few times, but the band was terrible and in my grown up dress and new face suddenly the decorated gym looked like just what it was—a high school gym. Brandon must have either read my mind or felt exactly like I did because not even an hour after we got there he put his arm around my waist and said, "Come on. We're outa this place."

He led me off the dance floor in search of Ryan and Carrie. "We'll see if they want to go with us; if not, I'll have the limo come back to pick them up later."

I silently followed as he weaved through the students packing the gym. We couldn't see our table until we were standing in front of it. Carrie and Ryan had returned to their seats, and looked up from their conversation when we appeared.

"Hey, Kris and I are leaving. You care to come with, or would you prefer I send the limo back to pick you up later?"

"You want to leave already?" Carrie asked, surprised. She looked at the clock on the wall.

Brandon spoke so I didn't have to look like the spoilsport. "Yes, I think we've had our fill. The ambiance is tired; we're over it. I think we're just going to cruise around town. Anything is better than this."

Ryan and Carrie looked at each other. Ryan shrugged. "It's your call. Wha'do *you* wanna do?"

A quizzical expression crossed her face, and then she brightened and shrugged. "I already took care of what I wanted to do. The proof that I was here will be in the pictures." That was Carrie; always concerned about the important things. "Wanna split, Ryan?"

"Sounds like a plan."

Carrie grabbed her handbag and the four of us made for the exit door.

"Shouldn't one of us tell Aeleise we're leaving and see if she and Nick want to come along?" she asked.

At the suggestion, Brandon's mild, calculating grin returned as if it had never left. "Yes, I think you're right, Carrie. Why don't we ask them to join us? The more the merrier."

"Okay. You guys wait here; I'll hunt them down."

Before Carrie could leave, Brandon gently pulled her back. "That won't be necessary. It seems they've come to us."

Aeleise approached with a ground-covering stride; Nick trailed behind her. "We've been looking for you guys all over this place," she said emphatically. "Where've you been?"

Brandon looked bored. "You must not have been looking too hard. We've been over at the table."

Aeleise said to Nick over her shoulder, "I told you we should've looked there first." She shook her head. "He kept insisting you guys weren't there. We've been wandering around this place like mice in a maze, trying to find you, and all along we've been on the wrong side." She smiled and rolled her eyes. "Boys."

"I was trying my best," Nick contested.

"I'm sure you were," Brandon said, his expression knowing.

I noticed how uncomfortable Nick became around Brandon. He turned to Aeleise in response to Carrie's invitation. "I'd rather stay; I haven't even had a chance to dance with you, Aeleise. But, it's your choice. We'll do whatever makes you happy."

Aeleise, flattered by his rare display of affection, gave him an adoring smile. They were staying.

Brandon's expression could only be called a smirk. "Why am I not surprised?"

I wasn't surprised by her decision either, but for an entirely different reason.

Aeleise broke her loving stare at Nick long enough to turn to our group, her eyes apologizing before she spoke. "Thanks for the invitation, but this is my first dance; I'd like to stay too. I hope you don't mind."

"Of course not," Carrie said. "We just wanted to extend the invitation. Have a great time."

"We'll see you at school," Aeleise promised and, still beaming, gave hugs to all of us.

Carrie and I said goodbye to Nick. Brandon extended his hand to Nick in contrived politeness, and Nick found himself forced to accept the gesture. They shook hands, and Brandon, in his ever-obnoxious way, held on longer than necessary. The maneuver guaranteed eye contact, and he met Nick's gaze with a taunting smile. "I hope you have a fulfilling evening, Nick."

Nick dropped his eyes as quickly as Brandon's hand. Carrie and Aeleise, none the wiser, chatted animatedly as they headed toward the exit. I quickly caught up to them, relieved for Nick's sake that she had decided to stay.

"Where do you guys want to go?" Brandon asked as the four of us piled back into the limo.

"How about that lookout point above the city?" Carrie suggested. "We can check out the view and drink whatever alcohol is in the limo bar."

"Everybody?" Brandon asked, looking at Ryan and me. "Does that work for you?"

"Fine by me," Ryan said.

"Sure," I said.

"Okay. Top of the World it is, then." Brandon pressed the button to lower the partition behind the driver. "Take us up past Newport Hills to the area where we can see the city. Are you familiar with Top of the World?"

"I am. I'll head there now."

Brandon closed the partition to give us privacy again. "We're on our way, boys and girls."

"Ryan, check and see what's in the bar," Carrie said.

Ryan leaned over to the other side console and opened the lidded compartment. "We have ice, water, Cokes..." He pulled out a crystal decanter full of amber liquid and pulled off the stopper. He sniffed it. "Some kind of whiskey, I think." He reached back in and pulled out another crystal decanter, the liquid inside it clear. "I'm assuming this is vodka," he said, and then smelled it. "Yep." There was plenty of both. He reached farther in and pulled out a bottle that had been buried neck deep in ice cubes. "And champagne."

"Help yourself," Brandon said. "You indulging tonight, Ryan?"

"It's a special occasion."

"What are you drinking, Brandon?" I asked.

"I don't drink, but don't let that stop you. Ryan, will you pass me one of the bottled waters, please?"

He handed the bottle to Brandon.

"What are you going to drink, Carrie?" I asked.

"I don't know. Ryan, can you make me a drink that doesn't taste awful?"

He laughed. "I'll do my best." He grabbed a glass that was taller than a tumbler and poured some whiskey and then some Coke into it. Ryan the bartender. "Try that and let me know what you think."

She took a swallow and gasped. "Did you add any Coke, Ryan?"

"Yeah."

She handed it back to him. "Well, could you add some more, please?"

"Wuss," he teased her.

"Hey, my stomach isn't made of iron."

He added more soda to her drink and handed it back. "Better now?"

She sipped it cautiously. "Yes, much. Thank you."

"Krista?" He looked at me. "What would you like? Are you drinking with us?"

I let out a sigh. "Sure." *Why not?* "Champagne, I guess."

"Coming right up." Ryan gripped the bottle and carefully eased the cork until it made a startling pop. He managed to keep most of the liquid from overflowing onto his tuxedo. He filled a long stemmed champagne flute for me.

"Thank you," I said, accepting the glass. I took a sip, and quickly made a face. *"Ugh.* It tastes so ... *bitter."*

Brandon laughed. "Haven't you ever had champagne before?"

"No."

"Well, I guarantee you, drink one glass of that and you won't remember if your next glass tastes bitter. Go easy on the stuff. It can pack an unexpected wallop."

"Thanks for the warning."

"Anytime."

Ryan had poured himself vodka and water in one of the taller glasses. Brandon casually leaned back against the seat, ankle resting on one knee, enjoying the ride and watching us all as we worked on our drinks. The limo slowed. We looked out the window.

"We're here," Brandon said as the limo stopped. "Grab whatever you want to take with you; we'll wrap it in our jackets."

Brandon and Ryan removed their jackets and concealed the alcohol; the limo driver came around the side to let us out.

"We'll be communing on the hill. To make it worth your while, if we run overtime I'll pay you double," Brandon said.

That pleased the driver. "I'll be here," he said.

Carrie and I followed Brandon and Ryan up the grass-covered hill. The night air was crisp and exhilarating. It tingled against my face, providing a rush of energy. By the time we reached the top of the hill, I felt surprisingly warm. We reached the spot closest to the edge and took in a breathtaking view of the city below. The night sky was black as sin, and covered in a blanket of stars that glowed brilliantly—distant crystals, infused with light. I had never appreciated the radiance of night as I did now. The boys set the alcohol on the ground.

"Put this on," Brandon said as he handed me his tuxedo jacket. "You're going to catch cold."

"I'm warm, really."

"It's just the alcohol, Kris. Put it on, please."

I frowned, but did as told.

"You too, Carrie," Ryan said, and wrapped his jacket around her shoulders.

"Thanks," she said, although I could tell she didn't want to wear a jacket either.

We sat on the grass, which wasn't very dewy yet—a plus, given our attire, although in truth, I doubted we'd ever wear these gowns again. Carrie sat on my right, and Brandon sat in front of her, while Ryan sat across from me. We quietly studied the view below: the red and white freeway-line beneath us, the illuminated windows of houses whose occupants were still awake. Now and then, a warm yellow glow would fall to black as the inhabitants of a house retired. I imagined families sleeping soundly.

"I'm glad we decided to leave," Carrie said.

I had to agree. "Me too; this is amazing. Do you guys come up here often?"

"Brandon does," Carrie said with a smirk.

"I beg your pardon," he said indignantly. "Who's telling *these* stories? Certainly not me."

"Oh, come on. You know you've been here before."

"Not as often as you seem to assume."

She just grinned at him. "Okay."

Brandon shook his head and opened his water to take a drink. I stared into the distance. I had finished my glass of champagne, and Ryan poured me another. His and Carrie's glasses also welcomed a refill.

"Go easy on it, Kris," Brandon said as he watched me accept the next full glass.

"I will."

He looked at me as if questioning my judgment, and then leaned back on his arms. He stared at us for a moment. "The view is lovely, I agree, but this has the potential to get extremely boring. What do you say — shall we liven things up? Keep things interesting?"

It was just like Brandon to become bored within minutes.

"What exactly did you have in mind?" Carrie asked.

"Yeah," Ryan echoed, "What'd you have in mind?"

"How about something simple? We're all familiar with truth or dare."

We all exchanged glances, and Carrie laughed. "Yeah, simple for *you* maybe. You have nothing to lose. You'll do or say anything."

"Afraid?" Brandon teased.

"No. Just telling the truth. I don't care, I'll play along."

"I'm game," Ryan said.

"Kris?" Brandon asked.

"Count me in."

He smiled. "Good."

Carrie egged Brandon on in a sarcastic tone. "Well, since this was your bright idea, Cookie, why don't you start?"

"Fine by me." He grinned. "Carrie, truth or dare?"

"Dare."

"I dare you to drink three mouthfuls of that little cocktail Ryan so generously made for you."

"Boy, dive right in, why don't you? What if I get sick?"

He looked at her pleasantly. "Then you'll throw up."

Leave it to Brandon to be literal.

"Are you going to do it, or whine about it?" he asked.

She glared at him. "Fine." She took three mouthfuls and made interesting faces as she worked to consummate her dare. She had broken a slight sweat with the last swallow.

"Good girl," he said. "Your turn."

"Ryan?" Carrie asked.

"Truth."

A smile crept across her face. "Is it true you slept with Jessa at Travis's party last year?"

"With *Jessa?* No."

"I *knew* she was lying." She shook her head. "*So* stupid."

Brandon looked at Ryan. "I guess you should feel flattered, Ryan. Jessa apparently wants you badly enough to lie about it."

Ryan just looked bewildered, then remembered it was his turn to ask a question. "Brandon?"

"Truth."

"Who was the last person you slept with?"

He laughed. "You would ask that. Shayne... and no, you don't know him."

My surprise must have shown. I probably wasn't good at masking my shock under the influence of alcohol. I'd never heard a boy state frankly that he'd slept with another boy. I took a deep breath.

Carrie asked, "What about the guy from the mall? Reagan."

Brandon said, "I assumed Ryan had something specific in mind. Ryan?"

"No details wanted, thanks. Your answer was plenty informative."

"So you *did* get together with him." Carrie grinned.

"Maybe," Brandon said, but his teasing tone and Smurf-like grin indicated a resounding yes. He turned to me. "Krista?" Just the way he looked at me made me nervous.

"Truth."

"Are you a virgin, darling?"

Between the combination of alcohol and embarrassment, I felt the heat rise to my face. "Yes." I took another sip of my champagne without meeting his glance. When I finally looked up, he was smiling at me.

"Your turn," he said.

I turned to Carrie. "And you choose?"

"Truth."

"Do you really like Marc?"

"Your brother?"

"Yeah."

She smiled, looking down at her glass. "Yeah. But promise me you won't tell him."

"I won't."

Carrie looked at Brandon. It was her turn to question. I noticed that her glass was almost empty. We were all buzzed—all except Brandon. Carrie had exceeded her capacity for alcohol, and I questioned her sobriety.

"Brandon?" she said, with a toying lilt in her voice.

"Truth."

She grinned foolishly in her altered state. "Is it true you're more impressively endowed than Aiden O'Hearn?"

"*My God*, Carrie," I gasped, eyes gone wide. I couldn't believe she had the audacity to ask such a thing.

Brandon laughed, and didn't appear offended in the least.

Ryan looked at Carrie as if she were nuts. "How would *he* know *that?*"

She kept her eyes fixed on Brandon, still wearing an interested grin. He took a sip of water and strove to keep a straight face. "Just answer the question, Brandon," she said. "Or are you backing out of your own game?"

He hesitated, then met her eyes. "Yes."

"*What the*—" Ryan looked incredulously at Brandon. "When did *you* get together with Aiden?" Ryan shook his head adamantly, suddenly serious. "No way—I don't buy that. I see him every day at practice. Since when does *Aiden* go both ways?"

Brandon gave Ryan his best poker face. "He doesn't." He left it at that.

Ryan shook his head. "I'm not even gonna ask."

Brandon looked at me. "I'm passing my turn to Krista. She's far too quiet."

I laughed, feeling giddy from all the champagne. After that last question, I got braver. Maybe Carrie would regret her last inquiry. "Right back at you, Brandon."

He chuckled. "Fine. Dare."

"I dare you to French kiss Carrie."

Carrie's startled expression matched Brandon's. He looked at Carrie, who had fallen silent. She was no longer laughing.

"Carrie?" he asked.

She shrugged, but sounded nervous when she told him, "Go ahead. I don't care."

Brandon closed the distance between them. The alcohol had hit Carrie hard, and he was clearly in control of the situation. He gently cradled her face and brushed his lips against hers, the kiss beginning slowly. His free hand traveled up her arm, feeling the bare skin of her shoulder and then the softness of her neck. Fingers played through her blond waves, and he lightly tugged at her hair. His tongue slid along her lower lip, then disappeared to explore further. Slowly, methodically, their tongues danced privately together in rhythm. Brandon looked like he knew what he was doing. When he began to kiss her deeper, she grabbed his arms, and he continued. She made an involuntary noise from the back of her throat that read clearly as a confession, and Ryan and I exchanged wide-eyed glances. Brandon slowly pulled away.

Carrie looked completely stunned.

Brandon turned to me. "Satisfied?"

Probably not as much as Carrie was. I nodded, almost uneasily. Carrie sat there as if she'd been pulled from a foreign dimension and wasn't sure what to do.

"You okay?" I asked her, my voice quiet.

"I'm fine," she said, not looking at anyone. Even in the moonlight, I could make out the flush on her cheeks.

Ryan looked from Carrie to Brandon. He was undoubtedly astounded by the intensity of their kiss, and I was right there with him. "I'm asking the next question," he announced, out of turn. He looked at Brandon. "*Christ,* Brandon—*screw* the dare. Truth—are you hard?"

"Gee, I don't know, Ryan. I dare you to find out." He gave him a smart-ass look that matched his tone.

Ryan looked down at Brandon's groin, but the way he was sitting, there was no way to tell. "You know I won't."

"Then I guess you'll never know." He gave him a cheeky smile.

"Stand up," Ryan said with a taunting grin.

"I don't think so. It's somebody else's turn."

"No it's not, it's still yours," Ryan said.

Brandon looked at him. "Fine. Ryan?"

"Truth."

"Does the thought of two girls kissing turn you on?"

Ryan's absurd expression made it seem as if the answer was obvious. "Well, yeah. Wouldn't it you?"

Brandon gave him a sarcastic look, and Ryan shrugged. Brandon didn't answer.

"Brandon?" Ryan asked.

"Again?" Brandon protested.

"Yes," Ryan said.

Brandon chose. "Dare."

Ryan smiled. "I dare you to ask Carrie to kiss Krista."

I don't know about Carrie, but I sure as hell froze.

Brandon gave Ryan a wicked grin. "Nice tactic. Have me do the dirty work." He turned to Carrie. "Carrie, I dare you to kiss Krista."

She looked at me nervously, trying to read my face, but I made sure it was utterly blank.

"I'm afraid I can't live up to your kiss, Brandon," she said tentatively.

"Nobody's asking you to. This isn't a contest."

She looked at me. "Kris...are you willing to do this? You don't have to."

"I don't care," I lied. "It's only a game, right? No one's backed down so far. I won't be the first."

There was silence.

Carrie glanced at me. "Okay," she said calmly, still recovering from Brandon's eager display only moments ago.

Full of uncertainty, she inched over beside me and gently kissed my lips. Nervous excitement washed through me. I had never kissed anyone before and I was on unfamiliar ground. She was cautious and slow, but I sat there like a paralyzed doll, not knowing what to do. It's one thing to watch it take place, but it's entirely another to actually participate. Her tongue slid along my lower lip, but my lips wouldn't move. My heart was thudding. I couldn't think. She slowly pulled back. I believe I just sat there, as dazed as she had been earlier, yet I knew our kiss was nothing in light of what she had just experienced with Brandon. It was practically *nothing*. No one said anything. I wondered what everyone was thinking.

Brandon broke the silence, his gaze resting on me. "This is no truth or dare question. In all seriousness...may I ask you something?"

"Yeah," I said, meeting his glance for only a second.

"Have you *ever* kissed anyone before?"

Heat rose to my face. "No," I said, not looking at him or anyone else, for that matter.

"I only ask because you looked scared. Is it because Carrie's a girl?"

"No...I don't think so. I just don't know what to do." I felt like such an imbecile.

"Did you like it?" Brandon asked quietly.

The air had gotten so still, so quiet.

"I would've liked it more if I knew what I was doing. After seeing the two of you kiss, I feel like a moron."

"Don't," he said.

"Brandon's had years of practice," Ryan said, trying to encourage me.

"He's had something," I said, almost too softly to be heard.

I finished the last of my champagne in silence. I knew that Brandon watched me. I hated that I didn't know what he was thinking.

"It's Carrie's turn," Ryan said, but the atmosphere had become nearly somber.

We looked at her. She still looked out of sorts—peculiar, almost ill. "I don't feel so well," she said.

"Maybe we should call it a night," Brandon suggested.

Ryan looked at me and then back at Carrie. "I think you're right."

———

Carrie decided to pass her drunken spell at my house, rather than go home in her present condition to a mother anxiously awaiting her return. We thanked Brandon and Ryan for the evening—interesting as it had become. It had been an enjoyable experience, and without question, it had been an enlightening—if not mildly bizarre—evening.

With my assistance, Carrie made it inside the house, and I steered her directly toward my bedroom. Our arrival went unnoticed. Josh wasn't home yet; since it was now past midnight, I doubted he had any intention of returning.

I closed the bedroom door behind us as Carrie took refuge on my bed. She slumped there without enthusiasm, and then wiggled her feet free from her shoes.

It was nice of them to take us," I said as I sat down beside her and kicked off my shoes.

She nodded. "It went by so fast."

"I think that's a good sign. At least the evening didn't drag."

"Mmm... true."

"Will you unzip me?" I asked.

She released the restraint and the tension confining my ribcage eased instantly. It had been fun to dress up, but I had never been so eager to slip into pajamas. Carrie swiveled her back to me, a silent request to reciprocate. I glanced at our gorgeous gowns, lying in a heap on the floor while we changed, and shuddered to think what Brandon had paid for them. I scooped them up and draped them over the back of my chair.

"Brandon would never let an evening lull," Carrie said, "not if he could help it. If boredom's a threat, he'll invent something—you can count on it." She chuckled. "Sometimes I think he views a moment's peace as a fate worse than drowning. Even when he's quiet, you know something's going on in his head."

"He's definitely not the sedentary type," I agreed. "His truth or dare game—"

Carrie looked at me. I regretted my mention of it. "You were serious tonight, weren't you? About never kissing anyone," she said.

"Like it wasn't obvious."

She moved farther back on the bed until her back met the pillow-lined wall. "I don't have much experience either," she confessed. "I never thought..." She let her thought trail off. "Brandon really took me by surprise tonight."

My eyebrows rose in recollection. "Yeah, it looked like it. He must be a good kisser."

Her gaze was mostly for the bedspread but her cheeks flushed. "Knowing his experience, I shouldn't have been surprised, but *God*. I mean we've kissed as a joke before, like when we first met you, but never like that. I wasn't ready for that—at all. Did I look entirely stupid?" She quickly shook her head. "On second thought, don't answer that."

I reassured her anyway. "You looked fine. Certainly nothing to worry about." Especially in light of my attempt.

"It just happened so fast. He kissed me and I couldn't even think. I wasn't expecting it to be so ... overwhelming."

"He wasn't exactly holding back; how could you *not* be shocked? If that had been me, I'd have been lost. I don't know how you did it."

Her expression clearly echoed my sentiment. "Me either. Technically, that was my first kiss ... like that, anyway."

I hadn't suspected. "Really? That was your first time?"

She nodded. Her face gradually paled to its normal healthy color. She pulled her entire mane over one shoulder.

"Have you ever had a boyfriend?" Once I asked her, I found it peculiar that the subject had never come up before.

She shook her head. "I've kinda been tossing around the idea, though. My mom isn't wild about the thought, but maybe with some coaxing…" She shrugged. "Maybe this year she'll let me date. I guess I'll see what happens. What about you?"

I hadn't given it much thought. "I don't know… maybe. The whole boy thing still makes me shaky. I'm just not used to being around them yet. Besides, I wouldn't have the first clue what to do with one anyway. I'd end up making even more of a spectacle of myself than I did tonight."

"It won't be that bad; you just have to get comfortable with kissing so it won't seem like such a big deal."

"Yeah, but there's only one problem with that. How do you learn when there's no one to practice on? We'd still need guys."

"Not necessarily," she said.

"You're not going to say we should practice on ourselves, are you? I don't care what those magazines spout—I just can't see myself making out with my arm and taking it seriously."

She laughed. "That wasn't what I was going to say. More like…" She hesitated. "We could practice on each other," she said, her voice uncertain, worried about how I'd react.

I looked at her and realized she was serious. Our dare to kiss had been a surprise of its own, but this suggestion was no less so. The concept left me questioning, not to mention nervous, but I tried to take a liberal stance. I was far from sold on the idea… but maybe, just maybe, it had potential. I'd rather look foolish before her than with a boy I liked.

"I never thought of that," I said, still unsure how I wanted to respond to her idea. Carrie had considerably fewer hang-ups than I did, and was certainly the pioneer in our friendship. "I suppose it would be closer to the actual thing."

I felt her studying me. "It doesn't weird you out?"

Just because she brought it up didn't mean she thought it was as natural as toast for breakfast. Because of that, I wanted her to be the first to answer. I wanted to hear how she truly felt about it. "Does it weird *you* out?"

"No, not really."

After a moment I lied and said, "I guess it isn't that big a deal."

"I was surprised you went through with it tonight. I think Ryan and Brandon were, too."

My forehead wrinkled. "They'd never say anything about it to anyone, would they?" Game or not, I didn't want word to circulate.

She shook her head. "You can trust them."

Hearing that, I felt better. "I think I'd feel more comfortable without the audience."

"Well, we could try it."

"You mean now?"

"Now's as good as any time," she said.

I don't recall how it happened, really; that part seems to evade me. But there came a moment of slamming clarity when all I knew was that it was *happening,* and there I was—heart hammering so violently that it left my ears ringing, and anything else occurring in the world at that moment was as forgotten as my first breath in this world. I experienced a suspended reality—a combination of light-headedness and disbelief, like an intoxicating high right before the crash. And yes, the crash came—a jarring and most unsubtle fall.

I'd been raised—drilled, truthfully—with codes to live by. I'd just broken a major one.

Our Holy Sisters, which for years had been my sole sounding board, my self-contained world, securing a lifestyle my mother expected me to embrace. A lifestyle as stringent as the one they led, where guilt was the invisible Eleventh Commandment of the Catholic Church.

I did believe all I'd been taught, didn't I?

It was different this time; we weren't acting on a dare. I knew our motive; we were practicing the act, hoping to impress the right boy when it came time. But then something happened — in the mix of the moment, in the mix of the alcohol. It wasn't planned, but somehow our kissing experiment turned into something else. Things went further ... and once they had, once I returned to earth from the euphoria ... I wrestled with my feelings at that frank realization, questioning whether our said objective was entirely true.

7

Dusk was approaching when I arrived home from cheer practice on Thursday. Exhausted, I walked in the front door, tossed my pom-poms on the living room chair and headed for the shower. I had been dreaming about a hot, clean shower the entire walk home. I lingered happily in the water, letting it hit my aching muscles. I emerged from the bathroom wrapped in a towel and ready to rest.

I opened my bedroom door and jumped back with a squeal, startled to see Marc in my room.

He turned around to face me. "Oh—sorry."

"*Jeez*—scare me, why don't you...what are you doing in here?"

"Returning your diary," he said, looking at me carefully. "I hate to tell you, but Josh was in here. You need to remember to lock your door."

"My diary?" My stomach fell, an instant reflex. "What are you doing with my diary?"

"Look. I think we should talk."

"Right now?"

"Yes."

"Can I at least get dressed first?"

He rose to leave. "I'll be in the living room when you're done." He closed the door behind him.

I glanced at my diary the moment he left. Locked. Josh probably hoped he could open it, but I carried the key in my purse, and it went with me everywhere. I threw on a pair of sweats, then headed toward the living room. Marc stood by the couch, obviously waiting for me. I had a perfect view of his back.

"Okay, I'm here," I said, and flopped down on the nearest chair. "What is it you want to talk about?" I ran my fingers through my towel-damp hair. "Well?" I pressed when he didn't say anything.

He turned to face me, his expression sober, and took a seat as well. "Kris...I don't know any other way to say this except straight out. I read your diary. Josh found it unlocked...read it. He told me what it said out of concern for you."

I was having difficulty absorbing the news. "I know what's going on, Kris."

"It's locked," I said. I wasn't going to believe this.

"Don't you wish. Check for yourself if you don't believe me."

I sat there motionless. My heart felt large in my throat. What if he decided to tell Mom.

"Kris, you can ask me anything. You know that, don't you?"

I nodded, my thoughts dazed.

"Then why haven't you asked me...about Carrie and you—"

"—Don't." I felt pale as a ghost. "Don't say another word." A second later, the surge of blood rushed to my cheeks. Shock and rage morphed into tears. I sprang to my feet and ran toward the illusory safety of my bedroom.

Marc intercepted me at the doorway.

"Leave me alone!"

He didn't budge. "Running away isn't going to change that I know."

I couldn't stop crying now. When he wouldn't let me pass, I turned to run toward the other exit that led to my room.

He grabbed my arm and didn't let go. "Kris," he begged.

"How could you, Marc!" I choked out between tears. "I might expect it from Josh, but *you*? I said, *let me go!*"

He released my arm. I ran for my bedroom, slammed the door, and locked it behind me. I threw myself face down on the bed and buried my face in the pillow. A second later, I lifted my head, tears streaming down my face, and looked at the nightstand where my diary sat.

Upon closer inspection, I saw he'd been correct. It was closed, but not locked. It may as well have been lying open. *Dammit! Damn Josh! And damn Marc!*

A moment later, he knocked at my door.

"Go away!" I yelled.

"Not until we talk."

"Does the word *privacy* mean *anything* to you?"

"Look, you have every right to be upset, but you have a choice—you can talk to me about it, or you can talk to mom."

"You told mom?" I shrieked.

"I was hoping I wouldn't have to. Now, will you *please* open the door? Please, Krista."

My fear of mom learning what had happened won out. I sat up. I was still crying and didn't want to let Marc in, but reluctantly, I unlocked the door.

What followed . . . ?

The most uncomfortable discussion of my life.

I don't know about anybody else but for me I don't think there will ever be any experience more embarrassing then talking to my brother about kissing a girl or any of the other subjects we covered that night which included what it really means to be gay versus what Marc called "a phase." He did not have to tell me that what happened with me and Carrie was an accident. I could have asked him how to handle the situation I suppose but I was feeling like about two feet tall and maybe four years old, having someone potty train me. Marc tried to go from there to sexual intercourse but I insisted Mom had covered all those basics (well, she had given me a talk about "it" once but it was hard to understand what she was saying and she did not invite any questions). Eventually I got away, just before I was dead from humiliation.

"Kris," he called as I headed for my room.

I turned around. "Yeah?"

"Here." He pulled a pad of yellow paper from the kitchen desk drawer and wrote down some information. When I walked over to him he tore the top page free and handed it to me. "That's Kaelie's number. You can call her anytime if you need to talk about anything. Don't be afraid to use the number, Kris."

"Thanks," I said, and pushed it deep into my pocket, knowing I would most likely never make use of it. "I'll see you in the morning. I'm going to bed now."

He nodded. "Night."

I shuffled through my bedroom door and crashed onto my bed. I was too tired to eat my energy bar.

———

Later that week I came home to find a note tucked halfway under my pillow. I withdrew it and read:

> I realize you may not be comfortable discussing these things with me, but I want you to have the information. If you want to talk or if you have questions, you know where to find me. I wish mom were here too, Kris. I know it would make things a lot easier. Check your nightstand drawer.
>
> Marc

Both furious and embarrassed all over again I went to my nightstand and withdrew the book he'd left there, then slammed the drawer closed, refusing to look at it.

My anger had subsided by the time I crawled into bed for the night. I'd finally realized—despite my reluctance to admit it—that I *was* curious. I brought the mystery book to bed with me and read until I fell asleep. I never said anything about it to Marc, and he didn't say anything to me; he was learning. He knew he'd made it clear that I could approach him with questions when I was comfortable. That earned him two brownie points.

I even showed the book to Carrie when she came over one day after school. She showed equal interest. We lay side by side on my bed and read it together. There was a lot of information. Almost everything was news to me. I never realized how little I knew. I'm not sure if it was shock, fascination, nervousness, or embarrassment that sometimes made us laugh or giggle endlessly. Maybe it was a combination of everything. Regardless of the reason, the book certainly kept us occupied.

In the days that followed, Carrie's behavior toward me was inconsistent. I remained confused about what had happened between us, and wanted to ask her about it, but couldn't bring myself to—I was too scared.

8

Carrie's Mom let me in and music blared from Carrie's stereo as I walked down the hallway to her bedroom. I entered to find her dancing—nothing unusual. I recognized Christina Aguilera's voice; that the sensuous notes were being belted out by a girl who was smaller than I was at eleven defied some kind of natural law. I gave Carrie a quizzical look. "Uh, since when did you learn Spanish?"

"Oh, I haven't," she said. "Brandon called; said he might stop by."

"The weather's beautiful today. I figured he'd be out surfing."

"Yeah, but the waves are flat."

"How do you know?"

"I called the surf report. If you can't find Brandon, it's your best bet to figure out where he's at."

I'd have to remember that. "What's Ryan up to? He's not with Brandon?"

"JV football had to stay late for practice."

I sat down on her bed as she danced back and forth between her walk-in closet and the stack of clothes resting in a three-foot pile on her dresser. They hadn't moved since the last time I was there. Her ponytail swayed and bounced in time to the music each time she shifted her hips.

"Want some help?" I asked. With her cleaning methods, she would be straightening her room for days.

"Sure, if you want to." She continued to rock away to the music, her off-key humming clashing with Christina's perfect pitch.

I grabbed an armload of hangers from her expansive walk-in closet, dropped them in a clanging mess on the bed, and began helping her hang clothes. We developed a system: I dressed the hangers, passed them to Carrie, and she skipped in and out of her closet hanging them in their proper places. We finished the task forty-five minutes later, and took a well-deserved rest on the floor. The moment we were comfortable, the doorbell rang.

Brandon entered a moment later. Well-groomed as always, he wore a simple white polo shirt, black shorts, and a pair of matching black tennis shoes. His hair hung loose around his face and looked as if it had been freshly washed. Bright, golden-glazed strands of honey-colored hair made his tan even more brilliant.

He raised his voice over the music to be heard. "What is *this?*" he asked, looking first at Carrie and then at me. "Why are my favorite twins resting on their duffs when the room sits in this state?" He looked around at the misplaced knick-knacks and books lying carelessly about, cluttering the floor and one side of her dresser.

"Nice to see you, too," Carrie said. "Actually, we're taking a break. Krista's been helping me organize my closet."

"How humanitarian of you, Krista. Looks like you still have a way to go." He stepped over a pair of pink and white sneakers.

"At least the bed is clear. Take a seat," Carrie said.

He carefully perched on the edge of the bed.

"So why aren't you outdoors soaking up the gorgeous weather?" I asked above the music. "I thought you *lived* for days like this."

"I live for waves, and there are none. And since I wasn't in the mood to meander about the city alone, I thought I'd stop by and see what other options were open. I didn't realize the two of you had made plans."

"We haven't, really. Other than finishing my room, I was just going to relax. Nick's busy too?" she asked after a moment.

"He has things to take care of with his girlfriend. Aeleise is enjoying his company right now. Doing what, I have no idea."

"I'm surprised you're not out cruising the mall for pleasant distractions. What—not in the mood for eye candy today?"

"Why do you think I'm here?"

Carrie tossed him some sass. "Well, I feel *much* better now. Isn't it nice to know we made Brandon's cut of approval, Kris?"

"Oh, definitely," I said.

Brandon chuckled. Finally he asked, "Do you mind if we turn down the volume a notch? Christina's voice is lovely, but it's difficult to hear either of you over her singing."

"Oh, sorry." Carrie scrambled to her feet and lowered the volume on the stereo just as a new ballad began. The room felt calmer.

"Thank you," he said.

I looked at Brandon curiously. "How did you know that was Christina? She's singing in Spanish and it's not even a song I recognize in English."

His eyes and tone regarded me as a simple creature. "Krista, the girl's voice is unmistakable in any language. I'm sure she could sing in Japanese and it would still sound just as incredible."

"I never realized you were a fan of her music," I said.

"I'm sure there are many things about me you've yet to discover." He gave me a chastising glance. "What—do you think I listen to show tunes all day or something?"

I laughed. "Did I say that? I was just surprised, that's all."

"Fair enough." He left it at that and looked at Carrie. "So...you never told me how things went the other day. Any positive news?"

I wasn't sure what he was referring to. Whatever it was, it didn't seem to brighten her mood. In fact, it seemed to dampen it considerably.

"Another no show," she said. She picked up the single pink tennis shoe within reach, and began tying and untying its laces over and over again. "Got called away at the last minute. Right." She resisted the explanation. "My mom wasn't surprised; she told me not to get my hopes up."

"I'm sorry," Brandon said.

She shrugged. "There's always a next time, right?"

She let the shoelace relax and leaned back on her hands to consider, her expression brooding. An instant later her attitude changed and she stood up with a new matter-of-factness.

"I think fathers are lore of ancient mythology," she began.

I wondered how long she had worked on her theory.

"How do you figure?" Brandon asked, more out of amusement than a desire to hear her response. "In case you missed the Sex Ed class in sixth grade, children have to be fathered in order to exist. Let me refresh your memory: we didn't get here by means of a cabbage patch *or* a space ship—well, maybe you did."

"Don't be a smart ass. That's not what I mean; I know how babies get here."

"Well, that's a relief," he said dryly.

She rested her hands on her hips. "Be quiet a minute, will you?"

He gave her the floor. "Fine. You were saying?"

"I'm referring to father fathers—real ones. The ones that stay around, like for the purpose of raising a family. It's entirely different."

"What does that have to do with mythology?" I asked.

"Well, how many do you know that *exist*? Any guy can make a baby, but how many are still around after the fact? Evidence of that is thin," she said, gesturing with her finger as if she had researched the topic thoroughly and now shared an educated observation.

"What brought this on?" I wanted to know.

"I got to thinking the other day..."

Always a dangerous phenomenon—at the very least, entertaining. "Go on," I said.

"Well, I mean, haven't you ever noticed all the stray cats that Grams feeds?" Grams was her affectionate name for her grandmother.

"Yeah, so what?"

"Well, it's like, out of all those cats...I've spotted the mothers and they each seem to have three or four kittens. Why are they always the ones who make sure their kittens are fed and that no harm comes to them? Not once have I seen any of the males. It's like they're ghosts or something; they materialize out of nowhere, and disappear just as quickly once they've completed their mission. They have no sense of responsibility after the fact. They're off again in the wind—*poof*—on to the next thing. There is no family—it's all illusionary. I'm almost sure of it."

Brandon and I looked at each other. I certainly hadn't spent any time studying the lifestyles of four-legged creatures.

"Whose idea was it to expect them to stick around?" she continued, "And how many families *really* stick together anymore? Ryan is the only person out of all my friends whose parents are still married—and who knows if it's happily? What's to keep either of them from taking off when it suits them?"

"Love," I said.

"I don't trust it."

"Are you going to doubt men forever, based on your limited observations?" I asked.

She sighed. "I just don't think anyone should be surprised in the least if their dad's not around," she continued. "I mean, I think leaving one's mate and having multiple partners is an innate male behavior. Let's use Brandon as an example—"

"*What? You compare me to a cat?*"

"Isn't it true that every time you've slept with someone, you're over them immediately afterward? It's like 'on to the next' is almost your motto, right?"

"I don't have any '*motto.*'"

"But you do lose interest shortly after you've had sex with them." She made it a statement.

"I still talk to Seth on occasion."

"You *slept* with *Seth?*" I asked, unable to veil my astonishment. Seth was on the JV team. He had full sleeve tattoos. My mother would have hated him.

He chose not to respond to my comment. His eyes locked with Carrie's.

"Yeah," she said, "only because he didn't want a commitment, and because he gave great—"

"*Carrie!*" Brandon's already wide eyes went wild at her announcement, stopping her before she could say more. He grabbed the stuffed giraffe on her bed and hurled it at her with amazing force. She ducked, but Brandon had extremely accurate aim.

"It's the *truth! You* said it, not me!"

"That information was *not* intended for broadcast. I told you in confidence!" Turning to me he added, "Silence from the peanut gallery."

He turned his attention back to Carrie. "What's that got to do with anything?"

"All I'm saying is that it's in a guy's nature to get what he wants and then bail. Guys are always looking for the next best thing. Cat, human—*whatever*. It's the whole 'grass is greener' deal."

"It's an interesting observation, Carrie." It was all I could think of to say. "But I'd hold off writing any papers just yet."

"Well, thank you for sharing another one of your truly profound insights into my contribution to the world," Brandon said coolly. "Perhaps next time you'll be kind enough to exclude me from your comparative research. It's always nice to learn that you think of me so highly, and to know I've been of assistance in your search into the mysteries of the universe."

"Oh Brandon, I didn't mean to offend you. You know I adore you entirely."

"Hmm," he grumbled. "You have an odd way of showing it."

"Really, Brandon," I said, trying to soothe his bruised ego, "she didn't mean anything by it."

"Easy for you to say; she didn't just compare your sex life and relationship skills with the fleeting instincts of an alley cat."

"I don't have a sex life *or* a romantic relationship," I reminded him. I was suddenly glad.

"Well, if that's the latest of Miss Einstein's discoveries—and even if it's not—I think I shall take my leave of you two ladies and your novel ideas until tomorrow."

"You're not angry, are you?" Carrie asked him.

"No, just...I don't know."

"What are you going to do?"

He shrugged. "Maybe check out Ryan at practice, see if he needs a lift home. Who knows—maybe I'll search out one of the neighborhood cats, ask its opinion on your theory. I'll catch you guys later."

"Bye," I said, and gave him a quick hug. Carrie did too.

"Bye, you two."

He looked dejected as he closed the door behind him.

9

Carrie first shared the news with me as we walked home from school Monday afternoon.

"Krista," she sighed, eyes dreamy as she gazed at the sky, "I think I'm in love."

I cocked my head at her. "What?"

"I met him."

"Whom?"

"Him," she said, and practically swooned. "Jalen McAllister."

Unmoved, I asked, "Am I supposed to recognize the name?"

"He's a senior at Fairmont. You don't know who he is?"

"No. Should I?" Fairmont was our rival school; why she assumed I'd be familiar with the students there was beyond me.

She looked slightly annoyed. "You know, the guy I pointed out—the one we saw talking to Jessa's brother at last week's game. Remember him?"

"Vaguely," I said, recalling that night. "And you met him how?" Carrie could be uncommonly creative when inspired.

She gave me an impish smile. "Well, when I saw them together, I asked Jessa who Collin was talking to; she said it was his friend from Fairmont." She slipped her thumbs beneath the shoulder straps of her glittering, baby-blue backpack. "Then Jessa called yesterday and invited me over to her house. I could pretend to be offended that the only reason she wanted my company was to grill me about Josh, but we both know Jessa without an ulterior motive isn't Jessa." She shrugged. "Anyway, she picked me up and we went back to her place, and twenty minutes later, guess who shows up?"

"Let me guess—Jalen."

Her smile was as wide and bright as a rainbow. "Yep. He stopped by to see Collin."

"How fortunate for you," I said with a small laugh. "So, what happened?"

"Well…"

She rambled on about the details of the meeting. My interest returned after she said, "So, get *this*—out of nowhere Jalen tells me that he and his friend Eric are going to the Fairmont party, and that if I had a friend who wanted to go, we could go with them. I told him I knew someone who would *love* to go. So… he gave me his *number!* Can you believe it, Kris? I almost *died!*"

"I thought Collin was twenty-one or twenty-two. That would mean he graduated from Fairmont like… three years ago. Is he going to the party?"

"How should I know?" she said, irritated by the shift in subject. "I didn't ask him. I'm not talking about Collin."

"Well, if Jalen and Collin are friends, he must be considerably older."

"I told you—he said he's a senior. That's not *that* much older."

I looked at her. "A senior."

"Yeah. What?"

"You don't even know the guy."

"I know *that*—but I want to. That's the point."

I didn't say anything.

"So, what do you think?" She sounded excited.

"What do I think about what?"

"About me going to the party with Jalen!"

"Don't you think it's a little strange he's not already going with someone? Nothing against you, Carrie, but he's a senior, you say he's gorgeous, and he's going to ask a freshman he doesn't know to a party you just now heard about?"

"Maybe he doesn't know I'm a freshman. Who cares? Besides—I didn't *just* hear about it. Jessa's mentioned it a few times," she said defensively. "She's going to be there with Micah and *he's* a senior. What does it matter?"

At least Jessa and Micah will be there. "I don't know," I said. "I guess stranger things have happened." We were almost at my house. My arms ached from carrying books; I juggled them, switching them to the other side.

"So, what poor shmuck do you plan on dragging to this party?" I asked. This sounded like something right up Morgan's alley.

She smiled triumphantly. "What do you plan on wearing?" she asked.

I stopped dead in my tracks. "Pardon me?"

"Oh, come on, Kris. We'll —"

"Carrie, you didn't!" But I knew she had. She had actually accepted a date with this guy Eric on my behalf. "How could you do such a thing without asking me?"

She didn't say anything.

"I don't want to go — find someone else." I walked away.

She scampered to catch up with me. "Please, Kris. It'll be fun."

"*No.*"

"You're the only friend I could possibly bring. No one else could pull this off. No one else has any panache."

"You should've thought of that before."

"I'll do your biology homework all week," she promised.

I shook my head. "Tempting, but I'd rather sweat it out."

"I'll do *anything,* Kris. Please."

"Carrie, you know I don't want to hang out all night with some guy I don't know."

"I'll go with you to Aeleise's and sit through Daemon's Bible study." Boy, she *really* wanted me to go with her. I looked at her strangely.

"Don't look at me like that. I've seen the way you look at him." Daemon? I started going to bible study at Aeleise's a few months before. It made perfect sense. After all my mother was a missionary and I was only recently out of parochial school. But if I were really honest with myself I would admit that it was the leader of the study, Aeleise's brother Daemon, who kept me going religiously — so to speak. That gorgeous guy who had taken our homecoming photos was a lure to bible studies. Was God having a joke on me?

"Have you completely *lost* it?"

She laughed. "Okay. Whatever."

That irritated me. Suddenly the thought of seeing her suffer through Bible study became appealing for that reason alone. I knew how much she detested it. I paused to reconsider.

"I don't even know the guy, Carrie."

She translated my remark into a victory. Excitement beamed across her face like laser. "It's only one night. How bad can it be?"

Did I really want to speculate on that? "I'll think about it," I said.

"Thank you, thank you, *thank* you, Kris! I owe you big-time. We'll have fun, I swear."

"Bible study...*and* church," I added, knowing I had her. She didn't even flinch.

"You got it."

———

I'd just arrived home from Carrie's when Josh, making a rare visit to the laundry room, saw me heading for my bedroom.

"Rumor has it that you and Carrie plan on going to the Fairmont party the seniors are throwing." He poured two heaping cups of detergent into the load, and then nudged the washer lid shut.

Boy, word traveled fast. And how did anyone know I was the girl Carrie had told Collin she'd bring along? "Rumor? Where'd you hear that?" I asked, feeling suddenly edgy.

"Oh, someone from school filled me in." That would be Jessa. I was sure of it. She must have been on Josh's telephone the minute Carrie left the house. Jessa would have known immediately who Carrie planned on bringing to the party. He turned to look at me. "Kris, you can't go to the party."

"Why not?"

"You're the one who just *had* to be to be a member of the dance team; Your friends talk, Kris, and word is already spreading about you and Carrie planning to get chummy with the crowd from Fairmont."

"They're having a party. So what? I never said I was going." Well, that was the truth, technically.

"Well, I'm telling you right now that you're not."

"And who died and made you king?"

"Don't push it. I already said no. It looks bad for the school, and it's not even safe for you guys to be there. It's a senior party—almost everyone there will be eighteen and over—and I know the guys who are throwing it. I'm telling you . . . it's bad news. They're losers, Krista. Trouble. You're fourteen. Why would anyone their age want to see someone as young as you or Carrie? Get with the program, Kris. You're in way over your head."

I was angry with him for trying to dictate my every move. He wasn't Mom. He wasn't even Marc. Even so, his words remained in the back of my mind.

———

Wednesday, after practice, Nick and I went to Aeleise's house for bible study. Carrie couldn't get out. It would be an intimate group—just the four of us. The evening seemed to start out fine, but then Daemon brought up the issue of honesty. He read a passage from the Bible, just as he often did, but with this particular selection, Nick obviously fell out of his comfort zone.

Daemon wrapped up with, "All relationships—at least ones that work—are built on a foundation of trust. Whether it's friendship, business, dating, or marriage, relationships are a partnership—they all require honesty and integrity."

Daemon saw Nick's uncertainty. "Something's on your mind. What is it?" he said.

Nick spoke slowly. "Well, what if the truth hurts other people? Wouldn't it be better then, to keep it to yourself?"

Daemon tilted his head slightly; the hair partly covering his eyes fell away, no longer hindering his view. "No one likes the idea that they may bring hurt to others, but I can't think of anyone who'd choose being lied to over knowing the truth, can you?"

Nick didn't offer a response, didn't meet his eyes.

"Anyone who is truly your friend will respect that you're able to be up front with them."

Nick fidgeted, preoccupied with his thoughts.

Aeleise looked at him. "You don't look well. Are you all right?" She placed her hand on his. "You're clammy." She brushed back his bangs. "You're sweating." Concern filled her voice.

"My mom's just getting over the flu. I—I think I may have caught it."

Daemon looked at Nick, then at the obvious concern on his sister's face. "Why don't we call it an early night?"

Aeleise lightly touched Nick's arm. "I'll drive you home. You should be in bed."

"I think you're right," he said.

Daemon decided to drive me home. We all agreed to meet again the following day. Nick didn't show.

10

As the days passed, Carrie and I saw less and less of Brandon. I attributed this to his new interest in Nick. Ever since he had accepted Nick's offer to go swimming, they had become inseparable. Must have been a successful swim session. Although Nick didn't surf, he enjoyed being outdoors and seemed perfectly content to spend hours at a time doing nothing other than watching Brandon surf the various hot spots.

Not surprisingly, Aeleise saw less and less of Nick. He, who was once present at every Bible study, slowly but steadily withdrew from the group. It was no secret to me how hurt she was, but she took care to hide her disappointment as best she could; she believed he would come around. I doubted it. I frequently dropped by her house to visit, and did my best to cheer her.

Often I'd see her brother attempting to do the same. Before long, he and I formed an alliance, and together we were able to take Aeleise's mind off things. One afternoon, after helping us with our homework, he left for the evening.

"What is it your brother does for work?" I asked Aeleise after he had left.

She erased the answer to the trigonometry problem she was working on and brushed away the debris. She began again; her pencil moved rapidly on paper as she figured the solution and socialized simultaneously. "He's a private pilot. But he spends more time working for the church and the youth group than he does flying. Occasionally he'll take on a private client or the odd job, but he mostly flies for recreation." She looked up at me from her paper, tapped the end of her eraser thoughtfully against her lips. "You should ask him to take you up sometime."

"He looks young to be a pilot," I said.

"He's twenty-eight. That's not young considering there are fifteen year olds who are pilots nowadays."

Twenty-eight? I thought he was nineteen or twenty. He certainly didn't *look* two years younger than Marc.

True, he forever kidded around with Aeleise the way Marc did with me, but Daemon had his differences, too. Through time spent in his company, I had learned his views on many things, and his were far more conservative than Marc's. I often listened to Aeleise and him debate over subjects I hardly considered.

Aeleise was good at debate; a member, with Brandon, of the sophomore mock trial team, she got plenty of practice. Debate was all they did. An important skill to possess, I was beginning to discover. Aeleise was also the only friend of ours willing to challenge Brandon in a game of trivial pursuit.

"I don't know why everyone is so intimidated by Brandon's intelligence," she said dismissively. "I think it's great. At the end of every game, we both walk away knowing more than we did when we started. It's the same with mock trial; he's a fierce competitor. You can't be lazy when you're his opponent; he forces you to think." She sighed. "Now, if I could only get him to debate religion ..."

In California I seemed to learn more off the school campus than I did in school. For me, the cultural diversity of California was a culture *shock*. However, even here there were some things the classes just didn't cover — like the occasional encounters Carrie hinted at taking up, which so far I had resisted. Her wanting to pursue a physical side to our friendship left me completely at a loss. How could she be looking forward to spending an evening with Jalen McAllister or Ryan for that matter and still be curious about kissing girls? I thought about the "phase" Marc had referred to in that "talk" we had. I wish I had asked him how long a phase lasted.

Eric called that night and luckily, I answered the phone. The moment he spoke, I knew he was considerably older. He was much too self assured to be a boy my age. Only Brandon, who was two years older anyway, was so smooth. Eric also had a rich voice. I learned from Josh years ago—after one of his blind dates had gone poorly—that it's always dangerous to pair a person's look to their voice before meeting. It invariably leads to disappointment. Therefore, I played it safe. I imagined Eric as a pimply waif, with blond, matted hair like that of an unkempt dog, and crooked teeth that had an odor so foul, it drew flies.

There was no long discussion; he and Jalen would pick Carrie and me up at 9:30 the night of the party. Now all I had to do was figure out how I was going to get past Josh. When had I turned into such a sneak, I wondered. Had public school changed me so much? Was I hanging around the wrong people? I refused to believe that. My friends were loyal and awesome. Maybe I was going through a phase.

———

The last bell sounded; I had no time to waste. I headed down the hallway with an armload of books. I planned to find Nick at his last class, before he had the opportunity to slip away. He was avoiding Aeleise. Now he was trying to avoid me; I knew that. Actually, other than Brandon, he had been effectively avoiding all of us. I wanted to know why.

I spotted him as he walked out the door. He didn't see me; I would just have to fix that. I fixed my eyes on his teal shirt so I wouldn't lose him. Quickly hiding myself within a group of people, I advanced quickly until I knew I was ahead of him. I did an about-face and stopped directly in front him, catching him off guard. He stopped—I hadn't given him any other option. I caught and held his gaze

"Hi." I smiled at him, hoping it didn't look as fake as it felt. I really wanted to yell. He hadn't said anything, didn't even acknowledge me except for that look in his eyes. He turned to walk away. I rushed up beside him. Although we were friends, I wasn't sure we were close enough for me to say "What the hell!" so I settled for, "Are you okay?"

He didn't answer. I struggled to match his pace. With his stride being one to my two, I was getting my cardio for the day. "Did any of us do something wrong?" I asked.

"No." He hadn't even bothered to look at me.

"Do you want to tell me what's the matter?"

"Nothing's wrong; I'm fine."

Boy, he must *really* think I'm a fool. I grabbed his arm and pulled him to a halt. "Nick. You're not telling me the truth."

"Krista, don't."

"I'm not letting you go until you tell me what's going on. Why are you avoiding Aeleise? Do you have any idea how much you're crushing her? I know you're not a jerk, Nick." I decided to say it anyway. "So *what the hell* is going on?"

He shook his arm free and looked at me, angry at my persistence. I knew he was holding back something. I only prayed that it wasn't an effort to contain tears; I hadn't prepared myself to see Nick cry.

"Nick, please. Tell me what's going on," I said, lightening my tone. God wasn't giving in to my requests today; the worst happened, and his tears fell freely. I repositioned myself so no one else could see him. "Come on," I said, and led him around the back of the school building, to a side where no one ever went. He leaned his back up against the stucco wall. "What's going on?" I asked lightly.

"I don't want to talk about it. Really." He looked around. "Especially not here."

"No one's around, and no one will be."

"Is Aeleise putting you up to this?"

"No. But I'm sure she'd like to know what's going on."

"Don't be so sure about that."

"She's *crazy* about you, Nick. She *adores* you. If something's wrong, she deserves to know about it."

"Even if it will tear her up? No. I don't think so."

"So you've lost interest in her? You want to break up—is that it?"

"*No!*"

"Then what's the problem? Why won't you make this easy?"

"Because it's not something *easy,*" he said.

"Is there someone else?"

He didn't say anything. I prayed he hadn't cheated on her.

"Another girl?" I pressed.

"No."

I threw up my one free hand, exasperated. "Then what? It's obvious that whatever it is, you're upset about it too."

"I don't want anything to get back to her, Krista. I'm trying to work things out. I really want to be able to stay with her." He certainly wasn't going to win any Academy Award for that statement; it was far from convincing. "Things are just complicated right now, that's all."

"If you *want* to be with her, then what reason could you possibly have for avoiding her?"

He said, "I want to hang out with my friends more right now." He looked at the ground, feigning interest in a crack that had given way to an obstinate patch of grass erupting beneath the asphalt.

"Last time I remember, you and Aeleise *were* friends, but if what you're trying to say is that you want to hang out with the guys more, fine. She's not stopping you, so how does that affect you and Aeleise?" I shifted my books to rest on my hip.

With a dirty white sneaker he kicked a piece of crumpled notebook paper that had blown in front of him. "I don't know how to say it."

"Just *say* it, Nick."

He looked straight at me. "I don't even know you well enough to trust you."

"You're right." I couldn't argue that. "But I guess you'll have to make a judgment call. I'm telling you now that, no matter how much I'd like to do otherwise, anything you say stays between us."

He considered my statement, and took plenty of time to do it. His eyes were beseeching. "Krista, *promise* me you'll keep this to yourself."

"I promise."

He hesitated, then spoke cautiously. "If you had a boyfriend you'd been dating for a while, and you *knew* he was in love with you, how well do you think he'd take it if you were to suddenly tell him you're attracted to girls? Can you imagine his reaction?" He shook his head. "I doubt it would go over well."

So we were walking in similar ballparks.

"Then add to that mess that the girl you want to be with also happens to be one of *his* good friends. Can you see where that might pose a problem?"

I set my books down on the weathered blacktop. "Nick, who are you talking about?"

He inhaled deeply and slowly let it go. It was so long before he uttered another word that I wondered if he would answer me at all. When he spoke, it came out soft enough that I almost didn't hear him. "Your ... *surfer* boy."

"Brandon?" You're interested in Brandon?" Obviously I knew this. I pretended surprise.

"Like there's anyone who isn't."

"What brought on this realization?" I asked, still feeling shell-shocked.

"A few things," he said, resigned.

I looked at him expectantly. "Are you enjoying dragging me through hell here or what?" He was quiet for a minute. "I blew it off at first; spent more time with Aeleise, started going to their Bible studies ..." He shook his head. "But then I started hanging out with Brandon and we spent a lot of time together."

His voice fell quiet, cheeks flushed in embarrassment. "Then I dreamt about him."

"Okay, and what?" I asked, trying to determine why he found that significant. "Now you think you're destined to be with Brandon, or something?"

He still found the ground fascinating. "No," he said, agitated. "It just tripped me out. I'd never dreamt about a guy like that before. It was ... weird."

"Dreams usually *are* weird, Nick."

He shook his head. "Never mind. You won't get it."

"Then explain to me. What am I missing?"

"You're not a guy, Kris. There are some things that ... as far as I know, you'll never experience. That's as much as I'm saying—I'm not gonna get into this."

"You're serious." I hadn't meant to say it aloud.

"No, I'm lying," he said sarcastically.

I shook my head, tying to think of what I wanted to say. "I'm sorry ..." *Why did Brandon always have to be right?* "I just didn't—" *believe Brandon.* I couldn't tell Nick that. "Yeah, well, neither did I, until then. Well, maybe I *had* thought about him once or twice before." He shrugged unhappily. "I just don't look at Aeleise that way."

He hadn't looked at me once. I could tell he had mixed emotions about accepting the facts. I sympathized with his predicament. "Does Brandon know?"

"You could say that."

That surprised me. Brandon hadn't revealed that he'd proven his hypothesis true. Brandon delighted in flaunting his triumphs, yet he hadn't said a word about it.

I didn't say anything for a minute, but then it didn't seem fair not to share my situation with him after his brave admission. "Look, I need you to keep this to yourself as well, Nick ... but you're not alone. Carrie and I are working through a similar situation. It hasn't been easy."

He looked up at me then, a look of surprise on his face. "Yeah?"

"Yeah."

He seemed grateful for my honesty. "Shit, Kris."

I suppose that was one way of phrasing it.

He was trapped in an unfortunate situation that would inevitably leave someone hurt. The way he made it sound, if he had to make a choice ... I had a feeling I'd be passing the box of Kleenex to Aeleise before long. Still, I read uncertainty in his eyes.

"Aeleise—what am I going to do about Aeleise?" he worried,

running both hands over his face. "You probably think I'm full of shit, but I really *do* care about her, Kris."

"I know you do." I could tell by the subtle tremor in his voice that he found it difficult to keep his emotions under lock; he wasn't about to cry again—at least not in front of me.

"This whole thing is fucked up, Krista. Aeleise is so good to me. The last thing I want to do is hurt her."

I knew he would never intentionally hurt Aeleise. Unfortunately, there was no way around that. "I know, Nick. One step at a time. Let's both just take this one step at a time."

11

Friday night—*the* night. Carrie and I charged into her room to get ready. Carrie jumped on the bed and I followed right behind her.

"Krista, can you believe that we're actually going to the party?"

"I have to admit, I hadn't expected my social life to pick up so soon." I stared at the ceiling as I lay on my back, actually considering the possibility of having a good time.

"What should we wear?" She sprang to her feet and over to her closet in one quick movement. "We *have* to look gorgeous tonight. I want to wear something that will give Jalen a lasting impression." She pulled out a few outfits, comparing them against herself in the mirror. "What are you going to wear, Kris? I think you should wear something of mine."

"What did you have in mind?"

"Well, I've been thinking… what if we went dressed a little more daring than usual? You know," she reminded me, "we *are* going to be around older people—a whole different crowd. I don't want to look like we just got out of junior high."

"Of course we won't," I assured her. I figured with the right clothes and makeup, we could add a few years to our age. "What do you have that would look good on me? Throw me something to try on."

"Here, try this." She threw me a shimmery black slip dress. "It'll look great on you."

I picked up the dress and held it in front of me. "Is this *all there is?*"

"Don't be silly—it's perfect. Let me see it on you."

"All right." I dropped my clothes and wiggled into her slinky dress. It felt sensual and fit perfectly.

Carrie's mother was so different than mine. She wasn't like a girlfriend or anything like that. She was more like not paying attention a lot of the time. I knew Carrie was really sad about her father disappearing out of her life pretty much and to have her mother basically invisible. My mother had more involvement in my life and she was thousands of miles away.

"Stand back and let me look at you," she said. I stood back and she nodded approvingly. "That's the one. It looks incredible on you, Krista. It fits you *perfectly*. You *have* to wear it." Her eyes glowed. She handed me a pair of heels that appeared far too complicated to be considered practical—but then, I don't believe the word practical had a place in Carrie's grand scheme for the night. "Here, try on these. I bought them specifically for that dress. I hope they fit you."

"I hope I don't break my neck trying them on. Can you actually *walk* in these, Carrie?"

"Mmm-hmm. Takes a little practice, though. Don't worry; you'll have time to get used to them."

She watched anxiously as I crisscrossed the laces around my calf and wound them about my leg in a steady ascent toward my thigh. I tied them right below the knee. Maneuvering carefully, I stood—now six inches taller.

"Wow," I said as I balanced on her near-stilts.

"Wow is right—you look *amazing*, Kris. But, lose the bra—at most, you'll be able to get away with a G-string." She shook her head. "God! Eric is just going to *die!*"

Wondering whether I should take out life insurance against the shoes, I looked at my reflection in the mirror and smiled. "I like it. I think I will wear it. Thanks, Carrie."

"My pleasure," she said, still smiling. "Now, help *me* find something to wear." She sifted through more clothing. "What do you think about this one?" She held out a two-piece outfit sized to fit a doll.

"Where did you get *that?*" I gasped.

"I bought it a while ago. I've just been saving it for a special occasion." She smiled, her eyes still on the scraps of silver fabric. "Do you like it? What do you think?"

I laughed. "It looks lethal! Try it on. I've got to see you in this."

She giggled and untied the dress she had on, letting it fall to the floor. She stood tan, slender and naked before me.

"I need your help to get this on," she said, walking toward me. She handed me two thin metallic chains. "Here—hold these up for me while I slip into the front part." She slid in between my arms with her back to me. Her skin felt like silk as it brushed against me. I caught the sweet scent of her new perfume, lingering faintly on her skin. "Now you have to cross the chains in the back, and then hook it up front again."

"Okay." I carefully draped her breasts with the silver metallic material and then hooked it.

"Perfect—we're halfway done; now all I need is your help getting into the skirt." She handed me the last piece of the ensemble and grinned devilishly at me. "Will you do the honors?"

I played right along. "Gladly," I said, and gave her a smile of my own.

I knelt and carefully wrapped the silver micro-chain fabric around her tiny hips. I clasped it carefully, making sure her belly button remained exposed. The skirt barely covered her from behind. The eye-catching outfit made her body a beacon, teasing from every angle. Had I been of the opposite sex, the effect would have been only too obvious.

Carrie's doorbell rang at 9:30. Her mother was on a date, which was convenient. We ran downstairs and gave each other's appearance a last minute look over, then eyed each other nervously and took a deep breath. This was *the* moment. I had prepared myself to expect the worst, and I had my handbag ready to swat her if Eric turned out to be unbearably disgusting.

I nearly died when she opened the door. I stood there, stunned, as they introduced themselves. I began to think Carrie had summoned otherworldly help to inspire their invitation. They certainly couldn't be wanting for dates. Blond, blue-eyed Eric looked like he'd been torn from the pages of Vogue magazine—and noting his 6'2" height, I was glad I'd worn heels.

Jalen had dark hair and green eyes; he was no less handsome than Eric. I almost wished they hadn't been so good-looking—I felt a little inadequate, afraid we'd never be chic enough for them.

We arrived at the party by 10:00 P.M., each of us appropriately draped on our dates. The party was in one of the mansions in the Upper East End of Newport. Whoever the owners were, they had plenty of money. People greeted Jalen and Eric the moment we walked in the door. All eyes were on me and Carrie as Jalen and Eric led us to the bar.

"What would you like to drink?" Jalen asked us.

What could we say? Neither of us had ever been old enough to buy alcohol ourselves. Carrie and I looked at each other.

"What ever you suggest," she supplied quickly.

"Something fruity?" he asked.

"Sounds great."

Eric looked at me.

"The same, please," I said, wondering what we'd just ordered.

Although Carrie and I were younger than the rest of the crowd, we were two of the best looking girls there. I was surprised, but pleased. We had done well; our choice of clothes had paid off. Even so, the atmosphere remained intimidating. I looked around for Jessa, but didn't see her. No familiar faces. Not one.

Eric returned from the bar and handed me my drink.

I cautiously tasted the green concoction, and was relieved to find it delicious. A few more sips of this and perhaps my nerves would calm. Jalen and Eric socialized. Everyone seemed to know them; almost everyone came up and said hi. As we stood by the bar, a tall, lanky boy with strawberry-blond hair approached Jalen and pulled him aside to talk privately. A moment later his friend left and Jalen returned. He and Eric escorted us to a couch across the room.

"Will you two be all right here for a few a minutes?" Eric asked me.

"Sure, we'll be fine."

He gave me an appreciative smile. They crossed the room and disappeared up the staircase. The moment they were out of sight, Carrie and I moved closer together.

"What do you think they're doing?" she wondered.

"Who knows? Who cares?" I said, unconcerned. I was just happy to have Carrie's attention all to myself for the moment. "How are you feeling?" I asked, noticing that she'd wasted no time in finishing three-quarters of her drink.

"Good. How about you?"

"I feel okay. The drink is helping." I held up my glass.

She smiled. "Good, huh?"

"Yeah."

"I'm going to get another drink while we wait. You want one?"

"Sure. But no more after that, okay?"

"Last one—I promise." She trotted off to the bar.

As her tiny frame slipped through the crowd, I couldn't help but smile. Warmth slowly suffused my body and I welcomed it; I'd been freezing in her slip dress.

Carrie returned a moment later with two full cocktails. "Madame," she teased as she handed me my drink with a bow.

"Why, thank you," I said.

We continued to drink and chat. Before long Jalen and Eric returned and we wandered through the house, cocktails in hand, checking out the scene. When we ventured into a smaller room down the hallway, the ambiance was far different from the room we had just left. Here, blue lights made the room darker, and the music pulsed with a slow, deep, rhythmic beat. I could make out the scent of marijuana beneath the competing scent of incense. Three people sat on the couch, sharing a joint. Despite that, I could tell Carrie liked the room as much as I did. Since Jalen and Eric seemed content to stay, we decided to stay as well.

"Who's your friend, Jalen?" one of the guys asked, looking at Carrie.

"Carrie, this is Scott."

She shook his hand. "Hi," she said politely.

"Pleased to meet you." He gave her a seedy grin. His focus then shifted to me. "And you are?"

"Krista," I said, and didn't offer my hand. Eric lightly put his arm around me.

"Nice to meet you, Krista," Scott said.

The girl to Scott's left passed him the smoldering joint; he put it to his lips and took a long hit. He held it out to Jalen while he held his breath. Jalen took it.

"Do you want to smoke?" he asked Carrie.

The girl on the couch hadn't taken her eyes off Carrie. She was smirking.

"Sure," Carrie said, sounding anything but. I looked at her in astonishment. Jalen must have realized by my reaction that Carrie had never smoked pot before.

"Have you ever taken a shotgun hit?" he asked her.

"No."

"It's easy. I'll show you." He pulled her closer. "After I hit this, open your mouth like you're going to kiss me and inhale. I'll blow the smoke into your mouth."

I couldn't believe she intended to go through with it. She followed his instructions to the letter, and it went just as he said it would. Jalen passed the joint to Eric.

"Do you want to try it?" he asked me.

Carrie turned to me with a look that required no words. *Dammit.* Why was I going along with this when I didn't want to?

I was trembling. I knew I should never have agreed to come. "Can we try it the same way?" I asked, trying to sound like I wanted an excuse to kiss him, rather than revealing that I had no idea what I was doing. He gave me a curiously suspicious smile. I don't think he bought it, but he humored me anyway.

"Yeah," he said, and eyed me, one brow raised, as he took the hit. He leaned toward me and met my lips with his.

I inhaled as Carrie had. I was afraid I would start coughing.

Eric passed the joint to the other guy sitting on the couch. I never did learn his or the girl's name. The joint passed around in a circle two more times. My anxiety had completely left me; I began enjoying myself. We giggled, and the giddiness took over, leaving us with the maturity of four-year-olds. I knew we looked foolish, but I lacked the ability to control it. I listened to the pounding, enticing rhythm flowing around us, seemingly begging us to dance.

Carrie took my drink and set it down next to hers. She grabbed me by the hand, pulling me up to dance with her in the center of the room. With Carrie, I easily lost myself. We were comfortable with each other, and the alcohol, the pot, and the atmosphere drove away our inhibitions. She pulled me close to her, placing my hands on her body. Her skin felt smooth beneath my hand as I cupped her waist, and the sweet smell of her hair as it lightly brushed my face made me drowsy. I forgot about everything else for the moment. I didn't know or care where I was. I just wanted to stay like this forever—with Carrie against me, warm and soft. Her lips looked so inviting that it took everything in me not to kiss her right there. I knew by the way she danced that she felt the same desire. She moved to kiss me, and I was prepared to let her.

Suddenly I felt a hand at my waist. I reluctantly turned toward Eric. What was I doing? I looked at Carrie and noticed Jalen standing behind her. Reality check. I removed my hands from Carrie's hips and remembered my date.

He smiled. "You two dance well together. You must be really close."

Apparently he had enjoyed our little show. I looked around and noticed that the other people in the room had disappeared. It was just the four of us now. I liked that.

"You could say that," I said, looking wistfully at Carrie. She was already in Jalen's arms. I wanted to be in his place so badly. These feelings about Carrie were new. After we had kissed that first time she was the one who would bring it up when we were together and a few times we had "practiced" some more. I admit it. I was curious and confused no matter how many books Marc gave me. But the wanting to touch her and draw closer I felt just now was exciting and it was very scary. What kind of woman was I becoming?

"Are you two ... ?"

"Really good friends," I supplied quickly.

"Right." He smiled. His twinkling eyes laughed, telling me he thought otherwise. "Do you want to get out of here? We could leave and give them some privacy." He nodded in their direction.

I looked back at Carrie and Jalen to find them locked in a kiss. "Sure," I murmured. "Let me tell her we're leaving." I walked over to the lip-locked couple, fighting my urge to tear them apart. I concentrated on making my voice sound even, unaffected. "Carrie, Eric and I are going to find someplace else to hang out. Are you cool here?"

"Um-hmm," she practically moaned, not bothering to interrupt her kiss to answer me.

I returned to Eric, who was waiting patiently. I hoped that, wherever he took me, we wouldn't be surrounded by a mass of people—I wasn't in the mood for crowds. He took my hand and led me down the corridor. We found an empty room—a beautifully decorated bedroom that boasted a small but elaborate adjoining bathroom. I assumed it was one of many guest rooms, but whose house was this? He closed the door behind us and we walked over to the lofty bed in the center of the room. Beautiful surroundings and a beautiful date—so far, so good.

I had to admit, I found it difficult to get past my initial tinge of jealousy at how easily Carrie accepted Jalen's affections. I felt confused, hurt, and maybe even envious of Carrie's attraction to Jalen, but she was obviously enjoying herself, and so would I. I wondered if her thoughts ever lingered. After all, I had exciting company of my own, and although I had a strong physical desire for Carrie, I believed that with effort, I could transfer those emotions smoothly to Eric, and find myself equally intrigued.

So here I was, alone with Eric—a guy every other girl in America would die to be with. So why didn't I feel the same? If it was normal to like guys, then I wanted to be normal too; apparently Carrie was normal. If Carrie liked it, there should be no reason I couldn't. I tried to be objective about it, to view Eric as a tool.

I looked at him. He would do. I had him all to myself, so I might as well make the most of it.

We sat down together on the bed.

"So, is this your first time at a house party?" he asked.

I really didn't feel like making small talk. I had the desire to roll my eyes, but restrained myself. "Yeah."

I wondered if he'd be dull the entire evening, or just slow to make a move. Anger and drink made me feel reckless. I wanted to prove to myself that I could find Eric intimately appealing. He was undeniably hot—I certainly didn't mind looking at him—but truthfully, he did nothing for me. I tried to force myself to find him desirable. If I drank enough, perhaps I could.

I eyed his lips. I thought about kissing him. Would it be much different from kissing Carrie? I removed my shoes with my toes and moved toward the center of the bed. I made myself comfortable, arranging my body in what I hoped was an alluring pose.

He looked at me curiously ... which led me to believe my attempt at sexy wasn't convincing. He hesitated, but then finally took the hint. He moved closer. I knew that watching Carrie and me had aroused his interest. I hoped his desire hadn't wandered far; I was ready to experiment.

I got my answer. He moved in to kiss me. My heart jumped as he approached. My body jerked in reaction as he slowly parted my lips with his tongue. I wondered if my lack of experience would be obvious. If so, he didn't seem to care. This was my first kiss from a boy, and it was far less subtle than Carrie's; the aggressive energy behind it was far more sexually charged. It overwhelmed me, and I worked to push my fear aside.

He pulled me closer to him; his hand firmly braced my back. I felt so miniscule next to him. My heart pounded in my ears. His other hand moved toward my breast. The new sensation thrilled and unsettled me at the same time, but I didn't stop him. I held my breath as he felt me, shocked by his sudden forwardness. Then, just as suddenly as he had begun, he stopped. I wondered what was wrong.

Nothing. He began unbuttoning his shirt. My nervousness returned as he tossed it aside.

The moment I laid eyes on his chest, I was reminded of the racy cover art that adorned trashy romance novels. I don't know what I had been expecting, but I knew I needed just one moment to think things through clearly. I also knew I'd find it impossible to form a clear thought with him in my field of view. I politely excused myself, stammering a plausible reason for my snap retreat. I prayed I'd masked my nervousness well as I entered the sanctity of the bathroom. I locked the door behind me and caught my breath for just a minute. Maybe I *was* in over my head.

I placed my hands on the sink counter and leaned in to the mirror. I stared hard at my reflection. I needed a serious pep talk. I took a deep breath and looked squarely at my twin. "Okay, Krista," I began, "you can do this. You're fine. He's hot. It's a little awkward, but not necessarily bad—so, why not go for it? Do you think Carrie's wasting any time with Jalen? Of course not; why should you? Exactly. It's settled," I said matter-of-factly.

I stood, straightened myself, and tossed my long chestnut hair behind my back. At least I looked confident. I flushed the toilet for good measure, and then calmly strode out the door. He had pulled back the covers on the bed, and waited for me where I had left him. Only he'd stripped down to his boxers, leaving very little to the imagination. I was almost afraid to take a step closer, but I forced myself to walk over to him.

He stood, showcasing another smile, and pulled me against him. He towered over me now, as I stood without the aid of Carrie's shoes. He bent down and I succumbed to his kiss. Running his hands over my body, he gently pulled down the straps of my slip dress. In a second it fell to the floor. I stood naked against him, save the thong I wore (for all it was worth). The warmth of his skin pressed against mine, and I quickly realized there would be slim chance of me gaining control of the situation. He was nearly three times my size. I followed his lead as he moved us onto the bed.

He pulled away for a moment.

"Could you hand me my wallet?" he asked, pointing at it beside me.

"Sure." I handed it to him.

My mind was spinning, but at least he had remembered protection. I was relieved by his precaution, but worried about myself—where was my head? Everything was happening so fast, I wasn't sure what I was doing. I berated myself for forgetting something that important.

He opened his wallet and produced a small, square, plastic bag. He opened it, dumping the contents onto the nightstand. To my surprise, he withdrew a credit card and a dollar bill. There went my condom theory.

I panicked. The joint had been adventure enough; I didn't like the looks of things.

"You like coke?" he asked.

Did I miss something? I mean, wasn't sex his goal all but a second ago? I was nervous, not to mention confused. Things were moving in the wrong direction—fast. Was I relieved or angry? Had I done something wrong?

"I've never done it," I said. I suddenly felt very unsure of myself as I sat there in only a triangle of fabric.

He focused his attention on the nightstand, carefully dividing the white powder into several lines. "You'll love it," he said without looking up.

I just looked at him, feeling entirely annoyed. The coke fully absorbed his attention. I could have been a poodle, for all he cared. He leaned over his creation, inhaling a single line through his nose. He closed his eyes, losing himself in contentment. He turned back to me with a beguiling smile and, holding out the rolled dollar bill, indicated it was my turn. When I hesitated, he patted his leg and motioned me to come over. I felt out-of-sorts—I didn't like playing second to something that looked like flour—and although I was happy to have his attention again, his suggestion made me uncomfortable.

"Come here." He beckoned again, inviting me over.

I moved closer and he pulled me onto his lap. The last time I had sat on someone's lap like this, I was visiting Santa. He slid one hand gently around my waist and handed me the dollar bill with the other. I wasn't sure why I suddenly liked being this close to him. I took the rolled up bill and looked at Eric. He placed his other hand on my thigh. A surge of nervous anticipation ran through me.

He smiled. "You'll like the way it makes you feel," he assured me, sensing my apprehension. "Just hold one side closed and inhale with the other."

I looked at the line he had laid out for me to do.

"You'll love it, Krista. I promise." He ran his hand up and down my thigh. At least *now* I had his attention—or was it the other way around?

I frowned. "Why do I feel like I'm in a bad after-school special?" I wondered aloud.

"What?"

"Never mind." I bent over the counter, put the dollar bill to my nose, and inhaled the line. I dropped his improvised straw onto the nightstand and waited, unsure what to expect. A second later, my teeth and tongue went numb. Was this normal? When would the good part happen? I waited, but it didn't get any better.

I was still sitting on his lap, and he seemed pleased. He flashed me another one of his winning smiles. "Well?"

"Is my mouth supposed to be numb?" I asked, feeling slightly panicked.

"It's one of the side effects," he said.

He pulled me back on top of him, and we resumed where we'd left off. *Finally.* He pulled me under the covers with him, and skillfully proceeded to remove my panties without missing a beat. He kissed me deeply and I nervously prepared myself for what would follow. The weight of his body pressed on top of mine. I figured the rest was up to him now. We'd gone well beyond my knowledge of foreplay.

He kissed me more gently now. Struck by anxiety, I wondered when he was going to take off his boxers. If we were going to do it, I wanted to do it and be done. I felt slightly sick. If he didn't hurry up,

I'd lose my nerve and never know. Perhaps he needed encouragement. With effort, I whispered the lie in his ear.

"I want you to be my first, Eric. Aren't you going to take off the rest?"

Surprisingly, he rolled off me. I couldn't figure him out. It seemed as if his desire came and went in waves. Was he or was he not attracted to me?

He looked at me skeptically, and then asked, "How old are you?"

"How old are *you?*"

"Krista..."

He never got the chance to finish what he had been about to say. The door slammed open. Josh stood in the doorway.

"Get the *fuck* out of bed and get your shit! We're leaving!" He enunciated every word perfectly, leaving a painful sting. I was horrified. Surely, this couldn't be happening. He looked at the coke on the nightstand. *"NOW!"*

I was too stunned to move. Eric mumbled under his breath, *"Jesus Christ!"*

"Josh—" I said, barely able to speak. I didn't want this to be possible.

"Krista!" he yelled again.

"I'm not dressed, Josh," I said, panicking.

"No shit! Put your clothes *on!"*

"Josh..." I pleaded.

"Krista, you have three seconds to get your ass out of bed, or I'm pulling you out of bed *myself!"*

I knew he wasn't kidding. I decided to cooperate. "Fine—turn around, then!"

He ignored me. His eyes now burned on Eric, and they remained there, unwavering. Afraid of what Josh's reaction might be if I waited a second longer, I hopped out of bed and grabbed my clothing from the floor. I dressed quickly. Neither Josh nor Eric said a word.

Once I was dressed again, Josh glared at me. He shook his head in disgust at my dress and took off his letterman jacket.

"Put it on!" he demanded.

I took his jacket and did as told. The jacket covered the entire length of my dress. Josh grabbed my wrist and yanked me out the door. I had left Eric lying in bed, not a single word spoken between us. I was sure I'd never hear from him again.

"Where's Carrie?" he wanted to know. "I *know* she came with you."

"The last time I saw her, we were in the room down the hall."

"Show me."

I pointed to the door. He dragged me by the wrist behind him.

There was no one in the room.

"Where else would she have gone?"

"I don't know. Maybe somewhere to be alone with Jalen," I suggested.

"Dammit, Kris!"

We went searching up and down the halls, checking every room. There were so many rooms. Josh still had hold of me, making sure I couldn't wander off. All of the rooms were unlocked. Some of the rooms were empty. Some of them were packed with people partying. And some of them were occupied by couples looking for a place to be alone.

The most remote hallway we checked had only three doors. The first opened on a bathroom, the second on another empty bedroom, and the third door wouldn't open.

Josh pounded on the door. "Carrie, are you in there?"

Neither of us heard anything. Josh put his ear to the door.

"Stand back, Krista." He motioned me behind him, out of his way.

Josh kicked the door in, using all of his body force. He disappeared into the room. I followed him.

We stopped and took in the scene before us. Carrie lay alone in bed like a carelessly tossed Skipper doll—all hair bows and no clothing.

"Carrie!" I cried, and rushed to her side, shielding her from Josh's view.

Josh stood still. "Shit."

Jalen's coat and shirt were on the floor beside her. His shoes were across the room. Everything *but* Jalen. Josh seemed to shake himself, then hesitantly approached the bed. Carrie's eyes, heavy-lidded, struggled to open. They fluttered at Josh, but held no sign of recognition. Her eyes were empty, and she had yet to respond.

I touched her face, brushed aside the hair covering her eyes. "Carrie," I whispered, to see if she could hear me. As I looked into her eyes, I realized that I was not feeling well, either.

"Where's Jalen?" I asked her, but my question hung unanswered in the air.

Josh came closer to the bed, stepping over beer bottles, cocktail glasses, and clothing. There was an array of substances on the night-stand, two of which I recognized as coke and marijuana.

"Carrie?"

Josh stood at the foot of the bed now, looking at a barely coherent Carrie. "That son of a bitch!" Enraged, he snatched the sheet and covered her. He displaced me, moving into my position to sit beside her. He took hold of her face, looking into her eyes. "Carrie? Can you hear me? Are you all right?" She didn't say anything.

"Where's Jalen?" he asked. She still said nothing. Her eyes went in and out of focus as she tried to pay attention to him. Josh's eyes scanned the room. He said in a low, fervent tone, "Krista, I need your help."

Carrie did not look well.

"Find her clothes — quickly!"

I ran around the room, searching under pillows, sheets, and the bed. I produced the tiny chain-link dress that she had worn earlier that evening. I handed it to Josh.

"You're kidding, right?"

I shook my head.

"I can't put this on her!" he said incredulously. He handed it back to me. "Put it in her purse." He took off his shirt. "Krista, come help me get this on her."

Josh sat her up and held her. I maneuvered the shirt over her the best I could.

"Where's her underwear?"

"She didn't wear any," I told him.

"Grab his jacket, Kris. Over there." He pointed at the floor. I handed it to him and he wrapped it around the lower half of her body, tying the arms together. "Make sure you have all your things. We're not coming back."

I double-checked. "I have everything."

"I need you to hold the door open, Kris. I'm going to have to carry her out."

I ran to the door and held it open.

We went out the side entry of the house so we wouldn't call unwanted attention to ourselves.

"Where's Jalen?" I wondered aloud as we walked to the car.

"He's long gone, Kris," Josh said soberly. "Grab the car keys. They're in my front pocket."

I grabbed the keys and unlocked his truck.

"Get the side door for me. I'm going to need your help getting her in. We're going to lie her down."

I ran to the other side and pulled her back toward me.

"Stay back there with her, Kris."

He hopped in the driver's seat and locked the doors from inside. We started on our long drive home.

"Are we taking her home?" I asked.

Josh was pissed. "I can't drop her off at home like this! No! She'll stay at our house!"

I sagged in relief.

"I warned you, Kris!"

"How did you know where we were?"

"Jessa called and said she'd be late meeting you at the party. I knew this was the only party going on." He shot me a knowing look.

I would have to thank Jessa later myself. I ventured, "I thought you were going out with Todd tonight."

"I was. Jessa called before I left." He shook his head. "When are you going to learn that I've been doing this way longer than you have? Any scheme you dream up, I've had years to perfect. It doesn't take long to figure you out, Kris. You may slide by Marc—or even mom—but I know how you operate, and I promise you, I'll catch you every time. You couldn't fuckin' listen, could you? You'd better hope she's okay!" He looked at me through his rearview mirror. He calmed for a minute. "Are you okay?"

"Yeah," I said quietly. I felt awful. "You won't say anything to Marc, will you?"

"It's going to be hard to sneak Carrie in as if nothing's happened, don't you think? Don't count on it."

"But I wasn't—"

"I don't want the details, Kris. You can take it up with Marc."

I sulked. I knew I'd be dead. Especially when Marc saw Carrie. I stroked her hair as her head rested in my lap. She was starting to come around. Barely.

We drove for what seemed like forever. Even without traffic, it took us more than half an hour to get home. Maybe Marc wouldn't be up. That, I knew, was wishful thinking. The light from the living room shone as we pulled into the driveway.

Josh parked the car, then carefully collected Carrie in his arms. I grabbed our purses and ran to open the door for Josh.

Marc sat on the couch with his back to us, watching a show on television. It looked like I might get lucky. We headed for my bedroom without a word.

Marc *did* look back. He watched Josh carry in Carrie; they exchanged looks. I started praying.

My room was in a total state of disarray. Clothes, magazines, makeup, shoes, and just about every other little thing that I looked through on a regular basis covered my bed.

"Jesus, Krista! Your room is worse than mine. Open Marc's door. I'll put her in there."

Josh carefully laid her down on Marc's bed. He grabbed a blanket from the corner chair and sat down beside her and covered her with it, carefully tucking the edges in around her. He brushed aside the wisps of hair that covered her face. I was surprised to see Josh showing such compassion.

Carrie rested.

As for me, I followed at Josh's heels as he went to the living room to seal my death sentence with Marc. And he did not spare a thing. By the time Josh was finished talking Marc knew everything, from finding me naked in bed to the cocaine, Carrie's drugged state, who the boys were. There was no question. I was burnt toast.

12

I remained in the hallway after their discussion. It was urgent that I speak with Marc. Josh scowled at me as he retreated to his room. I can't say I blamed him. I leaned against the wall. "Marc?" I called. He turned to me.

"Marc, I need to talk to you. There's—"

"I need to talk to *you*, Krista," he interrupted, his voice harsher than I wanted to hear. "Come here."

I trod nervously across the carpet and stopped at a generous distance from him.

"What the hell happened tonight?" he asked.

"Marc, please—I know what you're going to say. I owe you a huge explanation, and I promise I'll explain, but I *really, really* need your help right now—or rather, Carrie does."

"What's wrong with Carrie? Other than she took some unidentified drugs."

"I don't know, exactly. She says it's her stomach—she's in a lot of pain." I admit my vague description downplayed the situation considerably.

"Her stomach hurts," he repeated.

I nodded.

He waited for me to continue. I thought about all I had seen on the nightstand when we found her—and all that we drank. "She begged me not to say anything, Marc, but I don't know what to do. If we went to see anyone else, her mom would find out. Her mom *can't* find out, Marc," I insisted. "She wasn't supposed to go out tonight, but, well... we did. And now she doesn't look so good."

"Krista, quit dancing around the subject and tell me what the problem is."

"I don't know... can you just help her, Marc—make sure she's okay? She hasn't said much. I don't know what to think. I don't know what she took."

Marc said nothing as he studied me. What could he say to that? He took a deep breath. "I swear, Kris..." Anger wavered on the edge of his voice. He stopped himself, forcing the emotion to subside. "All right, why don't you go in and keep Carrie company while I get my bag. I'll be there in a minute. Let her know I'm coming."

I returned to his room. Carrie was where I had left her, only now she looked frightened, and was clutching the blanket as if chilled.

"I went to get help. Marc is on his way."

"*What?* Krista, *no!* Please—" she pleaded. "I don't want to see anyone!"

"Carrie, it's going to be fine, I swear. Marc is a doctor. We need his help," I insisted. "You're going to have to see *someone.* He's helped me, Carrie. I wouldn't tell him anything if I didn't know I could trust him. I promise, I'll be right here. But you need to let him make sure you're okay. You took a lot of shit tonight. You don't look so good. He might have to give you something to throw up what's in your system."

"I don't want your brother to know I was doing drugs!"

"I know, I know. But truthfully, our gig is up. Josh told Marc everything. Please, Carrie, just trust me. I'm going to be with you the entire time, I promise." I knelt down beside her.

Before she had a chance to open her mouth, Marc knocked on the door. "Krista?"

"Yeah, it's okay. Come in," I said, making the decision I felt was right despite her protests.

He opened the door quietly, shutting it behind him. "*Jesus,*" he said when his eyes rested on Carrie.

The room fell silent except for the whirling sound of the air conditioner, and the leathery creak from Marc's medical bag as he shifted it in his hands. He surveyed the situation for a moment. Carrie was still wearing Josh's shirt as she sat tucked beneath the blankets.

Marc was hesitant to speak. Something in his manner told me he'd walked into a position for which he wasn't prepared. But my faith in Marc's ability was unshakeable.

"You asked for my assistance," he said to me. His eyes shifted to Carrie. "Hi, Carrie," he said in his usual relaxed manner, though I knew he was working hard at appearing casual. "Krista says your stomach hurts." He set his bag down and remained by the door.

"Is anyone going to help me out here?" he asked when neither of us said anything.

"Carrie…" I urged gently. When she didn't say anything, I said, "I don't think she knows what she took."

Unexpectedly, she lowered her face into her hands and began to cry.

"Marc—" the word came strangled into the air, with a meaning I couldn't decipher, a tone so unusual and foreign it didn't sound as if it came from Carrie at all.

My ignorance in this exchange was unimportant. Marc was obviously well versed in the language, because with that, he walked over to her, sat beside her, and pulled her into his arms.

"Shh," he whispered repeatedly as he held her.

I watched her body first crumple, then wilt, her face disappearing against his chest.

"Krista," he said, his voice calm, yet somber, "How long did you leave Carrie by herself?"

"I didn't. She was with Jalen."

"Well, how long was she alone with him?"

I told him what I knew. "I didn't see anything, Marc. Carrie was alone, completely out of it when we found her. Jalen was gone."

He waited, as if expecting me to continue with my explanation, but what more could I say? And without talking to her about it, the exact details of her evening were as much of a mystery to me as they were to Marc.

"Did he wear a condom, Carrie?" Marc asked.

I became panicky at his question. I flicked a nervous glance at her. "*Marc,*" I protested. Carrie hadn't offered an answer, and I didn't expect one from her.

He shook his head. "Just how out of it were the two of you?" He returned his attention to Carrie, still stroking her hair. "I'm taking you to emergency, Carrie. You need to be seen by someone who can examine you thoroughly. I'm sorry, I know you don't like the idea, but I know an excellent doctor who's a woman and happens to specialize in the type of care you need. You'll be in great hands."

He withdrew a notepad and pen and scribbled what appeared to be notes.

"Don't worry. No one will contact your parents," he said when he saw the anxiety materialize on her features. "Once you're properly cared for, we'll discuss how we're going to handle this."

She relaxed.

"Kris," he said, his voice gruff but even. He handed me two white pills that resembled Tic Tacs. "Get her some water and make sure she takes these. They'll help with the pain. That's all until we leave—no soap, no washing."

Marc slowly rose. He turned at the door and said, "I'm going to make a phone call. We'll leave in ten minutes. Krista, give Carrie something to wear." He walked out, but then looked back over his shoulder. "Five minutes, Krista. Then I want to talk to you. Alone. I'll be in the study." It wasn't a request.

I watched him close the door behind him. Carrie sat up. I moved close beside her.

Carrie buried her face against my shoulder. "I just want to go home, Kris," she said, the words muffled between tears and the material of Josh's jacket.

"It's okay," I said, smoothing her hair. "You'll be home before long."

She nodded slowly. "How am I ever going to face Marc again?" she asked, anguished at the thought.

"Neither of us made smart decisions tonight, Carrie," I said, trying to console her. "You don't need to worry about Marc. He isn't going to dislike you over what happened tonight — he's concerned about you, that's all."

"But I see him almost every day." She cringed, mortified at the thought.

"It'll be fine. Really. My five minutes were up. "Carrie, I have to go see Marc. I'll be right back," I promised.

"Just help me understand. This is so unlike you." I looked away. Somehow, Marc hurt was always worse than Marc mad.

"This is *me,* Kris. This is *me* you're talking to — not mom. Since when have you ever been stupid enough to do drugs? I want to know what's going on. I want to know what happened tonight. The truth. *I* am the one responsible for you while she's away. I want to know who these guys are that you and Carrie have been hanging around." His voice rose. "*Look* at me, Kris! I'm talking to you!"

I reluctantly looked up. I had never seen the severe look that now pinched his features.

"How does it happen that Josh can find you and Carrie entertaining company, *nude,* at a party?"

Were you hoping you could be as lucky as Carrie is right now? What do you think — does she seem all right to you? Do you think she was hoping for that experience?" He paused for my answer, but I couldn't find one. He pointed sharply in the direction of his room. "Kris, she's so fucked up right now that if you were to ask her what happened tonight, she truly couldn't tell you — she doesn't have a clue. You have *no* idea what *really* happened, do you?"

"No. Not really."

"That could have been *you* in there, Krista!"

"You're yelling at me!" I whined.

"I have every right to yell! Your best friend is lying in there in tears, wishing she were anywhere but here right now. Have you no concept of that? Why don't you ask her how much she enjoyed her time alone with Jalen? And if she tells you anything other than that it sucked and it was a disappointment, then she's not telling you the truth. Krista, whatever dream-like notions you have about sex, I'm telling you right now — what Carrie endured tonight has nothing to do with love, *or* romance. It isn't even *close* to acceptable. There is no reason for her to be in the condition she's in—not even if it was her first time. Maybe you don't understand the severity of the situation. That's what we call *rape, Krista!*"

His words slugged me in the gut and I stood silent. I remembered how much Carrie liked Jalen, how excited she had been when he had invited her to the party, and how into him she was at the party. I thought about them kissing. Rape to me was something violent and obvious, something far different in my mind. It never occurred to me that things could get completely out of hand. Even now, as she sat in Marc's room, she hadn't mentioned anything to me about Jalen. But she had been disoriented—just beginning to sober up. Still ... wouldn't she have told me if that was what had happened? My mind raced. Why hadn't that thought crossed my mind? I felt sick.

"You should be thankful Josh found you when he did!"

I fought back tears.

"What you're playing around with is serious, Krista. It carries a responsibility and it can have life-changing repercussions. The two of you are playing in a grown-up's world, and you're not grown-ups." He stopped abruptly, as if seeing me clearly for the first time. "Who did your makeup?" he demanded incredulously. "You're wearing more makeup than Kaelie wears at a photo shoot!" He looked at me from head to toe. "Take off Josh's jacket."

I was afraid to move. He was getting angrier.

"Krista, I *said,* take off Josh's jacket!"

My eyes welled with tears. I let the coat fall to the floor.

He stared at me in disbelief. I thought he was going to slap me. *"What the hell is that?"* Carrie's slip dress had done its job. It clung to me, showing off everything that I had wanted Eric to see, and every-thing I didn't want Marc to see. "Look at the way you're dressed! What is that supposed to be—lingerie? Because it looks like lingerie to me! Where's the rest of it?" he demanded. "I can't believe you would leave the house like that—you look like a poster child for Lolita! You're *fourteen,* Krista, not twenty-four—and even if you were twenty-four, I wouldn't want you wearing *that!*"

I cried openly now. Marc had never yelled at me like this before; he'd always been my liaison, the mild-tempered confidant I religiously ran to when things were rocky. He paused long enough to notice how scared I was, how truly upset. When he realized that, he forced himself to cool down, looking away from me so he could compose himself. He sat back down. When he spoke again, he sounded calmer.

"Krista, I love you—you're my sister. I'm telling you this, not because I want to stop you from having fun, but because this is not how it's supposed to be. Why shortchange yourself on something that could be wonderful?" He handed me the box of Kleenex from mom's desk.

I wiped my eyes. "I need to find Carrie some clothes, Marc," I said, feeling devastated by the entire situation, needing to leave. Part of me didn't even want to face Carrie, didn't want to bear the knowledge of what had happened to her when I'd abandoned her. But that was cowardly, and I wouldn't let myself fail her twice.

"I want you to answer two questions for me first. Who are the guys you were with, and *are* you sleeping with either of them?"

My gaze fell to the floor. "Carrie was there with Jalen and I was there with Eric," I said, defeated and distant. "They're both seniors at Fairmont, from what I've been told, and no—I haven't slept with him. Is there anything else, or can I go now?" I waited while he decided.

"There is one more thing. I don't want you or Carrie seeing either one of them anymore. Ever. We *will* talk more about this later, Krista. Are you clear on that?"

I nodded.

"Help Carrie get ready, but as soon as we leave, I want you to clean up and go to bed."

I nodded.

"Yes. You can go now."

Once Marc left with Carrie, I phoned Brandon, feeling more than unsettled about the night's disastrous events. I was concerned about Carrie, and he was closer to her than anyone else I knew.

"Is she okay?" he asked, his voice going quiet at the disturbing information.

I relayed what Marc suspected, or rather, knew. Brandon remained silent longer than expected. "I don't know why Carrie would even chance it, after I already told her how fucked drugs are. She knows how out of hand my life became when I was using."

"You used to do drugs? When?"

"A few years ago, before I found surfing. It isn't important anymore. Tell me again why *you* went to this party."

"Carrie begged me to go."

"Next time say no. Does she really make you that weak?"

"Weak?"

"You went when you didn't want to, right?"

"I guess."

"You *guess?* So you're saying you wanted to be there—wanted to hook up with this guy?" I could hear his doubt, almost chiding, on the opposite end of the line.

"Why wouldn't I? He was cute," I said defensively.

"Right. Next you're going to tell me it didn't bother you to see Carrie with someone else, right?" he shot back, his voice sarcastic. "I don't think so. That's crap and you know it."

"What's *that* supposed to mean? How would you know?" I squinted my eyes to slits.

"Trust me—I know."

"Okay, whatever, *Mr. High and Mighty.*"

"Don't get hostile on me. I'm just trying to point out some things to you, give you a clearer picture, if you will; you get lost in those rose-colored glasses you're sporting all too often. I've given you something to think about."

"Well, last time I checked, I had perfect vision, so don't worry about me."

"I guess that all depends on where you're sitting."

Did Brandon think he was a CIA agent, or what? I didn't say anything.

"Fine—have it your way, but I pick up on the incongruities. Wanna challenge me?"

"I'm not into games—not those kinds," I said.

"All right then, I'm going to bed. I can see I'm getting nowhere. Kris...just be careful, okay? Carrie's a great girl, but she doesn't always use her head. I don't want to see you get into any more messes."

"I will, Brandon."

"Hey Kris...thanks for calling," he said before hanging up the phone.

13

Brandon called Saturday morning and invited me to join him for lunch that afternoon.

His ride had been recently washed and waxed—a ritual he performed often. Brandon took great pride in his possessions and maintained them at near-mint condition. At sixteen, he was the luckiest boy I knew. He had his own beautiful car—a sapphire blue BMW—and no car payment. The words "spoiled" and "Brandon" were synonymous and often used interchangeably.

As I hopped into the car. "Up, Up, and Away" by The 5th Dimension played on his CD player.

"Hungry?"

"Starved."

"Good, so am I. In the mood for Italian?"

"You have to ask?" I said through a grin.

His smile broadened. "Not really; I just thought I'd give you an opportunity to throw me off track. Angelo's & Vinci's it is, then."

The restaurant was one of our favorites, and well worth the considerable drive outside of Laguna—the small, family-owned establishment made some of the best Italian dishes in Orange County. When we arrived, the parking lot was only half full. Our server led us straight to a table.

"May we sit somewhere with more privacy, please?" Brandon requested.

We followed her to an isolated corner of the restaurant. "Is this okay?" she asked.

"Perfect. Thank you."

Brandon seemed out of sorts, distracted—he was quieter than usual, and stared at the menu without actually seeming to read it.

I finally asked, "What's wrong?"

He gave me a wan smile. "Nothing."

"Come on. What is it?"

He took a deep breath and let it out slowly. "I need to talk to you about something."

I wasn't used to such a tentative approach from Brandon—tentative just wasn't Brandon's way.

"What about?"

"You," he said frankly.

The intensity of his gaze made me uneasy. I felt like I sat beneath a microscope. "Me? What about me?"

"Krista, you know what I'm talking about. You haven't said anything about it, but I know you better than that. I would think that you, of all people, could talk to me about it."

My heart picked up its rhythm and I became aware of my breathing. *Please, Brandon, don't turn our luncheon into a nightmare.*

"I don't know what you're talking about," I said carefully.

He continued to look at me, but didn't speak. He had caught me off guard, and I hated surprises.

"If there's anything you want to say, then you'd better just say it," I said.

I wasn't accustomed to the warmth easily recognizable in his eyes. "Why are you doing this, Kris? Is it really all that bad?"

I dropped my eyes. I could feel the heat rising to my cheeks. Of course he would bring me to a restaurant, where there was no escape, no chance to avoid his questions. Good ol' Brandon. I didn't answer him.

"Do you think something terrible is going to happen if you just admit and accept that you like girls?"

I was stunned into silence. The server approached with our drinks. The tension at our table was severe enough that she sensed it, and after setting down our beverages, she scurried away.

"Are you going to say anything?" he asked.

He had tricked me into coming here. Without looking at him, I announced, "I think this conversation is over," and threw my napkin on the table.

"Why are you avoiding my questions, Kris?"

I flashed him a hostile look. "Why are you *asking* me this?"

"Because I care about you, and we're friends."

I tried to whisper, but it came out a hiss. "I don't see how us being friends brings you to any of the assumptions that you're making."

"Are you really going to sit here and deny that you have a crush on Carrie?"

"All day long," I said.

He shook his head slowly. "Why are you doing this to yourself?"

"Why am I doing *what* to myself?" I snapped.

"Torturing yourself like this. Don't you think it was hard for me, the first time I realized I was gay? I had nobody to talk to, Kris. *Nobody.*" His eyes were beseeching, willing me to accept him as a confidant. "Is that what you want for yourself? It's lonely, Kris. Maybe you don't know that yet."

I knew all too well. But he was off the track. What I wanted was so confusing that even if I cared to talk to Brandon about it that was impossible. It seemed like that word 'phase' that Marc had first talked about hit the nail on the head. Ever since the night of the party I had seen everything concerning sex differently. If Carrie could have been so passionate about Jalen, then did she really like girls? If I was interested in a first time with Eric, what was up with me? Most important, since the consequences could turn out as they had for Carrie, why even consider being intimate with anyone at fourteen? But I was not ready to talk to Brandon about this.

"Can't you just *talk* to me about it?"

"What do you want me to say?"

"Just *talk* to me."

I dropped my gaze and leaned back from the table. "I can't."

"Can't, or *won't*?"

"Either. Both. I don't know. This is just too much right now."

He stopped, allowing me time to gather myself, since I wasn't exactly the picture of calm. After a few moments, I looked at him again, and his eyes held mine. He said, "Whether or not you admit it to me today, you and I—we both know it's the truth."

Arguing was useless, but I was far from any great confession. "I want you to leave Carrie out of this," I said quietly.

"If that's what you want."

"I do."

After a moment, he spoke again. "Kris, even if you never decide to tell me, I hope for your sake you'll at least be honest with yourself."

Our server brought the appetizer. She made room on the table, pushing utensils aside, and set down the hot dish. I didn't look at her or Brandon. I had thoroughly lost my appetite.

"Can you just take me home, please?" I asked.

Brandon looked disappointed. "Yeah," he said, his voice heavy with resignation.

I stood and Brandon followed suit; he withdrew his money clip from a trouser pocket, peeled off a fifty-dollar bill, and handed it to our server, who had been prepared to take our order. "That should cover it," he said.

The server looked at us like we were crazy as we walked out the door.

14

"Where were you yesterday?" Brandon asked when he saw me the following Monday at school. "I tried calling and Josh said you weren't home."

It was true; I hadn't been at home. I'd made a point of busying myself, trying to forget the unpleasant discussion Brandon had initiated on the weekend. I was doing everything in my power to avoid him.

Carrie and I seemed to be avoiding each other, too, which was weird. She had gone to the hospital with Marc and neither one of them told me what had happened. Marc said it was confidential and the one time I had seen Carrie outside of school she got really strange when I asked her about the hospital. She had not returned any of my phone calls since then. In fact I had had thought about calling her to remind her she owed me a bible study but I did not think reminding her of that particular bargain would be very cool.

"I was at Aeleise's. Her brother's Bible study group was meeting and I decided to stay and check it out."

Brandon rolled his eyes. "Sounds scintillating; soon you'll be a regular. So, other than preaching 'The Word,' how does he spend his time? Daemon, isn't it?"

"Yes. He's a pilot."

"Hoping to become a member of the Mile High Club?"

"What's the Mile High Club?"

"Ask Daemon, I'm sure he'll be able to tell you all about it." He shrugged. "Who knows, if he isn't already a member, perhaps the two of you could join together."

The last club I'd belonged to was the Girl Scouts. But a new club might be fun. And it would look favorable on my school records when it came time to apply for colleges. If I could manage to squeeze in another constructive accomplishment, I knew mom would be pleased.

I next saw Daemon while waiting for Aeleise to return from Nick's house. Her parting words had been, "Make yourself comfortable; I won't be long," and then she was gone.

She had left goodies in the kitchen for her brother and me to enjoy, so we sat at the kitchen table, snacking on fruit and Aeleise's freshly baked oatmeal raisin cookies. Daemon grazed over his food, taking small bites here and there, as he thumbed through a magazine.

I had completely forgotten about Brandon's question until Daemon exchanged the magazine he was perusing for one across the table—the latest issue of *Flying*. As he began to flip through it, I remembered Brandon's suggestion; this was the perfect time to ask.

"Daemon, what's the Mile High Club?"

He paused, then continued paging slowly through the magazine.

"Brandon said I should ask you—that you'd know."

He lifted his eyes.

"He thought it might be of interest to me," I said, and then casually continued. "He suggested that if you weren't already a member, maybe we could join together."

He had yet to say anything. I tried again. "Are you already a member?"

I could sense that I had said something wrong—but what?

He said, "Brandon has a unique sense of humor." But Daemon wasn't laughing; his eyes were serious. "No. I am not a member of the Mile High Club."

"Well, what is it? Is it something we can join?"

"Kris, neither of us is joining anything that has to do with that club."

"Why not?"

He looked at me from across the table, and with one movement, wiped his napkin across his mouth so thoroughly, it was as if he were trying to wipe off foul-tasting lipstick. He wadded it up, tossed it with disdain onto his plate, and then took an audible breath. "Because ... I became a pilot to fly planes, not so I could act like some kind of wild rock star in the air." He shook his head. "The Mile High Club is nothing more than a group of people who get their kicks from having sex while flying. That's not what I'm about, Kris."

And I had just asked him in all eagerness to join. I felt the heat rise to my cheeks. I would kill Brandon.

"I'm sorry," I managed to say through my discomfort. "I didn't know that was what it was about."

"I know you didn't—but why do I suspect that Brandon did?"

Knowing Brandon, I didn't doubt Daemon's assumption was right. I would have to thank him for making me look like a complete fool in front of Daemon. Sometimes I wanted to strangle Brandon, golden locks and all. I quickly changed the subject.

"How are things going at the church?" I asked, doing my best to smooth things over. I could only hope he would recognize my efforts.

He put down his magazine. "Things are going remarkably well. You'll have to come check it out sometime." He took a sip of his orange juice, set it back down on its coaster. "Aeleise tells me that you used to attend a Catholic school. Have you found a church here yet?"

"Not exactly," I said. "With my mom gone, I guess you could say I've kind of slacked in that area. And, well, Marc hasn't exactly insisted that we try to attend, so we haven't."

He nodded, then asked, "Are *you* interested in finding a church?"

"Honestly ... after going to school with it for as long as I can remember, I'm enjoying the break." My brows furrowed. "Is that horrible of me?"

"No, it's understandable. It happens more often than you think. Even I went through a burnout phase. Maybe a change of pace would rekindle your interest. Are you open to going to a Christian church, if for nothing else but the experience?"

I wanted to keep an open mind. Besides, it would give me an opportunity to spend more time with Daemon over the weekend. I shrugged. "Yeah. I don't see why it would hurt."

"Well, then, how about going with Aeleise and me this Sunday?"

"Sure."

His expression warmed. "Great. I have a feeling you'll be surprised. I think you'd really enjoy the youth group."

"Maybe I will."

"Well, this is good. I'll look forward to seeing you there, then." He checked his watch. "Unfortunately, I have to go. I have a private client I have to take to San Francisco and then I'm off to Catalina. I probably won't see you again for a few days."

He pushed away from the table and rose. "It was nice to catch up with you before I had to leave," he said. He smiled and I gave my best effort at a smile back. I wasn't sure why the subtle melancholy set in. There was no reason for it, I told myself. "Stay out of trouble while I'm gone," he said.

"I will. Have a fun and safe trip."

"Thank you." He looked down at my plate. "Don't hurry on my account. Relax and finish your food. Hopefully Aeleise will show soon."

"Thanks. If not, I'll lock up when I'm through."

"I know you will—I trust you."

He grabbed his things and headed for the door. Before I knew it, he was gone and I wished I had given him a hug. Maybe I was being weird; I certainly felt weird. I picked at my cookie and stared at his empty plate across from mine, and the few leftover crumbs that hadn't made it to his mouth. I slouched on the table, still staring at his plate, and then decided to leave. I had no desire to wait around any longer for Aeleise. I tossed both our paper plates into the trash, locked the door behind me and walked home, vexed by my unexpected depression.

My depression morphed into anger when I saw Brandon at school the next day. I tugged on the sleeve of his gray sweater and confronted him in the bustling hallway between classes. "Very funny. Make me look like an ass, why don't you! *The Mile High Club!*"

He laughed. "Daemon liked that, did he?"

I glared at him. "Not at all."

"So he's not a member, then?"

"You *know* he's not!"

"I shook hands with him *once.* I've never talked to him—how would I know?"

"It's called judgment of character—and you can't play stupid on this one. You *know* that's not anywhere in line with his beliefs. Why did you do that?"

"I like to keep you on your toes."

"Well, don't bother."

"So what shade of red did he turn?" he asked, unable to keep from smiling.

"*Him?* How about *me? I'm* the one who asked him how the two of us could join!"

He chuckled. "He knows you had no idea what it was. Don't worry about it."

I scowled at him. "Don't do me any more favors, Brandon."

I stormed away to my third period class, wishing I knew how to swear in Latin.

———

It was unusually hot for an October morning. Carrie and I accompanied Brandon to the beach, a welcome way to start the day and for Carrie and me to put that horrible party behind us. One of Brandon's strong points, I have to say, was how he could be sensitive to what was going on with his friends. He knew Carrie and I had tension going on between us, so he had gotten us together in his own special way.

I had yet to see him dance on the waves, but today, that was all about to change. I looked forward with excitement to finally seeing what drove him to the water every morning without fail. It was something I had never fully understood. It was a glimpse into Brandon's secret world.

There were surprisingly few people on the beach. I enjoyed the solitude. It was a beautiful day and I was in love with the warm breeze that kept passing by to say hello. Carrie and I decided to take advantage of the sun's warming rays. Some color would do us both good. We lay on large beach towels Carrie had brought from her house, both different versions of Ariel from "The Little Mermaid." I should've brought my own. I rubbed suntan oil onto her back as she stretched out across the towel. She rested her chin on folded arms and we both watched Brandon head for the ocean. He was dressed in a full wetsuit; although the air was warm, the water was not.

Brandon shrank to a silhouette against the sun. I continued to rub the lotion into Carrie's skin. "He's good, isn't he," I asked, making it more a statement than a question as I watched him run into the surf, surfboard in hand.

Carrie raised her chest to prop herself up on her elbows. She watched him enter the water and disappear into the waves. "One of the best around here," she said matter-of-factly. "His sponsors think he's got enough potential to become world champion. He's already won the U.S. Amateur Championships, and he's placed fifth in the World Amateur Championships. You have no idea how difficult that is to do."

She added, grinning, "Just wait until you go to one of his competitions — you'll see." The breeze danced with her hair; the airborne strands glinted like golden threads in the sun.

"He's that good, huh?"

"Yep." She nodded. She was admittedly one of his biggest fans, a joke they shared and laughed about often. I knew there was more truth to it than they probably saw. It was sweet. "And just wait till you see his entourage."

I looked down at her as she continued to stare at the sea. "Brandon has an *entourage?*" I suppose I shouldn't have been surprised.

"Yeah." She laughed. "I never know whether to laugh or throw up. It's a trip to watch — impressive group, too. Too bad their efforts are wasted energy. If they only knew."

We shared a small laugh. I imagined an ever-growing group of gushing teenage girls crowding around him, screaming, yelling, and calling his name, all in a frantic attempt to grab his attention. Poor Brandon.

"He's a really good sport about it, though," she said. "So many of the local surfers are jerks to their fans. Brandon loves the attention, girls or otherwise. If he doesn't have to hurry off somewhere, he'll take the time to talk to whoever wants to meet him. You should see the way some of these girls' faces light up—you'd think they'd fallen in love and been kissed by Brad Pitt. It's crazy, but cute."

I thought it was unusually sweet of Brandon to be giving of his time. Although flattering, I imagined it was difficult and somewhat exhausting, having to be sensitive to their crushes when he had no desire for them whatsoever.

"None of them know?" I asked.

She shook her head. "He has to be smart about it, career-wise. Not good for the surfing image if he wants to keep his sponsors."

"Oh," I said quietly. I thought that sounded bleak. I wondered if it bothered him. I imagined it must. Did Brandon always have to hide who he was, except when in school? Even there, not everyone knew he was gay, but at least there was no risk of him being expelled from school or losing an education because of it. It seemed unfair to make his sexuality that big of an issue. What did that have to do with his talent or ability as an athlete?

"Even if his sponsors did drop him, it wouldn't stop him from surfing," Carrie said. "He's completely driven. It's what he loves, part of who he is." She dug her fingers into the sand, warming the tips of them. She slowly drew patterns in the sand, and her voice droned vaguely, as if she were somewhere far away as she continued to talk. "Surfing is really the only creative outlet he has; aside from loving the sport, it's how he releases stress. Instead of using drugs, he uses surfing as a positive way to cope with his demons. Some people go to therapy; Brandon has surfing."

Demons? "What demons?" I asked. I wasn't aware he had any.

"Ask him sometime. I'm sure he'll tell you."

"What am I supposed to ask him?"

She dropped her chin until her glasses fell lower on her nose, and peeked her sea-foam, blue-green eyes at me. "Ask him how he liked living with Jamison."

"You're being awfully cryptic, Carrie."

"That's all I can say. Just ask him, if you're curious. He'll tell you—you two are close."

I let it go. If the time ever seemed right, I would broach the subject with him. For the time being, I was just content to spend my day enjoying the sun, Carrie, and the entertainment Brandon provided. I didn't know the first thing about surfing, but it sure looked amazing, and he looked more powerful than I could ever have imagined. I watched in admiration as his distant form took on wave after wave.

15

Some school weeks seemed to go on forever. It was yet another lunch hour. On my way to meet Carrie, I spotted Brandon walking along the corridor and recalled our conversation at the beach.

I stopped him on his way to his locker. "Why haven't I ever been to your house?" I said.

"Is that a request to come over?"

"If you're inviting."

He looked at me as if trying to read something. "Meet me after school, then, by the library? I can finish my art history homework while I wait."

"I'll be there by two forty-five."

"Two forty-five? What about after school practice?"

"I'm playing hooky."

He gave me an impish smile. "Boy, you must really want to come over."

"That, and I haven't memorized the last thirty-two counts of our new routine."

He laughed. "I should've known." He set his watch, making it beep. "Very well. I'll see you at the designated time."

"All right, James Bond."

When I entered the library at the agreed-upon time, Brandon rose from the table where he'd been sitting and greeted me with, "You're punctual."

"There are firsts for everything. Besides, I know how unaccustomed you are to waiting."

He seemed to like the sound of that. "Well, let's be on our way. The field trip awaits."

I followed him to his car. He opened the door for me—he was always polite—and we set off.

He pulled into his driveway and stopped the car just past the curb. It seemed odd, but I didn't question it; perhaps he enjoyed the lengthy walk to the house. He seemed hesitant as we closed the car doors, and his stride was slow and reluctant as we walked up the drive. He fumbled for his keys as we reached his front door.

"Welcome to my stupid house," he muttered.

If I hadn't been well-versed in deciphering mumbles, I never would have understood his words. His "stupid house" was a fantastic glass work of art designed by an architect with a palate for the extreme—cold and austere, yet imposing. It was impressive. It was money.

"Stupid house?"

"Fine—stupid household, then. I suppose that's more true to fact." He sounded bored by the topic.

"Why?"

He shrugged and pushed open the door. I shivered as I stepped inside; at a guess, the temperature hovered at a brittle 55 degrees. I stood, a miniaturized maiden inside an incredible glass structure with soaring ceilings and recessed lighting. Slate gray windows filtered the view of the exterior world, allowing the inhabitants to see out while deflecting the curious stares of those outside. It was an executive dollhouse; a three dimensional combination of modern shapes and sweeping lines. It belonged to the new generation of fairy-tale princes, to an affluence beyond upper class. It was an eerily silent structure.

Without warning, the front door closed and locked automatically behind us. I jumped.

"It's designed to do that," he said.

As we crossed an expansive foyer that led to a variety of ominous rooms, I couldn't stop gawking. It was oddly stirring, like the drawings of M.C. Escher—a thought-provoking combination of math and imagination. I later learned that his father—an architect brilliant enough to have built Egypt's pyramids—had designed it.

Brandon led me into the living room, where we left our book bags on a semicircular couch of gray leather. He unzipped a new navy fleece sweat-jacket he had picked up from his latest sponsor and tossed it on the couch beside them.

The house felt empty.

"My mom doesn't arrive home from work until around four," he said.

"Will she care that I'm over?"

"Not at all. She'll be delighted. She is always delighted when I bring friends home."

Judging by the house, that seemed unlikely. The house was not what I would consider a home for entertaining—it displayed no warmth, no reality at all. It could host museum tours, perhaps, but hardly a festive event.

"Do you have many people over?" I said.

"Rarely." And then added in a casual, dismissive manner, "I don't like people that much."

It seemed an odd thing to say, coming from a person with an endless supply of friends.

"So, you want me to show you around?"

"Please."

"Where to first?"

"Your room?" It seemed the logical thing.

His mouth formed a curve like the belly of a boat. "I knew it! I was right all along." He laughed. "Just kidding. Come on."

I walked beside him down the car-width hallways, until we came to the double doors that sealed his room. He unlocked them with a remote control key he withdrew from his pocket, and the doors slid apart, then fused together behind us at another touch of a button, like the doors of a space ship. He had an expansive room which was partitioned off into distinctive sections. Each displayed a glimpse into the aspects of his life.

The room reflected his devotion to surfing. He had five different surfboards—all showing signs of use—a closet full of wetsuits, a collection of surf videos stacked beside his DVD player, a wall covered with surf posters, and a display case full of trophies he had won in surf contests.

He laughed when I admired his king-size waterbed, draped in a velvet leopard-print comforter and adorned with accenting pillows, and told him it was the first one I had ever seen. "It's the best I can do without sleeping in the ocean," he said.

The wall to the right of his bed caught me by surprise. Like those in the rooms of many pre-teen girls, it was covered in a collage of teen heartthrobs. My eyes roamed over the mysterious smile of Johnny Depp; the arresting eyes of Brad Pitt; Tom Cruise with his all-American charm; the ever-popular Leonardo DeCaprio and various half-naked male models displaying flesh in provocative black and white cologne ads.

"Nice wall." What more could I say?

"I know." He grinned, not at all bashful—"B" is for Brandon, who is bold and brave and likes his boys.

He had lots of expensive trinkets: a professional camera; a laptop computer resting open and ready on the nightstand; a complete Bose surround sound system; a Sony Playstation; a telescope; an extensive library of DVD movies and CDs; classic movie memorabilia; an electric guitar; three skateboards; model aircraft sets; fencing swords; a huge flat screen television; an enormous fish tank, home to three large eels—I liked the eels; a virtual library of books; and, hidden in the shadows of his walk-in closet, proof of his affinity to Disney's Peter Pan. I pretended not to see it, but thought it terribly cute. He demonstrated the revolving bookcase that operated by remote control and disappeared into the paneling of the wall. It harbored a hidden safe. I did not discover its contents.

We heard the loud sound of the front door closing.

"My mother," Brandon said. "You sure you want to meet her? We can always go out the back way."

"I'd love to meet her."

"Brandon?" Her voice echoed throughout the house as she called for him.

"All right, come on," he said, and then louder, "Coming."

A tall, thin, leggy brunette stood by the wet bar with her back to us, devoting all of her attention to some papers she was holding. I choked on her Poison perfume from twelve feet away. She didn't look up to see Brandon as we walked into the room; instead she paced this way and that, eyes still on the papers.

"Yes?" Brandon said.

She studied the papers as she spoke. "Darling...be a doll, won't you, and fix me a Bloody Mary." She looked familiar, but I couldn't place her face. "You know how I like it. Don't be shy with the vodka."

"Of course." He sounded cool, almost formal, as if on his best behavior.

She had yet to look up, and therefore didn't see me. We made for the wet bar as she continued to shuffle through her stack of papers. She loosened the top three buttons on her blouse with dexterous fingers, and the cream-colored fabric draped open. She nervously lit a cigarette of ridiculous length and wielded the prop, showcasing her newly painted, passion-red colored nails. Smoke curled about and away from her fingers.

She looked up then, and noticed me as if I were a newly delivered piece of furniture in the room. I recognized her at that moment, and worked to control my excitement.

"Brandon, honey, aren't you going to introduce me to your friend?" All smiles, she came up to me, her saucy walk as memorable as that of any elite runway model, and admiringly touched my face. Not the type of greeting I'd expected.

"My, aren't you a stunning girl," she said, nudging my chin up for a better look. The stench of nicotine on her fingers turned my stomach, and I discreetly held my breath. Her eyes sparkled with interest, and a smile played over her lips.

She spoke to Brandon as she combed my features. "I just don't get it, dear; you have such exquisite taste in women." She finally retracted her claws, and then called to him over her shoulder, "I don't suppose this means you're finally coming around?"

She quickly lowered her voice in girlish confidence meant for my ears only. "He just needs a little encouragement." She gave me a teasing wink and a smile.

"Mother, *please.*" He looked both irritated and embarrassed by her indiscretion. "This is Krista, my *friend* from school."

"Well, it's a pleasure, Krista. I'm Faye."

She flopped on the couch. "What do you two study together, dear? Home Economics?"

"Mother," he said stonily, "I don't *take* Home Economics. Neither does Krista, for that matter. I'm sure she has ambitions in life beyond baking Apple Brown Betty." He handed her the drink with a contemptuous smile. "You know, similar to you."

She accepted the drink, ignoring his comment completely, and stirred it delicately with her finger. She downed it with the absorption of a sponge, and then set the tumbler on the glass-topped coffee table in front of her. Lipstick clung to the glass, a puce stain. She tossed back her thick chocolate hair and urged her shoes to the floor with her toes. Her long, nylon-covered legs stretched nearly the entire length of the couch; she toyed absently at one earring. Her skirt had crept slowly up her thighs to reveal a length of leg that my mom would've grounded me for displaying. But then, I wasn't a soap star.

"Your father will be stopping by shortly. He says he has something for you." She took a drag of her cigarette and tapped the ash with a flourish into a Waterford ashtray.

Brandon tensed. "I have plans with Krista." In truth, we had nothing planned beyond visiting his home, but I knew better than to contest his excuses. He asked his mother suspiciously, "Do you know what he wants?"

"You know that coward never talks to me, I'm merely here to relay the message. I'm sure it will be quick; it always is."

Brandon sounded displeased when he said, "We'll be in my room."

"Is there a reason why you failed to mention who your mother is?"

We sat on the floor in his room. He was showing me his collection of rare coins.

He didn't bother to look up. "I don't know one thing about your parents, do I? Parents aren't exactly the hot topic of conversation, last time I checked."

"True. But somehow, somewhere along the line, I think *someone* would've brought it up."

Brandon shrugged without interest. "Not many people know." He pulled a coin out from its protective sleeve for closer examination, and then handed it to me. "She's just my mom to me; it's to everyone else that she's *Maxine Duvet*." He said the name with drama.

I took the polished gold coin and looked at it closely, admiring both sides as it gleamed in the light. "So beautiful," I said as I studied it.

"I am quite proud of it."

The coin grew warm in my hand.

"It's not of any interest to me," he said, "but we can go to a taping sometime, if you'd like."

"A taping?" I said, still inspecting the face of the coin.

"My mom; if you ever want to watch a taping of her new show, I'll take you, if you'd like. You know the *Days and Years* soap is finally off the air, right? She's working on a new one that has yet to be run."

"Oh…yeah. I liked that soap, though. I used to watch it all the time with my friend from Ohio, Lindsey. We'd sneak into her sister's room and watch it from there."

Brandon laughed. "That's too funny—sneaking around to watch my mom play an alcoholic on TV. You can see the real thing here without the screen. Life imitating art, so to speak, or vice versa."

I handed the gold piece back to him. "What's her character like on the new show she's working on?"

"Why, another alcoholic mother—surprise, surprise." He laughed, but it sounded more like a sniff. "Her experience makes her convincing in that role." His voice trailed off. "Maybe one day her range will reach beyond that."

I tried to read past his stony expression, wondering if he meant as an actress or at home.

His mother appeared at the door, striking a perfect "S" pose. The *tap, tap, tap* of her nails against the frame requested his attention. "Your father is here," she said to Brandon. "Be quick about it, will you, hon? I'd like to get him out of here before I need to leave for rehearsal."

Brandon made no move to get up.

"Chop, chop, Brandon!" she said. "I have places to be."

He looked up at her with his polar glare. "I'll be there in a minute."

She threw him an exasperated look and left.

"You want me to wait in here?" I asked.

"No, it's okay—you can come. You wanted to meet the parents, right?"

"Only if you're okay with it."

"I'm forewarning you, he's going to hope you're my girlfriend. He's not quite as accepting as my mom is concerning my sexual proclivity."

"I understand; it doesn't bother me."

His father did a double take at the sight of me. Interested and hopeful, he gave me an exuberant smile as he approached us from the next room, his arm extended in an overly enthusiastic greeting. "I'm Mitchell. Always a pleasure to meet one of Brandon's friends."

He was impeccably dressed in a tailored suit in the darkest shade of gray—it seemed to echo the feel of the house. He was handsome, with dark eyes, but although the shade of his hair matched the familiar honey color of Brandon's, it was obviously the work of artifice, lacking the sun-kissed highlights from time spent outdoors. Mitchell was tall, fit, and pleasantly imposing. To me he looked like a successful middle-aged playboy. But his apparent perfection didn't seem to penetrate any deeper than the surface. He was just *too* perfect.

"We were just getting ready to leave," Brandon lied. "You wanted to see me?"

"Oh, yes ... well, I wasn't expecting you to have company; we can discuss this later. I'm on my way out in a few minutes myself. You two have fun." He turned and made for the other room, calling over his shoulder, "Brandon ..."

"Yes?" He sounded decidedly unenthused at the thought of having to see his father again so soon.

"A moment with you, please."

They turned a corner, out of my view. His father's lowered voice rendered his words indistinguishable.

Brandon returned in record time. He indignantly strode over to the couch, head slightly lifted in an air of offence, or was it pride? He sat, crossing his ankles on the coffee table, and tossed a wad of money on the table. He laughed.

"He really is a piece of work." One side of his mouth twisted into a sour smirk. "I'm supposed to show you a good time." He looked at me and I knew the intentions behind his words. "With five hundred dollars we should be able to find something suitable to eat, don't you think?"

"He gave you *five hundred dollars* for *dinner?*"

"For whatever."

"Kind of extreme."

"Always." He leaned his elbow on the armrest, and thoughtfully toyed with his hair. He resembled his mother in his mannerisms. "I want to get out of here. Do you have time to hang out? It's still early enough; we could bail this place and go to The Promenade downtown ... get something to eat, do some shopping."

I hesitated.

"C'mon, it'll be fun. Be my platonic date for the evening. Let me play Barbie with you. I know some amazing shops." The idea seemed to lift his spirits.

"Why don't we just go to dinner if you're hungry?"

"Dinner *and* Barbie—and I won't take no for an answer. I want to show you a good time—*my* way. It'll be a blast and it'll make me feel better." He gave me puppy dog eyes. "Are you going to make me pout? *Please*, Kris?"

I couldn't help smiling at the uncharacteristically sweet look on his face; Brandon *never* begged. I sighed. "Fine."

He was pleased with his victory. I wondered if anyone ever refused Brandon.

It was a long but scenic drive to the Promenade, and we passed many people out enjoying the day.

As we breezed through the doors of an upscale shop, a fortyish, platinum blond saleslady flashed us a practiced smile. "Welcome," she said brightly.

I noticed she directed her greeting at Brandon. She seemed familiar with him.

"Check things out," he said to me. "Grab whatever catches your eye. I have some ideas as well." He perused a few racks of clothing. "You're about a size … two, maybe … four—right?"

He had an extremely accurate eye. "Yes," I said.

"Just making sure."

I was in the dressing room trying on clothes when the door burst open without warning. I nearly hit the back wall in effort to cover myself. Brandon was not the least bit concerned by my reaction.

"The store is closing in fifteen minutes, and there are still things you have to try on. Here." He thrust four more selections at me. "Hurry."

I still couldn't believe he just entered the dressing room without warning. I cowered in the corner, embarrassed. I accepted the clothes with one hand while strategically covering my breasts with the other.

He gasped.

"My *God!* Is that your *waist?*"

"Well, I haven't seen anyone other than *you* barrel into the room."

"The belt," he blurted. "I have the perfect belt—it'll bring you to *tears*, it's so perfect!" He was out the door.

He hadn't said word one about the boys' tighty-whities I wore. Shocker. I'd expected to be ridiculed, now that he was aware ... but no. And then it hit me — as I stood there in nothing but my underwear, all he could see were the endless fashion possibilities. I really was his Barbie. He seemed possessed as he rushed out the door in search of the belt he feared he'd never find another excuse to buy.

I started laughing. To be nearly naked, on display as it were, and his sole concern revolved around a *belt?* I liked this guy.

I'd just slipped into the body contouring slacks he'd selected — in a shade of blue pastel — when he returned to the dressing room, the rhinestone belt in hand. His face was as radiant as the belt's faux diamonds. The oddest things brought him immeasurable pleasure.

"God, I can't wait to see this on you."

I covered myself again as he joined me in the mirrored changing room and shut the door behind him. He draped the belt over his shoulder and approached me purposefully.

"They're worn lower on the hips ... like this. Very disco." Like a fashion stylist, he dropped to his knees in front of me to make the proper adjustments. He unzipped the front of the slacks.

I was almost too stunned to utter a word. I finally said in a questioning tone, "Brandon ..."

"Yes?" He was busily adjusting the fit, lost in the project at hand — his quest for perfection.

I watched him curiously; I decided to let it go. I let out a resigned huff.

"You'll have to wear different underwear, but at least this will give us an idea." He folded my boys' briefs down two times, transforming them into bikinis. He zipped up the slacks and then pulled them down further to expose my hips. "Like this, see? *Much* better." He retrieved the glittering belt from his shoulder, draped it low around my hips, and arranged it in its proper position. He stood, beaming. "I can't believe how absolutely perfect it looks. Turn around."

I slowly turned for his closer inspection.

"Your butt looks amazing. Face me again."

I did as told.

"Step back and give me your hands." He held his out to me. When I hesitated, he prompted, "Don't be shy, Kris. I'm just trying to decide which top you should try on. It's hard to tell when you're all scrunched up like a pillow. We have exactly five minutes to see what works and get out of here."

He stood back, considering.

"Here, try this one. You have great tits . . ." His voice sounded sterile, clinical—it held no hint of desire. He grabbed a sheer, cream-colored blouse and helped me slip it on, then tied it between my breasts, shortening it to expose my entire torso. He stood back to admire his creation. I'd never seen such a ridiculously wide smile—other than on Lewis Carroll's mythical Cheshire cat.

"You look *flawless!*" he said in quiet awe. "It's a must."

I turned to face the mirror. I had to admit, I liked the look. I was astonished to find I looked nearly seventeen. I also knew without a doubt that Marc would *never* in a thousand years let me leave the house in it. That dampened my spirits.

"Don't worry," Brandon said, reading the look on my face. "I know what you're thinking, but you can wear a sexy bra underneath."

I doubted Marc would be any more pleased by that suggestion.

"Hurry and take it off so I can pay for everything while you finish changing." He scooped up all the clothes and rushed out the door without a word.

Brandon was all smiles as we left the store. "I'll take you to my favorite place to eat," he said. "Critically acclaimed food and the surroundings . . . beyond beautiful. You'll love it."

I was sure I would. Brandon had impeccable taste. He transferred all three bags he was carrying to one hand and took my hand in the other.

I checked the time and knew I should check in at home since cheerleading practice would have just about let out by now. Marc was not there but Dominic, our housemaid who was also there to watch over me when no one else was around, answered the phone and said he was expected soon.

The restaurant was amazing. Brandon requested a table in the atrium, and the hostess led us to the most intimate and exclusive space at the back of the restaurant. Our table was completely surrounded by lush climbing plants and hundreds of flowers in shades of lavender, rose, yellow, and white, peeking demurely between the thick foliage. The faint sound of trickling water emanated from a waterfall nestled amid tumbled rocks, which fell to a tranquil koi pond. The magical atmosphere made me feel as though I had stepped into a fantasy world. Light, unobtrusive music floated in the background.

The night sky above us was surprisingly crisp and dark and smelled of sweet gardenias. The lighting was soft and dim. Ivory candles enclosed within frosted crystal spheres sat on every table, paired with femininely decorated vases of the same shade; in each vase lilies and orchids embraced. Firefly lights, tucked deep within the dense greenery, appeared star-like from a distance.

Brandon smiled warmly. "I take it this meets your approval?"

I could only nod. He laughed softly, pleased by my reaction. As we took our seats, I noticed most of the people in the restaurant were considerably older than Brandon and me—it was a charming change of pace.

"How did you discover this place?"

"It's one of my mother's favorites. There was a time we used to come here often, but that was years ago."

I thought about Marc and Kaelie. I would have to share this with them. I knew he would love to bring her here. It was the perfect setting for a romantic date.

Our waiter provided leather-bound menus with royal blue tassels, and we viewed the selections. There were no prices listed.

Brandon laughed when I asked about it. "You don't get out much, do you?"

Did he encounter this often? I knew the school cafeteria wasn't passing out any leather-bound menus.

"You should never make your selections by price, Kris. Always get what you want. Why live any other way?"

When our waiter returned, I ordered pesto tortellini. Brandon selected lobster and steak.

We enjoyed our meal and conversation, and afterwards Brandon insisted we order desserts and coffee. I wondered how I would manage to take another bite. Everything had tasted delicious.

Finally content, Brandon set down his cup and lounged back against his chair. Most of the patrons had already left.

He looked at me with calculating curiosity, then asked unexpectedly,

"Do you want to stay the night?"

"At your house?" I said dumbly. My voice didn't hide my shock.

"Sure, why not?"

"Well..." I stuttered as I searched for an excuse. I had never been good at thinking on my feet. "I don't know—I mean, I have no clothes to sleep in and—"

His smile, patiently amused, dared me to come up with another lame excuse.

"We can *buy* you clothes, Kris, and I'm going to the same school as you in the morning."

This was uncharted territory. I had never before stayed at a boy's house overnight. Would Marc even allow it? Besides, joking or not, Brandon had made questionable sexual overtures to me in the past. I wasn't sure if I was comfortable with the idea.

Brandon looked amused. He laughed openly at my awkward struggle to find the words I thought would rescue me. "I find it most entertaining, watching you wither." He shook his head. "Why don't you just say what's really on your mind? You're afraid I'm going to come on to you, right?"

He just laid it out on the table, direct and expectant. I felt silly answering such a pointed question, so I didn't. He leaned forward, a shit-eating grin on his face.

"It's okay to say yes, Kris." He leaned back in his chair, crossing his legs as he made himself comfortable. "Did you see a single picture of a girl *anywhere* in my room?"

I shook my head.

"That's because there are none. *I'm* the closest thing you'll find to a girl in that room." He raised his hands in mock arrest, and then hid them behind his chair. "I'll keep my hands to myself—I promise."

I laughed at his efforts to reassure me. He could be unquestionably charming at times. "Well, I can ask," I said.

He handed me his cell phone at "Well."

"Boy... you don't mess around."

"Not until *after* I get what I want." He tossed me a smirk. "Make your call."

I dialed my house and when Marc answered, I said, "May I stay the night at Brandon's?"

"Brandon's?" he asked with a hint of surprise. "It's a school night, Kris."

"I know. Brandon will drive me in the morning."

"Will his mother be there?"

"Yes." I omitted the detail that he should consider her presence an empty reassurance.

He considered aloud. "I suppose Brandon is as harmless as they come. Fine, you can stay—on the condition that you're on time to school."

"I promise," I said.

"Kris, if you miss school, this will be the last time."

"I swear I won't."

He finally said, "All right; have fun."

"Thank you."

"Uh-huh."

We hung up. I looked at Brandon as I handed him his cell phone.

"Well? The verdict is?"

"Mission accomplished. Permission granted."

We finished our dessert and coffee; Brandon grabbed our new acquisitions and we made for the car. He refused to let me carry my own shopping bags. Mom would've thought him a true gentleman—a product of sound upbringing and strong family values. Manners ranked high on mom's list of respected qualities. Although full of spice and sass, Brandon was a gentleman—when he wanted to be.

The sun was rapidly tiring, leaving behind a persimmon-colored sky. We'd had a full day, and were both starting to wind down. Brandon even took it down a few notches. We were inside his house by 9:00 P.M. It was as silent and untouched as ever—his mother had yet to arrive home. He carried our Promenade purchases through the house to the sterile living room, and we sat on the unyielding, stone-colored horseshoe of a couch to relax.

Brandon turned to me. "We have six guest rooms you can choose from," he began.

My face must have revealed something, because he paused, then added, "Or...you can stay with me if you'd rather." He seemed hesitant. "I don't mind sharing my personal ocean space with you." He gently added a familiar taunt: "I guess you're cool enough."

To me that option seemed far more appealing than spending a night alone inside this vast, bleak, airplane hanger of a house. "Yes, please...if you truly don't mind."

"I already said I didn't. Come on."

He reclaimed the bags and I followed him into his bedroom.

I wondered how many people had slipped between the sheets to share a bed with Brandon.

"Do you want something to sleep in?" he asked.

I realized that I had forgotten to purchase sleepwear on our shopping expedition.

"You're not going to sleep in your street clothes, are you?"

The term "street clothes" smacked of "hooker" to my ears. I frowned as I stood in front of his bed, but then realized he meant nothing by it.

"Do you have anything that will fit me?"

I half expected to find an array of nighties waiting in his closet for my selection. I was pleased there were none.

He walked casually to his dresser and pulled from the eighth drawer a selection of oversized surf T-shirts, boxer shorts, and sweat pants.

"Anything in here should fit you. Would you like to come look?"

I picked out what were his smallest sized T-shirt and sweatpants, and retreated to his bed.

"What are you going to wear?"

"Well, not my usual attire, to be sure."

"What's that?"

"Nothing," he said comfortably.

My heart rate quickened.

He laughed gently. "You look spooked, Kris. Don't hurt yourself thinking about it."

"Huh?" I had stopped registering words at "Nothing."

"You're concentrating awfully hard—trying to get a visual?" His jibe made me blush. "Don't worry. I give you my word, I'll be sufficiently clothed."

I relaxed.

"Still afraid I'm going to attack you?" he asked. I shook my head. "Good. Well, make yourself at home. Do you want to shower before me, or wait until morning?"

"I'll take the morning slot," I said.

He smiled. "I'll be out in a few. My nighttime ritual, you understand."

He disappeared into the bathroom and the door locked with a click. I swiftly changed into my borrowed attire and crawled into bed. I scuttled beneath the soft, leopard-print comforter, surprised to find bright pink sheets. It was like crawling inside the belly of a beast. I stared at the soft cotton sheets that rolled beneath me in rhythm with the waterbed. Jelly-bean *pink*. My eyes shifted to the clever eels in their tank, and I watched them move like snakes through the water in smooth, slow-motion glides, their keen eyes unresting, their mouths open. Beautifully dangerous.

I was tiring quickly. The click of the door alerted me that Brandon had finished with his bedtime preparations. I looked up to find him standing in the bathroom doorway, a cloud of steam behind him. He had stopped to look at me. He was dressed from head to toe in blue and gray sweats, taking it to the extreme by wearing the hood. He looked ridiculously cute; I had to laugh.

"Isn't this an uncommon sight to behold—a beautiful girl waits for me in my bed."

"I think you enjoy making me nervous," I said.

"You aren't really, are you?"

I didn't answer.

Brandon seemed hesitant to approach his own bed, so I pushed forward the words, "No, not really."

I knew he questioned my honesty, but he slowly came to bed anyway. He gave no hint of his intentions until he deftly grabbed a pillow and socked me over the head with it. I squealed at the unexpected blow and immediately retaliated with a pillow of my own. Within seconds a full-blown pillow fight raged, and I was failing miserably. I couldn't contain my laughter, and finally fell back out of sheer exhaustion. Brandon stood over me, pillow in hand, and laughed triumphantly as the faux sea raged beneath us.

"Ha! Brandon the victorious! *Say it! Say it!*"

My stomach cramped from laughter as tears trickled from the corners of my eyes. "*All right—all right!* You win! I surrender!"

"As you should."

He flopped down to sit beside me, and I watched as he rose and fell with the motion of the bed.

"I think you're insane," I announced.

"I am … insanely tired." He fell backward and let out an exhausted sigh. "Let's get some sleep, shall we?"

I laughed. "Yes, I guess that'd be a good idea."

We crawled under the covers, the mood considerably lightened, and my apprehensions behind me.

"Do you have enough room?" he asked.

"Yes." I moved closer to him. "Face this way," I commanded. He obeyed.

I scooted back, nestling against his chest, and cozied myself comfortable. It was a tricky fit, working against the constant motion of the bed.

"Lie still, already. Jesus, Kris."

"I'm sorry, I'm not used to your waterbed; it takes a while to get situated."

"Well, are you through doing the cha-cha now?"

I elbowed him hard. "Yes."

He went concave on impact, and then coughed out, "That *was* my stomach!"

"Sorry—I was aiming lower." I wasn't really.

"Well, I'm glad you have shitty aim, then. Is that your way of telling me to back up?"

I giggled. "Shut up and give me your hand." He surrendered it to me and I pulled it until his arm was wrapped around me. He seemed surprised by my actions, uncomfortable with the contact. His body was taut behind me. He said nothing for several minutes.

"I'm not complaining, but... I thought I was supposed to keep my hands to myself."

"Does it bother you?"

"No—I'm just... surprised, that's all. You *want* me to hold you?"

"Don't make me feel like an idiot, Brandon."

"Do you *ever* answer a question directly?"

I pulled his arm tighter about me.

He said, "I guess I'll accept that as a yes."

"Brandon, I had a really good time with you today. Thank you so much for everything."

"You're welcome." I could tell by the drop in his voice that he was unaccustomed to words of gratitude. "I'm glad you had fun... I did too."

The waves made me sleepy. "Night, Brandon."

"Night, Kris."

I remembered then that Carrie had suggested I ask him about someone named Jamison, but that would have to wait until another time.

16

Brandon and I had bonded quickly. He was the most unusual boy I'd ever met; he was certainly the most unusual boy I had had ever taken as a friend. We'd been spending a considerable amount of time together, and it pleased me to know we were becoming closer; I became more comfortable about sharing some of the more personal aspects of my life. I still didn't know much about him. He knew countless things about me and my life, and by comparison, I knew relatively little about his.

Regardless, I felt like I could share secrets with him, and I finally 'fessed up about Carrie and me. I told him how I wanted Carrie's friendship but was finding myself avoiding her because I did not know how to gently tell her that I was not gay. Once I told him, I suddenly realized just how grateful I was to have a confidant other than my diary.

"Kris, I know where you're at. Sorting out how you feel about things isn't easy. Take it day by day; that's all you can do. He knew I wasn't ready for any deep discussions yet, and I was grateful that he didn't push the matter.

Friday after school, Brandon was in unusually high spirits. As usual, he was impeccably dressed. He wore knee-length, tan shorts tailored to perfection, a navy blue, button down surf shirt that looked great with his coloring, and expensive, dark brown leather sandals. Imported from Italy, no doubt.

"Brandon, do you ever study or bring home a book?" I asked.

"As a general rule, no. I leave school at school."

I wish we could all be so lucky. Brandon was gifted: an intellectual who bordered on frightening. Pour cunning into the mix, and ... well, he breezed through his schoolwork and exams as easily as the Grinch stole Christmas. It was disgusting. I had learned from Carrie that he had tucked away over $2,000 last year during finals, writing other students' papers at $200 a pop. Easy change for kids in our neighborhood, and a sound investment for a good many of them. Brandon had made graduation possible for more than a dozen students who had no business leaving high school. He told Carrie it saved him from boredom when the waves were flat. He didn't need the money. His father gave him plenty of cash.

I followed Brandon to his sapphire car; he opened the door for me and I hopped inside. There was sand on the floor where he had tossed his wetsuit after his early morning surf.

"Sorry about the sand."

"Like I care."

We headed to his house, drove up the driveway and stopped the car in the tomb they called a garage, under the house. An underground entrance deposited us in the kitchen; from there we entered a living room large enough to hold the Governor's ball. It was approaching 5:30; as usual, no one was home.

It was the weekend. Maybe that's why it was easier to excuse it away. You're allowed to cut loose on weekends — it's like an unspoken law. It's what we all look forward to, right?

Mirrors lined the walls behind the wet bar, and I watched two Brandons fill glasses with ice and a healthy amount of Jack Daniels. I wondered why he even bothered with the splash of Coke he added. Before I had finished two swallows of my drink, he had polished his off as if he were merely taking a shot, and proceeded to replenish his glass.

He didn't say anything for a few moments, and then he glanced at his drink, downed it, and filled his glass yet again — this time not bothering with the mix. The three ice cubes bobbing in the whiskey held his attention as he deliberated. He took another healthy slug, apparently anxious for the liquor to work its magic before he started speaking.

"Has Carrie ever told you anything about my sister Jamison? About my living with her?"

Here it was without my saying a word, Brandon's story. I shook my head, got very interested in my glass.

"At eight, I went to live with Jamison. My parents wanted me out of the house until they figured out what to do with my brother."

"You have a brother? You never mentioned that."

"I know."

"Older or younger?"

"Older... by seven years." He gave a short chuckle, unaware his fingers had tightened around his glass. "See, *he* was planned—he was the son they *wanted*. That pregnancy was as mapped out as one of my father's floor plans. I, on the other hand... I was the unfortunate result of a drunken night of bump-and-grind." He continued in his falsely casual tone. "How did my father put it... oh, yes—a mistake." He took a hard swallow of his liquor. "I should be a walking endorsement for birth control, the way my father talks."

His eyes shifted to the floor and he released a low laugh. I wondered how he could laugh. "Come with me. I'll show you something."

I followed him to his bedroom. He picked up the remote control resting on top of his television and pointed it at his bookshelf. It turned toward us like a carousel. He pressed another button and the safe door unlocked and sprang forward. I would learn of its contents after all. He walked over to it and his hand disappeared into the box. He withdrew from it a single picture and handed it to me.

"That's Dean. It's my only picture of him. I don't know why I keep it. My parents don't even know I have it."

Time had yellowed the picture of a boy, roughly ten, who stood in his soccer uniform, sharing his moment of victory beside a proud father. Both held a trophy between them. I drew the photo closer and recognized the younger features of Brandon's father. I waited for him to elaborate. When he didn't, I asked him, "Is there a reason why you wouldn't want them to know you have it?"

He said nothing for quite some time. I looked at him, waiting patiently. There was obviously a reason, but would he share it?

"I'm lost, Brandon. Am I supposed to guess? Do you want to play charades? Obviously, something is up. Is there some sort of prize if I guess correctly?" I asked, hoping that lightening the mood would help. I was most decidedly wrong. I reached for his glass to take a sip and he pushed me away with surprising force. Already I felt confused by the situation; his action hurt.

Deep grooves etched his forehead. "No, Kris. I'm not gonna play some game about this." This, from the game-master himself. "You don't understand—people don't talk about this shit, Kris. At least, we don't."

"Then tell me, Brandon. We're the only ones here."

It was as if I were watching a transformation—a morphing from one person into another—right before my eyes. Brandon's voice lost its cynical edge, which had always been far too severe for someone his age, and the lines of restrained anger tightening his face melted into the soft confusion of a bewildered child. Brandon looked no more than nine as he spoke. It was the most unnerving thing I'd ever seen.

"I thought he'd pissed in my mouth. I wasn't old enough to know what coming was."

I blanched—went cold—then realized I had quit breathing. Had no words to convey how I felt.

I allowed him to talk. Perhaps it was enough just to listen. Maybe that was what he had needed all along. I absorbed every chilling detail, every stain of his humiliation, every imprint of his despair.

"He made me swear not to tell, and if I did, he was gonna kill my cat and make me watch—and then kill me. Every time my mom left the house, I'd just start crying because I knew what would happen next—I knew he'd come searching for me. When no one came to help me, I realized crying was useless. Eventually... I quit crying."

As I listened to him, it was all I could do not to cry myself. But how could I allow it when my tears cost me nothing? These horrors hadn't happened to me, I hadn't lived with his anguish. To cry would be to cheapen his pain, as if it were something that tears could wash away.

"He and his friends took turns with me; I was passed from one person to the next, both guys and girls. It went on for years, but I can never see their faces. All I see is Darth Vader's face—he stared back at me from Dean's Star Wars poster. I'd fix my eyes on him the entire time—it was the best I could do to keep my mind off what was happening." A strange movement tweaked his lips, not quite a smile but disturbingly close. "I must be the only person I can think of who can't stand Star Wars—any of it. I suppose I should feel grateful it relieved me of the details."

Jesus, Mary, and Joseph.

I feared I was being a bad friend; what words of solace could I offer him? I struggled to find something to say. *I'm sorry* wasn't enough, for despite all the pain and sorrow I felt for him, I could never truly understand his suffering.

"How did it finally end, Brandon?"

He absently stirred the ice cubes with his finger as he said, "One day my mom walked in and caught him fucking me. His friends weren't with him that time. She went ballistic, started screaming and yelling, and then crying; I remember her locking him in a room. She called the police, and they came and took Dean away. I ended up in the hospital."

He hadn't looked at me once since he'd started talking. "I knew she told my dad, though he never said a word to me about it. But he bought me that car when I turned sixteen, and he's always ready to dish out plenty of gifts and money. My mom sent me to live with Jamison until they could figure out what to do with Dean. He was fifteen when they finally sent him to Juvi. I switched schools for a year and moved in with my sister so his friends who had been in on it would have no way of finding me. I've never seen him since. He was legally an adult when he was released. My parents consider him disowned."

He stopped. Stunned, I tried desperately to think of something to say. Any words of consolation seemed petty and inadequate. Sex had been used as a weapon against him, and had made a wound so deep it wouldn't heal. Trauma had created a void within him, had kept him severed from intimacy; fear and suspicion held him captive, and tainted his trust and his notions of love. I took in his lost and sullen expression and saw a boy I'd never seen before. I wanted to reach out to him but I didn't know how. Neither of us had ever been demonstrative.

He had a deep well of emotions all tied up in that single picture of his brother, a desperate wish to make sense of it all.

"I'd forgive him of everything if he would just tell me that he's sorry; more than anything, I just wish he'd ..." His voice trailed off.

My hand shook as I handed him back the picture. I felt inadequate. Compassion wasn't enough. He'd been cheated—his childhood, his innocence, stolen—and what was stolen I couldn't replace.

"Krista ... no one other than my family is armed with this knowledge. Now you know."

I looked at him, not bothering to hide my concern. "Armed? Brandon, I would never use something like this against you."

"You could if you wanted to hurt me."

"Brandon, on my soul—I will never repeat a word of this. Not under any circumstance. Please believe me."

"I do believe you, Kris."

"Carrie knows you grew up with Jamison."

"She doesn't know the real reason."

Why didn't you tell her the truth? You two have been friends forever. You don't trust her?"

"It's not that; I trust her."

"But?" I coaxed.

He took a deep breath and let it out slowly. "Carrie's fragile, Kris. I've known her for years and I've seen her reactions to everyday things—TV programs on things like cruelty to animals, starving children, you name it—she carries it around with her afterward for weeks. Things affect her dramatically because she's so sensitive. I'm afraid she wouldn't be able to let it go, and it's not something I want to dwell on. He looked at me. "You, I believe, are more resilient. And that's another reason why I hope you think very carefully about how to handle her feelings about what is going on between you."

Although he had never seen it, I could cry too. I was just more adept at hiding it.

"I told Carrie I used to have a drug problem; I did. I left it at that. I didn't tell her why I started using; at the time, it was the only thing that dulled the pain. But then I found surfing and it was so much better than anything I'd ever felt before. It became my drug instead."

An interesting way of looking at it.

"Surfing is my religion. When I paddle out, it's just the ocean and me, and we're one. I'm at complete peace with myself out there. And when I'm riding a wave, for those few seconds, everything's just ... *perfect*. I decided I'd rather surf than spend the rest of my life in rehab."

"Wise decision."

———

During an afternoon visit to the Faust's, Daemon and I relaxed under the patio umbrella in their backyard, sipping lemonade and studying the board in one of our customary games of chess—a stimulating way to pass time until Aeleise returned home. I enjoyed hanging out with Daemon; he was unpretentious and charming, which made him easy to talk to. Lately, I had seen him nearly as much as I saw Aeleise.

He sat in the chair across from me, staring at the chessboard. Daemon's hair took flight in the warm breeze, fluttering down over his eyes as he concentrated. He brushed it aside at the same time he made his move.

"Your turn."

He enjoyed the sport. I enjoyed his unshakable confidence. I considered my next move. Choosing a pawn, I moved ahead one space. So daring.

"Daemon, why don't you ever talk about girls?" I had often wondered.

He squinted at me. "I didn't realize I was supposed to be saying anything about girls. What would you have me say?"

"Well, don't you like them? Don't they interest you?"

He chuckled. "Yes, I suppose it's safe to say they do. Have I given you any reason to think that they wouldn't?"

"Well, it's just that I've never seen you with anyone, and you never mention anybody. I'm just surprised, I guess. Don't you have a girlfriend?"

"Not at the moment, no."

"Odd." I mistakenly said it aloud.

He continued studying the board, considering his next move. "Well, don't let it trouble you. I suspect I like women as much as the next red-blooded male."

"But no one interests you?" I pressed. "You don't ever date?"

"I don't have anyone in mind at the moment, but I've dated in the past." He treated the subject in an offhanded manner, as if it was of no particular interest to him.

"Have you given it up?"

He lifted his eyes from the board to look at me quizzically. "No, not entirely . . . I just have other things that occupy my time." He rested his arm on the table. "I'll admit dating doesn't rank high on my list of priorities right now." His gaze lingered on me, and he rubbed his chin, then slid the heel of his hand up to cover his blossoming grin. "This is quite the inquisition; why the sudden interest?"

"I don't know," I said, retreating. "Would you prefer we not talk about it?"

He sobered. "It's not that." He sat up straighter. He sounded perplexed. "It's just not something I'm asked often. What do you want to know?"

"Who were they? Were you ever serious with any of them? Etcetera, etcetera."

"Ahh—the third degree. I see." He laughed. "Am I your latest science project?"

I smiled. "Maybe."

"I dated one person; there was no 'them.'"

"Well, did she have a name?"

"Danielle."

"How long were you together?"

"Just over a year."

A whole year. "That's a long time. You must have been close."

He frowned. "Apparently not close enough."

I waited, but he didn't share further. No matter, I didn't mind digging. "What happened?"

"Things didn't work out. I wish they could have." He shook his head with regret. "Things would've been fine if we just could've reached an understanding about the intimate aspect of the relationship." He sighed. "Unfortunately, we didn't share the same view regarding what was acceptable physically—it became an issue. When it came right down to it...I couldn't give her what she wanted, so she chose to go her own way."

"Are you still friends?" I hoped for a positive response to lighten his mood.

He shook his head slowly. "I wanted to be. I tried, but she wouldn't have it. Said she couldn't handle it." The drop in his voice alone revealed how hard he had taken the breakup.

I paused to think about that. "So that was the *only* issue that caused a riff in the relationship?"

He nodded.

"So what kind of physical boundaries do you set for yourself concerning romantic relationships?" It seemed a logical question, considering his conservative upbringing and unyielding devotion to God.

"Like what? You mean define how far I'll go?" He frowned, uncertain. "What exactly are you asking?"

"Um..."

"Um?" he repeated, teasing me. "Is that what you want to know?" When I didn't reply, he laughed. "Ah, yes—the ever curious and precocious Krista."

I was relieved he wasn't offended. "Yeah."

"You couldn't just ask me if we had sex?" I grew uncomfortable, and he chuckled again. "You're funny, Kris."

"I'm not trying to be funny," I said, eyes shifting to the chessboard.

"I know."

"Well?" Was he going to share, or just laugh at me?

"What do you think?"

"I don't know for sure."

He moved his knight to claim my bishop. "Yes you do. Think, Kris—do you know me, or don't you?"

I knew what he believed, but did he never slip up? No one's *perfect*. My eyes pleaded with him. Couldn't he just give me a straight answer? "Well, maybe you led a secret former life," I said. "No checkered past—nothing?"

His eyebrow rose at me. "I'm sorry—I thought you knew I was previously a gigolo, Mondays through Fridays, and a practicing Satanist on weekends."

I laughed.

"Sorry to disappoint you...no, we didn't. I'm afraid I'm not *that* interesting."

Oh, not true—I found him *most* interesting...fascinating, really. "Weren't you tempted?" I asked. "Either of you?"

"Every minute," he said matter-of-factly. "That was the problem."

"So what did you do about it?"

"Prayed for strength."

"That's *it*? That's all it took?" I was suddenly impressed by the power of prayer.

"Yes, prayer helped," he replied with an impish grin.

"So then you've *never* had sex," I stated, genius that I am.

"No, I haven't. What's that look for? You should know by now how seriously I take my faith. You act like being a virgin is a bad thing."

"I'm a virgin," I said defensively.

He smiled. "I should hope so." He leaned back in his chair and looked at me thoughtfully. The breeze picked up, stirring the wind chimes and bringing the scent of honeysuckle. "So, are you going to share with me the reason behind your probing?"

"Oh..." I decided at that moment. "I was just curious."

"If you say so."

Nervous, I quickly looked at the chessboard. We finished off the game twenty minutes after Aeleise returned home. Daemon won. He usually did.

———

I showed up at Daemon's the next day in one of the fashions that Brandon had helped me select. With the assistance of a waving iron, I had transformed my straight chestnut hair into a bounty of bouncing ringlets. I had applied a smidgen more makeup than usual. Okay...a lot more—powder and paint make a girl what she ain't. I felt confident I could pull off a sophisticated sixteen, seventeen...maybe.

When Daemon answered the door, he did a most unsubtle double take. "Krista?"

"Hi." I smiled brightly through my mango flavored lip gloss.

"Hi." He stepped back and ushered me inside with a swoosh of his hand.

I couldn't read the tone of his greeting.

My multiple silver hoop bracelets danced a lively *jingle, jangle* as I made my grand entrance. I had already perfected the walk in the tricky heels. They weren't too high—just a lift. He closed the door behind me. His expression left me feeling like the disco queen who had walked into the church social. I was foreign, and he seemed leery, suspicious of me. I had hoped for a more enthusiastic reaction. I wanted him to like me. But now I felt worried; if I played the organ donor, would he reject my heart?

"I barely recognized you," he said after a moment. "What's the occasion?" He looked handsome in a dark gray thermal shirt loosely tucked into dark slacks. His hair was slightly tousled.

"No occasion; just thought I'd stop by and say hello. Are you busy?"

"Not at the moment, no." His tone revealed nothing.

"What do you think? Do you like it?" I made a quick turn for his review.

He looked me over quickly, careful not to look too closely, or anywhere in particular. His face was a blank mask. "I think you're going to have every guy hitting on you, state to state."

"I'm staying in California."

"It's a figure of speech." His voice held no humor.

I knew that.

"This is a...new look for you," he said diplomatically. "What prompted it?"

"Brandon and I went shopping. He helped me pick it out."

"Why doesn't that surprise me?"

"You don't like it," I said, crestfallen.

"I didn't say that. I simply think it's a little too provocative for someone your age to be wearing. It leaves a lasting impression, if that's the desired goal. Do you want guys to look at you like that, Kris?"

"Like what?"

"Well, considering it scarcely leaves anything to the imagination...I gather most men will be wishing you were in their bedroom."

I found myself blushing at his comment.

"You should be blushing, Kris. It's about as subtle as a Britney Spears video." His expression clearly echoed his disapproving tone. "Have your parents seen you in this?"

"What parents?"

"*Your* parents."

"No. My mother wasn't available to give her opinion," I said coolly.

"I didn't think so. Well then, may I suggest you let Marc review this...brave ensemble before you leave your house again?"

"He wouldn't care," I retorted. *Right.*

His eyes were stern. "Are you confident enough to place a bet on that?"

Just then, Aeleise came to my rescue from her bedroom. "*Wow!* Where'd you get your outfit, Kris? It's—*wow!*" Her clear blue eyes were wide and impressed.

Thank you. My spirits lifted. "You like it?" I asked, smiling while she circled me for the full effect. Unlike Daemon, she scrutinized every square inch. She pulled back with an ecstatic grin. "It's fabulous!"

I returned her smile. "Thanks. You can borrow it sometime, if you like."

Daemon cut through our cheer. "You can admire it all you want from afar, Aeleise. But you're not putting one *toe* in that outfit, so don't bother asking to borrow it."

Aeleise took her eyes off me long enough to give him an exaggerated pout.

"*Aeleise...*" he said in warning, shocked she would even consider it. He frowned, watching as she continued to scour my outfit in delighted fascination. "*Try* to remember yourself. Right now you're gawking at her the way most men would."

"I'm sorry. It's just so...*amazing*. I've never seen you look better, Kris."

"Thank you." Aeleise: my only fan.

She turned to her brother. "Daemon, you don't like it? You don't think she looks spectacular?"

His words even felt cool. "It's quite an outfit. One intended for someone far older. At least I should hope so." Daemon could certainly wring a sponge brittle. "Kris, just what are Brandon's intentions behind these...*spectacular* clothes?"

"Not a thing," I said.

"I find that hard to believe."

"No, honestly Daemon. It's not like that," I insisted.

"No? Well, he certainly likes to see a lot of body for someone who professes no interest in it."

"Brandon just likes to take his girlfriends shopping sometimes," Aeleise supplied.

"I don't really know how to explain it," I said.

"I do," he said, his face deadly serious. "You're his trophy."

Why was Daemon being so...*sour?* "I'm not a trophy," I said hotly.

We locked eyes in a standoff.

"If you say so."

Aeleise, playing referee, said, "Peace, you two."

She walked between us and grabbed me by the wrist. I resisted, keeping angry eyes on him, then reluctantly let her drag me away. He held my eyes in challenge. I was still looking at him as she pulled me through her bedroom door.

"What just happened? What's with Daemon?" I asked, annoyed.

"Oh, don't let him upset you. It's fine. I'm sure he just finds the outfit...uh...distracting. It's super cute—no, *hot*, Kris."

I wasn't feeling so hot. More like hurt by his hostility.

"I'm so glad you came over," Aeleise said as we sat on her bed. "I just got off the phone with Nick. He said he wants us to get together."

My instinct told me to be concerned about this get-together, but I couldn't confirm my suspicions just yet. We'd simply both have to wait.

I returned to my house angry and upset. Nothing was going as planned. My new outfit was a bust; my efforts were certainly noticed, but not well received. Everything had an uncanny way of backfiring on me.

17

Thursday afternoon, Mr. Grindall took our entire History class to the school library to select books for our upcoming book report assignment. The topic was "Prominent Figures of the Past." I hadn't yet decided between Cleopatra and Joan of Arc.

The air-conditioned library was cool, and smelled faintly of old books. I wandered down an aisle, looking for a title that would catch my interest. In the quiet of the room, I heard whispered conversations and the sound of shuffling feet.

I found two books that showed promise and carried them to a table. I was flipping through one of them when someone slid into the seat directly across from me. I looked up to see Brandon's mischievous eyes peering at me over *The Valley of the Dolls.*

"What are you doing here?" I whispered.

"Getting a first-rate education," he whispered back, "and you?"

"We're researching for a history assignment."

"Ahh…" He lifted my book to inspect the cover. "Joan of Arc?" His eyes shifted to the other book. He leaned forward for a closer look. "Cleopatra." He nodded. "Definitely more you; leave Miss Joan for our Carrie. Won't she delight to discover how people tortured those suspected of witchcraft in the past?"

I scowled and shook my head. "You're horrible, Brandon."

"But you love it," he taunted in an undertone. "Come on, grab your books and come with me; I want to talk to you."

"Where are we going? This *is* still class," I reminded him.

"Just around the corner, don't worry."

I pushed out of my chair, picked up the book on Cleopatra, and followed Brandon to an empty area of the library.

"What is it?" I asked.

He turned to face me. "An invitation."

"To what?"

"I thought I'd throw a modest overnight shindig at my sister Jamison's beach house on Saturday. She'll be gone. You interested?"

My initial excitement subsided once I realized Marc would probably frown on the idea. But he *had* let me stay at Brandon's before—under supposed supervision. Could I pull it off again? I perked up, knowing I'd supply Marc with compelling reassurance—even if that reassurance meant fabricating Jamison's presence at the beach house. "Yeah, sounds fun. Who all is invited?"

"You, Carrie, Nick, and me." He smiled. "I thought a nice, cozy gathering might be appropriate for this weekend. Intimate evenings are so much more enjoyable than loud, chaotic get-togethers."

I agreed. "Nick, huh?" I teased. "I bet. As always, up to no good."

He assumed a wounded expression and moved his fingers to his heart. "Me, up to no good?"

Brandon was many things; innocent wasn't one of them. "Your protests are lost on me. Did Carrie agree to go?"

"Affirmative."

"Good work, Brandon. Count me in."

"Splendid. Two down, one to go."

"You think Nick will accept your invitation?"

He grinned. "I know he will."

I shook my head, smiling myself. "Are you always so sure of yourself?"

"Of course"

"So, are you just as confident that Nick will accept your advances?"

He laughed quietly. "My, my. Getting slightly ahead of yourself, aren't you? Already planning my activities for the evening?"

"No," I whispered, "I just know you too well. You've been in hot pursuit of an opportunity to whisk Nick away for ages now. Tell me I'm not right."

He smiled. "Why not? You know he's interested."

"Fine."

"Kris, we've been hanging out nearly every day together. You can't be surprised."

"Just confirming my suspicions," I said airily. "You really think he'll be open to the idea with Carrie and me present?"

He shrugged. "We have been getting to know each other during those swimming lessons."

I was glad I wasn't Nick. I'd be frightened to play along with Brandon's exotic and fanciful ideas. "Damn, you're a handful, Brandon."

He gave me a wicked grin. "More than a handful, actually."

I wasn't prepared for his crude innuendo, and I felt the heat in my cheeks. My voice dropped to a whisper. I couldn't look at him. "I can't believe you just said that. That's not what I meant."

He laughed. "Is it really that shocking? I thought you had learned to expect my bluntness by now."

I didn't think I'd ever get used to his lewd remarks. Obviously, he'd never had his mouth washed out with a bar of soap.

He said, "I meant it as a joke."

I doubted that was entirely true. I stared at Cleopatra's face on the book cover. "I don't know if I like your sense of humor."

"Well, I'm not looking for your approval," he whispered, leaning in to me.

"No kidding."

"Just as long as we understand each other." I could hear his smile without even looking at him.

"Perfectly; so save your witty comments for your boy toy."

"As you request." I could tell he was pleased with himself.

The more I knew of Brandon the less I understood. How could someone who had been so traumatized still stay open hearted. I began to believe that with all his lewdness and posing Brandon was the bravest person I knew. He could still go after love or whatever, even lust, after all that had happened to him. I might be fourteen and inexperienced but I had read the classics and I knew that the heart could be weak or strong. Brandon had come through his childhood and gotten to the other side. I could learn a lot from him.

He stood straighter, giving me room to breathe. "I'll see you at the beach house, then."

———

Saturday dawned sunny. By noon, we were at the beach house, perched like a dare on the edge of a cliff. Carrie lay back in the plush lounge chair beside the pool, head tilted toward the sun's warming rays. She wore her white heart-shaped glasses trimmed with rhinestones, and they reflected sunlight in tiny, blinding beams. She soaked up the sun in a pose perfect enough for *Cosmopolitan*, wearing her new—yet surprisingly modest—one-piece swimsuit in a color that matched her Betty Boop-like shades.

Five minutes immersed in the painfully frigid water in Jami's pool were enough to cool me off. After one final dunk, I climbed out, my hair pasted to my neck and back. "Want anything from the house?" I asked. Brandon had made it clear that his sister expected us to make ourselves at home. She was in Barbados with her fiancé and trusted Brandon to treat her house with respect.

"Something to drink. Do you need a hand?"

"No—you focus on your tribute to the sun. I can manage," I said with a smile, and walked toward the house.

The cool air inside the beach house greeted me when I pulled back the sliding glass door. The sudden shift in temperature hit me like a cold shower, and I was anxious to return to the sunshine. I clutched my arms around myself and padded down the hallway toward the guest bathroom. I entered—and stopped dead in my tracks.

The bath opened into an adjoining guest room, and through the half-open door, I saw them. Freshly showered and wrapped only in a towel, Nick stood no more than twelve feet in front of me, completely unaware that I had entered the bath. I was in darkness while they were bathed in soft light. Brandon rested against the sink counter, gazing at himself in the mirror.

I stood there dripping wet, not daring to make a sound. I wanted only to retreat without notice, but I had forgotten how to move.

"Don't disappoint me by leaving," Brandon said as I quietly turned to leave. Though this was directed at Nick, I felt like he was talking to me. Instinctively I turned back.

"Come here," he commanded Nick in a low, welcoming voice, a tone I had never heard until now. Although Brandon's words weren't for me, they felt like a soft caress. He watched Nick doing as he had been told, approaching him tentatively. I took a step backward, and Brandon glanced at me subtly. His eyes glittered; he suppressed a smile. It had gone unnoticed by Nick, and Brandon said nothing.

I felt foolish. He held his hand out to Nick. He pulled him closer, until they were lightly touching. Despite the cool air, I sensed a heat of a different sort, generated by the two of them. I could sense the energy—a combination of desire and tension that hung in the air.

I was so out of there.

———

Carrie and I sat outside, talking and picking over an arrangement of fruit. The daylight evaporated quickly. The sun yawned farewell and swiftly bowed out, a fiery ball sinking into the distant ocean. Carrie pulled back her glasses until they sat perched atop her head. She peeled back the bottom edge of her swimsuit, satisfied to see the tan line that promised to develop into a deeper golden bronze within days. The air felt suddenly cool against my skin.

Carrie sat up, wrapping the enormous spa towel about her shoulders. "It's getting cold. Let's go inside."

We found the boys kicking back in the living room. Nick sat cross-legged on the floor, his attention riveted to the television as he played a game on the Playstation. Brandon slouched comfortably against a corner of the couch, watching.

My eyes shifted just in time to see the well-endowed heroine who represented Nick onscreen take a fatal bullet in the chest; she collapsed in a pool of her own computer-generated blood. The words GAME OVER flashed repeatedly.

"Okay, that's it. I'm done with this." He pushed the controls out of reach.

"Where's Aeleise?" Carrie asked. "How come she didn't come along?"

Nick stalled, wanting for a response. Brandon replied for him. "I didn't invite her."

"*Brandon,* why not? I know you guys aren't best friends, but you *are* good friends. You invite her boyfriend and not her?"

"I'm not breaking any laws here. He *is* allowed to exist without her, you know. Just because they're together doesn't mean they have to be joined at the hip."

"Kick back. I wasn't accusing him of anything, I was just curious," she said, surprised by his aggressive response.

The subject of Aeleise didn't sit as well with Nick. He downed his drink.

"So, are we having a slumber party in the den, or are we sleeping in separate rooms?" Brandon asked.

My eyes went to Carrie. "Slumber party, for sure," she said.

"Slumber party it is, then. I'll go fetch us some blankets and pillows for bedding."

"I'll help you," Nick said.

Brandon paused, studying Nick. Finally he said, "All right. Come along, then."

They both disappeared into the hallway. I assumed Nick was looking for an excuse to steal some private time with Brandon. "Will you braid my hair?" Carrie asked from her snug little corner of the couch.

"Sure." I loved playing with her canary-bright mane. It reminded me of *Little Golden Books* and stories of Rapunzel read to me by mom, once upon a time. She moved from her spot on the couch to take a seat between my knees on the floor in front of me. A feeling of lazy content came over me as I parted her hair into sections with my fingers.

"I wonder what happened to Brandon and Nick," she said, too relaxed to be more than mildly curious. "They've been gone for a while now, haven't they?"

As if on cue, Brandon came into the room alone, carrying pillows and blankets. He dumped them unceremoniously onto the chair.

I resumed where I'd left off, running the brush through her thick tresses. Brandon drew himself up to sit sideways in the overstuffed chair across from the one loaded with bedding, his legs dangling over the edge. He seemed disengaged.

"You look unhappy," I said, taking in his bored expression.

He studied his manicure as he spoke. "I hadn't planned on babysitting this evening."

Oh oh. This was Brandon's curse. Now that he had Nick where he wanted him, he was going to tire of the poor guy before Nick knew what hit him. He looked at the two of us. "Carrie, you look about ready to pass out. Maybe I should lay out the blankets so you can lie down."

She nodded. The three of us laid out half a dozen pillows and enough layers of blankets to make a hearty lasagna.

Nick rejoined our group. Carrie and I lay on our stomachs, our pinkies entwined discreetly. Brandon sat staunchly on the couch with Nick beside him.

I looked over my shoulder at them. "Come down and sit with us."

Brandon slid off the couch to sit beside me as if it were a chore. Nick slid down on his other side. "Better?" he asked.

"Yes."

The comedian on the tube was going strong and Brandon hadn't broken a smile once.

"What's wrong?" I asked, lowering my voice.

"Nothing."

We sat up talking, while watching and critiquing music videos. Nick and Carrie, lulled by the alcohol, soon slipped into sleep beneath the covers. Brandon and I slouched farther into the nest. He turned on his side to face me; resting his head high on his pillow, he waved to me over Carrie's head. My body silently shook with laughter and I smiled at him and waved back.

Lowering his voice, he said, "Fun, huh?"

We both knew it wasn't. I wanted to pull Carrie toward me and hold her, but I knew that those feelings would pass, the phase thing, and then I would feel different. I wondered if Brandon was thinking the same about Nick.

I kept my voice low. "It would make things so much easier if we could all be straight-up with each other. I feel like I'm walking on eggshells. How about you?"

"I'm right there with you," he said. "Although for me, this is pretty much standard operating procedure." He accepted it, although not happily.

———

I hadn't felt her leave my side, but I recognized her shrill voice in the dark. Carrie's shriek nearly raised the hair off my back. I sat up, realizing that both she and Brandon were absent from the nest. Nick remained lost in his dreams. I got up and followed the sound of Brandon's voice into the hall, fumbling in their direction, not knowing the location of the light switch.

It was too dark to make out specifics, but a deep shadow appeared to be Brandon. Carrie had her back pasted to the corner wall as if she could will herself to sink through it. The sight of Brandon in no more than silk boxers had caught her unprepared, apparently.

"Carrie," he said softly, "Carrie, it's Brandon. Are you okay? I didn't mean to scare you, I——"

"I know, Brandon...I know. Just go back to bed."

He turned toward the living room. I placed my hand on her shoulder and moved in closer, gently persuading her into my arms. Her face burrowed against my chest, and I smoothed her hair.

Brandon had slid beneath the covers—slipped between the blankets beside Nick and encircled him with his arms. I gently coaxed Carrie into bed beside them. I lay with her in my arms, wide awake and staring into the slivers of light that cut between the blinds. I kissed the top of her head, letting my lips linger, relishing the scent of her green apple shampoo. I paused, an unexpected sound calling my attention.

I had *assumed* they were fast asleep — not true. Some twenty inches away, Brandon and Nick — mistakenly thinking the darkness would conceal them sufficiently — had started a party of their own.

I woke before Carrie the next morning, wanting to catch an early view of the ocean in solitude. In bare feet and pajamas, I padded out into the kitchen. I had hoped I would be the first up, but Nick and Brandon were already dressed and fixing breakfast. The enticing aroma of bacon and coffee filled the air.

They both looked up at me with matching saccharine smiles. Nick spoke first.

Brandon, sitting on the counter, said, "Hi, sunshine."

I didn't expect to feel the heat wash over my face as it did. "Good morning." My eyes drifted to the floor.

"What's wrong, Kris?" Brandon asked. "You're flushed."

I gave my best performance of nonchalance. "Nothing. It was just so hot in there under your duvet."

We just stared at each other for the length of five heartbeats, and then it was done. He knew everything I had seen, without a word spoken. Nick didn't see the color cross Brandon's face. He should have; it was rare to see Brandon blush.

At least he had the grace to look embarrassed.

18

On Monday, I went home with Aeleise for bible study. It was obvious Nick had not yet been honest with her about what was going on because she still was bubbly about him. It was an awkward position for me to be in and I tried to keep the conversation away from matters of the heart.

Daemon's silver Mercedes was parked in the driveway, and the front door to the house stood ajar. Inside, we found books *everywhere*. Their normally pristine living room looked like a library explosion.

"Just ignore the mess," Aeleise said, and led us upstairs to her room.

We dropped our book bags to the floor with a thud.

"What's your brother doing?" I asked Aeleise.

"Organizing the chaos downstairs, I imagine."

"Do you think Daemon needs any help?"

"You could ask him," she said. "If he wants our help, will you let us know?"

"Sure." I went in search of Daemon. I found him at the bottom of the stairs, transporting an armload of books to a box across the room. He set them in a precarious pile on the table beside it and turned around to face me.

"Hey, Krista."

"Hi," I said, and came closer for a better look. "What are you doing?"

"We had a book drive this week. Everyone donated their old Bibles so we can hand them out to people who can't afford them. You're looking at the turnout."

"Looks like it went well."

He had a pleased glow to him. "It really did."

"Do you want some help? Aeleise wanted me to ask you if wanted her and Nick to come down."

"No, I've got it handled. You guys do what you had planned. I appreciate the offer, though."

"Do you mind if I stay down here and help?"

"I suppose I could use an extra pair of hands."

"Tell me what to do."

He reached for a Bible, showed me how to check its spine, and sorted it according to version. "People are always looking for proof of miracles," he said, "but to some, something as simple as receiving their own Bible *is* a miracle. So Aeleise and I try to do what we can to help."

He added, "Everyone needs a passion."

I started handing him books, one at a time, and he placed them into boxes. I picked up one and the cover fell off, along with a few pages.

"Some of the older ones are in bad shape. Set those to the side and we'll see if they can be repaired."

I started a separate pile—a hospital ward for damaged books.

Eleven boxes into packing, my mind began to wander.

"What's wrong?" he asked.

"Nothing." I handed him another Bible. "Just wondering something."

"Oh, yeah? And what's that?" he asked good-naturedly.

"Does your wardrobe contain any clothing in a shade other than black?"

He gave me a charming smile. "Is that a formal complaint?"

"No, just curiosity."

"It's simply a personal preference."

I nodded. "Fair enough," I said, though I still found it peculiar. I handed him the last two books from the pile. "That's it."

His sudden frown was too cute to be considered true distress.

"What?"

He brightened. "The good news is... we have more."

"What's the bad news?"

His frown returned. "They're upstairs."

I laughed. "All right."

"You game?" He sounded surprised.

"Always."

He smiled and rose. "After you," he said.

"Keep going," he told me when we reached the top of the stairs. "They're in my room."

His room? I had never thought about his bedroom before. The bedroom was such a personal place, a disclosure of preference and personality that would surely provide me a clearer window through which to view him. How pristine would I find it? I recalled a field trip I'd taken with my class through the convent at my old school. Would his quarters be as barren, as austere as a monk's cell? Would they be as sterile as the life he led?

I stopped on the threshold, as if blocked by an invisible shield guarding his domain. My eyes went wide.

"Come on," he said. "You can come in."

I took two cautious steps forward.

Daemon's room was unlike any other room in the house. In fact, it was unlike any other room I had ever seen. Decadent. Buttered rum cake and brandied cherries—that was the first image that came to mind. I stepped inside the gothic masterpiece and inhaled deeply. The air was rich with the scent of strawberry incense.

The room was dark, the deep burgundy wallcovering reminiscent of the Victorian era. Golden crown molding made the room appear like a framed painting. Raven velvet drapes fell in seductive waves around his bed and shrouded the windows, blocking out all unwanted light. Two antique mahogany bookshelves were stuffed full of leather-bound books. I slid my toes over the rich, deep-stained hardwood floor; one more step, and I'd be plunging them into the pile of a Persian rug.

His high bed commanded attention in the center of the room. There was nothing subtle about it. It seemed to have its own life, like the abstract tree it resembled. Steel vines twisted hungrily upward, winding about the wrought iron fencing that served as head and foot-board; metal roses bloomed. The bed lay cloaked in black velvet and satin, topped by a multitude of velvet pillows in shades of eggplant, plum, and black. *It must feel heavenly between those sheets.* But I would never know.

An old gothic cross hung high above Daemon's bed, as exotic as the one that hung around his neck; elaborate candleholders clutched ebony and ivory candles, their weeping wax frozen; in the corner a chess set was balanced aloft by a golden statue of an Egyptian slave kneeling in submission. A box of Godiva chocolates sat on the night-stand beside a perspiring carafe.

I pointed to the curvaceous silver carafe and the two finely en-graved goblets on either side of it and asked, "What's that?"

"Water. Are you thirsty?"

The question struck me as incredibly wicked, as if it were some-thing I should have never been asked. I suppose "thirsty" worked, but "hungry" seemed far more accurate.

"No, thank you," I said softly.

For the X-rated thoughts it produced, Daemon's room should've required parental supervision. The atmosphere was overwhelming, intense.

I turned about slowly, taking it all in. This was *Daemon's* bedroom?

"Not exactly what I expected," I said carefully.

"Really? And what were you expecting?"

I raised my eyebrows. "Not this. Something much...simpler, I suppose. I'm not complaining. It's breathtaking."

It was nothing short of a gothic seduction set—an arena of ro-manticized death that, paired with Daemon, revealed a shocking twist in what I thought I knew of him. If he were a vampire, I would've willingly bared my neck.

"Well, thank you." His boyish smile was sweetly triumphant, com-pletely unarrogant, and very much at odds with his room. He walked to the far side of the bed. "It's over here," he said, and motioned me toward him.

I had forgotten our reason for coming upstairs. The dull, medium-size packing box sitting like an isolated oddity beside the bed reminded me. The Bibles. For some reason, that they waited in this room troubled me. But there was nothing sinful in lush decoration, I told myself.

I felt a new kind of excitement—a thrill that I couldn't quite explain.

19

I spent more and more time at Daemon's. I don't know what brought it on, or how it crept upon me with such ferocity, but before I knew what hit me, the damage had been done. Daemon. It was all about him.

I hadn't expected to find myself endlessly distracted by thoughts of him. It was a frustrating and unproductive way to pass time. By day, I indulged in daydreaming; by night, I tossed and turned in sleeplessness. It brought new meaning to the word *obsession*. I didn't have to close my eyes to see his staring back at me — eyes so purely black, so full of compassion, so bright with interest. I felt entirely lost. I could recall at leisure the scent of his cologne, the way his hair fell forward to conceal his features, the path his hand traveled through his raven locks to sweep them back.

He caught me staring once, much too captivated and for far too long for any reasonable excuse, and acknowledged my gaze with a quiet smile. I immediately looked away. I don't know what he thought at that moment; I only prayed he hadn't noted how my heart rate quickened, or my guilty blush. He was utterly unaware of the potency behind his occasional lingering glance. A smile from Daemon could warm me down to my toes.

At times, it was pleasant agony. But often, there was nothing pleasant about it. There were occasions when I didn't eat. My only appetite was for Daemon, and my appetite consumed me.

God ... to be close to him. There were stinging moments of clarity when I felt his body next to mine, so close his presence made me flush in awareness. My mind was fertile soil—ripe and flourishing with imagination about things of which I had no true knowledge. My schoolwork suffered. I'd open a textbook only to find my mind drifting over even the most casual thoughts of him, which forced me to reread the same five sentences again and again.

I was aware of the teacher, the slight hum of a lecturing voice in the background. Then Daemon's voice, promising an escort to a place more captivating, calling me.

"Krista … Krista …"

"Krista!" Ryan startled me like an electric shock. I unintentionally snapped the pencil in my hand. His eyes went wide.

Realizing what I had done, I tried to pull my head together. I looked at him, but I had memorized Daemon's face so completely that I could call it to my mind's eye as I pleased. Ryan morphed easily into Daemon and I had no clue what he was talking about.

"Kris?" Ryan waved his hand back and forth in front of my face.

"Hmm?"

"What's wrong with you? What are you so deep in trance about?"

"Nothing," I lied. No reason to add insult to injury … Ryan had been trying to get me to pay attention to him since Homecoming but that was just not going to happen.

"I just never realized how striking your eyes are." It was a cruel thing to say, knowing he was sweet on me, but it wasn't entirely untrue; he had fetching eyes. He brightened appreciatively.

"In that case, you're forgiven."

No need to mention that his ice-blue eyes had faded into Daemon's midnight orbs.

———

Marc wanted to know why my grades were suffering.

"I'll get them back up, I promise," I said.

And I did get them back up. Or rather, Brandon did.

"You're going to lose your spot on the squad if you don't pull yourself together," he warned as he did my homework.

I knew he was right, but that didn't help. I didn't know what to do about it.

"What's *really* going on with you, Kris?" When I didn't answer, he made his own assumption. "This is about Daemon, isn't it."

Full of guilt, I wordlessly shifted my eyes to my lap.

"Kris, you're screwing yourself over about something that isn't going to happen. Don't spend your time daydreaming about mindless folly. Let it go."

I looked up at him, eyes weighed with the import of his words. I didn't want him to be right.

He shook his head. "Don't set yourself up for a fall."

I tried to follow his advice. I made it through two weeks without attending Bible study in order to avoid seeing Daemon. On the days I went to Aeleise's for practice, my eyes and ears were on alert. At the first hint of him, I vanished into the bathroom or, if I couldn't escape in time, I made our encounter as brief as possible, and avoided making eye contact. It felt rude and I hated doing it, but I figured this was the best way to get over him, even if it felt as if I was at war with myself.

On one occasion, my self-trickery failed me. I entered Aeleise's backyard and found her and Daemon in the pool, hitting a ball back and forth through the air. Aeleise noticed me at the same moment Daemon delivered a successful serve, pegging her in the head. She shook it off, then waved, all smiles.

"Hi, Krista! Come in; it's great!"

Daemon turned around, pushing aside the dark wet hair that hid his eyes. "Hey, Kris."

I sat down in a patio chair in the shade of an umbrella. "Are you guys going to be in there long?"

"I'm out. I need to get ready for work." Daemon got out of the pool and grabbed a towel that lay at the water's edge. I noticed the first sign of color in his wardrobe: his long, crimson swim trunks clung to him in revealing ways. I looked at my fingernails. "The pool's all yours," he said to us as he wrapped the towel around his waist.

Aeleise called out to me, "Krista, grab one of my suits from upstairs."

I wasn't sure I wanted to swim, but I called back anyway, "Okay." Maybe I'd change my mind. As I moved to get up, Daemon pinned me in my chair, his hands planted on its arms on either side of me. I wasn't going anywhere.

He bent forward until his eyes were level with mine, merely inches away, and smiled playfully. "Nuh-uh — not so fast. Who *knows* when I'll see you again?"

My heart raced at a frantic tempo. His water-saturated lashes and coal-colored eyes appeared even more dramatic in the sunshine. What I had cautiously tiptoed around for weeks was now unavoidable. My heart beat at my ribs like a trapped thing. I was unaccustomed to being at such close range. His warm breath on my face smelled of cinnamon. I concentrated on my own breathing. "How long are you going to avoid me?" he asked.

Beads of water from his hair, delightfully cool, dripped one after another onto my bare thighs, slowly collecting to form a warm pool between them. "I'm not avoiding you. I've been busy." My voice sounded breathy and unconvincing. I hated it.

"Don't lie to me, Kris. You're not even looking at me. Did I do something wrong?"

"No."

"Then why haven't you been coming by after school? Is my company boring you? I've noticed your careful side-step routine — you dart from a room as soon as I'm in it."

Was it that obvious?

"Am I right?"

I stalled for an answer. "That's five questions in less than one minute. You're exceeding my one per minute max."

He laughed joyously. "Oh, really? Well, I'm practically your brother, so I'm allowed to play twenty questions if I like." He grinned.

That was the problem. I didn't need another brother. I forced a smile. "Quarter finals are coming up," I supplied quickly. "I want to be prepared." It was true. I wanted to do well — I just hadn't started studying yet!

"Finals aren't for another month."

My eyes darted to Aeleise as she swam, oblivious to our conversation.

"A little extra studying never hurt anyone."

His eyes laughed; he gave me a knowing smirk. "Uh-huh. Don't be such a stranger, okay?" He pushed away from the chair and headed indoors.

I waited until his cream-colored towel had disappeared inside the house before I wiped my sweaty palms on my shorts. Aeleise grabbed onto the side of the pool and came up for air.

"Aren't you coming in?" she pushed her tangled hair out of her face.

"I guess so," I said. "I'll be right back."

Once in her room, I rifled through her drawers until I found her collection of swimsuits. Decisions, decisions. Bikini, full piece, colorful or black. The faint sound of the shower traveled across the hall as Daemon prepared for work. I chose the black full piece and slipped it on.

I headed for the hall closet to grab a towel; the suit I had chosen was modest but I still felt too naked to be running around so bare in Daemon's house. I opened the cupboard to find . . . nothing.

I turned toward Aleise's room just as Daemon emerged from the bathroom. The color of his towel had changed to baby blue and hung low on his hips.

"I'm looking for towels," I stammered.

"There should be some fresh ones in the bathroom," he said nonchalantly as he continued on to his room.

I walked into the steamy bathroom that still held the scent of his aftershave. Daemon's dripping scarlet swim trunks hung from the towel rack where I'd expected to find a towel. I turned around, then jumped back when I found him standing there. He reached for the overhead cupboard, the movement causing him to lean against me. His body brushed against mine. My stomach fluttered at the unfamiliar feeling of contact. I could smell the scent of his aftershave.

"Here." He handed me a plump baby blue towel that matched his.

"Thanks," I said, still rather taken aback by his sudden appearance.

He gave me a small smile and closed the door behind him. I locked the door—a delayed reaction—as my mind chewed over the realization that Daemon had been nearly naked against me.

I joined Aeleise for a brief dip in the pool once Daemon was gone, and as we swam we discussed where to hold Jessa's upcoming birthday party. It was challenging to grasp that she and Jessa were such good friends. Their lifestyles and beliefs clashed so severely that it was hard to imagine them bonding at all. But Aeleise seemed able to mesh amiably with anyone.

We considered having the sleepover at Aeleise's, but quickly decided that the only place that seemed to offer an unconfining atmosphere was my house. Marc was easygoing compared to Daemon, and we trusted that he wouldn't attempt the role of overbearing parent. My house became the official site for Jessa's party.

The night of the party showed a 100 percent turnout. Popularity by association—no one wanted to turn down an "invitation only" event with Jessa as the star.

Around a pile of junk food in the center of the living room floor sat all Jessa's closest friends—Adara, Darian, Milla, and Aeleise, who were sophomores and, with the exception of Aeleise, closer to Jessa than I was. There was also a select group of freshmen from my class. We'd been stuffing our faces all night with popcorn, cake and candy while we sat campfire-style discussing the latest happenings in our lives. Finally, around 11:00 P.M., we'd had enough of food. Aeleise and Chloe both groaned that they had eaten so much, they felt sick.

We were all dressed for bed. Some of us wore boxer shorts and oversized T-shirts, while Morgan, Danya, and Jessa wore more feminine sleepwear. Jessa was on display in the nightgown her older sister, Emma, had given her as a birthday gift. It was a beautiful shade of lavender, made of satin, chiffon, and lace, and was lined with a bra that helped create cleavage. It seemed like a glamorous choice to me—something reserved for evenings, evenings that belonged to the world of men's romantic fantasies. The low-cut front accentuated her breasts, making them appear far more voluptuous than they actually were, while a side slit revealed almost the entire length of her tanned leg. Her sister knew well her attraction to Josh, and the gift draped over her body clearly had been chosen with Josh in mind—it certainly wasn't practical.

We all moved closer together, tightening the social circle we had created. The conversation focused on school, cheerleading camp, the dance team, and who was dating whom.

Danya congratulated Morgan on her latest decision to dump Trey. "*Finally.* I though you would never get rid of him, Morgan."

Morgan smiled mischievously. "Well, it does help when you already have your sights set on another."

Everyone perked up. "You're already dating someone else?" an enthusiastic Darian asked.

"Not yet. But I hope to be soon."

"Who is it?" Danya asked.

"I bet I know," said Chloe, smiling.

"Do tell, Morgan," Milla urged.

Morgan smiled and popped an M&M into her mouth. "Todd."

"I *knew* it!" Chloe squealed.

I looked at Morgan, eyes wide. "Todd? As in *Josh's* friend, Todd?"

"The same," she confirmed, smiling.

"Wow," Milla mused with a crafty smile. "I've heard some interesting things about that one."

"About who? Josh or Todd?" Darian asked.

"Both," Milla said.

"But he's so much older than you, Morgan," Carrie reminded her.

"So much the better. I'm tired of dealing with immature boys. After dealing with Trey, I deserve some excitement."

"Don't get too far ahead of yourself," Aeleise warned.

"Thanks, mom," Morgan said in a sarcastic voice.

"Oh no," I moaned, "this isn't going to be another one of your hour-long monologues professing your affections for my brother, is it?"

"Oh come on, Krista," Jessa said. "Forget for a second that Josh is your brother." *How does one do that?* "He and Todd are two of the hottest guys at school and you know it. Julie and Crystal told us how good in bed Josh and Todd are."

"Really?" Morgan said with enthusiasm.

"Really," Jessa said matter-of-factly, but she looked at me when she answered the question. She turned to look at Morgan and smiled. "I've had my eye on Josh since day one."

"And so have plenty of other girls," Danya chimed in.

Jessa shrugged. "No matter."

"What happened to Ryan, Jess? I thought you were all gung-ho to hook up with him," Adara said.

Jessa's eyes shifted to me. "I don't know. Maybe we should ask Krista; she and Carrie seem to spend a lot of time with him. So, what's the story—are either of you ... seeing him?" Her eyes rested on Carrie now.

"Neither of us is seeing anyone," I said. "Ryan's just a friend."

"Like you don't want more," Jessa said.

"You're right—I don't."

Darian said, "Unlike some people, Ryan's a mystery. I can't figure out if he dates or not."

"You're telling me." Jessa sniffed. "I put that boy to the test last year and got *nowhere.*"

Ahh ... so she's finally decided to come clean about it.

"I don't know what his problem is," Jessa continued. "He can be so uptight sometimes."

"Unlike your latest rogue pick," Milla said.

"You're one to talk—you're just as interested."

"Just not willing."

Jessa directed a cool glare Milla's way.

"Oh, come *on,*" Darian said, coming to Milla's defense."

"What are you trying to say?" Jessa asked, eyebrow arched in challenge.

"Popular opinion says they're male sluts," Darian said bluntly.

"What?" I blurted. "My brother is *not* a slut, Darian."

Darian didn't reply.

"I wish he would be one with me," Jessa murmured with an impish smile.

Chloe's eyes went wide. "*Jessa*—watch what you're saying."

"What? Krista knows I want Josh," she said, too innocently.

Milla put in her two cents. "Yeah, and I know why. I heard he's something to see."

"*Milla!* Both of you—*shut up.* Show some respect," Aeleise snapped.

Just then, we were startled into silence by the sound of the patio door sliding open. Josh walked into the house and headed for the refrigerator, looking to cool off after a workout on his weight set. He wasn't wearing a shirt and his tanned shoulders and chest glistened with sweat. He had forgotten I had invited friends over for Jessa's birthday, and didn't notice us there in the sunken living room, behind the partition. We waited quietly as he stood at the refrigerator, pouring a drink.

I noticed Jessa's eyes traveling over Josh's body. I kicked her lightly. Someone deliberately cleared her throat. Josh turned around.

"Hi, Josh," Milla said sweetly.

"What's up, Milla?"

"Just hanging out."

"Right…well, I'll get out of your way. Sorry to interrupt your party," he said, realizing he had an audience.

I got to my feet, started toward the kitchen. "Thanks, Josh," I interjected. I wanted him out of the room as quickly as possible.

"*No*—don't go," someone said. "Things were just starting to get interesting."

I turned to see who'd spoken. Darian. I shot her a look of warning. "Josh, just go. *Please,*" I added, getting nervous. "Leave the room."

Josh looked at me, and then at all of us, strangely.

"Don't be rude, Krista," Jessa interrupted. "Why, we were just talking about you, Josh. Now that you're here, we can ask you ourselves."

"Jessa, *don't!*" I stood and positioned myself between them, waving Josh toward the hallway. I looked at him. "Josh—just *go.* I'm serious." I got no response. "*Please.* You have the worst timing."

"On the contrary, Krista. I'd say your brother has *excellent* timing." She smiled mysteriously at Josh.

"What's going on?" he asked.

"Nothing," I said quickly.

"You're not being honest, Krista. Why not let him in on our gossip? I mean, after all, it *is* about him."

I wanted to strangle her.

"Because it's stupid shit, Jessa, and he doesn't need to hear it!" I almost shouted.

She didn't care. She had her own agenda. She stood and walked toward him. Entering the kitchen, she stretched out against the counter so Josh could admire the lacy negligee she wore. "So, are they true, Josh? All the stories we've heard from knowledgeable sources?" She smiled coyly.

"*Shut up, Jessa!*"

"What?" she asked me, feigning innocence. "I'm sure he already knows; I'm sure he's proud that everyone at school agrees he and Todd are at the top of this year's male ho list — Most guys would kill to have that reputation at our school."

Was she brave or stupid? I voted for the latter.

I heard the girls' sudden intake of breath.

Josh looked at her. "Really? I never realized you were keeping track, Jessa." He didn't let on that he didn't appreciate her comment, but I knew.

All the girls were quiet.

"I'm just working from the information that Julie passed along. She had only the best of things to say about your ... skills, Josh."

He laughed, but it wasn't out of amusement.

"Krista knows, don't you Krista?" she said.

My God! What was she doing? She'd turn her birthday celebration into a funeral at the rate things were going. The conversation had become a three-ring circus with Josh in the center ring. Josh would fry her for it.

He looked at her first and then again at me. All eyes were on him. I could tell he was ready to snap, but I couldn't be sure what he would do.

Only I knew the restraint he used to control his voice when he he turned his attention back to Jessa. "Maybe you'd like to find out for yourself if the talk is true?"

Someone giggled.

"Then again," he said, "maybe you should just cool down."

A hush fell over the girls.

Jessa stood frozen, her back pressed against the kitchen counter. Josh moved toward her, close enough for intimacy. "And while you're at it..." He lowered his face to hers, allowing his voice to drop low. "You can put your panties back on."

He turned to walk away. Suddenly remembering the reason for our gathering, he looked back at Jessa; he gave her an ironic smile. "Oh, I almost forgot—happy birthday."

—

When practice let out Monday afternoon, Nick went home with Brandon for another private tutoring session, while I left with Aeleise. She wanted to have a conference—over what, I had no idea.

We were in her bedroom when the phone rang in another room. "Do you need to get that?" I asked.

"Daemon will get it. It's probably for him anyway," she said, and resumed the topic she'd broached. "I want you to consider it, Krista. I think you'd make an excellent captain. It's early, sure, but—"

Daemon poked his head in the doorway, looking at Aeleise. "Sorry to interrupt, but the phone's for you—it's Nick."

She jumped up, her face bright. "I'll be right back," she said, and rushed out.

Daemon still stood in the doorway. "How's it goin'?"

"Fine... I think. Aeleise is convinced I should try out for captain next year."

He broke into a half-smile. "That's Aeleise—always thinking ahead. So, is it something you've ever considered?"

"Not really. It's a lot of responsibility."

He nodded. "But nothing you couldn't handle—if you wanted to."

"That's just it; I don't know if I do."

"Well, it's not as if you need to know by tomorrow."

Aeleise came rushing through the door, snatched up her purse and gave herself a quick perusal in the mirror.

"You going somewhere?" Daemon asked.

She turned to me. "I'm sorry, Krista. Nick says he wants to see me. I won't be long, I promise."

"Wait, wait," Daemon said. "You're just going to up and leave while you have company because Nick wants to see you? Someone's being rude."

"I'm sorry, Kris; I don't mean to be rude. I just..."

"Don't worry about it, Aeleise. I know you've been waiting to talk with him. I don't mind."

"Thanks, Kris." She gave me an appreciative smile, and dashed out the door.

Daemon pulled her back, holding onto her arm. "I can't believe you."

"I won't be long, I swear."

He let go of her arm, looking disappointed. She was gone in an instant. He shook his head and then looked at me. "I'm sorry. I don't know what's gotten into her. If you don't feel like waiting, I can drive you home."

"That's okay, maybe she'll be quick." But I doubted it. I had a feeling Nick was about to relay some unpleasant news. And if that was the case, who knew how long it would take him to get the nerve to tell her? Regardless, it certainly wouldn't be any sacrifice to spend some time in Daemon's company.

"You don't want to wait in here by yourself, do you?"

He didn't have to twist my arm. I followed him into the living room.

"I just need to finish putting away the groceries."

I looked toward the kitchen. "I'll help."

He smiled. "I'm indebted to you—you're always helping me out."

"Hardly—as if you don't help out everyone on a daily basis."

The groceries were already out of the bags and sitting on the table.

"This is all for you and Aeleise?" I asked, surprised.

"I try to make trips to the store count. I'm not a fan of grocery shopping."

"You'd never know it."

He opened the refrigerator and began storing away fruit in the crisper.

"Are you a vegetarian?" I asked when I noticed the hamburger patties were Garden Burgers.

"I like to watch what I eat. Aeleise, on the other hand..." He nodded toward the far end of the table. "That's all hers." Pop-Tarts, strudel, chips, ice-cream, bacon...

"Paradise!"

He chuckled. "A fellow junk-food junkie?"

"Completely. I live off cupcakes."

He laughed as he put away the orange juice and sodas.

My mind drifted to thoughts of the family portrait hanging in the living room; I wondered why I had never seen his parents. I asked Daemon about them.

"Like yours," he said, "my parents are living abroad."

I couldn't say why, but something about his phrasing—*living abroad*—bothered me.

"When will they be back?"

"When the time is right," he said lightheartedly. He put the last of the provisions away. "Anything for you?" he asked. I shook my head and he grabbed a water bottle for himself; we headed for the den.

"Actually, it will be some time before they return. I agreed to oversee Aeleise for the next two years. Until then, it's just the two of us."

"What are they doing abroad?"

"They're missionaries."

"Aeleise never told me that," I said with surprise.

"They travel to third world countries giving testimony, helping build homes for the poor—"

"That's amazing. No wonder you're so devoted to the church."

"To God," he corrected.

"I'm surprised Aeleise never mentioned it."

"Probably because she wasn't ready for them to leave. She's independent in her own right, but I know how much she misses them."

"Do you plan to follow in their footsteps?"

"I'd like to. Once Aeleise graduates high school, she and I plan to go overseas together. Our parents would've gone years ago, but they thought Aeleise was too young. It's fortunate she and I get along so well; it makes things easy. From what she tells me, our relationship is similar to yours and Marc's."

I nodded. "Marc and I are close — much closer than Josh and me." My mood dampened at the thought of Josh.

"Give it some time. You and Josh aren't far apart in age — that has a lot to do with it. I'm sure you'll grow closer with time."

"Maybe," I said doubtfully. "But then again, you don't know Josh."

"True, but I think I'm getting a fairly clear picture from all Aeleise has told me. I heard he was the unappreciative subject and quite the uproar at Jessa's birthday party."

I groaned. "Don't remind me."

"Sorry." He kindly shifted the subject. "So, she mentioned you have a home gym too."

"Mm-hmm — a small one that Josh uses, mostly. Sometimes I'll try it, but not often."

"I belong to a health club, but I'm not always in the mood to go. Sometimes I prefer to work out here. That's what I was getting ready to do before you and Aeleise showed up. I've taught Aeleise a few things to develop her strength. Has she ever shown you our gym?"

I shook my head. "She never told me she worked out on the side. I'm amazed she has the energy."

"Well, come on — I'll show you. Do you have time to work out?"

"I didn't exactly bring workout clothes."

"Aeleise wouldn't mind if you borrowed something of hers. You game?"

I sighed. "I guess so." If it wasn't disguised as dancing, I generally wasn't a fan of exercise.

He laughed. "Don't look so excited."

I headed for Aeleise's room. I found some older clothes that didn't strike me as anything she would wear out of the house, and changed into them.

When I returned to the gym, he was hanging upside-down from a pair of gravity boots secured to the ceiling. In his all-black attire with arms crossed across his chest, he looked like an oversized bat. I watched as he completed a series of inverted sit-ups that appeared painfully difficult.

He unhinged himself and got down, noticing me for the first time. "Hey—" he breathed, wiping his forehead with the towel nearby. "So, what would you like to try first?"

"You're the coach."

He smiled. "All right … I was just going to start on pull-ups. You wanna give that a shot?"

"No, you go first."

He walked over to the high bar near the back of the room, grabbed it easily, and pulled himself up until his chin cleared the bar. He made it look simple. I'd lost track of how many pull-ups he'd completed when he finally let go.

"You're up," he said.

I approached the bar feeling optimistic. I knew I had the strength in me to do this. I reached up, stretching to reach the bar, but couldn't make it. I jumped and missed.

"Need help?"

"I can get it," I said. I jumped repeatedly, just barely brushing my fingertips against the bar. Daemon took a drink from his water bottle. He watched with interest as I struggled. He tried not to smile at my frustration, but when he looked down and pretended to rub his eye, I knew that was what he was doing. I refused to ask him for help, but I had gotten no further in my repeated attempts. I tried to focus positive energy on my goal, but mostly I tried not to stomp my foot in frustration.

Daemon took another swig from his water bottle, then set it down on the bench. He walked over to me. I defiantly crossed my arms. I could deal with it.

"I admire your determination, but I'm afraid you're just a few inches shy of being able to reach it." He gave me a teasing smile. "Even if you can bounce like Tigger."

"Very funny."

"Why don't you let me help you?"

I stared at him stubbornly, making no effort to move.

He grinned. "Raise your arms, silly rabbit."

I hesitated.

"Do you want on the bar or don't you?"

I raised my arms over my head; my shirt rose slightly. He put his hands on my waist to lift me, and I was suddenly very aware of him and his hands on my bare stomach. My heart jumped to a new tempo — one far more frenzied. Daemon's touch made me nervous. I feared I was blushing.

"Do you want me to spot you?" he asked.

I shook my head once, quickly.

"Okay, then. You're on your own. Let's see how many you can do." He backed away, watching me, resting his hands on his hips.

I found a spot on the wall to concentrate on. I pulled myself up in a steady movement, completing my first pull-up. I kept going... and strained madly to finish the last one before I jumped down. I had completed eleven. My biceps were screaming at me.

"I'm impressed. You're strong for someone your age."

I hated comments like that; they were so indefinite. "Thanks," I said anyway.

Daemon worked out for quite some time, but I couldn't keep up with him. I watched as he demonstrated each exercise and what muscles were affected. Finally he plopped down on the weight bench. Beads of perspiration, like clear pearls, fell from his face. It seemed preposterous, but I managed to find that appealing.

"I'm going to hit the Jacuzzi," he said finally. "Do you want to join me?"

"I don't have a swimsuit."

He waved his arm in the direction of Aeleise's room once again. I was beginning to feel like a shoplifter in a department store. I wasn't so sure she would appreciate my borrowing her clothes. Well, Daemon would take the rap for that one, if it ended up being a problem.

"Okay. I'll see you there," I said.

This time, the only swimsuit I found in the drawer was a bikini. Great. I grabbed a towel, wrapped it around me and made for the Jacuzzi.

Daemon was already comfortably immersed when I entered, screwing up my plan to slip into the water without letting him see my body. I paused, looking at his dark wet hair. That he looked so stunning didn't make me feel any less self-conscious. Neither did the sight of his red trunks beneath the steaming water and bubbling jets.

"How's the water?" I asked.

"It's great. Check for yourself."

I tested the water with my toes. It was hot, and I was eager to get in. I couldn't think of any clever way to maneuver through the situation, so instead I blurted, "Close your eyes a minute." My anxiety made it sound like an order.

He cocked his head. "Why?"

Now I felt silly. What could I say? The truth would sound ridiculous.

He smiled and closed his eyes. Relieved, I unwrapped myself and placed the towel within reach by the edge. I stepped into the water and sat down quickly, fighting a gasp when I slipped into the sudden heat. The water came to my shoulders. I felt wonderful.

"Okay," I said quietly.

He slowly opened his eyes and looked at me. "I never knew you were so shy. It's cute."

The water didn't come up as high on Daemon and left his chest exposed. I tried not to notice, feeling foolish when I didn't succeed.

"Should I make you close your eyes, too?" he teased.

"Too late," came my most regretted admission. He seemed to realize my discomfort, and let my slip go unremarked—other than displaying a small smile that appeared almost embarrassed. Good. Glad to know I wasn't the only one.

"You look uncomfortable. Everything okay?"

"Of course," I said, striving for a casual, upbeat tone.

"Why don't I believe you?"

This was the first time Aeleise wasn't around during an aquatic social. I decided that I liked it much better when she was present. I shrugged.

"What's on your mind?"

The heat seemed to confuse me; it took a considerable amount of concentration to keep my mind clear. That question seemed unusually dangerous. The whirling jets gurgled loudly as I sought an answer — any answer. Preferably one that was believable and not incriminating. I could only shrug again. Just brilliant. Daemon's presence had a way of interfering with my ability to think.

He leaned back farther, splaying his arms along the Jacuzzi's edge, exposing more of his chest.

"So, what do you think about Nick?" he asked. "Is he a nice guy?"

"Nick? Well … yeah. He's great."

"Do you think he's good for Aeleise?" His brow furrowed. "She seems awfully focused on him."

I found the safest thing I could say without betraying him. "Nick is … unique. He tends to be quiet and generally keeps to himself. He's extremely shy. But I do know that he truly cares about Aeleise."

He nodded, assessing my statement. "In the few times I've met him, yeah — he does seem like a good kid. I'm just trying to look out for Aeleise. This is her first boyfriend. Sometimes I wonder if she's getting too serious too quickly."

"I don't think you have anything to worry about. Nick is extremely involved with school and his extracurricular activities. Honestly, I'm surprised he even has time for a relationship." That was the best forewarning I could give him. "Aeleise happens to be his first girlfriend, too."

"Well, I guess that's a fairly even match. So, all in all, I don't need to worry about it?"

"I'd say not."

That put him more at ease. "I guess I shouldn't be asking about him without her knowing, but I need to look out for her; I worry about it. It helps to have an objective opinion from someone who knows him better than I do. I hope you don't mind."

"Not at all. Marc would be the same way."

"Well," he said, with a wrinkle to his brow, "It's just that if I were to ask her about him, she would only give me glowing reports. I think she has it in her mind that she's in love with him. That's what worries me."

And it should. "Did she say that?" I asked.

"Not in so many words... but yeah. I know my sister well enough to understand her hidden messages. I think she's afraid that I might be upset if she were to come straight out and tell me how she feels about him. But enough about Aeleise. How about you? Do you have someone special in your life?"

"Me?" His question surprised me. I shook my head.

"I find that hard to believe."

My eyes shifted to the jets that enthusiastically whirled about me.

"Do you like anyone?"

I shifted uncomfortably, sitting on my hands, continuing to gaze at the water. "No one obtainable."

"And why's that?"

"Because... he's older and doesn't know I exist."

"Well, maybe you should go out on a limb, let him know how you feel. You only live once."

"I'll think about it." Before he could delve any deeper, I knew now was the time to leave. "I should get going. Marc wants me home for dinner. He's playing chef tonight."

"All right, give me a second to throw on some clothes and I'll take you home."

"No," I said quickly. "I enjoy the walk—fitness and all," I explained lamely. "Thanks for the training session. I had a good time."

"Well, you can come back any time you want; Aeleise or no Aeleise. The offer stands."

I shoved my nervousness aside with a smile. "Thanks. I'll see you soon."

"You'd better."

I got the phone call at 5:30 the next morning. Aeleise's distressed voice confirmed my suspicions—Nick had broken up with her and she needed a shoulder to cry on. I knew it was going to be a sticky mess. I just wondered how much he had told her.

I spotted her outside the dance room while we were practicing technique. She was trying to peek in the from doorway so she wouldn't be seen.

I quickly motioned to Aeleise to follow me so we could talk privately. Her shoulders sagged; she looked like she'd been dragged through hell and back. Her normally gorgeous, sleek black mane looked disheveled. Her eyes were red and bloodshot, her face puffy and pale, blotched with pink patches across her cheeks and nose.

"Thank you so much, Krista. I know I shouldn't have interrupted your class."

"Don't worry about it, Aeleise. My God—you look wrecked. No offense."

"I am . . . I am." Tears streamed down her face. "I can't stay at school today. I won't be able to keep it together if I see Nick. I haven't seen him since . . ." She was crying too hard to finish the sentence. Her gaze dropped to the concrete.

Though she'd told me the news over the phone, she had been too upset to go into details. "What did he say, Aeleise?" I asked.

She looked up at me. "That—that he couldn't give me what I wanted. That I deserved better." Her eyes glittered with pain and bewilderment. "How can he possibly think that? I don't understand what brought this on. I told him he was all I wanted, that I was happy, but it was as if he didn't hear me. Nothing I said could change his mind." The tears came faster; she wiped them away. "He was acting so strange.

I feel like there's something he isn't telling me. How can he just decide this overnight? We've never even had a fight."

I swallowed hard, wanting to console her, but unsure how, given the circumstances. I couldn't lie and tell her everything would be okay, give her false hope that they'd end up together again. I hugged her, and her body shook against me as she cried.

"I'm so sorry, Aeleise."

She finally pulled back, wiped the tears from her face. "Did he ever say anything to you? Anything that would make you think it would come to this?"

I was relieved when she didn't wait for my answer. "He swears it's not another girl." Her forehead creased in distress. "It can't be about sex, can it? He doesn't even like to talk about the subject. Not that I'd do it—sleep with him, I mean."

"I doubt it, Aeleise. Like you said, Nick's never seemed too concerned about that."

"I know. That's what I don't get. Things seemed great between us. It just doesn't make sense."

"I wish I knew what to do, Aeleise. Wish I had something comforting to say."

"No, you've been great, Kris—really. I appreciate you taking the time to talk to me." She wiped her eyes again. "You need to get back to class. I'm sorry."

"Don't be. If you want to talk more about it later, call me. I'll be home."

She nodded. "Thanks."

I gave her a final hug, then ran back to class.

———

I wondered if the news had reached Brandon yet. I was sure he was waiting for the day when he could hang out with Nick without false pretenses. When I got home from school, I phoned him.

"When did you find out?" he asked.

"Just this morning; Aeleise gave me the news."

"Bad?"

"Yes, very."

We were silent.

Brandon exhaled loudly. "He didn't show up at school today. Well, I'm sure he'll tell me in due time. As worried as he's been about dropping his safety net, I imagine he's spiraling as we speak. Thanks for letting me know."

"No problem."

"Mmm...I forgot to ask you—since you don't return Ryan's interest, you don't mind if I intervene on his behalf, do you? I have someone in mind I'm going to encourage him to pursue—but only if you're *sure* you're not interested, considering you're the primary focus of his affections at this point."

"I'm sure. Thanks for asking, but I just can't see anything further developing between me and Ryan."

"Fair enough. Just wanted the go-ahead. I'll talk to you later, Kris."

20

Sunday night. I sat perched on the chair behind my desk with only the faint glow from my reading light. By 10:00 P.M. the night air was crisp as it floated through my bedroom window. I had been by myself for hours now.

I closed my math book and abandoned my homework. I couldn't concentrate; wandering thoughts continued to distract me. I bit my lip and thought about my options. I wanted to talk. I *needed* to talk, and Brandon was the only person in whom I could confide. It was late, but I picked up the phone and dialed, praying he would answer.

After the third ring, Brandon said, "Hello?"

"It's Krista."

"Hey, gorgeous." He sounded remarkably awake.

"I can't sleep."

"Daydreaming about Daemon?"

"Try bored. Josh is on a date and basically told us not to expect him home. Marc had an emergency call from the hospital. Just thought I'd see if you wanted to come over—hang out."

After a moment he said, "Sure."

"You're the best, Brandon."

"That's what they all say."

I couldn't help smiling. "See you when you get here."

I hung up the phone, then sat back on my bed and began thinking. I was scared to be alone in the house at night, but I had other things on my mind, too. Tonight would be the perfect opportunity to talk to Brandon. I had a daring question for him—that is, if I got up the courage to ask him. I'd been tossing around an unlikely idea in my head ever since he had surprised me with his boyishly sweet kiss. Just as Carrie and I practiced I began to wonder how things might be if I were doing the same thing with a boy.

Was it horrible of me to consider it? Was it something I had no business asking? Would he hate me or be offended if I did? I was afraid. I couldn't be sure how he would react. Well, there was only one way to find out.

Twenty minutes later, Brandon rang my doorbell.

"Coming," I yelled, sliding down the tile of the foyer in my stocking feet to come to a skidding halt at the door. I flung it wide open.

"Hey, you," he said through a brilliant smile. He wore well-fitted blue jeans and a silky, short-sleeved, button down shirt in a deep shade of blue. He looked beautiful in blue. He came inside and closed the door behind him. We hugged in greeting, and I inhaled a sweet hint of his cologne.

"Thanks for coming."

"No problem."

"You can pick the movie," I said as we walked into the living room. "Over by the cabinet." Brandon headed toward the entertainment center while I went into the kitchen.

I returned with two cans of Coke, then flopped down Indian-style on the couch. "Did you find one?" I said.

Smiling, he handed me *Can't Buy Me Love*.

"*Again?* We've only seen it a hundred times."

"But Patrick Dempsey's irresistible in this role." He gave me one of his ridiculous grins.

"Fine. But I've never understood your taste in men."

Brandon put the movie in, then sat down beside me. I tossed him a bag of Skittles. The usual hard-fast rules about not talking didn't apply to this movie, since we knew it by heart. Sometimes it seemed as if we played it solely for background atmosphere. I made myself comfortable as the opening credits began to roll.

"How's Carrie?" he asked.

Carrie hadn't been at school for the past two days. In fact, her school attendance over the past month had been erratic. I really had no answer. When I had called Carrie's house, her mother stated that she wasn't accepting phone calls. So far, she hadn't let me in on what was going on.

"She still hasn't talked to me about it."

I turned my attention back to the television and watched half-heartedly.

The movie had been on for a while as I considered my dilemma. I wrestled with the idea of approaching the subject; it had the potential to turn things weird, real quick. Brandon laughed at a scene from the movie.

I made a tentative beginning. "Brandon."

He turned to look at me. "What's up?"

"I kind of... need to talk to you."

"So talk."

"How many girls have you slept with?" *Not very subtle.* "You don't have to tell me if you don't want to," I added quickly.

He studied me. "That question's left field even for you," he said.

I shrugged.

"So what's up?" Grabbing the remote control, he lowered the volume.

"Just curious, I guess. You've never really talked about it."

"There isn't much to tell."

"But you have..."

"Yes. Twice."

I reached for my soda trying to act casual. "Did you like it?"

"The first time was kinda weird," he said as if he were summoning some far-off memory. "Very vague. I don't know... I was really drunk. Barely have any recollection of it at all."

"So if you liked guys, why did you bother with girls?"

"I guess because I was kind of lost. I knew I felt differently, but at the same time, I was afraid someone would find out, so I tried to ignore it. Basically went along with what everyone else was doing. All anyone ever talked about was how great sex was. There was always talk about what girls did what." He shrugged. "My curiosity got the better of me. I figured I was missing out on something."

"And..."

His lips crooked into a smile and then he laughed. "It was... interesting."

"When was that?"

"Two years ago."

"Were you nervous?"

"Considering I had no idea what I was doing, yeah, I'd say so." After a moment he added, "Well, at least I tried it."

"But I saw a talk show that made it sound like gay men are totally turned off by women."

"You watch too many of those damn talk shows. I can't speak for everybody, but not all gays feel that way." Brandon studied my eyes. "Am I going to have to drag out what's bugging you?"

My stomach fell and my heart rate quickened. A lump formed in my throat.

"Does this have to do with Carrie? You know... I'll help in any way I can."

He might live to regret those words. "Thanks," I managed to say. This was it. If I was ever going to have the nerve to ask him, it had to be now.

"Are you feeling well?" he said suddenly.

My voice, barely audible, struggled to get the words out; I had officially reached panic mode. "I need to ask you a favor." Looking down at the couch, I picked at the fabric. "A big one."

"All right. What is it?"

I couldn't look at him, but I mustered up all the courage I had and took a deep breath. "Would you..." I stopped, cleared my mind and tried again. My voice was barely audible. "Will you be my first?"

Heat rushed to my cheeks so fast that I thought I would surely pass out during the awkward silence that followed. I felt like an ass. I flicked a nervous glance at him. His face was utterly blank.

"I'm sorry. I shouldn't have mentioned it." *Why* had I opened my mouth?

"Kris, you can have any guy you want. Why me?"

"I trust you. I don't know … all these things have been going on with Carrie … it's so confusing," I said. "Anyway, I—I want it to be you." There. I said it. "Will you do it?"

There was no way to know what he was thinking because he didn't answer me for a while. His voice had lost all humor. "You kinda caught me off guard." He looked at me again. "How long have you been thinking about this? Have you actually thought this through?"

I ignored his first question. "I have. I'm completely sure." I wasn't, but I had to do something. "If I've offended you …"

"It's not that."

He sat perched on the edge of the couch, tipped forward with his elbows resting on his knees. He stared at his hands, brows pursed in concern. "You're serious."

"Dead serious."

"I can get the keys to the beach house on Monday. We'll—"

"No." I swallowed hard. "It has to be now. You know Carrie and I are leaving for dance camp next week and I want to know…well I don't now what I want to know but I want it to happen before then. And tonight, no one will be home tonight."

He fell back into the couch, almost pale. *"Tonight?"*

"I need to know before I see Carrie again."

Brandon opened his mouth but silence filled the air. He closed it when he couldn't find a thing to say.

"Kris …"

"I understand. It was ridiculous of me to think …" I looked down, shifting my attention to my fingers. I finally made the admission. "At the party, I tried with Eric, but—"

"What? You really *must've* been on drugs! That's craziness, Kris. I can't believe you even considered it."

His vehemence surprised me, and I sat there, silent.

"You're afraid," I said finally.

"Terrified." He rubbed his hands together. "For more than one reason. If anything went wrong, I'd hate myself for it. And won't *you* regret it not happening with someone you really like, maybe even someone you love?"

"I thought you didn't believe in love."

"We're talking about you."

"I just want to experience what most girls do. Doesn't that make sense?"

"Make *sense*? You really don't believe this a typical request, do you?"

"I'm not expecting it to be perfect. I know the first time is generally a disappointment. I read *Seventeen* magazine."

His expression was wary. Maybe he didn't want me to decide my sexual preference based on an experience with him.

He rubbed his hands over his face. "We'll see what happens," he said. He turned to me. "I don't have any protection. Do you?"

"Josh does somewhere."

We headed for Josh's bedroom. His door was closed, but he had left it unlocked. I pushed it open to find a tornado of clothes, schoolbooks, candy wrappers, empty soda cans, and disheveled bed sheets.

We tiptoed carefully around the minefield. Brandon began searching the dresser drawers, careful not to upset anything. I hesitantly dropped to the floor, pressing my face against the carpet beside his bed. I stretched my arm out, reaching far beneath his bed but all I found was a gym bag and some sports magazines. I pulled the gym bag out and placed it on the floor in front of me. I unzipped it and stared at the contents, dumbfounded. "Uh—Brandon?"

"Hmm?" he said, not looking back from his examination of a drawer.

"I think I've found it," I said, not touching the contents. "Yes, I'd say I definitely found it."

Brandon came over and peeked over my shoulder. "That looks like a lot more than some condoms," he said, amused.

I placed the bag between us. "What *is* all this stuff?" I asked, eyes gone wide. This was far more than anything I'd come across at the beach house. I picked through the contents of the bag. A copy of *Hustler,* a movie without a box cover, condoms, empty condom wrappers, a bottle of lube, and a *Penthouse* magazine.

I looked up to Brandon's wry smile. "Looks like you found your brother's private collection," he said.

I thumbed through one of Josh's stash of magazines; my face flushed at the erotic pictures. I closed it abruptly. "Where did he get all this?" I asked. "My mother would *die*."

"Come on. Grab what you need and put his things back where you found them. We shouldn't be here in the first place," he said.

I grabbed a few unopened condoms, returned the bag with all its contents to its hiding place, and we left Josh's room.

Brandon was waiting in the living room.

I was nervous. *Really* nervous. Then I remembered that mom kept liquor in the house for guests and special occasions. I stood on tiptoe and reached above the refrigerator, straining for the cabinet that held the alcohol. I grabbed the bottle of Jack Daniels. I'd never tried it, but now seemed like a good time. I found a glass in the cupboard. Brandon walked up behind me as I began to unscrew the lid of the bottle.

He placed his hand over mine. "No alcohol," he said and turned me by the shoulders to face him. "If this is really what you want, you don't need that."

He was right.

"Are you sure this is what you want?" he asked.

"I'm sure."

He led me by the hand to my bedroom. My heart began to beat wildly as we walked through the door. Once inside, he locked it. Walking over to my nightstand, he set down the condoms Josh had unknowingly donated to us. He then walked over to my stereo and selected a slow CD. The volume was low. "Do you have a lighter?" he said.

"Over there," I pointed next to the empty vase.

I stood quietly in the center of the room as he walked about, lighting each candle until the room flickered with dancing flames and smelled of vanilla. He turned off the light and met me in the middle of the room.

We faced each other, unmoving. The atmosphere he had created helped. Gold light swayed and danced across his features. He moved behind me until my back was against his chest. My pulse quickened at the feel of him. His arm circled my waist, intertwining his fingers with mine.

"I won't pretend I know how to start this." He led me to the bed and we sat down. "If you change your mind, just tell me and we'll stop. I'm not a mind reader, so if you get uncomfortable, *please* ... let me know."

"I will," I said.

We moved toward the center of the bed. This was it. I looked up at him through my eyelashes.

He gave me a cute smile. "Nervous?"

"A little." I was terrified.

"Me too," he said. He leaned in and kissed me.

A tingling, almost electric, sensation ignited as our lips touched. I moved closer to him, my stomach full of butterflies. It was odd to be here with him this way. I didn't know this side of him; I certainly didn't even know this side of myself. He kissed me deeper, his tongue sliding over mine, exploring. I was tentative at first, but his kisses were urging. I felt light-headed, as if I could float. This was *nothing* close to what I had experienced with Eric. I lay back on the bed breathless, wondering what to do next. His lips brushed across mine.

"You all right?"

I nodded. He ran his hand over my night slip until it rested on my stomach.

"Kristina McKinley," he said warmly. No one ever called me that. "What's on your mind now?"

"I don't know what I'm supposed to do," I finally said.

"There aren't any rules. Just do what feels natural." He brushed my fingers against his lips. "What do you want to do?" he said, lying down beside me.

If I couldn't tell him, I'd never move past it. "I'm afraid to touch you." I said. Given the situation it seemed a ridiculous truth.

He smiled faintly, then placed my hand against his chest. It was the warmth of his body, his heartbeat beneath his silky shirt. That small contact made my pulse race. I wanted the shirt off. I searched out its buttons, clumsily working at them. Following my lead, he pulled his shirt from his jeans and undid the few buttons that were left. I brushed his shirt open. His skin was beautiful, a warm, sun-kissed, golden brown.

My hands traveled tentatively over his chest. The muscles he'd developed from years of surfing made him appear older than he was. I moved closer, let my lips meet his chest. He smelled delicious, almost sweet.

He slipped off his shirt. All I could do was stare. How could I have been oblivious to what every other girl in school seemed was so aware? Now, I really understood why everyone was hot for Brandon.

He moved my hand over his chest until I reached his nipple. He kissed me deeply as I toyed with it, and a small sound escaped from the back of his throat. His lips tasted sugary. My other hand wandered over his back. My nails grazed his skin, and he responded with a soft groan. In turn, his hands began to explore me. I watched his face, his fascination as he assimilated the differences between his usual experiences and this one, of having a girl against him.

His hand searched further over my slip, inching its way up my stomach until it found my breast. He brushed his fingers lightly over my nipple. The straps fell off my shoulders, and the rush of cool air tickled. He began to explore my chest the way I had his.

His lips left mine to search elsewhere. I held my breath as he kissed my neck; it wasn't long before his tongue found my breast. My fingers tangled through his hair and I gasped in response. He smiled at that and continued. I couldn't hold still; I started to squirm.

Freeing one hand, he peeled my slip down until I lay there in panties. He moved up from my breast and said "Am I moving too fast?"

I could only shake my head. I ran my fingers through his hair.

We began kissing again. But then he started kissing a trail down my stomach. When his lips reached my navel, my heart began to race.

His body was between my legs. He pulled me toward him and slid his hands beneath me. When his lips met the curve of my hip my fingers dug into the bed. He removed my panties, letting them fall to the floor. He worked to suppress a smile when he looked between my thighs and noticed I'd shaved. He resisted the urge to comment, but I could tell he knew why had done it. I could've hugged him for not teasing me.

A second later I realized where his face was. I quickly pulled my knees together. My cheeks infused with heat. I wasn't comfortable. He seemed surprised by my reaction.

"You and Carrie never...?"

I shook my head.

"I haven't either." He paused. "Did you want to?"

I didn't think I did.

"It's okay," he said. We were kind of awkward, just looking at each other. Then he asked me, "Have you ever had an orgasm?"

The question made my cheeks burn. I couldn't bring myself to look at him. I wasn't even exactly sure what an orgasm was.

He pulled back to look at me. "Yes... no...?"

I shrugged. Maybe, like Marc, he assumed I had figured that out on my own.

He gave me slightly impish smile, and then leaned into me; his lips brushed against my neck. "You would remember if you had. So I'll take that as a no." He pressed his body closer to mine and we began to kiss.

I was utterly naked and I didn't want to be the only one. "Brandon?"

"Yes?"

"I... I want to see you." I hesitated. "Are you worried—I mean, can you..." I stopped.

He raised my chin until we were eye to eye. He was mildly surprised, serious. "You don't know?" He pressed my hand against him, letting me feel him hard beneath his pants.

I closed my eyes because the confirmation made me nervous. I heard him unsnap his jeans and I made myself look at him. He pulled at one corner; the zipper slowly gave way. I felt high, dizzy. He kicked his jeans to the floor, leaving him lying beside me in only his tight-fitting briefs. I admired his body from head to toe. No wonder all of those unsuspecting beach bunnies threw themselves at him. I couldn't blame them.

Only one piece of clothing, a single cotton shield, separated us. I nervously traced his stomach with my finger. His demeanor had subtly changed. He was hesitant … and then it suddenly dawned on me; he was as self-conscious as I was.

He slowly removed his briefs until he lay naked beside me. I couldn't believe how difficult it was to look at him; my eyes didn't linger there long. The sight of Brandon naked made me anxious. What now? He seemed as uncomfortable as I was.

It was finally his turn to flush. Completely exposed to my scrutiny, he wouldn't meet my eyes. His reaction surprised me; I would have thought the bedroom was his playground.

I have Brandon VanAulstine naked *in my bed. How* had I ever found the nerve to ask him to do this?

"I guess you weren't joking that day in the library."

He smiled, slightly embarrassed at the recollection. "Sorry. I was being a jerk."

Maybe—but he hadn't been lying.

"Brandon …" I fumbled for words as I marveled at the sight of him before me. His entire body was incredible. I wanted to say something, but *what?* I could only bring myself to look at his chest; anything else, and I'd be tempted to run. "You look … incredible."

The color in his cheeks deepened.

I leashed my fear to touch him. I put my hand on him and watched his body respond. His skin was so soft. He caught his breath; he released it in a short, quick sigh. We kissed, our tongues moving against one another's. He gave up a moan as I held my hand on him.

I needed to know what to do. "Can you show me?" I said.

His hand covered mine and he guided it in a way that he found pleasurable; he let go as I discovered his rhythm. His hands gripped me tightly, and I knew then that he liked it. I noticed his rapid change in breathing as my hand continued to arouse him. I kissed him again and his mouth moved eagerly over mine, heat-filled and intense.

My mind raced ahead and I found the courage to make the next move. I gently urged him onto his back. I moved on top of him and realized I had no idea what to do next.

The candlelight danced in patterns across the walls. The music was faint in the background. With my finger I traced his lips. They were soft and full. I kissed him as I lay on top of him, while his hands trailed along my back. I felt him against my stomach. We kissed again and I moved my hips against his, making him moan against my mouth. He reached behind me, grabbing me tighter. His fingers were searching as we kissed, and when he kissed my neck, he slid his finger inside me. I gasped, gripping him tightly, an automatic response to the unexpected.

"You okay?"

I wasn't sure but I wondered what, other than the final act, was left to do. "Is it time yet?" I said. I felt pretty foolish.

"If you want it to be." He was tentative when he looked at me.

I nodded.

"I'll get a condom," he said. This was it, the final step.

He grabbed one from the nightstand and rolled it down the length of him.

"Okay," he said, looking first at himself and then at me.

I rolled onto my back, pulling him on top of me. He kissed me, deep, intense. He was taking his time, ensuring we were ready—or prolonging the inevitable, I'm not sure which.

"Kris...?" he whispered suddenly, hesitant, "is this really happening?"

I wish I could've answered him at that moment, especially since he sounded as if his mind had gone as cloudy as mine, but I felt dizzy, as if high on helium. Every thought was distant and airy, not quite within reach. I kissed him in reassurance and he accepted my answer clearly enough.

It seemed his nervousness had faded and mine had, too.

"Brandon..."

"Uh-hmmn..."

"I want to," I insisted in a single breath.

I felt him against me. He buried his face against my neck, and slowly pressed further, beginning to enter. My body tensed at the intrusion. I pulled back, scared of what I felt. It was no finger; it started to hurt.

"Are you all the way in? Are we doing it yet?" I said anxiously.

His voice at my ear. "I'm barely inside. Can you relax at all?"

I tried to clear my mind, to let go. I pulled his face to mine and kissed him deeply again. That helped.

"Kris..." he moaned, restraining himself.

I had already accepted that it was going to hurt, but I had made up my mind—I was determined to go through with it. I readied myself.

"It's okay. I want you to."

He slowly lifted his head.

"Now," I said.

He sank farther. Pain seared through me—I let out an involuntary cry. My nails embedded themselves like claws in his back. I couldn't think, couldn't breathe. I was aware of everything and nothing simultaneously. I felt nearly in shock.

He held still, afraid to move. "Oh God...I'm sorry."

He had stopped at my cry. Hesitating, he looked down at himself. I could begin to feel him pulling away.

"You're bleeding, Kris."

I wasn't surprised. I looked at Brandon's face, then realized I'd never thought to ask him if the girls he'd slept with were virgins. Maybe he had never experienced this before. Maybe it freaked him out. I tried to reassure him, tried to steady my already shaking voice. "Brandon?" I pulled him into me, holding him close. "Brandon, I'm okay. Really."

I started to worry. I couldn't be certain if he was frightened, shocked, or about to be ill. "Are *you* okay?"

He nodded, his face pressed against my cheek. He raised his head to see me. His eyes were a mix of emotions. His body still unmoving, he looked at me, unsure if he should continue.

"It's okay, don't stop." I brushed away the strands of hair that partially hid his face. "Really."

He looked at me and our eyes held steadfast. At my reassurance, he slowly began to move again. In his eyes was something unexpected—raw and naked honesty. Something was happening between us that I did not understand. We were connected by something indescribable. He closed his eyes and began to let go, allowing himself to give in to the physical sensation.

I held him close to me. Suddenly I was overwhelmed by the strangeness of him inside me, and how incredibly close I felt to him. He kissed me deeply, and it ignited every nerve ending in my body. The intensity grew and I began to let go. Pleasure replaced pain; it began to feel good. *Very, very* good. My breathing became deeper, he moved inside me faster. I gasped.

His worry escaped in a ragged gasp. "I can't last much longer." He slowed, trying to prolong the experience. His cheek brushed mine, and the warmth of his breath lingered against my ear. His voice was just above a whisper. "Kris, you're so close." He pressed his lips against my neck. "Close your eyes," he whispered. "*Feel* me."

I closed my eyes, drank in the sounds of his moans above me. I felt every inch of him move inside me, and suddenly, an unfamiliar pressure built with an intensity I never knew existed. I had no idea where he was taking me, but I let myself trust him completely in that moment, and when I did, I unknowingly dropped the barriers and what little safety I had. Unexpected emotions flooded me, making me feel things that, before this moment, I'd never known. It was as if we had transcended the physical, and he now touched parts of me that logically were beyond reach. It was frightening, and wonderful, and its intensity continued to build and build until I had to surrender to it completely.

His hips moved against mine and he sank deeper. *"Brandon!"* I gasped as my entire body clenched unexpectedly.

"I'm—" He gripped me tightly, muffling his loud and telling moan against my neck. He buried his face deeper as he climaxed. His body tensed then collapsed against me.

It was a moment before he caught his breath, then he carefully withdrew and removed the condom. He rolled onto his back, pulling me on top of him. The beat of his heart was ragged against his chest. Our bodies were slick with sweat.

"You okay?" he said. "You're shaking."

I nodded against his chest and managed to say, "Yes."

The experience had overwhelmed me; I'd expected something purely physical. Simple. I didn't expect it to tangle with my emotions. I felt all mixed up. I was happy. I was sad. I realized I felt completely vulnerable.

"Why are you crying?" he said as tears rolled down his chest.

I shook my head, not knowing.

"Did I hurt you?" Fear in his voice.

"No."

"What is it?" His arm tightened about me.

I had thought the experience would make my decision easier. It didn't. "I'm so confused, Brandon." The tears flowed freely, although I had no idea where they came from.

He was quiet for a minute before he said, "And I don't know that this helped matters any." A moment later, he said, "Are you sorry it happened?"

I looked up at him; his eyes stared, unfocused, at the ceiling until he looked at me. "No."

He gave me a weak smile.

"And you? Are *you* sorry you went through with it?" I asked, trying to keep a stranglehold on my emotions. I needed to know. I so hoped he wasn't.

He shook his head. "As long as you don't have any regrets, I—" His fingers trailed along my arm. "This wasn't what I was expecting at all."

We lay quietly together for some moments. I felt as if I had played bumper cars with my emotions. From out of nowhere had sprung foreign emotions that I didn't recognize, and didn't yet understand.

"What are you thinking about?" I said.

He stroked my back, taking his time to answer. "I'm glad you asked me, Kris."

I nuzzled my head against his chest.

That morning, when I had awakened, I'd been certain of two things: I, Krista McKinley, was a virgin with a good friend named Brandon. Now I was no longer one and had bewildering feelings about the other. Tomorrow would be an interesting day.

21

Monday morning, I arrived late to second period. I had slept through my alarm clock and missed both zero and first period dance classes. Not good. Brandon had told me the night before that he had to be up early to surf. It still amazed me that he could hop into 50-degree water first thing upon waking, and do it with a *smile* on his face. The thought alone made me want to stay curled up beneath my blankets.

When I eventually crawled out of bed, my body was sore in places where I never knew I had muscles. I reflected on the night before as I went through my normal daily routine of preparing for school. By now Marc was home. I wasn't sure about Josh. When I passed Marc in the kitchen we said our usual hellos but I was hardly present.

I was no longer a virgin!

I couldn't shake the memory of where Brandon and I had been only a matter of hours ago. It was as if I still carried him with me. I was glad I had asked him to be with me for my first time; I was even happier that he'd enjoyed himself as well. Privately, I couldn't help wondering whether he had felt half of what I had, or if that was my experience alone. After all, Brandon had taken the virginity of many. Sure, they'd been boys, but I didn't know if that made a difference to him one way or the other. Somehow I doubted that he was thinking of me, though my thoughts continually seemed to veer toward him.

I wondered if anyone would be able to see the difference in me. Despite my uncertainty, I smiled as I quickly finished the last of my orange juice, and then bolted for school.

I arrived to class just as Mr. Kraus finished taking roll. I offered no excuse for my tardiness; today I didn't mind being marked late. I felt different somehow. It was a peculiar feeling—as if everybody knew I'd just had sex for the first time. I knew I was just being paranoid, but it still didn't change my self-consciousness. It certainly didn't help matters any when a student runner from the front office interrupted class with a bouquet of balloons large enough to be an umbrella in a storm.

She approached Mr. Kraus at his desk. "Krista McKinley," she said, and showed him the accompanying card.

Mr. Kraus lowered his chin, glasses falling farther down his nose. He helpfully pointed me out to the lanky brown-haired girl, and said, "Krista, these are for you."

All eyes were on me as I thanked her. I flushed, trying to ignore the attention. I opened the attached envelope in my lap, sheltering it from peering eyes. Immediately recognizing the handwriting, I attempted to hide my smile, and failed.

The note read:

Good morning, Krista, Chickpea,

I couldn't resist sending you a surprise of my own after the surprise you gave me. Hands down, you win on the shock factor! Last night was most unexpected. I hope you don't have any regrets. I only wish I could've been Daemon for you. I know that would have made your night perfect. Don't worry; things will be okay. I'll see you at lunch.

Brandon

P.S. Quickly, dahling—better come up with an excuse for the balloons. Unless, of course, you don't mind people knowing about your gay Prince Charming. Ha-ha—I love putting you on the spot.

This message will self-destruct in 10 seconds. (Okay, so maybe you'll need to help it along, but you get the point.)
Kisses X3

I folded the note in half and stuck it in my notebook. I would throw it away when no one noticed. I didn't need any curious peers reading my letter after I tossed it in the trash. I had witnessed the lengths that some people went to get good gossip, and I wasn't taking any chances.

I was toting my balloons to third period when I spotted Brandon in the crowd at the other end of the hall. My first, instinctive reaction was strange—I'd become nervous, almost embarrassed at the thought of facing him in the light. Unexpected heat flushed my cheeks, but I made myself move forward. I couldn't let things become awkward between us. Before my emotions could gain a stronger foothold, I took a deep breath, and put forth my most animated attempt at normalcy.

"Brandon!"

He heard my call and turned around. When he saw me under the massive collection of rainbow-colored balloons, he laughed whole-heartedly. He ran to greet me.

"Don't *you* look cute." He grinned.

I stood, hands on hips. "You!"

"It's not breakfast in bed, but I wanted to say good morning."

I shook my head as I smiled appreciatively. "Sometimes you can be the sweetest person."

He held a single finger to his lips. "Shh. I won't tell if you don't."

I laughed. "Deal."

The first bell sounded for third period.

"Shit! I'm gonna be late—*again.*" He put his hand on my arm and smiled. "I gotta run, Kris." He gave me a quick kiss on the cheek. "I'm glad you like them," he added. A second later, he was running down the hall.

Before lunch, I stopped to drop off my books and found a note from Brandon slipped inside my locker. He wouldn't be at lunch; he'd gone back to the beach. Huntington was blowing up on the south side of the pier—simply too good to pass up. I laughed. One day he'd get himself into trouble. Feeling somewhat relieved that I wouldn't have to make eye contact with him again just yet, I pocketed the note, pulled my balloons behind me, and headed for the cafeteria to grab a snack.

Carrie was waiting for me, and we sat down together. She wore her pink jumpsuit with a new, fuzzy pink hat to match. "Who sent you these?" she asked, staring at my balloons.

"A secret admirer." It was the first thing off the top of my head.

"Who is it?"

"How should I know? That's why it's called a *secret* admirer."

"There was no card attached?"

"No," I lied easily.

"Wow. That's crazy, Kris. I bet you it's that guy who always stares at you during lunch." She looked around suspiciously for peering eyes.

I had no idea who she was looking for. "You think so?" I asked as I picked at my blueberry muffin.

"I wouldn't be surprised," she said, and threw away her entire lunch, keeping only the Twinkie. "You want to come over after school?"

"I can't. I promised Aeleise I'd go over her history homework with her. I'm playing quiz jockey to make sure she's ready for her next test."

"Yuck. Have fun."

"Always," I said.

———

I met up with Aeleise after school. From a distance, I spotted her — an isolated figure standing patiently outside the gym where we had agreed to meet earlier that day. When I walked over to greet her, she too was amazed at my flotilla of balloons. They sheltered us from the sun as we walked to her car. We stuffed the bobbing bouquet into the back seat.

I had dodged questions about the balloons all day without suspicion, and I'd contained my excitement, saying nothing of last night's event. I had even managed to ignore the emotions that existed just beneath my cloud of elation — the fleeting moments of anxiety, the dread that accompanied the feelings of harmony, the bitter that came with the sweet. A feeling of uneasiness had hitched a ride with my thoughts.

My anxiety grew as we neared Aeleise's house. I tried to shrug off the discomfort. I knew the moment I faced Daemon, alone or otherwise, guilt would once again wash over me, clinging to me like dish grease.

All unknowing, Daemon had the power to turn my evening of sweetness and newfound understanding into something catastrophic. He would consider my experience one of dishonor; I'd feel stained, unclean in his presence. The fear of him knowing threatened to suffocate me, but I couldn't lose my head. There was no way he'd know unless I said something, and I was adept at keeping my mouth shut when necessary.

I was glad that I would be leaving for dance camp in two days. I had an overwhelming desire to avoid Bible study. Or was it Daemon? Perhaps both. The once bright and dancing balloons began to appear dark and mud-colored, like a handful of weeds. I wanted to shed the reminder of last night's events, leave them in Aeleise's room so we could study in the den without distraction. I attempted a hasty escape to Aeleise's bedroom, but Daemon intercepted me in the hallway; his presence filled the room.

He smiled when he saw my floating symbol of mixed emotions. "Who's bringing home the circus?"

Aeleise supplied, "Krista has a secret admirer."

A pang of guilt struck me for wanting to hurt her at that moment, especially when I knew she was just genuinely excited for me, but her comment made me feel silly.

Daemon gave me a ridiculous grin. "A secret admirer, huh? Bet she knows who it is and just isn't telling us."

I gave him a fake smile as I made a beeline for Aeleise's room, and hoped it hid the truth. I cursed under my breath as I tied the balloons to her chair.

I returned to the den and we laid our books out on the coffee table. Thirty minutes into the evening, Daemon emerged from his room and silently joined us, conducting his own research at a desk across the room. He sat, quiet and unobtrusive, immersed in his own thoughts as he read and made notes on a lined paper tablet. I tried to ignore him, but I found it difficult to concentrate.

We studied until it got dark and Aeleise finally felt confident that she was prepared for any pop quiz. She rode along when Daemon gave me a lift home.

"Night, Krista. Thanks again for your help," she called from the car.

"You're welcome," I said, and entered my house entirely exhausted. I wanted to take a bath but I just didn't have the energy. Instead, I brushed my teeth and crawled into bed. I remembered I had forgotten to call Carrie. I would see her tomorrow. Tomorrow was another early day and I couldn't afford to be late twice in a row. I thought vaguely of Brandon as I scooted under the sheets. My head hit the pillow and I was gone.

I nearly bludgeoned the alarm clock when it shattered my slumber. Damn! I was still tired. Remarkably, my body still ached. I grabbed a bagel and juice, then returned to my room to get my book bag before leaving for school. It wasn't by my desk, where I usually left it. I searched the house — every room — but couldn't find it anywhere. I slowed down, allowing myself to think, and suddenly realized that my balloons were missing too.

I had left them at Aeleise's.

I ran to the phone and dialed her house. I prayed she hadn't left yet. Daemon answered the phone.

"Hi Daemon, it's Krista. Is Aeleise still there?"

"She left about ten minutes ago. Were you looking for your backpack?"

"Yeah."

"She took it with her to school, said to tell you not to worry."

I sighed. "Thank goodness."

"Your balloons are still here," he said after a pause. "She figured you could just pick them up the next time you came by, rather than carrying them around school all day again."

"Perfect. Thanks Daemon."

"At your service. Have a good day."

We said goodbye, I hung up the phone, then dashed out the door. I would have to run to make it on time, and run I did.

I ran into Ryan between classes; he reminded me school was only a half-day today. That put an instant smile on my face.

I asked him where Brandon was.

His brows rose. "He skipped school—left at sunrise to surf Trussle's, then said he's heading over to Nial's house." I had yet to meet Nial.

I nodded just as one of Ryan's football teammates interrupted our conversation; we said goodbye and parted ways.

When I got home from school no one was there. I took a quick shower, then decided to take advantage of this rare moment of peace and quiet and get some reading in on the new book I had started. I had just opened my book when the doorbell rang; I set the book down, wondering who it could be.

My eyebrows rose in momentary surprise when I saw Ryan through the peephole. I opened the door. "Hi, Ryan." I smiled at the unexpected company.

"Hi."

"Come on in." I opened the door wider.

"I hope I didn't come by at a bad time," he said, stepping inside. He was wearing my favorite ice-blue shirt with a pair of new blue jeans—not what he had worn to school today.

"No, not at all. I was just kicking back." I motioned for him to follow me to my room.

"Can I get you anything to eat or drink?" I asked as we sat down on my bed. Ryan chose to sit on the far edge, putting a healthy distance between us.

"No, thanks. I just happened to be in the neighborhood and thought I'd drop by. Thought I'd see if maybe you wanted to go to the movies sometime this weekend."

Just in the neighborhood? Ryan didn't live close enough to be 'just in the neighborhood.' Not unless he considered a two-mile walk from his house a casual stroll.

He said, "I was hoping maybe we could convince Carrie to join us."

His kindness warmed me. He knew she had been down, although he didn't know why. It made me think all the more of him; Ryan was a good friend.

"I think that's a great idea." I hadn't been to the movies in a while, and it would do Carrie some good to get out of the house. "We're leaving Sunday so it will have to be Saturday."

"Cool. Well, you two decide on the movie. Will you mention it to Carrie for me?"

"Sure."

He sat there for a minute, looking uncertain, and then said, "Oh...I almost forgot." He reached into his pocket and withdrew a small newspaper clipping along with what looked like a few candy wrappers. He handed me the clipping.

"Don't you like that girl who stars in all of those vampire flicks? I saw that in the paper; she's going to be doing an autograph signing in a couple weeks at the convention center. Thought you might like to know."

I looked at the article, already feeling excitement. I read the headline, then squealed with delight. I scampered over to his side of the bed and gave him a hug. "Thanks, Ryan; I can't believe it — she's going to be right in our neighborhood!"

I hopped over to my dresser and placed the clipping prominently beside my jewelry box so I wouldn't misplace it. I skipped back to my bed and reclined on it happily.

He chuckled at my enthusiasm. "Yep. You gonna go?"

"Am I going to go? What a question. *Of course!"*

He grinned. "I figured as much." He crumpled the candy wrappers in his hand. "Where's your trashcan?"

I pointed to the opposite side of my bed. He walked over to discard the wrappers, then stopped abruptly when he looked down. His back stiffened as he stared at the contents of the can. After a moment, he released the wrappers. He didn't seem in any hurry to turn around; when he did, his face was drained of color. Two seconds ago, he had been laughing right beside me. He was clearly struggling with his feelings, but he reacted as if he knew the value of remaining calm, even tried to mask what was obviously disappointment.

His voice seemed to sag when he suggested, "You might want to empty your wastebasket before Marc gets home."

It took me a moment to understand what he meant. Heat rushed to my face as I realized what he must have seen. Brandon had disposed of both condom and wrapper once they had fulfilled their purpose. I hadn't thought to get rid of them, or cover them. Nothing like an exhausted condom to leave a lasting impression. I couldn't believe I had been so careless. There was no excuse—I read Nancy Drew. Lesson number one: hide the evidence. I took a deep breath and let it out slowly. What to say now?

"When did you have company?" he asked, his tone subdued.

He was concentrating on sounding unaffected; he didn't want me to recognize the quaver in his voice. Unfortunately, he was nowhere near as skilled at hiding his emotions as Brandon was.

I lightly, carefully, cleared my throat. "Last night."

"Who was he?"

I didn't know if I should tell him, didn't know if I *could* tell him. Would Brandon tell Ryan what had happened between the two of us? Why hadn't I considered this before? I was slowly realizing that other people were going to be affected by the night Brandon and I had shared, and the news would not be well received.

As I took my time, playing a mental tennis match over what to say, suddenly his face went slack. My eyes followed his gaze.

Mother Mary.

"Whose belt is that?"

Brandon's belt hung over the back of my wicker chair. Even from across the room, it was obviously a boy's belt. Curious, Ryan slowly walked over to inspect it. He ran his fingers over the smooth, fine brown leather. It wouldn't be difficult to discern whose it was. Brandon was the only boy I knew to have every belt he owned proudly embossed with his initials. I wondered if it was for precious moments like these.

I took a deep breath, and then let it out. "It's Brandon's."

A distinct, sudden chill swept through the room. I watched the strained pulse in his neck. His throat constricted. I heard the feather-light frost in his voice. "Tell me this isn't what it looks like." Blue eyes, filled with equal parts raw ache and incredulity, turned to watch me too closely. "You're *not* sleeping with Brandon."

He looked crushed, like he'd been slapped. When I made no effort to comfort his worst fear, his voice nearly cracked with pain, hitting a squeaky high note much like a boy's prepubescent voice on the verge of change.

"You didn't, did you?" he almost pleaded. It occurred to me that Ryan had a crush on me. I don't know how more unconscious a girl could possibly be than me. Maybe everyone had seen it, maybe not but certainly Brandon had to know it.

I wouldn't be able to handle it if he started to cry. Still, I refused to hide the truth from him. I pulled my emotions in tight and barely managed to say, "He stayed here last night."

The belt may as well have slapped him. He barely shook his head then, his voice just above a whisper, said, "Jesus Christ — I've heard everything now." He stared blankly at the floor. "He didn't tell me."

Of course he hadn't. I spoke gently to his confusion. "You're his best friend, Ryan. Do you expect him to?"

Despite the twist of irony, there was an unspoken understanding when he met my eyes. "No ... I guess not," he said coolly.

"Are you going to tell him you know?"

He shook his head. "I'll leave that in your hands. If he can't face me about it, then ... that's his choice." His voice was heavy with disappointment. When he looked at me again, concern filled his eyes. He hesitated, carefully choosing his words. "Was he at least ... *good* to you?"

I knew Ryan well enough to know he wasn't inquiring about Brandon's prowess in the bedroom, or how I had enjoyed it; rather, he was asking about his bedside manner.

"He was a gentleman, Ryan."

He nodded. He was silent for some moments, and I watched the various emotions shift and change over his face. Confusion gave way to hurt.

"What in God's green earth made you turn to Brandon, Krista? Why?"

I hesitated, wondering if he would understand — if it would matter. "He's my friend, and I trust him. There's a reason why I wanted to lose my virginity; I wasn't looking for a boyfriend or a relationship. It seemed to make sense at the time."

"A reason?"

I shook my head. "It's personal."

He looked at me with wounded eyes. "I'm your friend, too — and I'm *straight*. Did you ever think of coming to me?"

I lowered my head, at a loss for the words that would seem sensitive to the situation or his feelings. The truth was, I had thought of him. But I'd quickly decided against it for a few reasons. Ryan was a virgin. It didn't seem too productive to me to have two clueless first-timers trying to figure out how the mysteries of sex worked. Then there was the suspicion that Ryan could develop feelings for me and apparently I was right which would only complicate everything. Brandon was impartial; it wouldn't affect him the way it would Ryan. He would be on to his next mission. Neat, clean, simple. Made sense to me. I was beginning to think I was the only person who thought that way.

"He's *gay*, Kris — and you *gave* yourself to him, gave him your virginity when it's not going to mean a damn thing to him!"

Maybe it would, maybe it wouldn't. "I guess I can live with that," I said softly.

He lightly fingered the belt, squeezed it in his fist, turning his knuckles white, and then released it, watching it fall to the floor. I had never seen Ryan so angry.

"He doesn't deserve that honor, Kris. He doesn't deserve to be remembered forever as your first."

I tried to calm him. "Ryan, please; don't get upset."

"How can I not be? Who are you kidding? We may never talk about it, but it's no secret between *any* of us; you know how I feel about you. I just figured if I kept on reminding you of that fact, I'd risk losing you as a friend. Now I wonder if I did the right thing by keeping quiet."

"Ryan …"

He looked at me, eyes full of sadness. "You don't have a clue, do you?"

"About what?"

"Do you have any idea just how many guys he's had sex with?"

I blinked, miffed by the unexpected question. "Well...no. Do you?"

"I'm his *best friend,* remember?" he said bitterly. "Of course I know."

I noted the subtle shift in the placement of words. He shook his head, brooding.

"Well, are you going to tell me?"

"It's not my place to say. You should ask him yourself—if you think you want to know."

I didn't say anything. I understood his implication perfectly. I could probably do without knowing. Considering Brandon's surprising skill, I knew he had to have taken many lovers. One doesn't acquire all that knowledge in evenings spent alone, or by playing Monopoly.

I really wasn't concerned. What happened had happened for a purpose; I wasn't expecting a boyfriend out of the arrangement. Had I, then maybe it would've mattered to me to know the names and faces of all those before me. As it stood now, I was fine with it. I didn't need to hear that Brandon had a list of priors that read like a roll-sheet.

He quickly shook his head, trying to resolve the facts in his mind. He couldn't. "I'm sorry, Kris. None of this is making any sense to me right now. But I guess that really doesn't matter, does it? I hope you'll understand if I'm not in the mood to go to the movies this weekend."

I nodded. I hoped this storm would pass quickly. I didn't like the idea of Ryan keeping his distance from me. He was one of my closest friends. I hadn't meant to hurt him.

"Ryan, don't be angry with Brandon."

Something in him snapped at that and I watched him fight for control. Angry, cool blue eyes stared into mine. "You can tell me anything you want, Kris, but don't think you can tell me how to feel. Angry doesn't quite cut it. Frankly, I'm *pissed*. I didn't see this coming. I'm afraid I'm fresh out of gracious responses. Forgive me." He brushed by me on the way out of my bedroom.

I followed right behind him. "Where are you going?" I asked anxiously.

"I've gotta go. I need some air."

"Let me come with you."

"*No.* I want to be by myself."

"But I'm worried about you."

He gave a quick, bitter laugh I'd never heard before from him. "That's touching. I'll remember that."

I followed at his heels as he walked down the hallway on his way out. He was so unlike himself it made me uneasy. "Promise me you won't do anything stupid, Ryan."

"I promise you, Krista—I won't fuck Brandon."

I stopped and winced at his words. I swallowed the ache forming in the back of my throat. I would not cry.

Just when I thought things couldn't get any worse, Josh walked through the front door as Ryan bolted for it.

"Where's the fire?" Josh asked, stepping back to let Ryan pass.

Ryan fixed his gaze straight head. "Hi, Josh." Ryan's voice was sober. He didn't stop.

Josh looked puzzled. "You takin' off already, Ryan?" He seemed disappointed. I don't know why, but he seemed to be Ryan's personal cheerleader lately.

Ryan looked at no one as he spoke; his words floated in his wake. "Yeah…I gotta jet. Catch you later, Josh. See ya, Kris."

The door slammed shut behind him.

Josh turned to me. "Whadya do now? He looked pissed."

"Never mind."

He shrugged. "Fine. But since you're here, I want to ask you something."

"What, Josh?" I said, my emotions straining. I was still trying to recover from the verbal slap I had just received from Ryan. I didn't have strength left for another argument, and lately, that's all Josh seemed to bring with him.

"What, other than condoms, did you steal from my room?"

I froze. Panic quickly replaced my need to cry.

"Look, I'm not going to kill you, although I'd *like* to, since I know you've been going through my room. But I guess I can't really say much, after going through yours. Stay out of my room from now on, and I'll stay out of yours. Deal?"

"Yeah." My voice came faintly from the back of my throat. I was still wondering how to respond to the first half of his question.

"Why were you in my gym bag? Is that all you were looking for—condoms? Or are there other things of mine that I'm going to find missing as well?"

"Why would I be looking for condoms?" It didn't hurt to try.

"Try to think of a worthwhile question, Krista. That one only has one answer."

He looked at me while he took off his jacket. He tossed it aside on the couch. I felt like he was preparing for a showdown; maybe he was. If so, I wasn't prepared.

He said, "You have two choices: you can either make this easy on yourself and answer my questions, or you can be a pain in the ass and I'll make sure your life is a living hell. I asked the question—you answer it. Don't try to play this off like you don't know what I'm talking about. I don't buy them for decoration, Kris. I know what I have in my room; the ones in my bag are missing and they didn't walk out by themselves. I *know* it's not Marc; he doesn't need to get them from me.

"Kris, I won't tell Marc."

"Sure. And I still believe in the tooth fairy. Anyway, who says they were for me?"

He shook his head. "You're doing it again. You're not helping yourself any," he warned. "I know they were for you because you'd never risk digging through my things otherwise. If they were for anyone else, you wouldn't have bothered; it wouldn't be worth the consequences of getting caught. The mistake you keep making is that you seem to think I won't catch you. Wrong *again*. Like I said before, I know how the game goes. I'll catch you every time." He looked at me, waiting for me to answer. "So...who was it? Ryan? Did you finally do something right, like see the light and give him a chance?" A clever, teasing smile crept across his lips. "Was that a lover's quarrel I walked in on?"

What the hell had the two of them been talking about? Since when had Ryan and Josh gotten so chummy?

"That's my business. I don't have to tell you a thing," I said.

"What's the big deal?"

"It's none of your business, Josh."

"It is when you're taking my stuff."

"I'm sorry. I'll find a way to replace what I took."

"Don't bother. I already have. I just want to know who you're doing."

"I'm not *doing* anyone."

"So you mean you're back to girls." He made it a scornful statement, something to throw in my face.

It made me angry. "What's your problem, Josh? Do you think I'm gay, or what? Is that what this is about?"

"Well, aren't you? That's what I'd call dyking out, with Carrie."

My face went pale at his words. I couldn't tell by his expression if he had said it just to hurt me. Either way, it worked. I tried to sound calm. "I wasn't dyking out with Carrie," I said, barely loud enough to hear.

"Well, that's what I'd call it."

I was so upset that the tension in my throat could no longer hold back the tears. The floodgates opened. "Why do you hate me so much?" I cried.

"Who said anything about hating you? I was just asking a question."

He really saw nothing wrong with his words; I wondered how he could be so insensitive, how we could possibly be from the same family.

"I'm not a dyke," I said, my voice bitter.

"Well, that's good news, then."

The front door opened and Marc walked in, back from the hospital at last. Josh and I still stood in confrontation in the hallway. What a reception. I was sorry in more than one way. He already looked weary.

He closed the door behind him looked at the two of us, then turned to me. "What's wrong? What's going on, Kris?"

I opened my mouth to speak but Josh cut through first, turning his eyes, full of condemnation, to Marc. "I notice you always jump to Krista's side," he challenged, his voice full of irritation. "What's with that?"

Marc's eyes scolded. "Yes, well, I thought you were capable of handling things by yourself, Josh," he said, exasperated by his need to explain. "If I need to start handling you with kid gloves, let me know."

That shut Josh up. He left the room in an angry snit, and slammed his bedroom door. Marc took a deep breath and turned to me again; the exhaustion was clearly visible on his face. "What happened?"

I simply wasn't in the mood to discuss things politely. "Nothing," I cried, then hustled to my room.

I called Brandon in tears. I should've known I'd get his machine. I left what was probably an incoherent message and hung up the phone. Chances were, he was still surfing—had to be. Now he would return to wade through my recorded waves of misery. I threw myself face down onto the bed.

Marc knocked on the door. "Kris?" He didn't wait for an invitation to enter.

"I don't want to talk, Marc. It's not that important."

"That's why you're in tears," he said.

"You just got home. Relax before you have to listen to our same old drama."

"Why don't you let me worry about myself?"

There really wasn't anything I could share with Marc. I couldn't trust what details Josh would give up. If I told Marc what he'd said to me, Josh would simply toss in that I had taken condoms from his room, and I definitely wasn't ready to disclose anything concerning that.

"What did Josh say?" I asked.

"Nothing. He said he just got home and found you in tears."

Remarkable. Josh had kept his mouth shut. I blinked, and then my head cleared. Who was I kidding? I knew he only did it to spare his hide; Josh just didn't want to hear one of Marc's lectures on showing respect for me.

"So what happened?" he asked.

"I want to talk to Brandon about it. Don't be offended."

He seemed to consider my preference. "All right, if that's what you want, I won't interfere. I'm here if you want to talk."

"Thanks."

He nodded and left the room.

I had just grabbed a Kleenex when my bedroom phone rang.

"What's wrong?" Brandon didn't bother with a salutation.

"That was quick," I sniffed.

"I was screening my calls; I didn't catch the phone in time. What's wrong?" he asked again.

"Josh..." I tried to speak but the tears complicated the task. "He..." It wasn't working.

"Kris, why don't we talk in person? I'll come pick you up. Give me two minutes to rinse off."

I managed to say, "I'll be waiting."

He hung up the phone.

Ten minutes later, he pulled up outside the house. He must've really rushed, to be here so quickly. I left my room and didn't stop in the living room when I called out to Marc, "I'm going out with Brandon." I pushed through the door and let it slam behind me.

I rushed out to meet him. The engine was still running; he could tell by my exit that I didn't want to stay here long. As I opened the passenger door and hopped in, I glimpsed a picnic basket in his back seat.

"Okay," he said, and turned to me. "Pause for a hug."

I gratefully accepted the comfort of his arms, now that I was safely inside his car.

"It's gonna be okay, Kris. Let's go up to the spot on the hill; we can talk and have a picnic."

I let myself out of the car to take in the view when we arrived. I looked down on the city and the beach below us; it seemed so far away and tranquil from a distance.

Brandon grabbed the basket from the back seat and we made our way to the shelter of a great, sturdy, old grandfather of a tree. Its trunk was coarse, gray, and wide, its skin etched with names and promises of love. I liked the tree. I found it comforting.

A salt and pepper-colored cottontail bounced by to hide in the bushes; another one that had been nibbling on the grass at the edge of the clearing sat up on its hind legs, ears perked at our presence, and then sprinted across the grass to join his companion. Brandon laid out a red square blanket large enough to accommodate our goodies and us, and we sat protected beneath the gently swaying branches. I sniffed, wiping away tears with the back of my hand. Brandon handed me a napkin.

"What happened, Kris? Start from the beginning."

I sat Indian-style, shoulders slouched, as I picked apart pieces of my soggy, tear-filled napkin. As I recounted all of Josh's harsh words, he listened without interruption, a look of concern coloring his expression. Once I'd shared everything, he looked quietly into the distance.

"God, I hate people sometimes," he said, his voice equally distant. He turned back to me. "I'm sorry, Krista. Really. I know what you're going through, and it sucks." He shook his head. "You may hate me for saying this, but fuck Josh, Kris. Don't allow him to make you feel bad about yourself. Don't give him that kind of power. I know it hurts to hear him say those things—he *wants* it to hurt. He hates that he doesn't understand, and that scares him as much as it does you. Know that's why he says what he does. Don't be afraid of it, Kris. Don't let other people hold you down.

"There have been plenty of occasions when people have gone out of their way to let me know I'm not welcome, and I'm sure there'll be more. If I let every instance when someone said or did something screwed-up to me take root and hold me back, I wouldn't have made it a year without trying to commit suicide. I've seen hate, Kris—in every shade of gray imaginable—and it hurts all the same."

He arranged plastic plates and silverware before us as he continued to talk. "I remember the day I finally got the nerve to come out to my best friend—this was before I met Ryan. I'd agonized for *months,* just trying to get up the courage to tell him. That was probably one of the hardest moments I lived through, and my worst misjudgment.

Everything I feared happened—and then some. He called me a faggot, and a whole list of other things I'd like to forget. He felt threatened—thought I hadn't said anything about it before because I wanted to hook up with him. It wasn't true, but it didn't matter. That's how he chose to see it. That was my *'best friend.'*

"The next day after school, he had me jumped by two guys I didn't know. Shit—I wanted to *die.*" He shook his head. "If it weren't for Ryan, who knows where I'd be now? He was the only person who came to help me when he saw what was happening—and he didn't even *know* me. That's how we became friends, and we've been friends ever since.

Oh great, now I had to tell him about Ryan.

I wasn't looking forward to telling Brandon, but I had to do it. Ryan had discovered the truth, and Brandon needed to know that.

Brandon set out a selection of finger sandwiches, fruits and chips, and then poured us each a glass of fruit juice. He nibbled at the food, but I'd lost my appetite.

Brandon had managed to calm me enough that I could speak, at least for the moment. "I have additional unpleasantries to share," I said.

"Just give it to me straight," he said, brushing the crumbs off his fingers as if preparing himself.

I sighed. "It's Ryan. He saw the condom first, then he found your belt on my chair; he put two and two together and figured it out. I couldn't lie to him, Brandon. He would've seen right through it."

He sat silent, his face expressionless. When he finally came around, his tone was solemn. "I would never ask you to lie, Kris. I can take the heat. I realized what I was doing when I made my decision. It is totally obvious that Ryan has had a thing for you since day one. But he's never done anything about it."

He stared off into the distance. I recognized that empty gaze; I had seen it before. He didn't see a damn thing in front of him.

"God," he said, his eyes still fixed in that trancelike stare, "he's *really* got to hate me now."

"I'm sorry."

He turned to me. "No, *I'm* sorry. Why are you apologizing to me? I'm the one who was careless." He sighed. "Well, what's done is done, right? Let me guess—he's picking out my headstone as we speak?"

"Close enough."

"Thanks for the warning."

"Well," I said, trying to find the optimistic side, "he did say he would wait for you to bring it up. I'm not sure if you view that as a plus or a minus."

"Interesting approach—none. Good to know. I'll have to give this some careful consideration. I imagine if I don't come clean to him soon, his anger is just going to fester to the point of a blowup. I rather hope to bypass that. Then again, it may be inevitable. After all, I did just sleep with the one person he worships since day one." He shook his head. "I crossed the one line…"

An unfamiliar brooding look vanished as quickly as it came.

Brandon stood up and grabbed both my hands. "Come on, Doll-face." He pulled me up with a hop. "Let's get out of here."

22

I headed to dance camp armed with my new experience. From here on out, I was supposed to know what I wanted. Problem was, things still seemed unclear.

The second night at camp, after lights out, Carrie snuck into bed with me, not saying a word. I said nothing either, both out of fear of being caught by the other girls (although we had done nothing wrong), and out of a sheer loss for words. She cuddled up beside me, and I could feel the rise and fall of her chest as she concealed her tears and I knew she was back there with Jalen the night of the attack. No matter what I did or did not feel for her, I would never let her ache all alone. I held her close to me all night. But in the morning, as so often before, when the sun showed its face, the truth stayed with the darkness; it was as if last night never happened. Once again, we never discussed it.

Five nights passed before she spoke of it. We spent our free time, the time between last practice and last meal, together, as always. Though still early evening, darkness came quickly, shrouding our fears and making us feel safe enough in the dim room to speak freely. The exhaustion from the day's exertions slowly crept upon me and I lay down to rest; Carrie crawled into bed beside me. I maneuvered to give her more room, and she cozied up against me even tighter. I lay back on my pillow, gazing at the ceiling, Carrie's head resting comfortably on my chest. Moonlight streamed through the windows and the doorway, touching the sparse contents of the room and leaving a soft glow on the ceiling where I fixed my eyes.

Her whisper pierced the darkness. "I liked him so much, Kris. I mean, I really liked him, you know? Sometimes I can't believe it really happened; I don't remember any of it. It's like that night's all mixed up in my head—like some dream sequence that turned out to be a nightmare, only I can't recall the details. I'm so ashamed of myself, Kris."

"He drugged you, Carrie. From that point on, everything that happened was beyond your control. He should be the one who's ashamed, even if he isn't. And I'm sorry I wasn't there for you." It hurt to say it.

"Don't," she said. "I'm sorry that I insisted you go."

I tried to think of something positive to say. Somehow, I doubted that a reminder that she had managed to escape without pregnancy or STDs would be uplifting. "I'm just glad you're safe," I said lamely.

"I never thought I'd ever be afraid to be alone with a guy, but I am. I hate that—I hate being afraid." Her voice trailed off into the cool night air. "I thought it'd be romantic, I thought..." She paused, began again. "The worst part about it is that I don't remember him being mean or rough or anything like that. To me, everything was perfect; *he* was perfect. There was nothing to make me feel otherwise."

That scared me the most. It stunned, *angered* me to know that her only memories of him were positive ones. Was that better for her, or worse? I just didn't know.

"Kris... the whole thought of sex with a guy makes me sick now. I don't know that I would ever want to do it." She shifted slightly, finding a more comfortable position. "Did that night scare you?" she asked. "I never asked you; what happened that night with you and Eric?"

"Nothing worth talking about," I said. "Part of me just wants to sweep him and that whole night under the rug. I wasn't happy at the time, but now I'm glad Josh came and found us when he did. We really were in way over our heads. I guess I see that now."

We lay there quietly for a while. Then Carrie asked, "How do you feel about guys now? Do you think you could ever still be with one?"

It seemed unfair to judge all guys by the actions of two. Not all men were like that, and I couldn't see blaming the entire male population for what they'd done. Jalen was guilty, no one else.

I hadn't told her about Brandon yet and I needed to. I had procrastinated, still unsure of how she would take the news. But guys and sex, two topics we rarely discussed anymore, were open for conversation at the moment, and I couldn't guarantee that there'd be another opportunity any more appropriate than now to bring it up.

"I've been meaning to tell you, but with everything that's happened, the time just never seemed right." I slipped my secret into the crisp night air. "I'm not a virgin anymore."

"What?" she asked, and then hesitated. "You slept with Eric? Why didn't you tell me?"

"I didn't sleep with Eric." Suddenly I wished I had; somehow, it sounded kinder.

"I thought you just said you did."

"I slept with Brandon."

For moments, it sat there, untouched.

"With Brandon?" She spoke slowly, as if to make sense of it; finding none, she asked in dismay, "Are you serious? He had sex with you?"

I nodded.

"He's gay," she said, as if stating his sexuality would ensure it remained true.

"I know."

An eerie silence hovered in the air for the length of ten heartbeats.

"Did you like it?" she asked quietly.

I wouldn't lie to her. "Yeah." I felt a little like I had betrayed her. Maybe I had.

"What was it like?"

"I don't know how to describe it," I said. "I don't know what I was expecting, but that wasn't it. It was unlike anything I've ever experienced before." I couldn't be sure what she was thinking. I hoped my answer didn't upset her.

"Were you nervous?"

"We both were. Everything ended up okay, though. He was really cool about it."

"Why Brandon?"

"Because I trust him, I guess."

"Do you like him now?"

"What—like a boyfriend? No. Nothing's changed. We're still just friends. It was a one-time thing."

She didn't say anything for a while. I listened to the thick sound of singing crickets outside our cabin walls. The moon, round and perfect like Tom and Jerry's cartoon Swiss cheese sat suspended in midair, glowing right outside our window.

"Did you like it more than us?"

She had caught me off guard. Never before had she acknowledged that we had progressed beyond friendship. It felt good to hear her say it.

"It was entirely different. I don't know how to explain it completely." I tried. "Carrie, I love the way it feels when I'm with you, but..." I closed my mouth before I could slip up and tell her I loved her—but not in that way. I couldn't go there yet. I ran my fingers lazily through her hair.

"I know you and I were just practicing. It started as a dare, remember?"

I was relieved that she understood how I felt.

"I'm happy for you, Kris." Her voice sounded vacant, as if only spilling out empty but necessary words. I wondered if she believed them. She continued with, "What about Daemon?"

"We're just friends. I really don't think about him that way."

"I think you're afraid to admit you're attracted to him," she decided. "I don't know why. He's cute. I don't know that he'd have sex with you, though. I rather doubt it."

"Well, I have no reason to be concerned with it," I said, although deep down, I knew she was right. I *was* attracted to Daemon, had feelings for him that I didn't know how to handle. But I was afraid to share those feelings about him with anyone—especially Daemon—and-sometimes... I even tried to hide those feelings from myself.

"Isn't he still a virgin?"

Was I at liberty to say? I didn't want to wait too long to answer. "Yes," I confirmed. After all, I knew he wasn't ashamed of the fact.

"Don't you think that's kinda weird? He's like...thirty. Do you think maybe he's not telling us something?"

"Carrie," I reproached her, suddenly feeling the need to defend him, "Daemon has no need to keep secrets from us. Some people are just better at waiting than others. We can't fault him for that."

"I guess you're right. I'm sorry."

I hugged her gently against me. My fingers lightly traced her back. It felt good to finally talk to Carrie again, to hold her the way I once had, and yet know it would not be misinterpreted. Comfortable with each other, we drifted off to sleep. We awoke to the rude sound of the alarm clock we'd set to give ourselves time to get ready for dinner before the other girls returned.

I peered out my bedroom window when I heard the engine, then tore down the hall and flew through the front door, leaving it to slam on its own. I saw the boys in Brandon's blue beauty. It was the first time I'd seen Ryan since he'd stormed out of my house, and it was a welcome surprise; I had missed him. And I had missed Brandon, too.

He stepped out of the car, removed his shades with a disarming smile, and threw the door shut behind him. He was dressed in light tan slacks and a black short-sleeve dress shirt. I ran to the driver's side and tackled him with a hug.

"Brandon! I *missed* you!"

He laughed, squeezing me tight. The light, sweet, scent of his Caroline Herrera cologne lingered on his neck. "The feeling is mutual." He kissed my cheek and reminded me in a whisper, "Don't forget brother Ryan."

I squeezed him tight once more and then bounded toward Ryan, who sat leaning against the car. He wore jeans and a long-sleeved sea green surf shirt that had two charcoal gray stripes running across the chest; it must've been new. I wasn't sure how well my greeting would be received. I decided to chance it and moved in for a hug.

"It's good to see you," I said warmly.

He didn't push me away, but he controlled our contact with restraining hands. I pulled back, my arms still resting lightly around his neck, and looked at him. For someone at a reunion, he didn't look very happy. I couldn't help being disappointed; I'd hoped for a more receptive homecoming. I wondered how long he'd hold his grudge against me.

My voice came quieter in response to his reaction. "I haven't talked to you in forever, Ryan—I've missed you. I guess I'd hoped you'd missed me, too." I worked to fight a frown. "Aren't you happy to see me?"

Ryan struggled for words. "Yeah…I—"

Brandon, relaxing next to us against the fender of his car, interjected with a teasing grin, "Lean any closer and you'll find out just *how* happy."

Ryan ignored him. "It's really good to see you too, Kris."

I smiled warmly at him and moved his hands to wrap them around me. "Then just hug me, will you?"

He gave me a real hug. Ryan had to be the only boy I knew who could be obviously turned on, yet still manage to maintain his sheer innocence. It was kind of cute.

Over Ryan's shoulder I shot Brandon a sassy look; his eyebrows were raised in amusement.

I invited them in.

Brandon spoke up. "Ryan needs to be at hockey practice in less than twenty minutes. He just came along for the ride; he wanted to say hi to you before we head to Carrie's."

I smiled. "That was sweet. I'm glad you did."

I grabbed a yellow note pad from the kitchen, scribbled my whereabouts on it and left it on the kitchen table so Josh would be sure not to miss it. I left my purse behind and stuffed my money in my pockets.

Brandon was already behind the wheel, his Armani shades in place. Ryan stood outside the passenger door.

The hockey rink Ryan practiced at wasn't far from Carrie's house. Ryan gave us a quick, enigmatic smile as he hopped out of the car.

Ten minutes later, when we arrived at Carrie's, she was ready to go—a miracle. She wore a powder-blue sweater, her favorite fitted white skirt, and white strappy heels. Small silver hoops with matching baby-blue beads graced her earlobes. As always, she looked feminine and perfectly put together—like a girly powder puff.

Brandon gave her a hug and told her how cute she looked. Carrie hugged him back with a small, polite smile. Her enthusiasm on seeing Brandon usually rivaled that of a sparkler; this reunion seemed remarkably flat. If Brandon was conscious of it, he didn't bring it up. *Of course Brandon is conscious of it.*

I gave Carrie the front seat, and we were on our way to the mall. Brandon had suggested that we make the most of our last free day before returning to school, so we planned to see a movie and grab a bite to eat.

The movie wouldn't start for a few hours yet, so we had plenty of time beforehand to browse our favorite shops and eat. Carrie lagged behind, uninterested, as Brandon and I shopped. She had been unusually quiet and seemed indifferent about hanging out—not at all what either of us had expected. I began to wonder why she had agreed to come at all.

When Brandon stated that he was getting hungry, I suggested the food court.

"I was thinking more along the lines of a *restaurant*—something *off* the mall," Brandon said.

"Come on," I teased him. "I want to see you eat like the rest of the population. Seeing you come close to brown-bagging it will make it all worthwhile."

He shrugged. "What can I say? If I get food poisoning, I'm taking you down with me," he warned.

Since he was making *such* a sacrifice, Carrie and I allowed him to pick the mall cuisine. Brandon decided on Chinese. We filled our orange trays, then headed for one of the few tables that weren't occupied in the busy food court. Brandon sat across from me, and Carrie took the seat beside mine. I handed out the plastic cutlery, then looked at Carrie, who stared at her plate. "Are you going to eat it, or just stare at it?" I asked.

"I'm not hungry."

"Then why did you order it?" I said.

"Why does anyone do anything?" she sighed, addressing the air rather than me.

Dramatics. Carrie and her dramatics. I looked at Brandon, who mirrored my mystified look.

"Is everything okay?" I asked, and fell right into the trap. She didn't answer. "Is something wrong?" I tried again.

She turned her head slightly toward Brandon and locked eyes with him. I had never seen Carrie look so cold. "How's your food, Brandon?" she asked icily.

"As expected, tasteless and lamp-warmed." He gave her an odd look. "Am I missing something?"

"Missing something? No, I wouldn't say you're missing anything. In fact, I'd say you've had your fill of everything."

"What's up with you?" Brandon asked, sounding irritated.

"What's up with *Nick?*"

Brandon hesitated. "He's fine. Why?"

Carrie smiled at him, too sweet. "He must be pretty open-minded. Does he know you like to fuck girls on the side?"

Brandon froze, unable to swallow his food. They just sat there staring at each other. The air felt so heavy, I thought I would choke.

"Say something, you prick!" Carrie hissed at him.

"Carrie!" I said, and kicked her under the table. "Don't be stupid."

She didn't take her eyes off Brandon. "I'm not. I'm being honest. Which is more than I can say for you!" She leaned into the table. "Go ahead," she said, "go ahead and tell me you don't know what I'm talking about. I *dare* you."

Brandon slowly put his drink down. Although Carrie was livid, she was also near tears. "I have no reason to lie to you," he said carefully.

"Really? And just *when* did you plan on telling me?" She shook her head, glaring at him. "Fuck you, Brandon." She pushed away from the table and ran toward the bathroom, in tears.

Shocked, silenced, we watched her leave.

"What the *hell* just happened?" he said, still watching her. He turned to me. "You *told* her? Why didn't you *tell* me you told her?"

"I'm sorry; it came up one night at camp. She was curious, and I told her. I never went into any details. She was fine that night," I added, bewildered. "I'm sorry."

"Let's just go find her," he said.

I grabbed Carrie's purse, which she had left behind in her haste to get away. We left our food and headed for the bathrooms in search of Carrie. We heard her before we saw her.

"I'll be right back," I said, and ducked inside, leaving Brandon to wait beside the water fountain.

I found her standing in the corner crying, paper towels in hand. I approached her, ignoring the other women in the bathroom who were obviously interested in our situation. "Carrie, at camp you were fine with everything. What happened?"

She shrugged. I understood. She had no idea what was going on inside her.

"Come on," I urged her gently. "Let's get out of here."

When we walked out the door, she saw Brandon standing there and froze. "What?" she said, her voice acidic, "Nick wasn't enough for you? You had to go and *fuck* my best friend?"

Brandon stood in the crowded mall and took the embarrassment that came with her words. Curious and condemning stares came from the strangers around us.

I couldn't let Brandon take the fall for this. I grabbed her arm and squeezed it tightly, whispering, "Look. Quit yelling at Brandon. It's not his fault. If you want to yell at someone, yell at me. *I* asked *him*, Carrie."

"Are you serious? *Why?*"

"Because I wanted to know." I looked at her puffy, red eyes. "Come on." I tugged her arm. "If you want to talk about this, then let's go somewhere where we're not the main attraction."

Brandon led the way with emotional detachment. I pulled a sulking Carrie with me. We stopped in an area of the parking lot where there were no cars.

She snapped the moment I let go of her arm, her rage flying at Brandon like a dervish gone awry. "You *asshole!* What—fucking guys doesn't do it for you anymore? Nick isn't cutting it? How *dare* you make Kris another notch on your belt!"

"She *asked* me, Carrie—it wasn't like something I planned."

"You could have said no!"

"Carrie…" He fought to keep the heat out of his voice.

"No!" Her fury bordered on hysterical. "Why don't you just admit it—you *wanted* to sleep with her! *You've wanted to all along!*"

"Carrie, calm down." He reached for her.

She smacked his arm away. "Don't touch me."

He pulled back, his body rigid with shock. "I didn't mean to—"

"Did you enjoy yourself?" Her voice was mocking. "Mr. 'I'll never sleep with another girl again.' *Ha!* What *bullshit!*"

His gaze dropped to the floor, his cheeks blooming with embarrassment. "Why are you doing this?"

She smiled cruelly. "I bet you loved it. I bet you *loved* screwing with her emotions, making her think there was hope." Her tone was taunting, but her eyes were not. "Did you like it, Brandon?"

"Stop it."

"No! I want to hear you say it!"

"What?" His eyes flashed at her.

She pointed in his face. "I want to hear it from *your* mouth. I already *know* Krista's side of the story. Tell me, did *you* enjoy it, you—you conniving prick!"

"Carrie!" I yelled.

She didn't back down. "Tell me!"

Brandon, stunned by her harsh words, said nothing.

"Did you like feeling her naked against you? Did you like being her first?"

"Carrie. Please—"

"Fuck you, Brandon! Did you like it?"

"Yes!"

She flew at him wildly with fists and nails, grabbing at his shirt, tearing it. "I despise you Brandon! I *hate* you!"

She hit him repeatedly, and he let her, only shielding his face behind his arms as he turned from each punch. She kicked him hard in the groin. Brandon doubled over with a cry of pain, defenseless. She continued to hit him.

I grabbed Carrie. *"Stop it!"* I shouted, struggling to pry her off him. "Would you just *stop it!*"

She struggled against me as I pulled her away. I let go of her when she was a safe distance from Brandon. She settled down.

Still crouched over, he looked up at her, his eyes bleary with pain. "I can't believe you're saying this to me!" he gasped. "Do I *ever* say anything about you and Krista?"

Her eyes went wide, horrified.

He nodded slowly, looking at her as it sunk in. "What, you think I wouldn't know? Use your head, Carrie! Do you really think Kris would ask me to sleep with her because she was dying to get inside my pants? Hardly! She was just as confused as you probably were!" He took a breath and slowly stood upright, wiping the sweat from his lip and brow. "Look, I'm sorry—what Jalen did to you was unforgivable. But if I recall correctly, before any of us knew what an *asshole* he was, you *wanted* to be with him. I don't see you giving any excuses for why you wanted to fuck Jalen! How can you be pissed that Krista was curious too? Shit, Carrie—you're too much."

He shook his head and turned away, shifting his weight as he violently raked his hands through his hair. He looked like an agitated animal pacing its cage. He took an audible breath and faced her again. "Look. We weren't trying to hurt you. We're all friends here. Let's not turn this into an episode of *Dynasty*, okay? Nobody is trying to hide anything from you, Carrie. Seriously."

He tried to pull himself together, tried to straighten his torn clothes. "So, does Nick know? Did you tell him?" he asked.

"Give me one reason why he shouldn't know."

"That isn't what I asked. I asked if he already knows."

She looked at him bitterly. "You mean does he know that you're a lying, cheating, prick? No. Unfortunately, he doesn't."

Brandon exhaled loudly.

"Knock it off, Carrie," I said.

Brandon looked at the asphalt, his voice tired and full of regret. "I appreciate your discretion with that, at least. I'd rather be the one to tell him about it. I guess it would be better if he heard about it from me," he mused.

I looked at Brandon. I felt terrible. I was the one who had gotten him into this entire mess. I hadn't meant to jeopardize his relationship with Nick. He shoved his hand into the front pocket of his slacks and grabbed his keys. We looked at each other, locking eyes. He looked away.

"Fuck!" He shook his head. "Come on, let's go. I need to get out of here. I need time to think."

We followed him silently through the parking lot until we reached his car. We got in mechanically. Not one word was exchanged during the entire ride home. I sighed. The Three Musketeers; happy as three peas in a pod ... that was us. Yeah, right.

———

I called Brandon the next day to see how he was doing after the blowup. He answered on the first ring.

"How are you coping?" I said.

His voice lacked his signature enthusiasm. "It's not a day at the beach, but I'm dealing with it."

"Did you tell him yet?"

"I told him."

"How'd he take it?"

"Not well." He paused. "Nick's been struggling with the "guy" thing for a while now. He's trusted me, and after what just happened ... I guess I can't blame him. How could he *not* feel insecure?"

"I'm sorry. I honestly wasn't even thinking about Nick when I asked you."

"Me either—which I guess says enough in itself."

"Are you guys serious? Does he consider this cheating?" I said.

"I don't know what we are anymore. All I know is, he's freaking out about it. Kris ... I already have a less than glowing track record with guys. Now I look like I can't keep my dick in my pants. At least those were Nick's fine words."

"You weren't with another guy. Does it really count?"

He humphed; I guessed it was supposed to be a laugh. "What planet are you living on? Yeah, it counts. It makes it that much worse."

"Why?"

"I can't explain it, Kris—it just does."

"Is it true what Carrie said—that you said you'd never sleep with a girl again?"

"It doesn't matter."

"But you said it...you meant it."

The anger in his tone traveled clearly through the phone line. "Well, I guess I got over it, didn't I? Let's not get into this—okay?"

"Fine." Brandon turned cold, as if at the switch of a light. It was unnerving.

"Don't be surprised if you hear from Nick," he said.

Great. "What do you want me to say?"

"No details. I've covered all he needs to know. If he starts asking questions, be smart about your answers. What happened between us, happened between us."

I agreed.

I prayed Nick wouldn't call.

He called.

"If you were a guy, I'd kick the shit out of you," he said.

Great way to open a conversation. This would be fun.

"If you liked him, why didn't you just tell me? I could've accepted it then."

"I don't like him—not like you're thinking."

"Well, then you're even *more* fucked up. How could you sleep with him if you don't even feel anything for him?"

I'd never known this kind of rage from Nick. But even while experiencing his anger, I began to hear the genuine hurt beneath it.

"I *trusted* you, Kris." His voice cracked, but he continued despite it. "You slept with him, even after you *knew* how I felt about him. I don't understand that at all. How can you separate the two? You supposedly have no feelings for him—well, *I do.* Yet, ironically, *you're* the one who's sleeping with *my* boyfriend."

Boyfriend?

"I wanted to let you know how much I appreciate that—along with the marks of your night together scratched like a damn *calling card* across his back! You obviously enjoyed his company."

I wasn't about to respond to that.

"I sure hope Brandon was able to help you resolve your sexual preference issue. I guess I'll know by who you're screwing next whether or not he gave a first-rate performance for the boys, huh?"

I felt how selfish I had been, how much I had hurt the people I cared about. My voice dropped to a whisper as, inadequate as they were, I said the only words I could. "I can't begin to tell you how sorry I am. I don't know what else to say."

"Answer me this: how can you be there for me one day, and completely go behind my back another?"

"I don't know," I mumbled.

"I see Carrie was equally touched by your experience."

"Yes … I've gotten the backlash from her, as well."

"You deserve it."

The phone went dead.

———

It didn't escape my notice when Carrie kept her distance. Not surprisingly, Brandon received the same treatment. He had made a point of stopping by her house every day to see if she would receive his company, but his visits met with no success.

Eventually, though, his persistence did pay off. One afternoon he came to my home with news; we retreated to my bedroom and he handed me a sealed letter from Carrie.

"She asked me to give this to you," he said.

"She *spoke* to you?"

"Only long enough to relay her message," he said, and I heard his disappointment.

"What is it?"

"Your guess is as good as mine. Why don't you open it and find out?"

I looked at the pink envelope with the sparkly red heart sticker she had used to seal the envelope, and smiled. Totally Carrie. I carefully peeled it back and withdrew the note.

It said:

It could've been anyone but Brandon, Kris — anyone but Brandon, and I could've dealt with it. What happened to trust? What happened to us? You shared our secrets with him. I'm confused. I'm lost. I can't even begin to understand his decision to sleep with you. I love you both, but you crossed the line with Brandon, Kris. What is it you share with him? If it's love, then I've lost my place as your best friend which is worse than anything. Come by so we can talk. I don't want to lose you to Brandon. Decide ... but don't waste time.

Carrie

My eyes never left the paper. Overcome, I read it over and over, and then over once more. I took a breath and then read it over. A tear fell on the pink pastel paper; I looked at it as if it had fallen from the sky. *Was she really asking me to choose between being her friend or Brandon's?* Would this have happened whether I had slept with Brandon or not? Somehow I thought it might have. Even if Brandon were a girl Carrie might eventually have gotten this jealous. It was not about feelings. It was about envy.

Brandon placed his hand on my shoulder. "Kris, what's wrong?"

I shook my head repeatedly in disbelief.

"What is it?" he asked again.

My eyes grew unfocused. The cloudy emptiness that filled my mind turned everything before me into a blur. Without asking, he took the paper from my hand and silently read it.

We looked at each other, not knowing what to say.

As requested, I met Carrie at her house later that day. She let me inside and we went to her room. Unsure what to say, I decided to wait for her to open the conversation. I sat on her bed.

Things were just about to get started when Carrie's doorbell rang; a moment later, her bedroom door came flying open, and Brandon entered wearing a spurious grin.

"Surprise," he said, and closed the door behind him. I guess he'd had a change in plans.

"What are you doing here?" she asked, obviously taken aback.

"Crashing your party," he said. "I would've R.S.V.P.'ed, but I wasn't given an invitation."

"That wasn't an oversight," she said, her voice cool.

"Yes, I figured as much. But considering your recent behavior, I don't mind saying that I respect your wishes about as much as I respect your tactics at the moment." He shook his head. "My, how you've changed, Carrie."

"Why are you here?" she demanded.

"To contribute my two cents. And if you pay attention, you might find their value to be worth considerably more." Brandon turned to me. "Hi, Kris," he added as an afterthought.

"Hi," I said, and remained silently flummoxed on her bed. Brandon strode over to her dresser and set his keys on top of it. He leaned back against it. "I couldn't help feeling slighted that you didn't even care enough to include me in on this noteworthy discussion you've orchestrated—especially when it concerns a matter in which I played an equally active part. Just what, pray tell, do you hope to accomplish by your meeting here today?"

Carrie's expression was cagey. "Did you tell him we were meeting?"

Brandon answered before I could. "No, she didn't. Carrie, you truly are a unique brand of bitter."

"What do you want?"

"For you to pull your head out of your ass, would be an appreciated start. For someone I've gone through thick and thin with, I couldn't be more disappointed."

"Well, then we both feel the same way."

Brandon said, "You know I would never intentionally hurt you. Neither of us would."

"Well, you did."

"I know, and I'm sorry. But that doesn't give you the right to toss out unfair ultimatums, and that's why I dropped by — to alleviate the need." He took a deep breath. "I'm going to do what's best for all of us right now — give you some space. You can't afford to let this strain things between you and Kris; you two rely on each other. I'll step back and you can find me when you're ready; you know I'm not going anywhere. I understand you're upset, but Carrie, you're blowing things out of proportion. How can you stoop to make those kinds of demands of Kris? You're going to force her to choose between the two of us? That's ludicrous, not to mention cruel. Don't fuck up everyone's friendship over this. Don't make Kris suffer because you're angry with me."

"I'm angry with both of you," she said.

"Yeah, I can see the fault is equally distributed here." His tone was full of sarcasm.

I said to Carrie, "I'm the one you should be yelling at, not Brandon. I'm sorry, Carrie. We're both sorry."

Brandon's eyes remained on Carrie as he spoke to me. "That's not the way it works, though, is it? She's hurt by your choice; she's *pissed* at mine — *pissed* at *me.*"

Carrie's eyes burned on Brandon. "You know how close Kris and I are. You should've known not to go there."

"Or the other way around," Brandon said.

"What's that supposed to mean?" she snapped. "I told you why I was mad. No one wants to find her best friends sneaking around behind her back, keeping secrets."

"Yet, you consider Ryan one of your best friends, and had he done what I had, you would've left *his* balls intact. You know Ryan would date Kris if he thought she'd say yes. Yet, you have no problem with that." He shook his head. "If this were solely about jeopardizing your relationship with Kris, then you'd stand to lose a *lot* more with Ryan. Your story has some holes, Carrie."

Neither looked happy as they stood there looking at one another. I felt like a bystander, trying to follow Brandon's take on the matter. He had a point.

"So, on that note... is there anything else you have to say? Clear the air? Or are you going to leave this entire thing unresolved, all smoke and mirrors before Kris?"

She shook her head. "There's nothing more to tell."

"That's it," Brandon said, and it was a flat and unbelieving statement.

"That's it," she said.

His eyes were severe. "Don't ever stand there and lie to my face, Carrie. You can tell me to fuck off, or call me an asshole—at least you're being honest with yourself then. But there's nothing I can't stand more than a liar. Don't start doing it now." He paused, waiting for her to say something, anything. She didn't say a word.

Frustrated by her stubbornness, he said, "At least be up front about it, so I can make a response."

Her expression was careful, guarded, like her tone. "I've said all I'm going to say. Like you always say—it's no one's business but your own."

They stood there in silence, holding each other's gazes. Brandon finally broke away in disgust.

"I'm out. At least I know the waves aren't going to feed me lines of bullshit."

He grabbed his keys and strode to the door. At the very last minute, he stopped. He turned around, his eyes serious for Carrie. "I would've said yes—had you asked me. But you never asked." He walked out the door, pulling it shut behind him.

23

Carrie and I spent the night at Aeleise's so we could attend church with her and Daemon the next day. Carrie didn't want to go when it came time — no surprise there — but kept true to her promise. Without getting into details, I warned Aeleise that Carrie and I were experiencing some tension over Brandon.

Although she assured me everything would be okay, Aeleise's voice sounded strange, unsteady, and there followed an odd stretch of silence over the phone.

"Speaking of Brandon..." she began quietly, "Nick told me yesterday that..." Her voice wavered. "That... he's gay."

What could I say?

"Kris... are you surprised?"

That he told her? "Yeah," I said quietly.

"So am I — I'm stunned."

Silence.

"He was crying — said he was sorry, that he didn't mean to hurt me, that he didn't want me to hate him. How could I possibly hate him, Kris? I love him. It just... hurts. Why didn't he tell me that before I fell in love with him?"

"Maybe he didn't know, Aeleise. Maybe he's surprised himself."

"How can he possibly know he's gay when he's still a virgin? Do you think..." she suggested tentatively, "that Brandon's playing on his insecurities? Nick hardly has any male friends, and — " her voice became worried " — if he trusts Brandon... He's just so *naive*. You know as well as I do that Brandon's brilliant enough to convince him of anything."

"I know Brandon's been guilty of his share of mind games, but I don't think he'd take it as far as this. I'm sure if Nick had the strength to tell you, then it's because that's how he truly feels."

"I'm sorry—I know he's our friend. I'm just...upset. And considering the rumors about Brandon..." She paused; I could practically see her shaking her head on the other end of the phone line. "He's about as safe for Nick as a cobra. Where'd I go wrong?"

"That's just the point, Aeleise. You didn't. There was nothing you could do."

My heart sank at the sight of Aeleise. Her eyes were pink and swollen in a pale, pasty face, as if she'd exhausted herself crying. Carrie and I hugged her. She looked so frail; it worried me.

"Do you want to talk about it?" I asked gently.

She shook her head, vacant eyes on the floor. "Not right now. I'm just glad you guys are here."

Someone rapped lightly on the door. I opened it to find Daemon on the other side.

"Do you have a minute?"

"Sure," I said, and stepped back, allowing him into the room. He looked at the door and I understood it as a silent request to shut it. I did.

"Something's been bothering me," he said. "I know you're close to Nick, and, well...I just wonder, how is he doing? I haven't heard a thing from him."

His worry surprised me, although I guess it shouldn't have. "He seems okay," I said. "We haven't really talked about the breakup."

He took a deep breath. "I can't say I approve of his lifestyle, or that I even understand his choice, but I'm not God, and it's not my place to judge. Sure, I'm disappointed for Aeleise, but I didn't have any intention of blowing him off. I think, if anything, it's more important to let him know that he's...still cared for, loved." His brows knitted again. "If you find a chance to talk with him, let him know he's still welcome. No questions, no weirdness. I'm still here if he needs me."

I felt a strange tightness in my chest as I nodded. "I'll make sure he gets the message."

His attempted smile fell flat. He let himself out the door.

I crawled into bed and thought about the confusion between Brandon, Carrie, and me. I hoped time would weaken the taste of our last meeting. I hated to see my two best friends feuding. I closed my eyes, intent on slumber, but my mind wouldn't rest. I plumped my pillow, flipped it on its other side, and vainly tried to sleep again. I tossed; I turned; then tossed and turned some more. I opened my eyes to all-engulfing blackness. It was after midnight according to the teal glow of the clock, the only light in the room. The soft, insistent ticking of the clock downstairs kept time to the sway of a pendulum.

I hated staying overnight anywhere other than Carrie's house. She and I always shared the same bed if we stayed anywhere together. At Aeleise's, we all slept in our own rooms.

I heard a noise downstairs. My overactive imagination began to feed my fears. I sat up and reached for the light, then made my way to the door.

I opened the door and looked into the hall. A faint glow at the far end revealed the stairwell, and I crept over and peeked down the stairs.

Daemon sat reading by a dim light in the living room.

Soundlessly, I descended the stairs and approached him as he continued to read. He was lounging in loose sleep pants in a black and gray plaid, and his favorite cross. No shirt. He probably didn't expect anyone to see him—Daemon didn't strike me as someone to exercise the freedom of shirtlessness. Other than the rare swim session, I'd never seen him this bare. Here, it seemed unusually bold, like I had been let in on a secret—*shh*—only I didn't know the reason for the hush. I moved forward hesitantly despite the warning going through my mind.

He looked up at the sound of my footsteps brushing the carpet. "You should be in bed."

"I can't fall asleep," I said. My bedroom here didn't have a night-light, Carrie, or my bear. It was pointless to try sleeping without one or the other. But I couldn't admit to him that I was still afraid of the dark; surely he'd think it seemed childish. I sat down on the arm of the overstuffed chair where he was reading. Then I glanced down at his book and realized that for once he was reading something other than the Bible. I leaned forward, my interest piqued. "*The Screwtape Letters.* What's it about?"

"I'll let you borrow it sometime, if you'd like."

Silent, I sat there, perched before him. Without thinking, I reached out and touched the intimate ornament sleeping against his chest. I inspected it closely, turning it over slowly in one hand. He watched my fingers as they explored and appreciated the detailed surface of stained silver. The carved metal had absorbed the warmth from his body.

I had finally touched it. It sat soundly in my palm.

He closed his hand around mine, startling me, and he looked me square in the eyes. My eyes stalled on his, and for an indecisive moment, neither of us spoke. My face flushed instantly, and I pulled away as if pinched, letting the cross fall from my fingers.

For a while we just sat there, I with my heart thudding in an irregular beat, saying nothing as we looked at each other. He finally broke the silence.

"I think it's time for bed, Kris," he said gently.

I didn't want to leave him, didn't want to go and fight the sleeplessness.

"Come on—I'll stay with you until you can fall asleep."

He set his book down and took my hand. My heart jumped into my stomach when his palm met mine. He led me back upstairs. He left the hall light on without being asked, and left the door ajar a few inches to allow in some light.

"Hop in," he said softly. He pulled back the covers and I crawled underneath. He pulled them up about me. "Settled?" he asked.

I nodded.

He pulled a chair up beside the bed and sat down. "Get some sleep, okay?" He smiled gently. "I'll be right here." He leaned back in his chair and propped up his feet on the edge of the bed. "If you wake up again and still can't sleep, you remember where my room is, right?"

I nodded. "Thanks, Daemon."

"Sure."

I closed my eyes.

I was slowly melting in the summer heat as I stood outside Aeleise's house. The fragrant smell of gardenias hung in the air, and a subtle breeze brushed past my skin and fluttered the hem of my dress. Strawberry Bubble-Yum watered in my mouth. Daemon was washing his car and I watched him intently... every part of him.

He smiled when he noticed my stare, and approached me. He wore tight blue jeans, and his white T-shirt had become transparent as it clung to his damp skin. I was startled by the coolness of his wet hands on my waist and the insistence with which he pulled me against him. His lips lightly brushed my cheek, and the heat of his breath tickled my neck as his voice throbbed beside my ear.

"I've been wanting to do this," he said, and then pressed his lips to mine, the kiss intensifying as his tongue brushed my lips, gentle but assertive, and while he kissed me, his hands traveled over my body with certain knowledge. Images in my mind blurred and shifted, becoming a dizzying kaleidoscope of Daemon exploring me as Brandon had.

"That's what I thought," he whispered.

I gasped and sat up. I was covered in sweat and out of breath. My sheets were soaked; my hair clung to my face. I looked beside me; Daemon was not in the room. A dream. It had been a dream. I let out a sigh and tried to calm myself. The dream had been so real it shocked me, leaving me feeling uneasy. A moment later, I quickly removed my pajamas, shivering as cool air met wet skin. What a bizarre experience! Had it not been for the sensations playing though my mind, I would've thought my body was breaking a fever. It left me feeling strange. Had Nick's dream of Brandon been this vivid? If so, I understood the depth of his initial distress.

Thank God everyone was asleep. I wrapped myself in the comforter—the only thing that was still dry—and, feeling unsettled, prayed silently, anxiously awaiting morning.

Sunshine was streaming in through the guest room blinds when I awoke. I sat up in bed, remembering the tumultuous night. I was still clad only in panties. I heard talking downstairs. I stretched, slowly rose, and stood before the full-length mirror. A heavy, black, satin-lined robe lay over the chair in the corner. I put it on and looked at my reflection. I lowered the robe to expose my upper body, and studied it from all angles. My shoulders were too narrow, and I could use more help in the chest area. Satisfactory, but far from impressive. I hoped I still had plenty of growing to do.

Daemon's reflection in the mirror startled me. My back was to the door and, deep in thought, I hadn't heard him enter the room. I covered myself quickly, pulling the robe up around my shoulders.

He stopped upon seeing me and abruptly turned around. "Sorry; I didn't realize you were changing. I was just coming to tell you—"

"I was just getting ready to come down for breakfast," I said quickly, hoping he hadn't witnessed my self-scrutiny and he wouldn't recognize my fib. I was getting good at lying through omission. I snugly tied the cloth belt around my waist. "I'm covered."

He turned around, looking at my reflection in the mirror.

"I'll remember to knock next time," he said apologetically.

His simple beauty hooked me instantly. It was a natural phenomenon, the way he could pull me with his eyes. I grazed over his reflection as he spoke. Preoccupied by his body and the vivid recollection of last night's dream, it was a moment before I realized he had asked me something—I wasn't sure what—at the same moment I made the unfortunate (and novice) mistake of allowing my eyes to stop at his most private area. I nervously looked away, praying he hadn't noticed. I had never blatantly searched his body before, but now... curse last night's dream! He watched my eyes inquisitively.

"I'm sorry...you said?"

"I asked if you slept well."

"Yes, thank you." I prayed he hadn't witnessed anything telling while he had stayed with me. How long *had* he stayed? "Thank you for helping me fall asleep."

He smiled then, and appeared further pleased. "Not only do you look like an angel when you sleep, you also look terribly cute in my robe."

I instantly felt foolish. "Oh, I didn't realize—" I stammered.

"Don't worry about it," he said. "I came to tell you we're having breakfast on the patio. Carrie and Aeleise...wanted to make sure you didn't miss their blueberry pancakes. Aeleise knows how much you love...blueberries." The sentence floated conspicuously between us.

My cheeks heated at his innocent words. "You make me feel funny," I said before I thought to sever the connection between mind and speech. I instantly regretted it, but it was too late.

"I do?"

I nodded.

"Funny..." he repeated, as if mulling the word over for hidden meanings. He looked at me carefully. "Maybe we could talk about it after breakfast," he suggested. "If you want to."

I looked into the mirror, directly at his eyes, and swallowed the nervousness that had suddenly hit me. I needed to dismiss a potentially embarrassing discussion. I couldn't possibly talk to Daemon about this—not a chance. "Yeah—I'm starved," I said, blowing off his comment entirely. My voice had risen an octave and become animated; I had magically regressed to twelve. "I'll be down in a second."

I held my cheerleading smile until the door closed behind him. It was nice to know that I could get some mileage out of all that practice, for truly important situations.

After I threw on my clothes, I ran a brush through my hair, then dashed downstairs to meet them outside. The patio table was nicely laid out with four sets of steaming pancakes, fresh orange juice, berries, and syrup. Daemon already sat at the table, sipping a cup of black coffee while he looked through the paper. I took a seat between Carrie and Aeleise, which put Daemon directly in front of me.

"Good morning," Aeleise and Carrie sang in unison.

He peered up from his paper. "Ah, Sleeping Beauty decided to join us." He set down his paper. "Good morning—again."

I was starving. I reached for a fresh blueberry—one of many that surrounded our pancakes.

"Who wants to lead us in grace?" Daemon asked.

I let the blueberry roll back onto the plate.

"I will," Aeleise said, smiling.

We bowed our heads and she began the group prayer.

I noticed the morning paper—or more accurately, the headline. There had been a drug bust, one of considerable significance. I recognized one of the two people in the accompanying photo.

Jalen.

As we sat waiting for the service, I marveled at the people surrounding me. A girl near my age sat cross-legged two aisles in front of me, to my right. She wore a denim miniskirt with pink, sparkly flip-flops. She swung her foot, waiting impatiently for the service to begin. Flip-flops in church? My mother would've suffered a coronary on the spot.

As far as I knew, blue jeans, shorts, short skirts, flip-flops, and halter tops were just not acceptable church attire—at Our Holy Sisters, they were practically illegal, and no one there would let anyone in such clothes through the doors for worship. God enforced a dress code, where I came from.

However, the church that Daemon and his sister attended was astoundingly less rigid, free of traditions and rituals. Here, they actually discussed the Bible and how it applied to our everyday lives, and I found that attitude refreshing.

A pastor rather than a priest led their version of service, and it resembled nothing close to a Catholic mass. He asked us all to rise and sing, yet there were no song missals. Instead, three large screens magically descended from the ceiling, encouraging us to sing along with the words projected onto them. They were songs I'd never heard before, and I nearly went into shock when everyone started clapping their hands, dancing, and swaying to the music. All around me, people smiled as if they were at a concert or a theater show.

For act two, five boys my age went onstage—because there wasn't an altar—and set up their drum sets, electric guitars, basses and microphones. The atmosphere resembled a rock concert as they played songs that reminded me of the grunge music popularized in Seattle. Granted, the words were different—lyrics in praise of the Lord presented in an offbeat manner—but there was nothing solemn or reverent about this service.

We were sitting in folding chairs. There were no pews, nothing to kneel on. In fact, we never knelt once. Was that permissible? Where were the altar boys? Did they disappear along with the altar? Where was the holy water? Where was the incense? Where were the Stations of the Cross? Come to think of it, where *was* the cross? Not to be irreverent, but Jesus wasn't hanging around anywhere. No tabernacle in sight, no Virgin Mary, no Joseph. Not even a confessional—I wasn't all too upset about that. There seemed to be nothing even remotely holy or divine about this place. All my memorized prayers fell useless; not one was ever uttered.

Everyone around me seemed happy to be here. I must admit, I didn't see smiles like that when I attended mass, but *still*. Was this enough respect for the Lord our God? Tank tops, shorts, miniskirts, flip-flops, bubble gum, and groovin'? I just wasn't sure.

Amazingly, Carrie seemed to mesh well with the whole scene. I hadn't expected her to throw away her crystals or magical charms and miraculously convert from this experience alone, but I was a little shocked by her reaction. She hadn't complained once.

The service seemed to fly by, maybe because I was simply too stunned and too busy observing the oddity of it all. I shrugged to myself. Who knew? I left feeling more dazed than confused, and wondered vaguely if I had been to church at all.

I was dreading cheer practice today. After several days without after school practice, I'd now be forced to face Nick.

Carrie and Nick were talking when I arrived. Although disgruntled, Carrie would look at me, at least. She broke away from Nick and headed in my direction, passing those doing warm-up stretches in preparation for practice. We were doing stunts today—not my favorite activity.

Carrie said, "Miss Delaney was just by. There's been a change in formation. Chloe can't perform because she didn't make the mandatory GPA—she's on probation—and you've been given her spot. That makes you flyer."

For a minute, I just looked at her, not saying anything. "Why am I taking her spot? Danya is smaller than I am."

"Don't ask me, that's just what Miss Delaney said."

"Great . . . so now I have to learn all her counts? Which side of the formation is she on? Mine, I hope."

Carrie shook her head. "Nope. Her starting position is the second row on the left. It's only a mirror image—it won't be hard to pick up. She's going to walk you through it, anyway."

I let out a deep breath. I couldn't stand heights. "This sucks. I don't want to be flyer."

Her eyebrows rose. "You're not the only one who thinks it sucks. I know someone who hates the change more than you do."

"More than me?" Was that possible?

"Yeah—who do you think your base is?"

She nodded to the right and my eyes followed her gaze. My stomach fell. Nick's face was scrunched up like that of an angry Gremlin as he and Chloe exchanged words.

Nick? I have to depend on Nick?

Miss Delaney's voice cleared a path through my anxious thoughts as she called for practice to commence. Carrie and I walked toward the group.

Nick gave me a cool glance so fleeting, it couldn't even be considered eye contact. Wonderful. The one person who considered me the Judas of his life was the same person I needed to trust with mine—literally.

I would've liked to laugh at the irony of it—karma, payback, Carrie's magic spells, *whatever*—but I simply couldn't. I'd be lucky if he didn't drop me on my duff or hurl me to Russia. Nick and I didn't exchange a single word the entire time. Not one. Probably because Chloe spent most of the time talking—explaining, then demonstrating the stunts before I'd attempt them myself. If we needed to say anything to one another, we phrased our comments and questions so that they passed conveniently through her. She was the perfect intermediary. The tension was palpable.

I told Brandon about my new fears at practice. Nick had already talked to him. He put my mind at ease. "Trust me, nobody wants to get on my bad side—*especially* Nick. No harm will come to you—he's been warned."

———

Shortly thereafter, Marc broke the news to Carrie about Jalen's arrest. They talked at length before I joined them.

She hadn't taken it well. Her expression was blank, her eyes vacantly zoned on my bedspread. "I can't believe they caught him doing that to someone else. I can't believe..." She shook her head briskly. Her eyes met mine, now full of dread. "I don't want to have to see him again, Kris. Not ever again. I can't."

The possibility of having to appear in court before a sea of judging faces made her sick with fear. But Marc impressed the importance of her pressing charges—not just for herself, but for the future protection of other girls. My attempts to comfort her had little effect, but Marc's reassurances and soothing presence seemed to provide what I couldn't. He promised her that whatever happened, he'd be beside her the entire way. Together they went to the police station and identified Jalen.

24

I was sleeping when the phone rang. I had not spoken to my mother since dance camp and was suspecting it might be her.

I fumbled for the phone. "Hello?" My voice cracked.

"Kris." Definitely not my mother.

"Brandon?"

"Yeah, it's me."

I squinted at the pink glow of the alarm clock: 1:57 A.M.

"It's two A.M.," I said.

"I know what time it is."

"What are you still doing up?" I propped up on one elbow and rubbed the sleep from my eyes with my free hand.

"I'm up," was all he said.

"And you're calling because ...?"

"You're the closest thing I know to Superwoman? Can you take on a rescue mission right now?"

There was an underlying tension in his casual words. "What's going on?" I asked.

He hesitated for a moment. "I need your help, Kris. I need you to come pick up Ryan and me."

"What's wrong?" I asked, suddenly worried.

"I can't explain right now."

"Where are you?"

"I'm in Coto de Caza. At a friend's house"

"Are you okay?" He didn't answer. "Have you been drinking?"

"Something like that. Can you do it?"

"Brandon, I don't even drive. How am I supposed to pick you up?" I considered possibilities, those I knew who owned cars. Still, who would be willing, at two in the morning? "I suppose I could try Josh or Marc," I thought aloud. "Josh does seem to have an affinity for Ryan these days."

"Exactly. That's why Josh can't be here."

"Why not?"

"I don't want to screw up Josh's affection for Ryan; he values your brother's friendship."

"You're not making any sense."

"We'll talk about it later. I need you to come alone."

"Alone? How do you expect me to get there?"

"I'll send a town car to pick you up. I wouldn't ask you if I didn't really need your help."

He was being so cryptic. "Brandon…"

"Can you do it or not, Kris?"

The strange sound in his voice suddenly made my decision easy. "Yes. I'll do it," I said. "I'll be waiting. They'll have to pick me up at the corner. If Marc catches me leaving, I can't think of any excuse he'd buy at two A.M."

"Good point. And don't worry, the driver knows how to get here."

I thought about Josh's refrain that he was always one step ahead of me when I was doing something wrong. This time I decided to give him a head's up. Marc had broken down and gotten us cell phones with a family plan. I knew Josh would never check his text messages until the morning so I sent him a text telling him that I was on a mission with Ryan to help a friend and we were taking a town car paid for by Brandon. Okay, it was a lie but if by any chance someone found my bed empty they could call the phone and find me safe and sound (and sober).

Brandon stood waiting at the curb outside a posh estate when we pulled up twenty minutes later. He walked over to the car and assisted me out. He took my hand and led me toward an iron gate that barred entry to a long curve of driveway limned with golden lamplight. We climbed the drive toward a dark mansion whose front entry was monstrous in scale. When we reached the large, oak double doors with their decorative crystal windows, we stood outside on the step.

Brandon let go of my hand, leaned back against the wall. I stood in front of him, wondering why he'd paused.

"Thank you for coming," he said.

"Thank me later. I still don't know why I'm here. What's going on?"

He turned his head to look at the extravagant double doors. "Ryan's inside and he's wrecked, Kris."

"What's wrong with him?"

He paused, as if reluctant to tell me. "He's on ecstasy and . . ."

"And what?" I asked, now impatient. I thought I had been summoned for an urgent matter; why was he stalling? Weren't we wasting valuable time?

"He's been drinking—more than he should have," he said.

"You look scared."

"I'm not scared."

I wasn't going to argue over something that showed clearly on his face. "Fine. Why was he drinking, or partying, at all? That's not even like him."

"I know. His curiosity got the better of him."

I studied Brandon. I hated to doubt him, but I had to ask. "Where did it come from? You didn't give it to him, did you?"

His eyes flashed—offended at first, then just disappointed. "No, Kris, I didn't give it to him. That would make a lot of sense—to preach the evils of drugs and then turn around and push them on my friends."

I let out a sigh. "I'm sorry I doubted you. So, how bad is he? Is he passed out?"

"No." He dropped his eyes.

I waited expectantly, knowing full well there was more he wasn't telling me.

"He's too far gone to think reasonably," he said finally. "Kris, at best, everyone in this house is wearing fifty percent less than I am.

I'm afraid of how he'll react if someone hits on him. He shouldn't be here right now."

"Who all's here?" I asked.

"There's me, Ryan, two guys you don't know—Kyle and Shayne—and then there's Nial; this is his house. There are a few others, but I don't know who they are."

I recognized the name Shayne. Was it the same Shayne once intimately involved with Brandon?

"Everyone's partying; Ryan started drinking, then took the ecstasy they offered him. I told him not to take it but he didn't listen." He shook his head. "He wanted to see what it's like. Well, now he knows—it's hitting him hard; he's already thrown up once. But..." He looked down at his shoes. "It's only going to get worse. This isn't the place he should be." He gave me his eyes. "It's going to be a bad scene, Kris. We just need to get him out of here."

He grabbed the gold-plated door handle and pushed against the door.

I followed him, and he quietly closed the door behind me. He hadn't said to keep our voices down, but it happened naturally and seemed to be appropriate in the situation. I felt as if we were sneaking in; for all I knew, we were.

We stood on marble tiles laid in an elaborate mosaic pattern throughout the grand foyer. The house stretched on forever; long marble-floored hallways extended on either side of us, and a monstrosity of a crystal chandelier hung above our heads. The lights were low, despite the hundreds of sparkling diamond teardrops. Their glow imparted a warm, sleepy feeling to the room, which opened on what looked like a living room, and beyond it, outside, a pool was illuminated by blue and green lights.

"Where is he?" I asked.

Brandon pointed down one of the halls. "I managed to get him into the bathroom before I called you."

"You couldn't find someone to help you move him to a bed or a couch somewhere?"

"Trust my judgment, Kris. I didn't ask for assistance, for good reason. My idea of help wouldn't resemble theirs—not once they saw his condition. I had to call you from the phone upstairs so I wouldn't raise suspicion. As it is, they think I'm taking him on a tour of the grounds. It will buy us the most time."

"Well, let's go get him, then." I headed in the direction he had pointed.

Brandon gently grabbed my arm. "Kris, before we do, there's something you should know."

"Okay ... that is?"

"He thinks he's in the Garden of Eden."

"Huh?"

"Not *literally*; I mean, he's chillin' in the buff."

That stopped me. I gave him a wary look. "Why is he naked?"

"Because he's higher than a kite and being naked feels incredible in his state. He managed to get his clothes off while I was upstairs. I just wanted to prepare you." He regarded me seriously. "Will you be able to handle it?"

To see Ryan unclothed didn't seem right. But if he needed my help, I'd deal with it. No doubt he'd be just as uncomfortable with the idea as I was. I nodded, striving for maturity.

"Ecstasy does a number on your senses, Kris. He's overwhelmed right now. I'm forewarning you, he may get handsy. If he starts to get out of line, whatever happens, just try to keep in mind that it's only because he's high."

Great. The last thing I wanted was Ryan pawing me. "Anything else?"

"That's it."

I took a deep breath and let it out. "Okay then, let's do this."

I followed Brandon down a dimly lit hallway until we stopped in front of a closed door. He looked at me one final time before he went in. I followed behind him and closed the door quietly; I kept my back against the door.

Sure enough, just as Brandon had warned, Ryan was completely bare. He lay on a gray, furry rug; he hadn't looked back when we entered.

I'd grown so used to seeing Ryan in his football gear, battling aggressively out on the field, that what lay before me now seemed fragile by comparison — he looked too vulnerable to ever have demonstrated that kind of brutality. Was this really the same boy?

Ryan nestled against the rug. He seemed extremely content, slowly rocking himself, running his fingers through the soft nap of the rug. He brushed his cheek against it.

Brandon looked at me, gauging my reaction, but I kept my face carefully neutral.

Brandon approached Ryan and knelt before him. "Ryan. Ryan," he said gently.

Ryan sighed, lost in the pleasure of it all.

Brandon touched his arm. "Look at me, Ryan. I need you to sit up. I'm going to try to get you out of here."

"I'm happy where I am," Ryan replied dreamily. "Just leave me here."

"I can't leave you in the bathroom, Ryan. Come on." With one hand, he brushed back Ryan's sweaty bangs to make eye contact. "We'll go home and you can get in bed where it's clean and comfortable." Brandon ran his hand up and down Ryan's arm in an attempt to win his cooperation. "Come on."

Ryan shrugged Brandon away. He slid his freed arm low against his body, then turned his face from Brandon until he was staring at the floor. "Don't touch me," he said, his voice falling unnaturally quiet. "Go away."

Brandon sat back on his heels, baffled by the order. "What?"

"I mean it, Brandon — this isn't cool. Don't think just because..." Ryan struggled to remain calm, but his anxiety seemed to be growing. "Just 'cause you and Aiden screw around, don't think I want to."

Brandon was taken aback. "Don't be an idiot, Ryan. I know that. You're *high*. It's the ecstasy. A troll could touch you and your body would respond. Don't be daft. I'm going to try and help you dress, so we can get the hell out of here." He reached for Ryan, ready to assist him to his feet.

"Don't." Ryan jerked back. "Brandon, don't... I'm not getting up; not right now."

Brandon rose, struck by Ryan's words. "I can't just leave you lying here on the floor, fucked up and naked in someone else's house. *Jesus,* Ryan. Be reasonable."

Ryan remained unswayed.

Brandon exhaled, irritated. "Fine. If you won't let me help you, then Krista will."

"Krista's here?"

"Yes. She came to help you."

"I don't want Krista to see me this way."

"Too late," I said. I walked over to him, careful not to let my gaze stray from his face. "Come on. We're taking you out of here." I held out my hand to him.

He slowly concaved like a shrimp, bringing his knees to his chest. "Oh my God," he said, voice lower than a whisper. His face flamed red as he prayed to the floor, "Please tell me this isn't happening."

I knelt beside Ryan. He cuddled against the rug as if it was his sole comfort—a world as soft and comforting as clouds of cotton balls. I placed my hand on his cheek and turned his face to me; he still refused my eyes.

I tried to reason with him gently. "Ryan, listen to me. Don't make this any more difficult than it has to be. This may seem like heaven to you, but the reality is, you're lying on someone's filthy bathroom rug, sweating and shivering. We can do better than this, Ryan. Come on; we need to get going." When I got no response, I tried again. "We'll go someplace where we can kick back and not have to worry about it."

Still nothing.

Brandon tried to lighten the mood. "Look, Ryan, if it'll make you feel better, when we get home, we'll both flash you so we can all feel like imbeciles, and then you can call it even. But let us help you. I know you would do the same for either of us."

I shot Brandon a stern look beneath my brows, surprised he had volunteered my participation in his unorthodox tactics. He shrugged and shook his head with a wry expression. I knew then that they were just words to Brandon, nothing based in truth.

"Whatever works," he said.

It caught Ryan's interest. Brandon's wit brought forth a silly smile from Ryan, almost a giggle in his unpredictable state. He finally met my eyes. His were glassy, his pupils dilated to nearly the size of dimes, leaving only the faintest edge of his crystal-blue eyes visible. The Husky had gone undercover. "You'd flash me just so I'd let you help me?" He grinned foolishly.

Lie or not, my heart relaxed, knowing we finally had something to work with. "Ryan, I'd do almost anything to get you off this filthy floor. You can be cute about it later. Now, come on."

I gave him my hand, and—*hallelujah*—he accepted it. He managed to shield his lower body, demonstrating skill akin to that of a contortionist as he moved almost in a huddle. I grabbed his other shoulder and helped him to sit upright as much as he would let me.

I scanned our surroundings. "Where are your clothes?"

His eyes drifted in and out of focus. "I don't know."

"They were here after I called, Kris," Brandon said, pointing to the corner as he looked at Ryan. "Who came in here when I went outside to wait for her?"

The look on Brandon's face had me worried.

Ryan's eyes were closed. "When did you leave to get Kris?"

My gaze met Brandon's. His jaw clenched, then he looked at the ceiling. "*Dammit*, Ryan!" He shook his head.

I sat with Ryan while Brandon searched throughout the house for his clothing. He rested his head against my chest. His body shook as he burned with perspiration. He huddled against me, and I wrapped my arms around his shoulders, tried to keep him warm. The vents above us raged silently, emitting a frosty breeze that permeated my clothes. I knew it was unhealthy to have Ryan exposed to this temperature in his condition. I marveled that he was so warm; I was freezing, and I was clothed.

Sounds traveled across the hall as Brandon scrambled about in a nearby room. My mind scrambled in the bathroom. What had prompted Ryan to disrobe? Where were his clothes, and had he been alone?

I heard footsteps approaching. Brandon had returned. He shut the door behind him.

"I found everything except the underwear," he said, sounding slightly out of breath.

"I didn't wear any," Ryan said, a careless air about him.

That solved that.

Dressing Ryan turned out to be like trying to dance with a Gumby doll. Once we restored Ryan to a fully clothed state, our next goal was to get out of the mansion. Ryan walked sluggishly with Brandon's aid as I helped facilitate our way to the front door. The hallways stretched on forever, an arduous expedition.

When we reached the front entrance, Brandon searched his pockets. "Kris, I forgot my keys. Can you hold him for a second while I go get them?"

I stood in the foyer supporting Ryan with one arm around his waist, one of his around my shoulder. This entire ordeal had proved unnaturally draining—physically and emotionally—for all of us. Exhausted, I looked to the floor as if it would somehow relieve me.

A sound grabbed my attention and my gaze lifted. Not more than twenty yards down the hallway, a boy stood in his underwear.

Barefoot, he padded along the corridor, then stopped at one of many doors, tried to open it, and found it locked. He leaned back against the wall, waiting for ... *what?*

Even from a distance, he looked dazed; his eyes, glazed, stared off into nowhere. His eyes had closed. It was a moment before he opened them and noticed us. His face held no hint of surprise, no desire for modesty; in fact, once he saw us, he headed shamelessly in our direction.

My stomach tightened instinctively.

As he neared, the appeal of his tan skin and pleasant build was undeniable. His hair swayed as he walked; it fell evenly above his shoulders, slightly wavy and golden enough to polish. From seven feet away, his eyes—the vibrant, turquoise-blue of a tropical ocean—struck me. He belonged inside one of Brandon's taboo magazines—the perfect centerfold.

Within moments, this dazzling nymph stood unabashedly before us in nothing but black briefs. He was older than Ryan, though not by much—wedged within that vague category between boy and man.

I stared. Catching the clouds in his dream-state eyes, I knew he had partaken of the party favors, too.

He stood before us, invading my personal space, at least; Ryan didn't seem to notice or care. He looked at Ryan, looked at me, looked at Ryan again. He was curious enough.

I locked eyes with him. His gaze faltered, revealed his uncertainty. He was as suspicious of me as I was of him. "Are you leaving, Ryan?" he asked. He had an appealingly rich voice that reminded me of after-hour commercials promoting adventurous, late-night phone calls.

"Looks like it," Ryan said, sounding too dreamy for my taste.

"You don't want to stay?"

Time to clear his confusion right up. I intruded curtly with, "He has other engagements to attend."

Golden Boy looked at me, his wide aqua eyes full of wonder at my announcement, further snuffing out any hope that there was any substance behind the flashy packaging. To him I was as foreign as a unicorn, and now, by denying him the object of his desire, I had uttered something beyond his comprehension. He turned back to Ryan.

"Is this your girlfriend?"

I grew defensive and snapped, "Yes, I am," before Ryan could say otherwise.

My outright lie dampened his spirit. "Oh … I thought — "

"You thought wrong," I said.

He studied me longer than was comfortable. Probably wondering why Ryan preferred my company to his. Then he turned back to Ryan. "Well, I had a cool time talking to you," he said in that intoxicating voice of his. He placed his hand on Ryan's arm. "It's too bad you have to take off; I wish you could stay."

I bet. I pulled Ryan away from him, ending the contact, and gave him my sweetest condescending smile. "I don't like people touching him."

He looked at me with a touch of surprise. "Sorry."

Sure he was. I glared at him.

He turned to Ryan. "Well, I hope I can see you again."

"Hope for something else," I said.

He gave me a disapproving look, then sauntered away in his undies.

I was pissed. How *dare* that strange boy eye Ryan as if he were a tasty piece of chocolate. I'd have a word with Brandon about this. What was taking him so long, anyway? My muscles ached beneath the taxing weight of Ryan's body; I was tiring quickly.

Ryan groaned and twisted his body. "My arm is falling asleep, Kris."

"I know; I'm sorry. Brandon should be here soon." Although letting him sit and lean against the wall would be a relief for both of us, it wasn't worth the effort it would take to get him up again.

Brandon swept around the corner. "Okay," he said as he approached, "I think I have everything. Let's split."

He dashed to my assistance just as my arms felt ready to give out. He hoisted one of Ryan's arms over his shoulder and I did the same with his other, sharing the burden of his weight between us. On the count of three, we lifted, and Ryan's feet barely brushed the floor.

We carried him out the door and made for the car, Brandon's sapphire beauty, which seemed like a luxury getaway car tonight. He opened the backseat door. "Kris, do you mind sitting in back with him while I drive?"

I slid into the seat while Brandon held Ryan, then assisted Ryan into the car, pulling him toward me.

Just before Brandon closed the door, he peeked inside the car. "I forgot one last thing, Kris. I need to run inside for a moment. I promise I'll make it quick." He was gone before I could open my mouth.

Ryan rested his head in my lap as he lay on his side. We waited in the dark.

It seemed as if we'd been waiting for Brandon forever.

I rested my hand on Ryan's shoulder. The sound of doors shutting came from nearby, and I looked toward the house. Brandon jogged down the lamp-lit driveway, eyes fixed on the pavement. He opened the driver's side door, got inside, and slammed it shut.

"Sorry about that. Ready?"

"What took you so long?" I asked.

"I just needed to say goodbye to my friends."

I stared at him in dismay. *"Friends?* What kind of friends throw parties like these? You were gone forever."

"Sorry, Kris." He looked back over his shoulder at his best friend lying in the backseat, and through the subtle movement of air, I caught the faintest scent of unfamiliar cologne. His face hung like a gray curtain; undisguised concern played along the creases of his forehead. "How's he doing?" he asked.

"I think he's fine. But let's get him someplace where he can get comfortable."

"I'm taking him to my house. Are you coming with us, or do you want me to drop you off at home?"

"I'm here, aren't I? I'm in for the duration."

He gave me an appreciative look, almost a smile. "Thanks, Kris."

I sat back in my seat and tried to relax—not easy to do. Three A.M. had passed long ago; we were out past curfew on a school night. Two of us were under the influence of alcohol; one was behind the wheel, the other was whacked on drugs. I prayed the entire car ride home that we weren't caught. God heard my pleas.

25

We finally arrived at Brandon's house and escorted Ryan to the guest room. Brandon's mother as usual was nowhere around.

I looked at Ryan. "We should get you into the bath. You'll feel better once you're clean and can slip beneath fresh sheets. How does that sound?"

"I don't know that..." he began, then sighed. He finished with, "It's too much work."

"It's necessary work. You're filthy, Ryan. Come—you'll feel much better afterward. I promise."

I held out my hand, but he didn't take it. He shook his head, unconvinced and dreamy-eyed. "I don't think I can, Kris. I don't feel with-it enough."

"We'll make sure you don't drown," Brandon said with a smirk.

"Come on." I took his hand and, with Brandon's assistance, got him to his feet. Brandon and I had decided that between the two of us it would be less embarrassing for me to help him than Brandon given that Ryan knew of Brandon's sexual preference. Even though the guys were close friends, Brandon's experience with Ryan was that he could be homophobic which was why his partying with the guys this evening was so biazarre. Anyway, I was nominated to give him the bath.

The bath adjoining the guest room was like a backstage dressing room with its Jacuzzi tub and, along the opposite wall, a string of hot lights over the mirrored vanity.

"How are we going to do this?" he asked.

"I'm going to help you, silly. Sit here."

I sat him on the closed toilet seat. He wilted like spinach.

Ryan watched me in a hazy, relaxed manner. His smile resembled that of a man who had just won the lottery and was still basking in the shock.

I drew his bath, and sat on the side of the dark marble tub, waiting for it to fill. We didn't talk; I watched him. The room began to fog with steam. I ran my fingers through the water, testing the temperature. Hot.

"Your bath is ready," I said. "Get in."

His brows knitted tighter. "I don't know, Kris. I've never done this before."

"Never taken a bath?" I teased.

"Not in front of a girl."

"Well, surely your mother bathed you when you were younger."

He attempted to give me his best wry look, but in his drugged state, it came out looking weary. "You're not my mother."

"Get serious."

"I don't think this is going to work."

"Ryan, what's the big deal?"

He looked up at me beneath his baby-doll lashes.

A stretch of silence followed; he made no move to stand.

"Can we get you into the bath before the water gets cold?" I asked.

He looked at me, then dropped his eyes to the floor again. He pulled his shirt off. I made sure he didn't topple over when he bent over to untie his shoes. He pushed them off with his feet, pulled off his socks, then took my offered hand so he could stand. Once he was on his feet, I steadied him by the shoulders as he worked his jeans off and clumsily stepped out of them.

Brandon sat on his bed, looking as if he needed sleep. "Everything going okay?" he asked when he saw me.

"So far. Do you think it's okay to leave him in there by himself? He seems out of it—as if he's in La-La Land or something."

"He is—he's peaking."

"That's a good thing, I hope?"

He barked a tired laugh. "That's the moment he's been waiting for."

"So we don't need to worry?"

"Not unless you're worried about him dying of bliss."

"Brandon, explain something to me."

"Yes?"

He gave me a teasing smile. "I take it you haven't *peeked*."

"*Brandon . . .*"

He chuckled, shook his head. "You *are* precious, aren't you."

"Don't patronize me; I'm serious."

"Ahh, yes," he said with a small smile. "You always have played by the rules."

"I just want to know if he's going to look or act normal anytime soon. He looks like he's in some heavenly slow-mo trance."

"He is. I have a feeling that the stuff he took is cut with heroin —which has a tendency to do that."

"*Heroin?* Are you joking?"

"I never joke about drugs, Kris. I didn't see what all they were passing around, but Nial—he's virtually the Willy Wonka of drugs. Anything you could possibly want is at your fingertips in that house. Nial's ecstasy is usually the purest money can buy, but there have been times when it's been cut with speed or heroin; they're just different highs."

"How do you know so much?"

"When I dabbled, I didn't do it lightly."

"I better go check on Ryan."

There was just enough room for me to sit on the edge of the tub. I grabbed the soap beside me, sudsed the washcloth, then began to wash his back. Self-consciousness crept over me as I tended to him. "You're so quiet," I said.

He rested the side of his face on his knees. Strands of dark hair clung loosely around his eyes; teardrops of water slid down his face to his knees. His arms were wrapped about his legs, but they were relaxed; his earlier tension seemed to have slipped away. His eyes were unfocused, though his gaze was directed at me. He blinked, serene and innocent. It was nice to finally see him peaceful. He absently held out a limp arm for me, and I washed it gently, sudsing his skin clean, then moved on to the next one. He never said a word.

"What are you thinking about?" I asked. He looked so tranquil I was almost jealous. "Wherever you're at, I wish I was there."

"Me too," he said.

"How so?"

My question brought him back from his drifting. Aware again of where he was and who was bathing him, he suddenly tightened up. "This is a bad idea," he decided. "It's nice of you to help, but I think you should go."

"If you want me to stay, I don't mind."

He shook his head, his eyes tired, vague. "You don't get it. This whole thing is wrong."

"How is it wrong?"

The silence lasted a healthy length of time, the only sounds borne from the movement of water about him, and the occasional isolated drops of water that joined the pool.

He opened his mouth as if ready to respond, but no words came out.

I leaned closer to see if he was okay, and the heat of the water rose against my face. "What is it?"

He stared at his knees. "I can't take anymore of this. It's driving me nuts!"

His answer, taut with restraint, emerged sounding strangled. I had stopped washing him without realizing it, unsure how to react.

He didn't look at me, but kept his voice calm. "I don't feel all together, right now; I don't trust myself to not try something stupid and ... I don't want to screw up."

"Screw up?"

He looked at me then, and I couldn't describe the look in his eyes. Hurt? Bitterness? Whatever it was, it remained there with fixed intensity. "Don't you get it? This entire situation is confusing me."

His forehead pinched. "I *want* you, Kris. You're close enough for me to touch — but I can't.

"Brandon's sitting in the next room and he's done everything with you that I've wanted to do, and I'm sitting here ... naked ... in front of you, fantasizing about it. It's maddening, Kris. Having you touch me, and knowing I can't touch you back, is the same as being teased. Don't do it — please."

My eyes widened and I leaned farther back. "I'm sorry. I didn't mean to — I wouldn't purposely ..."

He turned his face away from me so all I could see was the nape of his neck. "Can I be alone, please?"

"Sure," I said, feeling more than awkward now. Emotionally, I felt frayed. I had naked admissions from Ryan, and I wasn't referring to his lack of clothing. I wasn't prepared for the anger tied to his feelings, wasn't sure how to respond to him as a friend. Now that he had placed his feelings in my hands, what was I supposed to do with them?

"Let me guess — he had difficulty behaving himself?" Brandon looked lazily amused.

I just stared at him.

"It's to be expected, Kris." He touched my arm. "Hey, are you okay? He didn't get out of hand with you, did he?"

I shook my head.

"I shouldn't have let you go back in there. I'm sorry."

"I'm fine."

"No, you're not; I can tell you're upset. What happened?"

The words hummed in my head as if I had just heard them. "He told me, in a most unsubtle way, that —" I shook my head, deciding not to repeat what he'd said. I looked at Brandon. "Is it the drug talking?"

"If I'm anything close to guessing what he said, then ... no. I'm afraid that's the truth."

Brandon motioned me toward him, and I walked over to where he sat perched on the frame of his ocean-like bed. I stood between his legs and he wrapped his arms around my waist in a hug.

"This isn't one of Ryan's finer moments—I know it's difficult to see him this way. It isn't easy for him to be around you like this; he's been hoping for a long time."

I stood with Brandon's arms around me, his head resting against my stomach, my arms around his shoulders. I could feel how tired he was.

"We should wait for him in his room," Brandon said. "Let's go."

Brandon and I were seated on the bed when Ryan emerged from the bathroom. We rose simultaneously. Ryan leaned against the doorway for support. He had succeeded in wrapping a towel around his waist. The bath had been a good idea. Not only was he clean, he seemed more grounded in the familiar surroundings of Brandon's home.

Then he looked at me. His words were still fresh in my mind and, I gathered, in his, too—I understood when he quickly shifted his gaze, uncomfortable with what he'd shared. He looked at Brandon, obviously wondering if I'd shared his confession with him...His jaw tensed. I suppose he was in his right to feel resentful.

Exhausted, I walked past Brandon and took a seat in a small chair near the back of the room.

"Do you want to borrow something to sleep in?" Brandon asked.

"No. The clothes drive me crazy."

Tired, Brandon sighed. "Kris is staying the night, so be considerate."

"She's staying?"

"Yes."

"In your bed?" he asked, in a soft, accusatory tone.

Brandon looked at Ryan and said with a hint of dryness, "No, not in my bed. She'll be staying in the guest room beside you. Happy?"

"Yes."

Ryan walked toward the bed, staring at Brandon as he struggled to balance on unsteady legs. Something still bothered him, but considering the night's events, it could be anything. Brandon turned to leave and I got up to follow.

"You aren't going, are you? Don't leave on my account, Brandon. I was just warming up to the idea of us hanging out alone. I hear you're big on naked get-togethers; I thought that was your idea of fun."

Brandon turned around too calmly. "Do you want company?" he asked. "I thought you might welcome some time alone. Some privacy, perhaps?"

Ryan laughed softly, almost to himself. "That's okay. Unlike you, I won't die if I don't get off."

Brandon smiled cruelly. "No, just from perpetual frustration. Are you asking me to stay and help you? Is that what you want? Or are you merely angry that Krista isn't at your disposal to be your bed partner? There's a reason I told you not to take it, Ryan. Now you're finding out the hard way. Fun, isn't it?"

"We're best friends, right?" Ryan replied. "We can talk."

Brandon waited.

Ryan stared at the floor; a moment later, he looked up at Brandon and a small smile crept across his lips. The gentleness in his voice didn't match the look of contempt in his eyes. "So, tell me—am I the only friend left you haven't fucked?"

Brandon's face slid effortlessly into cool, impenetrable stone. "My patience is not endless, Ryan. Don't piss me off."

Ryan ignored the warning, grinned lazily. "I'm serious. I am, aren't I?" He smiled, and slowly ran his hand across his bare stomach, turning a normal act into something suggestively overt. "Were you hoping that would change tonight? Or... am I not good enough for you?"

"Ryan, if you could hear yourself right now, you'd be horrified," Brandon said.

"Tempted?"

"Offering?" Brandon asked just as snidely in return. He shook his head at Ryan's smirk. "Good night, Ryan." He headed for the door.

"I want to see Krista first."

Brandon turned around, irritated, and swept his hand in my direction. "Then turn around. She's been here the entire time."

Ryan looked back over his shoulder and smiled when he saw me, not at all embarrassed by his behavior or lack of clothing. I'd never seen Ryan act this way; I didn't like it.

"I'd like to be alone with her. Or is that against the rules?"

"I never set any rules, Ryan. Kris makes her own decisions. But if she decides to stay with you, you'd better watch yourself."

"*Watch* myself? She'll be naked in a room with *you*—a damn *predator*—and you're afraid to leave her alone with *me*? That's rich."

"Don't talk as if she's not in the room. No—normally I wouldn't worry, but you see, *I'm* not high or acting irrationally. You're being an *ass,* Ryan. Why don't you save your hostility toward me until later, when you can think clearly, and we'll deal with it then?" He waved his hand in my direction. "Go ahead, ask her if she'll stay; it's not up to me." He stared at Ryan, then added the warning, "But cool it."

"Worried? Jealous?"

I wanted to flee the tension and aggravation building around me, and should have.

"Try *concerned.* I know where you're at; I've been high on Nial's candy more times than you have functioning brain cells. I *know* how you feel and I *know* what's running through your mind—no subtitles needed."

"Really? I thought you didn't look at girls that way. Or did Crestmount's favorite fag suddenly turn bisexual?"

Brandon's face paled. His words came like calm ice. "Don't be a punk, Ryan—and don't speak to me that way. You're pressing your luck."

Brandon made his last restrained effort at civility. "Ryan, Krista's our *friend.* I know it's difficult under the circumstances, but try not to let your dick do your thinking. You'll end up doing something stupid, and you'll regret it in the morning."

"Of course she's our friend ... but *you're* the one who fucked her, and now *this,* coming from you?" He chuckled at the advice. "Are you saying that you regret sleeping with Kris?"

His words felt like a slap. I looked hesitantly at Brandon, surprised to see the degree of rage that swept through his body.

Stepping forward, he closed the distance between himself and Ryan. Anger burned in his eyes. He spoke slowly, his voice calm, steady, and oh-so controlled. "If you *ever* disrespect Krista, or speak that way in front of her again ... I *will* kick the shit out of you."

Ryan, stunned by the confrontation, didn't move.

Brandon turned to me, walked over, and took my hand. "Come, Krista. We'll give *Master* Ryan some time alone until he can find some manners."

I followed him silently out of the room. We went to Brandon's room and closed the door. He was still trembling with anger.

"I'm sorry. But *no one,* not even Ryan, can speak that way and expect me to accept it." He walked to his couch and sat hunched over with his elbows on his knees. He lowered his face into his hands and rubbed his expression away, as if trying to wake himself from the nightmare. He raked his hands through his hair, then shook his head. His face was tight, his body tense. "I don't know what he took tonight — or whether he does — but whatever it was, it was a hell of a lot more than ecstasy and alcohol. He shouldn't be that belligerent."

I looked at Brandon. I didn't know what to think anymore. I was glad he'd stood up for me, and I understood his anger, to a point. Ryan had insulted him on multiple levels; he'd upset me, too. But I also tried to remember Brandon's earlier words — that the drugs were making him behave this way.

I tried to make sense of it. What had caused such a caustic change in Ryan? What was the real reason behind his outrageous behavior? I sat on Brandon's waterbed, considering. My thoughts returned to the party we'd just left.

"How could you take him there?" I asked, feeling a hint of anger.

"Kris, I swear to you — I had no idea what Nial's plans were for the evening. We went there for an entirely different reason. I was just as surprised as you were."

"Then what was your reason for going there in the first place?"

"I was bringing Nial something."

"What?" I demanded.

He almost looked embarrassed. "I was bringing him the paper I wrote for my Art History class. He said he wanted to read it. That, and I wanted to pick up some new logic puzzles. He likes to challenge me—likes to see if I can figure them out." He shrugged. "It gives me something to do when I'm bored." His head dropped and he fidgeted with the hem of his shirt. "The whole thing just backfired on me. This wasn't supposed to happen."

I hadn't anticipated his answer. It sounded simple, but coming from Brandon, it was anything but. If he'd told me something petty and frivolous as expected, that would've given me an excuse to yell. But he hadn't, and I knew he was being honest.

A thought came to me. "Is he going to remember any of this tomorrow?"

"Hard to say. I'm sure some of it, he will; some of it, he may not. The mind's a funny thing, Kris. You'd be surprised what it can protect you from when things become too much. We'll have to wait and see."

I entered Ryan's room and closed the door behind me. The room was dim, lit only by the pyramid lamp glowing at its weakest setting. Ryan lay face down on the bed, still unclothed; he hadn't looked to see who entered. I walked over and sat down beside him. My fingers brushed his hair.

"If that's you, Brandon, I was kidding." His pillow muffled his voice.

"It's not Brandon," I said. "Is it okay that I'm here?"

He lifted his head and looked at me over his shoulder.

"Are you okay?" I asked.

He nodded and said, his voice low, "I'm sorry for what I said. I know Brandon didn't regret being with you."

"Don't worry about it. It's finished. I just wanted to make sure you're okay."

"Thanks."

He rose to his elbows, twisted his torso so he could see me. He studied me quietly with joyless, empty eyes. His disheveled hair made him appear especially young. "You look uncomfortable," he said.

"Well, you're still not wearing a stitch of clothing."

"Oh ... sorry," he said. He grabbed the closest pillow and shielded himself behind it, then pulled part of the comforter around his body.

He looked back at me, his eyes steadfast. "Are you ever going to tell me what it was like—being with him?"

His request startled me. "Ryan, that's not something you want to hear."

"Yes, it is."

"Why?"

"Can't I be curious? You guys *are* supposed to be my friends—he's supposedly my best friend—but ever since you came into the picture, he hasn't shared a word." His brows drew down across his forehead. "Do you understand that I *told* him how much I liked you, only to find *him* in bed with you the next minute? I couldn't help feeling burned. Do I have to be in the dark about the whole thing? I'd like to know what's going on."

"Ryan ..."

"I can handle it—really. I wasn't ready to hear it before, but I'm ready now."

I took a deep breath and let it out. What could I possibly tell him? What if Brandon was listening right outside the door? He'd hear everything I said. Not that he didn't already know the details; he'd been there too. But sharing that kind of intimate information felt awkward.

"I don't know what to tell you," I said.

His eyes were poised on me intently. "Well, did you like it?" he asked, getting right to the point.

I squirmed in my skin. I realized I had never told Brandon how I felt about that night—at least, not directly. Maybe inadvertently he knew that I'd enjoyed it—after all, I *had* inquired about his unexpected proficiency—but otherwise, I hadn't mentioned it. I couldn't help feeling as if I'd taken him and his willingness to help me for granted. He had done me a favor and I hadn't even thanked him.

"Uh ... yeah," I managed to say after a minute. I cleared my throat, continued in a mellow voice, "Sure ... I liked it." My cheeks warmed. I couldn't believe I was telling this to his best friend. I hadn't even gone into this with Carrie. Then again, she'd never wanted to know.

"Did you feel weird about it—I mean, it being Brandon and all?"

"It was…intimidating, I guess. He's already experienced and everything; it's not like I knew what I was doing."

Though he pretended to be only mildly interested, his casual tone didn't fool me. "So…did you drool over his body, like every other girl?"

"Why all the questions about Brandon?" I countered.

"I just want to know."

I looked at him carefully. Ryan was younger than Brandon—not much, but enough. Maybe he looked up to Brandon, or something. I didn't know. The memory of my night with Brandon remained vivid in my mind. A flashback hit me and I looked down at the comforter, tried not to blush. It didn't help.

When I looked up, Ryan was smiling at me. "That look alone tells me enough. I guess he's not your average sophomore."

"I'd say not."

"I wonder how it feels to have everybody want you that way."

His honesty surprised me. Ryan truly was good-looking, even if he couldn't recognize that. "Lots of girls like you. What are you talking about?"

"Lots of girls want to be my *friend*. It's not the same thing."

"Ryan, you and Brandon are entirely different people. Brandon's also older than you and he surfs every waking minute. You have no reason to worry. You already look great."

He cast his eyes down, hedging on the next question: "Have you already compared me to him?"

Okay, so I had seen both their bodies. But I wasn't taking notes or anything. "I'm not drawing any comparisons, so don't worry about it."

"Do you want to sleep with him again?" he asked quickly.

"It was a one-time thing. We did it for a reason."

"That doesn't mean you can't want to do it again."

I crossed my legs and abruptly sat straighter. "I'm through with this question and answer session," I said.

He smiled lightly, looking down at the bedspread. "Thanks, Kris."

"Yeah, whatever."

He rolled onto his back, laced his hands behind his head, and gazed at the ceiling. "He's my best friend and I envy him so much." I heard longing, not bitterness.

"Why, Ryan?"

He humphed. "Do you have a week? The list is long. I don't know." He shook his head, quietly frustrated. "You're just comfortable with him...in a different way. It makes me jealous as hell." He turned his head to look at me.

"Brandon and I have been through a lot together. It's not like I'm trying to exclude you."

He looked away. "I know. I'm sorry for the way I've been acting around you. I guess it's pretty immature."

"Don't worry about it."

"This isn't exactly how I imagined the evening would go."

"What did you think you guys were going to do?"

He shrugged. "I don't know. It's not like we made specific plans. Brandon just said he had to stop by Nial's. There were some guys there that he knew—Brandon introduced me. They seemed cool." He shrugged again. "They asked me to party with 'em, and...so I did. Then one of his friends started talking to me; we got into a heavy conversation. I'm not blind—I could tell he was interested, I just didn't feel threatened by it. Shayne was cool. I wasn't going to freak out on him just because maybe he liked me."

"Was he hitting on you?"

The look he gave me matched his dry tone. "By the time he had his hand on my thigh, I got the hint, yeah."

"Why didn't you tell him to back off?"

"I could handle myself. Maybe I let it go too far; I was nervous, and...I probably pushed it, but if things had gone any further, I would've put an end to it."

He went unusually quiet, and I sensed there was more he wasn't telling me. He turned a solemn face to me. "Kris, I think part of me was happy that Shayne paid attention to me. I didn't know who he was at first, but once I did, I wanted to make Brandon jealous; I wanted to hurt him the way he'd hurt me. I never would've done anything with him, but seeing Shayne made me angry all over again. I know how Brandon felt about him, even if he won't admit it.

"I think he overreacted. Nothing was going on; I was hot, that's all. I took off my shirt and a second later, Brandon dragged me out of the room. You don't think Brandon thinks I wanted to hook up with him, do you?"

"No. I know he doesn't think that, and neither do I. That's why he wanted to get you out of there. Neither of us wanted you doing something you wouldn't do if you were sober."

"Thanks, Kris." A moment later he asked, "Is this going to change things? Are you going to act different around me now, because of tonight? I don't want things to be weird between us."

"Nothing's going to change. I promise."

He nodded. "Kris...you won't tell anyone about tonight, will you? If anyone finds out I even went as far as to party with that crowd I'll crawl in a hole and die."

"Somehow I think that if I'm still alive after what Brandon and I did, you'll be just fine. But I swear I won't tell a soul."

"Thanks." His tension eased, and so did the worry creases above his brow. "Kris?"

"Yes?"

"Thanks for being so cool."

I stood up to leave. "Get some sleep, Ryan."

Brandon leaned one shoulder against the wall just beyond the door. He looked at me, eyebrows an inch higher than normal on his forehead. "Well, if that wasn't one of the most informative eavesdropping sessions I've had in forever and a day." He scratched his temple. "You handled the situation beautifully."

"Well, there you have it—your best friend's insecurities exposed. Did you enjoy hearing him bare his soul?"

He shrugged. "Why don't you ask yourself the same question? Carrie's no different from Ryan in that respect. Ryan simply doesn't wander to the other side to experiment with our friendship on a more...intimate level, if you will." His right hand swept back the shank of hair that had fallen in front of his face.

"Obviously, you're the standard by which he measures himself and his successes. That can't be too healthy."

Ryan was bright and talented in his own right, but Brandon possessed a rare gift. What Ryan worked hard at came easily to Brandon.

"I don't think it's quite as serious as you're making it out to be, Kris."

"No? Pay attention. Sometimes I don't think you realize the power of your influence on him."

He looked at me, silent to my comment, and then pushed away from the wall. "Let's get some sleep." He took hold of my hand again. "I'll walk you to your room."

I was disappointed I wouldn't be staying with Brandon, sharing his room or his bed. But I understood that with Ryan here, it wasn't a wise idea. Brandon walked me to the second guest room down the hall.

"Thanks for coming to the rescue, Kris. It was gutsy of you to do it. I was afraid that things were going to start getting weird."

"How weird?"

"Weird enough that I wanted him out of there."

"Does it have anything to do with the blond stud parading through the house in his underwear?"

He looked at me, face perfectly blank. "No."

"Was Ryan right? Is that why you separated them, out of jealousy? Did his tactics work?"

That prompted a reaction—a bitter laugh. "I assure you, it had nothing to do with jealousy."

He said no more about it.

"Brandon, who's this guy Nial, and why do you hang out with him?"

"He's just a friend."

"A friend? From what Ryan says, he's almost old enough to be your father."

"What does age have to do with anything?" he said defensively.

"Normally, I'd say nothing, but considering how much time you spend with him, can you blame me for finding it unusual? What could you guys possibly have in common?"

He didn't say anything.

"You don't *do* stuff with him, do you?" I had no right to make accusations against someone I'd never met, but middle-aged men hosting underwear parties for under aged boys?

His reply seemed well rehearsed, making it sound unimportant, a non-issue. "Quit jumping to conclusions, will you? What's the big deal? We hang out, go to the movies and stuff."

It was the *stuff* part that I worried about. "Is he interested in you?"

"I never asked him."

I sniffed at his flippant comeback. "You don't have to ask him, Brandon; you know the answer. For some reason you have this bizarre ability to tell whether a person's gay, curious—even what color underwear they wear on Tuesdays—within ten minutes of meeting him. Don't give me that."

He seemed agitated. "Krista knows me well," he mused aloud. It was a moment before he answered in a less than friendly tone, "He doesn't like men."

"And?"

"Krista," he said mildly, and I recognized the warning, "you know I don't kiss and tell." His eyes held mine. "Done."

A chill washed through me. I opened my mouth to say something and he cut me off, holding up his hand. I closed my mouth, unsettled by the warning communicated through glittering eyes. The flecks of his irises were a pure and burning gold, dangerous. I stood there, silent, almost afraid to move.

"Done," he said again. "Good night, Krista."

<hr>

I sat upright in bed. The darkness was a vast black hole. I shushed my fears and sat still, allowing my eyes a moment to adjust.

The moon cast a dull shine along the hall, its light barely adequate for my stealthy mission. I tiptoed across cool, polished concrete.

His room was devoid of moonlight, with only the subtle glow from the eel tank to guide me.

Brandon lay silent, oblivious. I slid under the covers, snuggled up against him, wrapped my arm around his waist. Bare skin against skin. My nose and lips brushed, soft as petals, along his bare back, and I inhaled the intoxicating scent of his skin. Brandon had been truthful, he really slept in the nude.

Brandon stirred. "Kris?" he said in a mild voice, thick with sleep.

"Yes," I whispered. "I couldn't sleep."

He reached for my hand. "You all right?"

"I wanted to sleep next to you. Is that okay?"

"I'm naked," he murmured.

"I know."

We lay quiet, still, and extremely aware. Only the soft gurgling of the eel tank broke the stillness around us.

I hadn't expected to be taken by temptation, but Brandon's familiar, naked body against mine was more enticing than anticipated. My hand traced his stomach, then found his chest, and I enjoyed the feel of smooth skin and well-developed muscles beneath my fingers. It was like exploring a fine sculpture that fit perfectly beneath my palm. He let my hand wander, allowed me to feel him. I grew braver and my hand slinked with purpose, dropped below his belly button. The beginning of soft hair tickled with my fingers. He gasped quietly—breathy and sudden; his breathing changed automatically.

He interrupted my journey by seizing my hand. "I'm hard."

I paused to evaluate his comment. "Is that a problem?"

"It could be."

"Do you want me to stop?"

"No." He firmly pressed his hand against mine, stopping me. "But maybe we should. Haven't you had enough excitement for one night?"

Unsure what that meant, I stopped.

"Do you think this is a good idea, with Ryan here?" he whispered, sounding more as if he was battling the question himself.

If anything were to progress further, the next move would have to be his. I wasn't answering his question.

"What do you want from me, Kris?" His voice sounded far more uncertain than I would have anticipated, and his question pitched me in the other direction.

"I don't want anything from you," I said.

"Yes, you do. You wouldn't be here if you didn't."

I just wanted to be near him, wrapped in his arms. But was that answer enough? It seemed too simple.

"What brought you to my room?" he asked again.

"You did."

"So..." His soft tone resonated warmly through the darkness. "Did you come to me for sex? Is that it?"

My heart did a tiny hop and a skip.

He paused, waiting for my answer. When I gave him none, he continued. "I noticed you didn't answer Ryan's question—when he asked if you wanted to sleep with me again. It's just the two of us talking now. So, do you?"

Count on Brandon to be direct.

"Why didn't you tell me you enjoyed it?" he asked.

I chewed on my lip. "I'm not sure."

"It would've been nice to know."

"I'm sorry."

"It's okay," he said. "I would've asked, but I didn't know how you'd react if I brought it up."

I lay there silently, unsure what to say.

"Were you embarrassed to say that you did?" he asked a moment later.

I thought about that. "I guess, maybe."

"And now, to admit that you want to again?"

Silence.

"Were you scared to be alone in the other room?"

I frowned. He knew I was afraid to be by myself?

"You need to help me on this one, Kris."

"Maybe it's not exactly sex," he mused. "Maybe you just want to sleep here beside me; I don't know." He really did sound confused. That was rare.

"You're making this difficult," I said, suddenly confused myself. "Maybe I shouldn't be here." I started to pull back my arm. "I want-ed—" I stopped, then tried again. "I want to cuddle with you. But I got sidetracked by your body." I felt foolish at my admission.

He rolled in my direction and shifted onto his back. I swear I could feel his smile in the dark. "I would love to cuddle with you, Kris."

The motion brought me awake. The water bed argued beneath us as someone settled on it. I didn't know what time it was. Brandon still cuddled me from behind, arm around my waist, sleeping soundly. It was dark. My body jerked when a hand touched me.

"Ryan?"

"Krista?" Ryan's whisper sounded uneasy.

A sudden stillness.

"What are you doing here?"

I was still waking and almost answered him, but then I thought for a moment. "Shouldn't I be asking you the same question?"

"I didn't realize you'd be here," he said, and then fell quiet. "Why am I surprised?" He didn't sound upset, just uncertain. Am I inter-rupting something?"

"No. We're just sleeping," I assured him. I reached out, and my hand contacted his bare chest.

He didn't say anything.

Brandon's arm tightened gently about my waist, letting me know he was awake. He kept quiet. I suppose he was as curious as I was.

"I couldn't sleep," Ryan said.

"Me either," I said.

"And," he continued, "I wanted to tell Brandon that I'm sorry. Sorry for everything—every screwed up thing I did and said to-night—but...I'm not entirely sure what all that is," he admitted quietly.

"It couldn't wait until morning?"

In a stretch of silence, I waited for his response.

"Sometimes it's easier to say things in the dark."

"Are you still high, Ryan?"

"I think so, but nowhere near as bad as before. I tried to sleep, but my mind keeps racing; my thoughts are all mixed-up —"

How many hours had passed?

"Do you remember what you told me in the bathroom?" I thought it wise to know, considering he was now lying next to me, naked.

His voice dropped even lower. "Yeah. But I promise I won't touch you, Kris. I'm sorry."

"For telling me?"

"Kinda, yeah."

Neither of us said anything for a moment, but then he made a move to get up and I touched him so he wouldn't leave.

"Do you want to stay, sleep with Brandon and me tonight?"

"You mean you're not going to kick me out?"

"Not if you stick to your promise."

I wrapped my arm around him.

I didn't say anything, but I wondered if things would've ended differently had I not been there. Brandon uncurled his arm from around me, then reached out and settled it on Ryan. Startled, Ryan's body jerked, but he remained quiet. My arm was around Ryan too, and I felt his body go rigid at Brandon's touch.

"It's okay, Ryan … it's cool."

The gentle reassurance in Brandon's voice seemed to mend something in Ryan. He relaxed into me.

We were all huddled like spoons, close enough that Brandon's arm could hold us both, and he left it resting on Ryan's stomach. And then something did happen. Ryan moved his hand and laced it with Brandon's. No one said another word.

26

I had no idea what time it was when I awoke the next morning. I only knew we had all missed school, and Ryan was in bed with me. Just Ryan. Brandon was nowhere to be seen.

Ryan slept soundly as he faced me on his side. He had shifted during the night, his arm around my waist, his right leg casually draped over mine, his head resting on my chest, as if he'd chosen me as the more comfortable pillow. How my arm ended up wrapped around his back, I had no idea. But he lay curled against me, as if I had knowingly accepted this position in the night.

Where had Brandon wandered off to? Dammit. Once Ryan awoke, what was I to say? Uncertainty plagued me as he lay cradled against me.

Brandon walked in, wearing only boxers. He hadn't gotten as far as a shirt yet. He approached the side of the bed where he had slept, and stood looking down at us. His mouth hinted at a lazy smile.

"Don't you two look precious?" he said, his tone low enough not to disturb.

I stared up at him, unamused, and he sat on the bed frame, careful not to create any motion in the bed.

"I suppose that look on your face would become even grimmer if I were to tell you that I found myself in that exact position this morning. Had you no clothes on, it would've appeared quite the ménage à trois." His lips curled upward.

"I'm not so sure that it still doesn't," I whispered curtly.

"It's too bad last night's events hadn't taken a different course. Under any other circumstances, if he awoke to find himself here, alone with you in *my* bed, it would be the ultimate highlight of his life. After all, he is, in a way, sleeping with the girl of his dreams." He smiled, but it wasn't exactly pleasant. "When he finds himself naked beside you, he's going to wonder what the hell happened."

Ryan slowly came to; he stirred slightly, and his lashes fluttered just before he opened his eyes. He took in his surroundings without moving. He must have registered where he was, and who he was with, because suddenly, he went unnaturally still, reminding me of a snake right before it strikes.

His voice, quiet and uncertain, seemed more a query of my identity. "Krista?"

"Yes."

His heart rate quickened as he lay pressed against me. He didn't move.

"Where are my clothes?" he asked nervously.

"I'm not sure. We may have left them in the bathroom."

"Could you get them, please?"

I nodded, but he didn't release me. He didn't seem about to move, either—or didn't remember how to, in his state of surprise. Maybe he didn't comprehend that his body was holding me down.

"Brandon?" I said.

"I'll go check," Brandon said.

"Brandon..." Ryan said quietly, as if trying to jog his memory.

Brandon stopped at the foot of the bed. "Did you sleep well?"

Ryan grabbed the covers and clutched them tightly about him. "You're pissed," he said.

Brandon was matter-of-fact, devoid of emotion. "Krista was most accommodating for you, Ryan. You're lucky she cares for you so deeply. You said deplorable things in her presence and yet she still tended you like she was your personal nursemaid, allowed you to sleep naked against her, and comforted you before you slept. Don't be embarrassed, Ryan—be grateful." He gave him a lingering look, and then said lightly, "I'll be back." He turned and left, leaving behind an awkward silence.

Ryan sat on the bed, staring down at the sheets. "I'm afraid to look at you," he finally admitted.

"Don't be. Nothing happened, and I'm not mad at you."

He seemed relieved by that. He looked at me then, eyes still lost, but I understood his confused state of modesty.

"No?" he asked.

"No."

He winced.

Brandon returned with Ryan's clothes and placed them beside him on the bed.

"Thank you," he said quietly, without looking up.

"How are you feeling?" Brandon asked.

"Uhm ... confused, and slightly foggy. My vision seems crisper," he said with an odd look on his face, as if he was noticing it for the first time.

"Yes, you had quite a night. Are you hung-over?" Brandon asked.

"I don't know." Ryan squinted; it looked painful. "All I know is that I have a bitch of a headache, if that counts, and I have no idea why I'm completely naked."

"I'll get you something for your headache," I said, and rolled off Brandon's bed. In the bathroom I searched through his mirrored medicine cabinets until I located the aspirin, and quickly returned with the remedy and a glass of water.

"As she's done throughout the night—your bidding," Brandon noted, looking at Ryan. "I'll leave you to get dressed. I'll be in the kitchen; what do you want for breakfast?"

"Nothing. I don't have an appetite."

Brandon's bleak expression shifted as he tried for a tired smile. "Why am I not surprised?" He sighed. "Any questions you want answered?"

Ryan considered silently. "Yeah, one."

"Go ahead."

"Can we forget about last night?" he asked, looking almost ill.

I gingerly took a seat on the bed frame so I wouldn't set the bed in motion. "Which part?" I asked him as I handed him two aspirins and the glass of water.

He accepted it with thanks. He took the pills and finished most of the water before returning the glass to me; I set it on the nightstand.

"Every part. The entire night."

Brandon's face was serious. "Then you remember everything?"

Ryan paused for a minute, thinking. When he spoke, his voice seemed to gradually deflate. "Honestly? Only bits and pieces, but enough that I know I want to forget about it."

"Okay," I said, willing to comply with his request.

Brandon didn't dismiss it so easily. "Ryan, you and I have things to talk about. I thought we'd cleared up certain matters between us, but apparently not well enough."

"I don't want to discuss anything. I already know I behaved horribly."

"Yes, you did," Brandon agreed.

"But we've already forgiven you, Ryan. You've already apologized," I said.

"Something tells me apologies aren't enough." His voice sounded harsh. He wasn't pleased with himself.

"Don't worry about it," I said. "You'll make this whole thing larger than life in your head."

The lines of distress were prominent on his forehead. "I don't want any details. What I don't remember, I want to keep that way."

Brandon and I looked at each other. What did Ryan remember, or fear he'd done, in order to scare him into complete avoidance?

"Now, to make sure there are no questions later..." Brandon withdrew a small white tablet from a drawer and scribbled something in pen across it. He made a sweeping flourish, and then pulled the top sheet off and handed it to me. He held a prescription pad; he'd just written me a doctor's excuse. He wrote another one and handed it to Ryan. "They'll excuse your absence if you take that in tomorrow."

I looked at the page he'd given me. The name across its top was *Dr. Nial Froman, M.D., Pediatrics.* I looked at Brandon, not sure what to say.

"He gave me permission to use that, in case I was ever in a bind. Just one of the perks of our friendship." He gave me the oddest stare, and I didn't know what to make of it. "And you thought there was no value in it."

The phone rang. Brandon let the answering machine pick it up.

Nick's voice came over the speaker. "Hey... it's Nick. I'm on lunch and I—"

Brandon picked up the receiver. "Hey. Something came up... Yes, she's with me... No, she's not going to make it... Nothing. Please don't start this again. No... I'll tell her, and I'll come over later... Bye."

He returned the phone to its cradle, turned to me. "Nick says hi, Kris." He chuckled. "Yeah, right after the inquisition. *You,* darling, fuck with his confidence."

"Not intentionally. I'd never try to do that."

"I know. You don't need to."

Ryan sighed. "Let's just kick it here until it's time to go."

Brandon said, "We could use the Jacuzzi. It would do you some good, Ryan. It'll help you sweat that shit out of your body. If you drink enough water, between that and the Jacuzzi, you should start to feel better. You may not feel it now, but you're going to be sore and worn out from all you took. Those drugs tear at your muscles, and if you want to get back on the field anytime soon, cut back on your down time."

He shrugged. "If you think it will help, sure."

Brandon looked at me. "Kris?"

"Fine by me."

27

Brandon and I got together the following day to catch up. Nick had had a nightmare about their relationship—one so intense, it had startled him awake, which in turn had startled Brandon awake when Nick jumped while in bed next to him.

His account reminded me of the night I had awoken in a panic after being trapped in a dream state over Daemon. I finally came forward with the one thing I had yet to share with Brandon—my confession of what I'd experienced the night I'd stayed at Aeleise's. It came out that afternoon, while we were driving to the coffee shop.

"Your *virgin angel.*" He rolled his eyes. "He's only bringing you to climax in your sleep, Krista—*Christ!*" He shook his head as he slowed the car for a yellow light.

I couldn't decipher his attitude from his behavior. Was he angry? Amused? Or did he just think I was pathetic? "But I never expected *that,*" I countered. "It was such a…*strange* experience—rather disquieting."

"I don't know why you're so surprised. You constantly fantasize over him as if he's some sort of sex god."

My eyes went wide and I playfully swatted him. "Brandon!" I knew he could be brazen, but *really!*

"What? It's the truth, isn't it?"

We turned the corner and approached the parking lot. Brandon had his car valeted, and we were at the Java Hut within minutes. The air was thick with the aroma of cinnamon, chocolate and vanilla, all mixed with the scent of freshly ground coffee beans.

Our waitress brought us steaming cups and left us to our discourse.

"Kris, what is it that you find so intriguing about Daemon?"

I paused to consider that. Daemon had many qualities I admired, but I chose the easiest one for Brandon to relate to. "Don't you find him attractive?" I asked.

The question seemed to annoy him. He poured a healthy amount of milk into his tea and stirred. "I'm sure he has his attributes," he said grudgingly, "but is that the only reason you like him? Because you think he's hot?"

"Of course not."

"What is it, then?" He sniffed. "Is he your proverbial 'good boy'? Or..." He paused, then gave me a harassing grin. "Perhaps it's the opposite — the mysteriousness akin to manhood?"

Riddles. "Can you please speak in English for once?"

His face dropped the teasing look. "Is it, you know — because he's a man?"

I couldn't put a finger on the unfamiliar tone in his voice.

"Man, boy — whatever. What difference does it make? It's all the same."

"I'm sure if it were permissible, Krista, he'd show you the difference."

"You're saying you don't consider yourself a man?"

"I'm sixteen. Don't flatter me, Kris. Neither of us is blind; nor are we stupid. Is that what fascinates you so? Our differences? Please tell me."

When had this become a comparison? Baffled, I looked at him as he absently stirred his tea.

"It is," he said. Disappointment weighed his voice. "You want to see his body." He cleared his throat. "I can understand that."

A moment later, he made a quick sound that might have been a laugh. He removed the spoon from the cup and placed it gently on the saucer. He pushed all three away. "His inexperience ... endearing, I suppose, considering how long he's managed to cling to his virtue. And then, of course, he's also never had sexual relations with men."

"What do other men have to do with this?"

"Nothing, Kris."

I knew he lied. "No—you brought it up."

"I wonder." His voice was sour, flat.

I looked at him expectantly. "Well?"

"Be straight with me—what would you think if Daemon had had sex with men?"

"I'd think it was his business."

"I've got eyes; I know what you see. From head to toe, he's impressive; I'll give him that."

"How would you know?" I asked, suddenly both astounded and irritated that he'd have such knowledge.

"He and I attend the same gym." He traced the edge of the cup with his finger. "I've seen him naked, Kris. He doesn't shower in his clothes." He restrained his smile, but his eyes teased as he added, "Just in case you were wondering." He raised the cup to his lips, took a sip. "So ask away—I'm waiting."

I wondered why he would drag out the subject. He didn't need to be telling me all of this.

"What?" he asked. "No curiosity? You don't want to know?"

I felt myself blush, and in that instant, I knew I didn't want any of the details. It seemed wrong for Brandon to divulge such personal information about Daemon. It wouldn't be something that Daemon would openly share with me, and therefore we had no business discussing it. To do so would make me feel as if I was violating his trust.

"No—I don't want to know." I shook my head. "Are Daemon's attributes truly that big of a concern to you?"

He glanced at the table, then shifted in his seat, trying to find a more comfortable position.

"Brandon," I teased with a small smile, "I do believe you're jealous."

"Maybe."

He abruptly sat up in his chair, shifting to a new mood. "Enough about Daemon," he decided. "Hey—I have a *great* idea. Let's go to The Hunter's Club. They've got great music and a great vibe."

I'd never even heard of The Hunter's Club. "Is there an age limit?"

"Twenty-one and over, but I know the owner. We'll be through the door before anyone else. You ready?"

I could've stayed longer and enjoyed the aroma of the coffee and the mellow tunes, but I was curious about this club. "Yeah."

When we arrived at the club, Brandon phoned in. I heard the voice on the receiving end of the call clearly from the passenger seat.

Brandon's grin was as wide as I'd ever seen it. "Marcel...?" he drawled in a playful tone. "I bet you can't guess who this is."

"It *can't* be—it isn't."

Brandon laughed with abandon; Marcel quickly joined in, overjoyed by the surprise.

"It *is*. My *God*—The Beautiful One has *returned!* I would recognize that voice anywhere, you *fool*—where are you?"

"Who's calling who a fool? I'm outside your club, you dingleberry."

"Get your ass to the back door. I'm coming to get you myself."

"I have a friend with me."

"The Blond Beauty?"

"No. A different beauty—but you can't have her, either."

"*Such* the dictator you are—always calling the shots."

Brandon laughed. "You like it that way."

"True. Fine child, meet me now. I'm waiting as we speak."

Brandon collapsed his phone and tucked it in his pocket. He pulled his car around to the back of the building and parked. This was the brightest I'd ever seen him.

When we reached the back entrance, we found a tall, slender man with close-cropped dark hair leaning against a brick wall, smoking a cigarette. He took a long drag and quickly blew the smoke out. He tossed the cigarette to the ground, snuffing its life with a twist of his shoe.

"You beautiful bastard—you haven't changed a bit." He opened his arms in greeting, and Brandon went to him, hugging him affectionately. Marcel pulled back to look at him. "It's *good* to see you...*so* good."

"You too."

Marcel's eyes caught mine, and he redirected his smile. "And this is the other beauty you spoke of?"

Brandon turned around and claimed me, pulling me forward. "I'd like you to meet Krista."

Marcel took my hand and kissed it. It wasn't anything mischievous—nothing close to the way Brandon had greeted me when we first met.

"Delighted," he said. "You must be okay, if you've made it this far."

Brandon gave him a playful shove. "She's better than okay, you goon. She's *fabulous.*"

"*My! Well*...enough of this shooting the shit in the gutter. Come inside, Bambi and *Fabulous.* Let's get out of this damn sun."

We followed Marcel and ended up in a narrow red hallway that seemed to stretch as far as the eye could see. The farther we walked, the louder the music became—a driving, pulsing beat coming from a hidden lair beyond the walls. We made a sharp left turn into another hallway, and I glimpsed the dark club, its blackness pierced by frenzied laser beams and flashing lights. We weren't headed there yet. Instead, we entered a room on the left and Marcel closed the door behind us, quieting the music significantly.

The room looked like a pimped-out office with a red couch and a matching easy chair, a desk, a few filing cabinets , a television and a table. A miniature refrigerator sat up against the far wall beside a makeshift altar of candles and incense.

Marcel gestured to the couch. "*Fabulous,* make yourself comfortable; Heartbreaker, you know how we do it."

I took a seat, and Brandon headed for the refrigerator to withdraw two old-fashioned bottles of Coke. He offered me one.

"Marcel?"

"Got all I need right here," he said, flopping into his swivel chair with relish. He reached for a pack of Marlboros lying on the desk, the box half-open, the contents half-missing. The ashtray at the edge of his desk, full of stubbed out cigarette butts, begged to be emptied.

Brandon joined me on the couch.

"So, did you come to torment my patrons?" Marcel asked Brandon as he lit a new smoke.

"I haven't decided yet."

Marcel laughed. "No, you haven't changed a bit." He looked at me. "He's a live-wire, this one. But I'm sure you've already figured that out."

I chuckled in agreement as Brandon took a swig of his coke.

"So, what the hell have you been up to? What kinda hell have you been raisin' — 'cause I know it's something."

Brandon smirked. "I've been remarkably low-key for a change. Honestly."

Marcel's brows rose. "Really? No more crazy after-hours parties at the mansion?"

"Well . . . not like before."

He cocked one brow and eyed Brandon as he audibly blew out a cloud of smoke. "Mmm-hmm," he drawled, as if he knew better. He pointed at Brandon. "You know what I think about Nial. I don't trust him — and I don't like that you hang out at his parties." He stubbed out his cigarette. "You've got nothing to gain there."

"I know."

"So why go?" Marcel grabbed another cigarette and popped it between his lips. He flicked the lighter and brought the flame to the tobacco, managing to light, puff, and talk all at once. "And I don't like that fucker Shayne, either."

He took a drag, kicked his feet up on the desk, then exhaled as he leaned back in his chair. "*I know, I know* — he's hot shit and you like him, but I'm telling you . . ." He gestured at Brandon, his cigarette scissored between two fingers. "He's jealous as all hell of you, and he's just waiting to find a way to get your ass in trouble. Find some other tail to chase."

"I'm not seeing Shayne any longer."

Marcel looked at me. "Is he telling the truth?"

"As far as I know."

Marcel nodded. "Well, I'm glad to hear it." He shook his head, eyes stern on Brandon. "Leave it to you to fall in love with some rake."

"I *wasn't* in love with him."

"Save it — I remember the tears."

Brandon stiffened, didn't say anything.

"Not another word, Lovey. I know."

I sensed a strange tension, and shifted the subject. "You're married?" I asked, noticing a picture of Marcel standing beside a woman and two children that looked too similar not to be his.

"Once upon a time, child, once upon a time." He flicked ash into the ashtray. "Davey still asks about you, you know," he said, looking at Brandon.

"Yeah? Tell him I say hi. How's he doing?"

"Why don't you tell him yourself? He's good. Loving being in sixth grade — thinks he's big man on campus now."

Brandon chuckled. "And Miranda?"

Marcel smiled, then nodded as he took another drag. He exhaled a cloud of smoke. "Still crushing on you, hard as ever. Getting better looking every day." He shuddered. "God, I'm just dreading the day she brings home her first date." He shook his head. "Not ready for that one. I'm glad she's still daydreaming about romance with you; at least I know there's no need to worry there."

Marcel's eyes shifted to me. "You fallen for Lover Boy yet?"

Stunned by the question, I just stuttered.

"Marcel..." Brandon set down his soda, then turned to me. "Feel free to ignore him."

"Oh, I'm just havin' fun. You know that." Marcel leaned forward and stubbed the cigarette in the ashtray. He began to cough, deep and raspy. He cleared his throat.

Brandon shook his head. "You ever gonna lay off the dirt sticks, Marcel? Don't you know those things will kill you?"

Marcel raised a single brow at Brandon. "You're lecturing me about *smoking?* Your time would be better spent protecting your own health. We've had this discussion before. I hope you've kept your promise. You're playing safe with whoever you're seeing?"

"I've been safe, Marcel. I wouldn't risk it."

He nodded. "Good. You just remember to stick to your guns, no matter how charming or beautiful you think some guy is."

"I won't forget," Brandon said, his tone serious.

Marcel leaned back, satisfied, and lightened the mood with a smile. "So, I suppose you came to gaze at the older boys, right?"

Brandon gave him a nefarious grin.

Marcel chuckled, shook his head. "You and those go-go boys. Go on, then; have fun—but keep your nose clean. And no exchanging numbers."

Brandon stood up and sighed. "Marcel, you take the fun out of everything."

"You know the rules."

"I know the rules." Brandon took my hand and led me out the door, pulling me toward the club and the clanging music, the chaos of lights and dancing bodies. We sat down at the bar and ordered virgin cocktails, on the house.

I strained to hear Brandon talk, but the music made it nearly impossible. He grinned as his eyes cruised over the hundreds of men before him. I had never seen anything like it; we'd entered a mysterious world that catered exclusively to Brandon's tastes. Guys were eyeing Brandon as if his clothing were cellophane.

An attractive blond with a killer smile wasted no time. He asked Brandon if he wanted to dance.

"Thank you, but I'm here with a friend."

I looked at the tank-top-clad, muscular figure standing before us, and knew Brandon's declination wasn't out of disinterest. "Brandon, go dance if you want to. I'll have fun watching you."

"I don't want to leave you here alone."

I looked at the surrounding patrons and laughed. "Uh—I'll hardly be alone."

He grinned as the man grabbed his hand and pulled him toward the dance floor.

I turned my attention to my drink and saw that Marcel was now standing beside me.

"He's a good kid," he said, nodding toward Brandon. "Wish I'd hear from him more often, but I understand; I remember what it once felt like to be young and unstoppable." He chuckled, then patted his body as if searching for something lost. He found the Marlboros in his back pocket. He lit one, watching Brandon dance in the crowd. "If it weren't for those half-wits he has for parents…" He shook his head. "It's not often I'd say a kid would be better off on his own, but in Brandon's case… hell, he's practically been on his own for years anyway." He scratched his neck. "At least he knows he's always welcome in my family."

I concealed my surprise at that revealed fact.

I liked Marcel. I even liked the way he looked at Brandon. There was something going on there, much deeper than discussed. He seemed genuinely concerned about Brandon's welfare, and that scored major points with me.

"As highly as Brandon thinks of you, I'm surprised we haven't met sooner," I said.

A corner of Marcel's mouth twitched in a peculiar smile as he watched his hand stubbing out his cigarette. "And I'm surprised we met at all. Brandon doesn't like to be reminded of his past."

He put his cigarettes in his shirt pocket, exchanging the pack for a fluorescent blue business card, which he handed to me. "If you ever get in a jam, or if this one does—" he pointed to Brandon "—you ring me up, hear?"

I smiled. "I will. Thanks, Marcel. It was nice meeting you."

"It was nice meeting you, Fabulous." He gave me a quick wink and walked away.

28

Later that afternoon, exhausted from cheering at an after-school assembly, Carrie and I decided to welcome the weekend at my house. We grabbed sodas on the way in, then crashed on my bed the second we were through the bedroom door.

We had been home only minutes when Marc appeared at my door. "Kaelie's stopping by and then we're going out to dinner. It's the anniversary of our first date. You got things covered here?"

"Yeah, I'm fine. You and Kaelie have a good time. Happy anniversary," I added quickly, and smiled. Lately I had really tried to put more effort into accepting Kaelie.

He smiled and I could tell he was in a good mood. "Thanks."

"And you bought her flowers?" I pressed.

"Yes, *nosey,* I did."

I grinned in approval. "Just checkin'."

"Now if you'll excuse me, *Miss Krista,* I have to get ready for my date." Smiling, he made a mocking bow, then headed for his room.

The doorbell rang—Kaelie had arrived. I heard Marc run for the door. I was looking forward to Carrie and I having the house all to ourselves.

"Well, moving away from that topic, what do you think about the new transfer in Latin? I hear he's in a punk band or something. I guess he plays bass."

I took a sip of my Coke. "Brandon told me about him. He has calculus with him during second period."

"Leave it to Brandon. He wastes no time."

"I know."

Carrie's tiny smile slowly stretched. "Brandon says he's in love with his lips. Personally, I was paying attention to his ass."

I hid my shock. Not only over her spark of interest in the newcomer, but that she and Brandon were apparently on speaking terms. "Brandon says...? The two of you are talking again?"

"Oh—" Her eyes dropped to the bedspread. "Yeah. I decided to take the rational approach and called him."

I nodded, realized she wouldn't offer more. What she said was enough. I was happy to hear that things were moving forward for her and Brandon, and plenty ready to positively reinforce this revived interest in boys. Maybe there was hope yet.

I reverted to the topic of the eclectic rocker. "I think the new transfer's name is Skylar. He is easy on the eye, I'll give him that," I said, and smiled.

She grinned. "You noticed too?"

"How could I not? It's pretty hard to miss. Besides," I mused, "lately my eyes have been doing their fair share of wandering. Like these past few weeks." I couldn't suppress the beginning of a grin. "You'd think I'd gone *mad* if I told you what I found myself looking at the other day."

"I'm listening."

"Daemon."

"Daemon?" she said with a perk of interest.

"I know I shouldn't even be thinking about this because he's our friend and all, but have you ever noticed the *package* on him?"

She picked at her nails, flaking off rose-colored polish that had started to chip. She brushed it off the bed. "No, I can't say that I've exactly been staring between Daemon's legs. Why—were you?" She looked up at me, a quirky smile on her face, and teased, "Pervert."

"I didn't mean to," I whined, trying to hold back a smile. "It was just, like... *there*. I *tried* not to look, but... I couldn't help it." I twisted the sapphire ring on my finger as a diversion. I cleared my throat, suppressing a grin, and admitted, "I suspect he's rather... well endowed." The laugh that followed sounded silly. I shook my head. "I must be crazy." I tried to keep a straight face, but broke into an encouraging smile. "Next time you see him, check for yourself, if you don't believe me. Tell me if I'm wrong."

I looked up from the ring to gauge her reaction, and she shook her head. *"What?"* I said. "You don't think Daemon could be well—"

"You have company," a voice announced behind me.

The hair on my neck stood up at the sound of Marc's voice. Apparently I had interpreted Carrie's sign language incorrectly.

"Krista," he said.

Carrie looked as if she had stopped breathing. I slowly turned around. My Coke slipped from my hands and crashed to the floor as I locked eyes with Daemon, who'd been standing there as I shared my observation.

"Oh my God!" I gasped, and looked away. My face burned, flushed scarlet.

Carrie scrambled for a towel while I tried to gather some dignity. I had no idea what to say. I looked up just enough to see Marc, eyebrow raised, give me a questioning look before walking away. Daemon stood there motionless, with equal parts of uncertainty and embarrassment on his face.

I spoke first, but I could barely meet his eyes. "Hi, Daemon," I mumbled.

"I could come back."

The damage was already done. "No, come in," I said, doing my best to regain my composure. "How are you?"

"I'm fine," he managed to say, and sounded relatively normal. "And you?"

Carrie, kneeling on the carpet while pressing the towel to the spilled Coke, said, "Uh, Krista … I'm going to talk to Marc for a minute, okay?" She swiftly rose. "Hi, Daemon," she said as she rushed by him, avoiding eye contact.

Neither of us had time to reply. She scampered out the door, the Coke-soaked towel still in her hands. I was stuck alone in my room with Daemon and my comments. Should I acknowledge or ignore my indiscreet words?

He saved me from that decision by speaking first. "I—um." He concentrated on holding a blank expression. "I brought you something. Something I wanted you to have."

I was grateful he'd chosen to ignore my words. "What's this for?" I asked as he awkwardly handed me a gift-wrapped package.

"I was just checking out the new bookstore at the plaza and I saw these and thought of you. I remembered Aeleise said you were reading from an older version that you sometimes found confusing. I thought you'd benefit from a version that was written for modern times. It's a little easier to understand. I hope you like them."

I slowly pulled the decorative paper from the package to reveal a brand new Bible. My name was embossed in gold on the cover. There was also a high school devotional book and a journal.

"Thank you, Daemon." Shame had swallowed my voice until it was just above a whisper. "It's beautiful. You shouldn't have."

"I'm glad you like it."

I ran my hand over the burgundy leather cover, quietly staring at it. "I love it."

There was silence. Neither of us knew what to say next.

"Well...I should get going," he said.

I looked up at him then. "Daemon—I'm sorry," I blurted.

"No, I'm sorry, for just dropping by unannounced like this." I didn't doubt his sincerity there. "I should've called first. I didn't mean to interrupt your...well, yeah." He fumbled for words, then moved to the door. "I'll see you at my house tomorrow, then."

I nodded.

He was gone.

The front door closed; he had left. I placed my gifts beside me on the bed and took a deep breath. I looked up to find Carrie leaning in my doorway, an impish smile on her face.

"Nice one. That was slick," she said. "So how did you get out of that one?"

"I didn't."

"I *tried* to warn you."

"I didn't realize it until it was too late."

"So what did he come by for, anyway?" she asked as she re-entered the room.

"To drop off these." I showed her my new books.

Her expression softened. "Oh Krista," she said sympathetically.

"I know."

The doorbell rang again. "That had *better* be Kaelie," I said.

Marc left with Kaelie for the evening.

We retreated to my bedroom once again, and I sank unhappily onto my bed. Carrie sat beside me and offered words of consolation. I appreciated the effort, but it really didn't alleviate the sting of all I had said. I tried to pacify myself by reaching for the pom-pom that I'd tossed on the floor, losing my fingers inside the tangled mess. I pulled absently at one of the many thousands of gold and white plastic streamers. It stretched inches, resisting, until it finally snapped. It lay limp, gold, and uncheerful on my bed.

Carrie retrieved the practice CD from her book bag. I grabbed my portable CD player and we made for the den, where we pushed aside the furniture so could practice our dance. We had lots of work to cover. Carrie had only begun to teach me the first half of our competition routine for nationals, and I still didn't have those moves memorized. It was going to be a long night, but I was enthusiastic about practicing. I knew it was a team effort, and I knew that they needed me to come through for them if we had any hopes of placing at the competition, let alone winning. Focusing on that helped me push aside all the unpleasant events of the day.

When it was obvious that I had no more strength left to pull off even a simple pirouette, Carrie called her mother to come fetch her. By the time I had pulled my body out of the shower and crawled into bed, I was feeling damn near close to jelly. I settled between the sheets and withdrew my gifts from Daemon. I sighed. I really did know how to make a memorable blunder.

I had yet to turn off the light when my door slowly cracked open. "You still up?" Marc asked, peeking his head inside my room. Lost in my thoughts, I hadn't heard him arrive home.

"No," I said, and didn't bother to hide the sarcasm. "I always sleep with my eyes open."

He pushed the door open a little wider. "Can I come in?"

I nodded and he entered, almost closing the door behind him. He pulled the chair out from my dressing table and moved it closer to my bed, setting it down backwards and straddling the seat to talk to me. As he leaned on the back of the chair, a silly spark gleamed in his eyes that reminded me of old times, and our past chats. His smile had that warmth that only true happiness brought on, and it made him seem younger than he was.

"Don't *you* look pleased with yourself," I said, smiling along with him.

He chuckled. "Do I?" he asked, then answered himself. "I guess I am."

"*So* ... how did things go?"

He nodded with quiet satisfaction. "I'd have to say things went ... really well. We had a great time."

"How'd you like the restaurant? Isn't it beautiful?"

His eyebrows reached for his hairline. "It was everything you said and more. Kaelie absolutely loved it. Thanks for the recommendation."

"You're welcome. Happy I could help." I was pleased with my first contribution to their relationship.

He rested his chin on his arms, crossed over the chair-back. His eyes looked almost quizzical as they lingered on me; he was considering something.

"Brandon took you there, huh?"

"Yeah. We went a long time ago. Why?"

He shrugged and I recognized the questioning look on his face. "It's a pretty pricey restaurant to be going out to, if you just want to grab a bite to eat."

"I forewarned you that I didn't know what the prices were like. Brandon refused to tell me."

"I can see why."

"Was it bad?" I asked, almost hesitant to hear the answer.

"The food was fantastic—better than expected. But at just under four-hundred-and-twenty dollars for the two of us, I don't think I'd be eating there every day."

My eyes went wide. "You can't be serious."

He laughed. "Oh, yes. And I have the receipt to prove it."

"Sorry about that, Marc. I never imagined."

"No apologies. We enjoyed ourselves—genuinely." The subtle tilt of his head spoke of indecision. "Does make me wonder about Brandon, though." A moment later, he was fighting a smile. "Guess he knows what he likes."

"Yeah. Indecision has never been a problem for Brandon," I said. I closed the book I had been reading earlier, and slid it onto my nightstand.

"Whatcha' readin'?" he asked, eyeing the paperback.

"A devotional book that Daemon gave me." I deserved to be doing penance.

"Something new?"

"Yeah. He gave it to me today, along with a new Bible. It even has my name on it."

"Is that what he had with him when he came over?"

I nodded.

Marc was quiet. "That was nice of him," he said after a few moments. "Not to put a damper on things, but I heard what you said earlier. I hope you're not getting any crazy ideas. Those were some bold statements to be making about Daemon."

"*Statements?* How long were you two standing there?"

"Longer than you'd like to know."

I said, "I know. I feel awful about it."

"You should."

"Did he hear everything?"

Marc's eyebrow rose, and he gave me that knowing look. "*Yeah, he heard you.*"

"What can I do now?"

"*Nothing*—you've already done plenty. If I were you, I'd give him a break and not mention it again." He pushed away from the chair, sitting upright. "I'm sure you've managed to make him sufficiently self-conscious; if he chooses to act like he never heard you, do the same and leave it at that." He stood up and swung the chair back where it belonged. He looked at me. "I suggest you find someone new to become the object of your fascination. Someone your own age."

He gave me a gentle smile before pulling the door closed behind him.

"Marc," I called out before he had shut the door completely.

He pushed it back open a crack. "Yes?"

"I'm glad you had a nice time with Kaelie tonight. I just wanted to say happy anniversary again."

He smiled. "Thank you. Good night."

29

When I entered the kitchen, I found Kaelie, Marc, and Josh sitting at the table. Josh gave me a teasing look. "I was *trying* to enjoy my breakfast."

I'd been awake ten minutes and already I'd committed an unpardonable crime. *What now?* "Good morning to you too, Josh." My attention shifted to Kaelie. "Ever had the pleasure of sharing breathing room with someone as charming as my brother?" I was quick to clarify, "I'm not referring to Marc, of course."

Kaelie withdrew, trying to fight a smile. "I've been spared of brothers; I just have my little sis."

"Wanna trade?"

"You might retract your offer, once you meet her. Eleven-year-olds have *way* too much energy."

"It's a risk I'm willing to take."

"You're hanging out there," Josh said, looking at me.

"What?" I said, letting my exasperation leak through. "What have I done to offend the mighty Josh *this* time?"

"The sixties are over. Put on a bra—*please.*"

The ever-subtle Josh. I could always count on him to make me feel miserable. Marc and Kaelie looked up. I had an audience of three staring at my boobs. Six eyes analyzing my cleavage—now I'd lost *my* appetite. How strange. It seemed a month ago that I didn't even need a bra. When was my mother coming home?

"Put on a different shirt," Marc said. "You can't go out in that."

"Why don't we go shopping today?" Kaelie offered. "Do you have time?"

Marc didn't wait for me to answer. "She has plenty of time. I think that's an excellent idea." He reached into his back pocket and withdrew his wallet. He pulled out a credit card and handed it to Kaelie. "Get whatever you need—clothes or otherwise. If you decide to make a day of it, then you can have fun exercising my card—both of you. In fact, why don't you ask Carrie if she'd like to join you to do some shopping as well?"

My face lit up. "Really?"

He nodded.

With that, I ran to my room to call Carrie. I loved it when Marc felt generous.

Once at the mall, we headed straight to Nordstrom's in search of intimate apparel. Kaelie knew the floor plan like an employee, and directed us unwaveringly to the proper area. Carrie and I made our selections while Kaelie reserved a changing room for us. I was quick with my choices, and retreated without Carrie to try them on. Kaelie asked if she could see how my choices fit, and I began to wish I'd worn separates rather than a sweater dress. I allowed her to come in, though I wasn't exactly thrilled about it.

She looked at me as I stood in my underwear—she looked *at* my underwear. Her eyes were supposed to be judging what was above the equator, but apparently, the undies were more captivating. Now my secret was out. She'd seen me in my boy's briefs—the tighty-whities commonly associated with younger boys.

I stood there, feeling self-conscious, waiting for whatever comment she'd send my way that would make me wish I could disappear. After all, Kaelie was a model. It was her job to wear the latest women's fashions. And somehow, I doubted boy's briefs made it to the runway.

She smiled. "I bet those are a hell of a lot more comfortable than this G-string I have riding up my ass."

I smiled tentatively and nodded.

"Maybe I'll have to raid your brother's underwear drawer."

If I hadn't been grateful for her reaction, I would've flinched that she was close enough to Marc to search as she pleased through his intimate apparel. I wasn't sure if she really meant it, but I appreciated it either way.

"It's just your luck that they're having a fifty percent off sale in men's wear."

I had to smile at that. Kaelie was slowly beginning to grow on me. Despite my resistance to her becoming a permanent fixture in our lives, Marc had done well.

Shopping bags in tow, we pushed through the exit doors, leaving the shopping mall in high spirits. The sun blazed overhead. We smiled, pleased with our purchases. They could've filmed the moment for a commercial: Barbie and friends go shopping. It felt that ridiculously fun.

I called Brandon to check his agenda. I was praying he was free so we could spend some time together. I hadn't visited with him for a while; not since our curious afternoon at the Java Hut. Nick had been monopolizing his company of late.

"I hear Kaelie took you and Carrie on a shopping expedition," he said when he answered the phone.

"What, no hello? How did you know it was me?"

"Sorry—caller ID." He got right back to the issue of shopping. "*Well...* what goodies did you buy?"

"Girl stuff."

"Did you hit the Chanel counter?"

I laughed. "Afraid not"

"So, what do you have planned for today? Are you and Carrie going to get together later?"

"Actually, no. That's why I'm calling you. I wanted to see if you're free to hang out."

"I can't. Nick and I already have plans. His parents gave us tickets to the dinner theater. He should be calling me any minute with the details."

I tried to leash my frustration. If it wasn't surfing, it was Nick — always Nick.

"That sounds nice. I hope you two enjoy yourselves." Even I noticed that my cool voice marred my attempt to be amiable.

"What's wrong? You sound upset."

"No, I'll just have to remember to book in advance. Nick beat me to the punch ... again."

"I'm sorry, Kris. I promise we'll hang out soon."

"Promises, promises."

"How about—" Silence interrupted his speech. "—eek? Shit. I need to answer my other line—it's probably Nick. I'll call you later, Kris."

Then he was gone.

So I was envious of Nick. Fine. Now that I had admitted that to myself and gotten it out of the way, I realized it did me no good. I had gotten more than I bargained for on the emotional end of the spectrum. I couldn't change the facts, and I should've considered what further repercussions might follow my night with Brandon before I'd acted upon it. Finding another diversion became crucial. I plunked down in the seat at my dressing table, fanning through my thoughts in a dizzying, haphazard manner.

Daemon was hot, Daemon was single. Brandon was happily involved with a sweetheart of his own. How could he know how jilted and lonely I felt? Well, I knew Daemon was holding a bible study tonight. There was going to be a time when I was going to have to face him and see how he reacted to the horribly embarrassing incident in my bedroom. And I might as well look my best. I selected a deep, cranberry shade of lipstick, leaned into the mirror, and slowly pulled the creamy crayon across my lower lip. I was unsure why I felt a dull thrumming of irritation in the back of my mind, but it was there.

Lower lip properly lacquered, I moved to the top, following the curve of my lip with slow and steady care. The sudden vision of Nick's lips struck my mind with the clarity of a picture. The lipstick snapped. I stared at my frozen reflection. I realized I had painted his lips with this very lipstick. Instantly I saw the heated reaction on Brandon's face; his words pulsed like a low-level recording between my ears: *"I'd like to lick it off your lips..."*

I tore a blue tissue from the box and scrubbed my lips with it, as if trying to erase the bitter reminder. I ground the remaining quarter-inch of color into the tissue along with the broken top, and hurled it into my wastebasket.

I needed another lipstick to cover the stain of the last; I was pulling out all the stops. I withdrew the jeweled tube that sat in the place of honor on my dressing table. I had waited for an apocalyptic moment to unveil it, and it had arrived. This wasn't any ordinary lipstick I decided as I expertly dressed my lips in a sultry shade of muted pink. This would be my charm tonight. I put it on feeling a new sense of purpose. Bible study or not, I was out to make an impression.

My door opened without warning; startled, I jumped. Brandon entered and closed the door behind him. He looked at me and his eyes went wide.

"*Whoa.* Where are you going? Got a hot date?"

"Yeah." My lips pursed in irony. "A date with the Bible."

He paused, reformatting the information to suit him, and blandly said, "Don't you mean Daemon?"

"If I meant Daemon, I'd say Daemon."

"What's wrong with *you?*"

"Nothing." I turned back to face my mirror. "I just wasn't expecting to see you, that's all."

"Do you want me to leave?"

"No," I said, and turned around almost too quickly. "No, stay—please. Have a seat." Maybe his timing was perfect; I could test out my ensemble on him. I smiled to myself.

He walked over to the bed but paused as he was about to sit down. He straightened and approached me. "What is that?"

I looked at him strangely. "What?"

"That smell." He walked closer. "Whatever you're wearing is making me hungry. You smell like..." He ran his hand through my hair, lowering his face into my waves; he inhaled deeply. "Vanilla cookies. What *is* that? You smell good enough to eat."

I humphed. "A secret recipe. I only wear it on special occasions."

"I remember smelling it on you once before..." He had an odd look on his face, almost a frown. "It drove me crazy then, too."

Obviously not crazy enough.

He returned to my bed and sat down. I still had a good hour before I needed to be over at Aeleise's for Bible study. I wiggled out of my tank top and shorts. I never thought twice about changing in front of Brandon anymore. I knew he couldn't care less. I tossed my outfit aside, barely making the already overflowing hamper of clothes in my closet. From my dresser I selected my favorite bra from those purchased when I went shopping with Carrie and Kaelie. I fastened it and then turned around to face him, modeling my new satin push-up bra in powder pink.

"Well, what do you think?" I asked him, proudly displaying my manufactured cleavage.

He looked at me inquisitively. "What's the special occasion?"

"No special occasion, really. I just wanted your opinion." Brandon already knew the landscape; I knew I could actually count on him to review my clothing rather than my body.

"Well, that depends. Are you trying to look like Barbarella? If so, then I'd say you've accomplished that fairly well." He smiled at me. "Kris, it looks good, but do you really think it's necessary? You already look great without it."

I shrugged.

"Do you plan to wear that now? Unless I misunderstood you moments ago, may I remind you that you're going to Bible study, not a Victoria's Secret fashion show?"

"I thought you'd like it," I said, disappointed.

"I do. But face it, you're not wearing it for me. It's also not what I'd consider practical for tonight." He leaned back lazily on my bed. "To what lengths do you plan on going to catch Daemon's attention?"

I let out a tired huff. "That's not what's going on."

"Isn't it?" He gave me a knowing smile. "I know *exactly* where this is heading."

"I just thought maybe I should try wearing something more ... mature."

"Sure, Kris. Whatever you say." He looked at me with dry seriousness; his final words of warning were delicately wrapped in disapproval. "A friendly, gentle reminder: statutory rape is never in vogue."

"What a horrifying thing to say!"

"What a horrifying truth," he replied calmly.

"This isn't about Daemon," I insisted.

He scoffed at my words. "The hell, it isn't. Carrie already told me about his unexpected visit yesterday. May I congratulate you on your timing?"

Indignant, I held my head high. "Don't I look at least a *little* older to you?"

He looked at me, shaking his head. "It has about the same effect as Skipper wearing Barbie's padded bra—you still know she's a kid by her face."

"Brandon!"

He chuckled. "Uh, news flash—a push-up bra isn't going to magically change your age; some facts remain the same. Sorry."

He was having far too much fun at my expense.

"I don't want to look like I'm ten anymore."

"Trust me—with or without the bra, nobody's going to think you are."

I turned around to face my reflection in the mirror, now concerned by my small hips. I frowned. "I still look like a boy."

"I've seen every inch of your body, and I assure you, there's nothing boy-like about it."

I gave him an exasperated look. "Don't make fun of me."

"I'm not making fun of you. C'mon, seriously now. You're being ridiculous. I don't know why you're in such a hurry to grow up. The thought of it positively bores me."

I frowned. "You just don't get it, do you?"

"No, I think you just don't get it." He dropped the humor. "Kris, being a woman is a lot more than having a fancy push-up bra to show off your assets. Do what you want, but it's not going to help the situation any. If you honestly think that by wearing that you're going to cloud Daemon's mind into thinking you're closer to his age, you're going to be disappointed. You may not think you're a girl anymore, but I guarantee you, Daemon still sees you that way. I just don't want to see you get hurt, Kris—and if you continue to pursue Daemon in this manner, you will be."

Brandon definitely wasn't telling me anything I wanted to hear. "Never mind," I said, annoyed.

I threw on one of my favorite T-shirts and a pair of jeans. I remembered that his visit was unexpected. "What brings you by today?"

"Forget it. It can wait," he said.

"You came out of your way to say forget it?"

"I was on my way to Nick's."

"Oh," I said with an air of coolness to cushion the burn. I should've known. "Of course. I'm surprised you're not with him now."

"His parents are making him finish his homework before he can do anything else. We stayed up late last night, and I don't think they were too pleased."

Late nights and Brandon; I so didn't want to hear what would come next. "I should get going," I said. "I don't want to be late."

He looked at his watch. "Isn't it early yet?"

I sighed and gathered my things. I didn't want to sit around and hear the steamy details of his love affair with Nick. I gave him a bold-faced lie. "We're meeting early today."

He looked thoughtful. "Oh … well I'll give you a lift, then."

"Aeleise's house is out of the way for you if you're going to Nick's."

He shrugged. "I don't mind."

I looked at him, and he studied me uncertainly. "Unless, for some reason, you don't want me to take you."

Now I felt foolish. "No, of course not. I'll accept a ride—if you're sure it's not taking up too much of your time."

He smiled and grabbed my hand. "Come on."

When we arrived at Aeleise's, I had him drop me off at the curb. I don't know why I didn't want him to pull up their driveway, but I didn't. I thanked him and told him to have fun on his date. I didn't doubt that he would.

30

Although it was late in the afternoon, it was still too early for Bible study when I arrived at Aeleise's. I wanted to spend some time with her. She was still struggling over her breakup with Nick. The discovery that Nick preferred Brandon over her definitely hadn't helped her self-esteem. She had tried contacting Nick again, just to talk. He wouldn't accept her calls. I thought it was unkind of him to shun her, considering she had considered Nick a friend. But what kind of friend disappears overnight?

As I walked up to the door of her house, I hoped she would answer. I hadn't seen Daemon since the embarrassing incident in my room. I had made such a fool of myself. There was also the disquieting dream, the memory of which continued to plague me. I was still unsure what to make of that.

The front door was open; I rang the doorbell and saw a shadow approaching on the other side of the screen door. Daemon. Shit.

"Krista. Come in," he said, and opened the door for me.

I entered, avoiding eye contact. "Is Aeleise home?" I asked quickly.

"She left about twenty minutes ago to print some flyers. Would you like to wait for her? I know she'd love to see you. She's been really down."

I really didn't want to stay, but after that, what could I say? If I left now it would seem rude. "If that's okay, yes."

"Of course it is," he said, as warm as ever. I followed him into the living room and he offered me a seat on the couch. "Please, make yourself at home. Excuse my mess—I seem to have overtaken the living room."

He moved to sit on the floor where he must have been when I arrived. He was dressed in sleek black: a tight, silky, long-sleeved shirt was tucked into pleated slacks. A black suede belt hugged his waist.

"Thank you," I said, and chose a seat on the floor instead.

Fat, sand-colored pillows dotted the floor around his Bible and some loose papers. He had his highlighter out beside his Bible. I figured he was making notes for the next Bible study.

"Can I offer you anything? Something to drink?"

"No, thank you."

He didn't seem to be concerned with last night's events at all. Perhaps he had already forgotten. Yeah, right. But he seemed like regular old Daemon to me, and so I relaxed.

"What are you reading?"

"I'm selecting passages for the next lesson. Next week we begin a new series. Want a preview?"

"Sure."

He smiled at my interest and patted the floor beside him, indicating that I should join him. I did. I had been taking our Bible studies more seriously, of late. They had become interesting to me as I tried to sort through my conflicting feelings. The Bible seemed full of information, information that made me think and consider. It gave me guidelines that, unfortunately, I was finding hard to follow. Nevertheless, I was curious and wanted to learn more.

Daemon stretched out on the floor beside me and paged through his Bible, locating the verses for the lesson he was working on. I made myself comfortable, lying on my stomach beside him.

He paused, then looked at me. "You smell good," he said with a curious look on his face. "Almost like...candy or something. What perfume are you wearing?"

I felt a spark of satisfaction. "It's vanilla."

He shook his head, as if clearing it. "Well, it's certainly..." He didn't finish the thought. "I'm craving sugar cookies," he said finally.

I smiled, pleased I'd given him something to think about. He returned to his task, searching through pages. He found what he was looking for, and stopped.

"I thought since the subject has been coming up often enough, and we have yet to discuss it, we should address what the Bible has to say about sex."

Warmth rushed to my cheeks. So it was on his mind after all.

He looked at me when I made no comment. "You're blushing."

"No, I'm not."

The corners of his lips curved in amusement before he turned back to his notes. Would he bring up the transgression I made yesterday? *Pray, not.* What would I say? *Sorry Daemon, but lately I've been preoccupied with thoughts of what you're harboring beneath your pants.*

He lay on his stomach as he read, arms crossed in front of his chest, propped up on his forearms with a hand cupping each elbow. I watched his lips as he spoke. This was all wrong.

Daemon read aloud Matthew 5:27-28, a passage that dealt with lust.

"May I interrupt a minute?"

Daemon raised his eyes from the book to look at me. "Of course."

"Can you clarify that for me? '...anyone who even looks at a woman with lust in his eye has already committed adultery with her in his heart.' I mean—isn't lust sometimes something beyond your control?"

He lifted one questioning brow.

"What about dreams?" I finally said.

"You mean like romantic fantasy?"

Well, that was a polite way of putting it. "Yes."

"Well, lust—no matter where it comes from—is always a sin. I realize that you can't control what you dream about, but it's my understanding that generally dreams have some relation to our thoughts."

His statement, true or not, didn't make me feel any better. Daemon mesmerized me, but I didn't want him to know that. Sure, he was good-looking, but so were plenty of other boys I knew. We were good friends—nothing more. So why was it Daemon who endlessly infected my dreams and thoughts? Whatever the reason, it now made me more self-conscious around him … and it bothered me. I studied him with a new awareness, trying to see if there could be any validity to my dream.

"Earth to Krista…"

I snapped to attention.

"You got quiet all of a sudden."

"Oh … I was just thinking about what you said."

"Did my answer help any?"

I sat there silently.

A moment later he said, "What's up, Kris? You're acting awfully strange. Is it something I said? Are you having issues with lust? Something you want to talk about?"

I wanted to cringe. The manner in which he spoke brought back powerful memories of my days in Catholic school. He sounded like a priest I once visited in confessional when I was eight. I hated confessional. I remembered how the nuns would drag me there by my arms, kicking and screaming. I shook the nasty memory from my mind.

"Don't know. Maybe." I toyed with the cashew-colored carpet, giving myself a moment to think. "Actually, I'm confused. I really don't know if talking about it will help."

"Well, I'm happy to listen, and offer what advice I can."

This could get tricky. True, this was Daemon's department—the role of trusted friend and guidance counselor. But it just felt iffy. "I don't know that I should bring it up. Who knows what you'll think."

"Krista, whatever it is, you should know that I'm not here to judge you. You can tell me anything you have questions or concerns about. That's what I'm here for. What is it?" he asked, and touched my hand in a gesture of concern.

It felt strange, uncomfortable, to feel the warmth of his hand on mine. He had no idea what I was about to say. I moved my hand away, and took a deep breath, wondering how to begin. It seemed there was no easy or polite way to say what was bothering me, so I just jumped in with both feet. I looked at him warily. "I had a dream. A very *vivid* dream. You were in it."

I waited to see his reaction. I hoped I wouldn't need to say more. To my surprise, his expression didn't change. Did he understand the implications of my admission? Apparently not. He seemed to be waiting for me to continue. Perhaps he thought he was only a bit player in my dream—some sort of divine dream, something full of angels and harps.

"Okay, go on. I'm listening."

I almost wished that he wasn't. I was beginning to feel guilty for indulging in thoughts of him, an unknowing participant. "Daemon…" I looked at his patient expression, his eyes welcoming me with the openness and warmth of Mother Teresa. I chickened out, shook my head. "This is crazy. I can't."

"You were doing fine. Quit worrying. You had a dream…I was in it…" he prompted.

I rolled onto my back and stared at the ceiling. I studied the creamy wash of stucco bumps above me, gathering my courage. Finally, I found my nerve. "In my dream, you and I…we…we were, uh—making out. And, well, when I woke up…" Heat rush into my cheeks. Did I dare continue? Perhaps a different approach? I put it on him. "I'm confused—I mean…Have you ever had a dream *so real* that you woke in a dead sweat? Has something like that ever happened to you?"

Daemon drew a breath. The silence seemed eternal, it was so uncomfortable. I immediately wished for some magical way to retract all I had said. When I turned back onto my side to face him, he was sitting up.

When he recovered his voice, all he managed to say was, "Uh…"

When he made no further answer, I began to think he had missed the question attached to my confession. I decided to ask again, but then his brows knitted and he said, "Excuse me?"

"I asked you if—"

He stopped me. "I heard you the first time, Kris. Don't you think that's a little personal?"

"Why?"

"Because it is."

I studied his eyes. "You're embarrassed."

He didn't answer.

"I've been thinking about you lately, and it makes me feel all out of sorts. I can't eat, I can't study—I daydream about you in class. Thoughts of you haunt me to no end—I can't even sleep. It drives me *crazy*. I feel like I've half lost my mind."

He frowned, processing the information. "Do you think it's possibly...just a crush?" he asked, as if afraid to flatter himself. "Have you ever really had one before?"

I shook my head. "I mean...nothing like *this.*"

"Well, it might be uncomfortable right now, but I'd try not to worry about it. I think your preoccupation will be short-lived. Infatuations come and go; you'll see."

"I never realized a crush could be so intense, so all-consuming."

His concern seemed to deepen, like the lines above his brow. He swallowed at my admission, nonplussed. If only I could read his mind, wipe away the trouble that clouded his eyes. But he seemed far away, as if floating somewhere beyond my reach.

I hesitated. "Can I ask you a question? Even though you've never had sex, don't you ever think about it?"

He took a deep breath. After a pause, he answered, "There are times when my mind stumbles over the idea."

He had shifted to lie on his side, facing me, propped up on one elbow. He was wearing his gothic cross—the ornate piece of silver hung low and heavy outside his shirt. Did he know how erotic it looked on him? I had an all-consuming desire to rip it from his neck and send it hurling. I fought the urge, and found myself enticed by his silky black shirt instead. The fabric hugged him intimately, clinging to his every movement and curve. It seemed as if it was made for only him.

I reached out and gingerly placed my hand upon his chest. He watched my fingers trace the line of the fabric, following the contour of his body. They stopped. He raised his eyes to meet mine, and said nothing. My finger danced with the fabric again, slowly grazed his chest.

"Close your eyes," I said.

His eyes, full of skepticism, studied me. Though hesitant, he said nothing, and finally complied.

"Don't open them," I insisted. "Promise me."

"I promise." He sighed. "Dare I ask why?"

He would know soon enough. I cocked my head, indulging in a closer look. From every angle, I stared at him, just drinking in his handsome features. His face was so exquisite, I ached just looking at it.

"Can I open them yet?"

"Not yet."

My heart raced. *It's now or never, Krista.* I leaned forward and kissed his lips. *Daemon's* lips, soft and warm. They gave me goose bumps.

If he'd suspected my intention, it didn't show. His eyes opened as I backed away. Now he stared at me — stared for a long while without saying a word.

"Aren't you going to say anything?" I asked quietly.

"Yes. This can't go any further."

Not the response I'd hoped for. I placed my hand on top of his and moved it to my breast. The warmth of his skin penetrated my T-shirt, and my body responded. "But you want it to," I protested. "Brandon says he can tell that you do."

He yanked his hand back, cheeks flushed in surprise. He took a moment to regain his composure.

My advances were unwelcome. "Haven't you ever thought about me?" I asked.

"Not in that way."

"And why not?"

"This can't be an issue between us. Look, you're a lovely girl — "

"*Lovely?*" I grimaced, hearing my grandmother's voice in the back of my mind. What was that supposed to mean? He'd have to do better. "Then why did you stop me?"

"Krista, you're a wonderful person ..."

"I don't want to be *wonderful* — I want you to *want* me. Don't you?"

The only thing that registered in my mind was that he hadn't said no. But then, he shook his head. His expression wavered.

"This isn't what you want. You're not thinking clearly, Kris."

I thought it was he who couldn't see clearly. I made sure he could see my eyes. "I'm thinking perfectly clear. I'm not the one hiding how I feel. What are you afraid of?"

He lowered his eyes and said nothing, leaving me to guess.

"Tell me that you've at least thought of me once—whether you meant to or not. Please tell me I'm not the only one struggling with this..."

"Krista," he said gently, "I need you to be honest with me." His eyes were serious, full of self-doubt. "Have I ever given you reason to believe that my intentions or feelings for you went anything beyond friendship? Because if I have, I apologize. I would never intentionally hurt you or lead you on."

I considered his words and knew that he had done nothing; it had merely been me hoping.

"When the time is right, you'll find the man you're meant to be with—the man you're meant to marry."

"How do you know you're not the right man?"

He looked at the carpet, the slight twist of his mouth resigned. "Because I know." He looked up at me then, and I recognized the look in his eyes. They held the same warmth and concern Marc had displayed the night he confronted me with my diary. I didn't like that.

"Be patient. He's out there." He leaned forward and kissed me gently on the forehead. The little sister kiss.

His lips had so much more potential, I thought, and felt a twinge of annoyance—his tepid kiss was just a reminder of Brandon's forewarning.

Brandon's amused expression—*I told you so*—appeared as vividly as if he were sitting there like a smug little elf, watching me.

My anger flared. "If you're going to kiss me, Daemon, at least *kiss* me."

Before he could retreat, I brushed my lips against his, and kissed him softly. His body went rigid at the contact, frozen in surprise, but he didn't resist; he let me kiss him, whether he meant to or not. My lips lingered over his. He pulled back and pushed me away.

"You were doing so well," I said.

"Do you ever hear a word I say?"

"When I want to." This wasn't one of those times.

"This isn't right, Krista."

"It was a simple kiss, Daemon. It's not going to send you to hell."

To me, he was the embodiment of the vampire lover—*my* vampire lover, who had unknowingly bewitched me. He had to know his beauty was shocking. How he'd been able to hold out for twenty-eight years was beyond me. Somehow, that seemed like the only sin.

Tense he raked his fingers through his hair and rolled onto his back. Bad decision. I got on top of him. I lowered my face to his, feeling his velvety skin against my cheek. I closed my eyes and drank in the warm, wonderful scent of his cologne that mixed with the heat of his body. His rosy lips, still wet where I'd licked, were full and sensuous. I wanted to taste them again. I nuzzled my cheek against his and felt the exciting rush of adrenaline hit me, sending me on an enthralling high.

"I saw you in a dream like this," I said, my voice just above a whisper. "I like the way it feels … to be this close to you."

The scent of our perfumes mingled, lingered between us. His heart beat violently beneath his shirt as the sound of my own pounded in my ears. I had engulfed him in a conflict of emotions.

I shifted, and when I resettled my weight, I accidentally brushed against his groin.

A quick breath escaped his lips; he closed his eyes, his jaw taut with an intensity I'd never seen before. A second later, he was hardening against me.

So he was human after all.

"Krista—get *off* me." He panicked and pushed me away from his hips. Without thinking, my fingers grazed over his slacks where he was responding. He grabbed my wrist to stop me, his cheeks flushed such a vivid scarlet.

"*Don't.*" He held my wrist.

It was a sobering moment.

I pulled back, realizing how far I had gone. Even his tone sounded foreign. The continuous tick-tock of the hall clock only worsened the silence.

"I'm sorry," I said.

"I don't even know what to say. I'm sorry..."

I didn't know why he was apologizing. It was my fault. "It's okay. Really."

"No. It's *not* okay," he said completely distraught. "*None* of this is okay. That's the problem. The worst part about this is that you don't even find anything wrong with it. Do you have *any* concept of the way you just touched me?"

"Why does it have to be wrong?" I asked. "Didn't you like it?"

"*Krista!* Is this a game to you? This *can't* happen."

But it already had.

He searched my face, his eyes still upset, but now full of concern. "You had a confusing dream that caught you off guard. You're just a little mixed up right now."

It was an odd experience and I did feel confused. Somehow, I'd changed things between us. Suddenly I wished I could erase what happened. I wanted to be near him again—comfortably, the way we had always been together: almost as if we were brother and sister. All of a sudden, that didn't seem so bad. But I'd been drawn to the idea that there was something unexplored about him, and I had confronted it.

He watched me, frowning, unexpressed emotions behind his eyes. "Maybe you'll understand the position I'm in, when you're older."

So, it had come back to that.

Something in those words angered me, flipped a switch. Brandon hopped into my thoughts again. Brandon had warned me that Daemon would think I was too young. I hated more than anything that he still thought of me as a child despite all my efforts to show him I wasn't. Hell, I had more experience than he did.

"You want me to understand; well, I *don't!* I just practically *threw* myself at you, and you weren't even *tempted!*" Ryan would have given anything to be in Daemon's position. It didn't make sense.

"Am I *really* just a kid to you?" I shook my head. "I may not be the same age as you, but I'm not the *girl* you seem to think I am. Have you ever even bothered to *look* at me?"

He didn't say a word.

"Congratulations," I said. "You didn't touch me. But don't treat me like some ... *flower* that will wilt if exposed to harsh weather. I'm not. I know more than you think I do, Daemon. But you treat me like I'm all about sunshine and bubble gum. I want you to tell me the *truth*. For once, I want you to tell me what *you* think — not the law, not God — *you*."

Without a thought, I removed my shirt. He saw me in my pink satin bra for only a moment before he turned away. I took off my bra and tossed it aside. I looked at him expectantly. "Surely you have an opinion, Daemon."

"You're one of my sister's best friends. Don't do this, Kris. Put your shirt back on."

"Daemon, look at me."

I made a final desperate attempt. "Daemon," I pleaded, "*look at me, dammit.*"

He said evenly, "Not until you're dressed."

I didn't move.

"I'm waiting," he said.

"Fine!" I snatched up my shirt and put it back on, not bothering with my bra. "I'm dressed. It's safe to look now."

"I think you should go."

I knew then that I had seriously messed things up between us. Suddenly, I felt miserable. I wanted to cry — alone.

As I turned and walked toward the door, I wondered if I had just ruined one of the friendships that I valued most.

31

Ashen clouds loomed overhead like discolored cotton candy; the clouds were crying, and so was I. The wind blew against me in angry, cold gusts, tangling my long, wet hair. My fingers were cold.

What an idiot I was to think Daemon and I could be together. What had happened to my decency, or my common sense, for that matter? Could I claim temporary insanity? Not likely.

I tripped over an irregular hump in the pavement.

My jeans were heavy and soaked through. My hair, pasted flat against my head, hung like a dirty dishrag. My T-shirt clung to me, wet and cold. Pink glittery letters sparkled and danced across my chest, forming the words *Sugar and Spice*. My nipples pushed at the fabric of my shirt like Jujube Beans. I turned the corner at the end of the block. Cars whizzed by me in a blur.

Daemon's words replayed in my mind: "Sex is for marriage, Krista. Wait until then." Daemon didn't even know. I would never be able to come clean about Brandon.

The sun was setting quickly. I paused, focusing suddenly on my surroundings. Lost in my thoughts, I had wandered far. *How long have I been walking?* The beach where I now found myself was a good fifteen minute drive from home.

I looked again at my surroundings, slowly turning in a circle. I recognized the donut shop up the street, and the gas station on the corner ahead.

I wasn't far from my secret haven — an abandoned lifeguard tower. It was visible in the distance. I went to it as if it were my grandmother's house and she was inviting me in for hot cocoa and fresh coffee cakes. I ran to it, dashed up the stairs and then slumped gratefully against the wall, catching my breath. Exhausted, I sat on the platform and watched the waves in the near distance. They were hardly distinguishable from the smoke-colored sky. Everything merged into one color. The sky lay still and heavy as lead. Against the sound of the crashing surf were the voices of seagulls.

I sat shivering, arms wrapped around me, knees against chest, trying to think of something, anything I could possibly do to make things go right.

I thought about Marc and Kaelie, about their marriage and what that would mean. I thought about Christmas without Mom. Josh would be off at college next year. Daemon thought I was a child. *Where does that leave me?*

I didn't want to be alone.

I would pray about it—heed Daemon and his ever-encouraging words to reach out to God for help. He said God always listened when called upon, and that no problem was too big or small for His attention. I believed him. I *needed* to believe him. It was all the hope I had left.

The sound of heavy shoes grinding on wet sand grew louder behind me as they approached. Had some stranger followed me? Nervous, I froze like a rabbit, listening. I sensed a presence directly under the lifeguard station now. *Does he know I'm here?*

I jumped to my feet. The station vibrated and shook. Someone was climbing the stairs.

I pressed my back flat against the wall. Heavy footsteps. Three steps, then they stopped. They moved again, purposefully, coming in my direction along the station's ledge. I retreated.

There was a weakened board behind me. My right foot fell straight through. Boards cracked, splitting beneath me as I fell. I screamed, hit the ground with a sharp thud. Pain shot through my entire body. The fall knocked the wind out of me. A flashing light show passed across my eyes, disorienting me.

I scrambled away on my hands and knees. I realized as I tried to stand that I had twisted my ankle badly and would not be able to run.

I saw him. He stood as tall as the fabled Green Giant—a black shadow atop the tower, atop my haven. He was looking at me, I was sure of that, even though, in the absence of light, I couldn't make out the details of a face.

He jumped toward me, becoming a dark figure flying through the air. I screamed. He landed with a thud.

"Krista!"

My name rang through the darkness. The figure stumbled toward me, his movements frantic.

I screamed again. He was only twelve feet away.

"Krista, stop! It's Daemon! It's okay—it's me!" he shouted.

"Daemon?" I called in a frightened voice, still unable to see clearly.

"Yes. It's me." He ran up to me and fell to his knees, panting and out of breath. "Are you okay?"

"Look at you! You're freezing and soaked through." He promptly removed his jacket and wrapped it around my shoulders. "Wrap your arms around my neck." When I did, he lifted me, cradled me in his arms, and carried me across the beach to his car.

I felt blue with cold. He turned the heater up to 90 degrees as we drove. I felt strange, as if I was in shock from the excitement and the fall.

"You're nuts," he said.

Probably. I looked out the window.

There was no traffic and we soon arrived back at his house. He carried me into the house, up the stairs, and through his bedroom to his bathroom. He set me on the toilet seat. "Don't move."

He walked to the bathtub and let it fill with hot water. He returned to me, knelt at my feet, carefully untied my shoes and removed my socks. He examined my swollen ankle and shook his head. "This needs to be looked at," he said. "Is Marc home?"

I shrugged.

He stood and removed the jacket he had wrapped around my shoulders earlier. "Lift your arms," he said.

Daemon the drill sergeant. I obeyed, and he lifted my shirt. The awkwardness I felt struck me as odd; only hours ago, I'd tossed aside my clothing without reserve. This wasn't quite how I had imagined it in my dream, but this was probably going to be the closest I would ever come to reliving my fantasy.

"Can you lean back on your arms?"

Yes, and I did.

He reached for the button on my jeans and I looked at him as if he had suddenly turned into a serpent before my eyes. "What are you doing?" I asked anxiously.

He looked at me without interest, his tone exhausted, serious. "Modesty. I'm impressed."

I gave him my best scowl.

"Believe it or not, I have seen a girl without clothing before."

"Who? Aeleise?" I said snidely.

There was no amusement in his eyes. "That'll be enough."

I sniffed a small laugh.

I let him undress me, struggling with my jeans as they stuck to my skin. When he freed me from them, he picked me up and placed me in the tub. It was wonderfully hot and filled with bubbles. I guessed that was probably to hide my nakedness. My teeth chattered at the sudden change in temperature, and goose bumps covered my flesh.

"Kris," he began uncomfortably. "About what happened earlier... I'm sorry if I hurt your feelings—or if I seemed harsh—but I wasn't prepared to be put on the spot like that. You have no idea how awkward I felt."

I looked at him briefly, saw the lines of distress across his forehead.

"I'm not trying to discount you as a child, it's just—" He shook his head. "How do I make you understand? Look... you say you want to know more about me, and I'm going to take you at your word. Normally I'd never share something this personal, but I want you to know what happened between Danielle and me, so maybe you'll see what I'm trying to say." He swallowed, kneaded his brow with one hand. "When we were dating, our relationship..." He shook his head. "There were too many times when sex became the focus of our time together. We never actually slept together, but we came close. It would've been easy to let things keep going further, because we both wanted them to. And on one occasion, things went further than they should have." He looked at me. "I didn't feel good about it afterward, and that's not the way things are supposed to be. You shouldn't have to regret something that's meant to be special."

He paused and I wondered what to say. The news about him and Danielle surprised me. I had pegged him as having no experience at all.

"I only wanted you to be attracted to me," I said sullenly.

"Why? We're friends. When did things change?"

I didn't look at him. I had no answer. I was tired, frustrated, upset.

"Intimate contact between us can't happen," he said. "As it is, I'm ashamed that it already has." He sighed heavily. "So ... do you want to tell me why you just did your best to give yourself pneumonia?"

"No."

He shook his head. "How come I haven't noticed before what a royal pain in the ass you are?"

"Such language. From you?" But truly, his words affected me. It was unlike Daemon to say something like that.

He walked over and knelt by the tub. "I'm just frustrated with you. Why can't you talk to me anymore?"

I pouted and said the first thing that came to my mind. "My hair is filthy."

He looked at me strangely. "Would you like me to wash your hair?"

I nodded slowly.

He began to gently lather my hair. I remembered how I'd loved it as a little girl, when my mother washed my hair. Daemon's ministrations made me think of her, and made me realize how much I missed her. My throat ached.

As Daemon rinsed my hair out, the pain, all the unacknowledged, unanswered pain welled up inside me. I wept without reserve, and let myself feel it.

Daemon lifted me out of the tub without any questions. He wrapped a fluffy white towel around me, sat down, and held me on his lap.

"Krista," he said as I gave myself over to his care, "I want to help you in whatever way I can."

He carried me into his bedroom and sat me down on the bed.

I told him about everything. About missing mom, being unsure when she'd return. About Marc's plans to ask Kaelie to marry him, which meant he'd probably be moving away. I told him how Josh would be graduating this year; not only wouldn't I see him at school anymore, but if he got the scholarship he wanted, he'd be moving away as well. I told him how I was homesick for Ohio and my friends there, and for days that were simple. I told him how I had mixed emotions about some of my new friends.

And worst of all, I broke my vow. I told him about the Fairmont party, and how I felt partly responsible for Carrie being raped.

"I have something that belongs to you," he said. He reached across the bed and opened the top drawer of his nightstand. He withdrew something small, folded, and slightly crumpled that fit in the palm of his hand. He handled this thing so gently, it was as though it pained him to touch it. I wondered what it was.

And then I saw it. He handed me the card from Brandon. My heart jumped into my throat at once. I found it impossible to breathe.

He knew. He *knew*. I couldn't look at him.

His voice was too gentle, too filled with disappointment and hurt. "When were you going to tell me?"

"How long have you known?"

"What? That Brandon's gay? That you slept with him? Or that you've been hoping to pursue things with me? I've known all three for a while now."

I was horrified. "You've known this entire time and you've said nothing about it? Why? Why would you pretend not to know?"

"I didn't pretend not to know. An opportunity to talk about it had never presented itself until today. I only brought it up now because I *do* know. Did you get what you wanted from it?"

"What do you mean?"

"Whatever it was you were looking for, did you find it?"

"You wouldn't understand."

"Oh, no? Why don't you give me a chance? I know you and Brandon are good friends; are the two of you friends the same as we are? Be honest with me. You at least owe me that. Did you come on to Brandon the same way you came on to me today? Did he fulfill what I wouldn't? Is that why you slept with him?"

"I asked him outright, Daemon. He did it as a favor." I couldn't stop the tears anymore.

"A *favor*? He made love to you as a *favor*?" I didn't need to see his eyes to know how incredulous he found it. He gently touched the side of my face so I would look at him.

"We weren't making love. We had sex," I said, trying to cheapen the experience. Although even as I said it, I realized that I didn't feel like that was entirely true.

"That's even worse, Kris."

"Don't look at me that way. I feel awful enough." He looked away from me. "It only happened that once."

His voice went quiet with concern. "Did he at least wear a condom?"

"Yes," I said quietly.

He nodded silently. A moment later, he turned to look at me. "Are you in love with him?"

"You know how I feel," I said between tears. "But telling you I love you is pointless now, isn't it? You'd never believe me after what happened, and you'll never love me back anyway."

There was a stretch of silence, and then he said, "Of course I love you, Kris; in my own way, an appropriate way. It's just . . . I almost wish you didn't have those feelings for me, because I'm not in a position to do anything about it."

"You really mean that?"

"*Yes* . . . and I'm *concerned* about you. I feel torn on a level you wouldn't understand." He took a deep breath. "It really . . . *hurt* when I learned about you and Brandon. I know it shouldn't have—but it did."

"I never meant to hurt you. I'm sorry."

"Don't apologize to me. You don't owe me an apology. You don't. Regardless of how I feel, the truth is that that's between you and the Lord now."

"I've disappointed you, haven't I?"

He sighed. "I've managed to live through many disappointments."

His comment made me sad. I turned on my side to sleep and he wrapped his arm around me, comforting. We lay there as spoons, my back cupped against his chest.

Although I rested, I wasn't able to sleep. My mind wandered as I lay there awake. Daemon drifted off to sleep, and I listened to the rhythm of his breathing behind me. The slight tickle of his breath brushed lightly against my ear and neck. It was then that I realized how incredibly difficult it was to lie close to him, fully aware of my attraction. It took excruciating effort to do nothing, to lie still.

I tried to occupy my mind with other thoughts, but each unsuccessful attempt returned to him. I saw him as I had in my dream—a flash of him in his wet T-shirt. Somehow, that was all it took. I stirred. I barely moved, but I had moved against him. I knew I could get him to want me, even though he would never admit it. Why I needed him to want me, I wasn't sure. I hadn't meant to disregard his earlier words. I was startled by his voice.

"Krista…" His voice, thick with sleep, sounded more like a concerned warning, more like a mild scolding from an elder than I wanted to hear. "Is there a reason you're trying to push the boundaries?"

I said nothing. I didn't know what to say.

"There are ways for us to be close to one another without having to turn this into something sexual." His voice was steady, but had not entirely lost its sleepiness. "Is it really sex that you want from me right now? Or do you just want to be held?"

"I—I don't know," I admitted.

"Well, I do. Now, hush and go to sleep. I'm not going anywhere." He pulled me in closer against him, and held me tightly, almost protectively.

I was surprised. And I was surprised even further when I realized how relieved I felt. I finally felt safe. I began drifting to sleep in his arms the moment I closed my eyes. I fell into a deep, deep, sleep, as if I hadn't slept in years.

32

I saw Aeleise at school on Monday morning. I approached her in the hallway between classes and she continued to walk on without stopping. I ran to keep up with her, but she never turned to acknowledge me.

Without looking at me, she finally said coldly, "You were in my brother's bed, Krista. I didn't like it." After a few hurried paces, she stopped suddenly and turned to face me. "Why Daemon, Kris?"

"Nothing happened," I said.

"Maybe, maybe not. But either way, that's what you want, isn't it —for something to happen?"

I didn't say anything... had Daemon?

She shook her head. "Great. That's just great, Kris. Hey—you think you could book me a night with Josh, or is he already spoken for this month?" She pretended to consider. "Then again, maybe I'd prefer Marc. He's close to Daemon's age."

"I'm sorry, Aeleise."

"So am I." She walked away.

When the school day ended, I walked to the coffee shop two blocks from campus. Mondays were slow at the Java Hut, which meant I often found Brandon there, relaxing with a book.

The little bell chimed as I pushed through the door, and I spotted him sitting way in the back. He was engrossed, at least two hundred pages deep in a copy of *Atlas Shrugged*. He absently sipped tea with one hand, and turned pages with the other. I liked to watch Brandon. I stood there silently with the sounds of jazz and cappuccino machines whirling in the background.

He finally noticed me.

"*Good God!*" He lifted my hand to inspect my newly painted black fingernails. "Are we in mourning?"

I withdrew my hand.

"Are you looking to join the ranks of the Goths at school? Should I find you a bottle of Robitussin now?"

"No," I grumbled. "They would never have me anyway."

"Then what's the meaning of... *this?*" He waved his hand at the layers of black chiffon I wore.

"I blew it with Daemon yesterday—absolutely *blew* it."

"Blew it with Daemon," he said evenly as he studied my face. "So, do I have to guess, or will you be kind enough to fill me in?"

I told Brandon about the entire disaster—how I'd candidly admitted my feelings to Daemon, only to follow that admission with a display of shamingly forward behavior; how he'd found me injured on the beach; and how our secret wasn't such a secret anymore.

"*Jesus*, Kris." He eyed my ensemble warily. "So... this is some tribute to Daemon? Well, at least you had the sense to wear Donna Karan."

I slumped into the chair beside him. He gripped the arms of my chair and pulled me around to face him. "Ignored my advice, I see."

"Brandon, if this is the part where you start in on a lecture, or tell me I told you so, I'll take a rain check."

He took my hands in his. "I'm sorry. I won't say anything—I give you my word." He squeezed my hands. "Come here." He tugged me lightly to sit on his lap, and his arms closed about me. "I hate seeing you look so defeated. I am sorry, Kris. I know you've had your heart set on him. I wish I could change the circumstances for you."

I was proud of myself; I didn't cry. It wasn't accomplished without effort.

He placed his hands on my shoulders, pulled back to catch my eyes with his. "But enough of this, gorgeous. You're in dire need of a wardrobe change. This overzealous nod to the underworld is *not* working, hon. Trust me — you'll thank me later."

He nudged me to my feet by rising himself, and claimed my hands again. "*Rise,* Vampirella."

I let Brandon drag me away.

33

When Brandon didn't show up at school the next day, I phoned him at home.

"He's surfing, dear," his mother's inebriated voice cooed sweetly over the phone.

I stared at the phone, dazed for a moment, and then, frustrated, I slammed it down. I asked myself why I was so angry over being unable to get in contact with him; he didn't owe me anything. We weren't dating. I didn't even know what I wanted to say that was so important.

The next time I saw Brandon, four days had come and gone. It was Monday after school; the air was hot, dry, and still. Almost everyone had left for the day. I spotted him halfway across campus, sitting on a bench in the grassy area of the lunch court. His back was to me, but I recognized him immediately.

A sudden rage swept through me from head to toe, unbalancing me; he was with Nick. Brandon reclined against the table, using his elbows to support himself, while Nick sat sideways on his lap. Nick, in profile, was smiling, engrossed in whatever Brandon was saying.

Neither had seen me approach. I made my presence known without subtlety: I deliberately chose my heaviest textbook, then dropped it without warning to create a loud *smack*.

It got their attention. Any hare would've been impressed with the height of their startled jump. They turned around. By the look on Brandon's face, I knew he wished he hadn't.

I gave him a sweet, condescending smile. I ignored Nick completely.

"Krista." He didn't bother to hide the discomfort in his voice. Good. He deserved to feel it.

"Hi, yourself." I kept my voice mild while battling my inner fury. "Where have you been? I've been trying to get hold of you for days."

"I know. I'm sorry."

"Why haven't you called me back?"

"I've been busy."

"Bullshit—you've been avoiding me," I said, and then realized I needed to regain control over my outbursts. "What did I do, Brandon?"

He lowered his eyes and picked at the drab, sun-drained yellow paint around a chipped area on the bench beside him. "Nothing. I should've called you."

"But you didn't."

"But I didn't," he conceded.

"Time out, you two. What's going on?" Nick asked.

My eyes remained on Brandon, not even acknowledging Nick's words. He was odd man out in this discussion and I felt no remorse; after all, he was the one sitting comfortably on Brandon's lap.

"Nothing that concerns you," Brandon said. "If you'll excuse me a minute, Nick, I'm going to take a round with Krista."

Nick shrugged. "Sure."

"I'm sorry I didn't call you."

"Where have you been? You haven't been to school in days."

"The waves have been insane. I've been surfing two sessions a day, sometimes more."

It was always surfing. "Where have you been at night?"

"At Nick's."

"*Every* night?"

"Yes."

Was I really getting jealous? Maybe, just maybe—but I didn't want to embrace the thought. I might allow myself to justify anger, but *jealousy*—no way.

He was studying me. "Don't ask questions you don't want to hear the answers to," he said matter-of-factly. "He had the place to himself."

I swallowed past that, knowing what it meant. Brandon loved sex. I knew he did. I already knew he'd been with Nick. This was simply the first time it presented a roadblock—the reason behind avoiding me or ignoring my phone calls. It stood in front of me as a formal acknowledgement. Four days without separation? They were without question a couple now; Brandon might even be embracing the uncommon idea of commitment to Nick. So . . . good for them.

"I understand," I said slowly. "So . . The happy couple. I hiccupped a bitter laugh. "He actually escaped the fate of being just another conquest?"

I worked to squelch the potpourri of emotions I feared would be detectable in my voice.

"Is that what you think you were? You weren't a conquest, Kris—and don't compare yourself to Nick. It's not even close to the same situation."

"Who said anything about me?"

He stopped abruptly, as if my words had struck him as unbelievable. He stared into my eyes. The brightest golden flecks of color in his irises appeared only when he was angry or upset, and now they gleamed like the gold of Sleeping Beauty's fairy tale locks. He spoke with measured slowness.

"Okay, Kris. I'll be as blind as you want me to be."

"What?"

He shook his head, began walking again. I stared at the path as it blurred before me.

"I don't know what I'm getting so upset about," I said, half to myself. "It's just not like you to disappear like that."

"Well, now you know—everything's fine."

It didn't feel like it.

We had reached the tables once again, where Nick waited. His tone was wondering, softer than usual. "Hey, Kris. I didn't get a chance to say hello."

I hadn't given him one. Surprised he had made the effort to be civil, I said, "Hi." My voice sounded weary.

He didn't ask any questions.

Brandon filled the uncomfortable gap. "Can I drive you home, Kris? We were going to take off anyway."

"No, thanks."

"I'm not going to leave you alone on campus. It's getting late. It'll be dark soon."

"I'm not afraid of the dark." I only said it to be a smart ass; he didn't need to know that wasn't the truth.

"Don't argue with me. I'm taking you home."

I didn't want to sit with them, to see the two of them together in the car.

Brandon grabbed my textbook off the table. "It's coming with me, and so are you."

He ignored my scowl and lightly took my arm to steer me toward his car. I obeyed grudgingly, wordlessly. Nick the silent partner trailed behind us, then opened the passenger door, prepared to get into the back.

"I'll ride in back," I said.

We were at my house within minutes and I hopped out of the car, thanked Brandon for the unwanted lift, and said goodbye—yes, even to Nick.

Brandon said he'd call me. I wouldn't hold my breath.

34

Wednesday after school, Ryan came over to the house to run plays with Josh. Josh would hurl the ball, sending it sailing past the living room window, and then I'd hear the distinctive grunt as Ryan caught the pass. Back and forth, back and forth. Over and over again.

The phone rang. I jumped up and answered it before it rang twice. It was for Josh. A new girlfriend named Meagan.

"Hold on a sec."

I went by the door and called outside, "Josh—phone. It's Meagan."

A minute later, he came panting up to the door.

"In the kitchen," I said.

Ryan, sweat-soaked and rosy-cheeked, came up to greet me at the door. He used his forearm to wipe the perspiration from his brow, and it left a nice dirt smear across his forehead. *Just like a five-year-old, hard at play.*

"Hey," he said.

"Want something to drink?"

"Yeah."

I motioned for him to follow me into the kitchen. Josh wasn't in sight, which meant he'd taken his call to the study. "Water or Gatorade?"

"Gatorade. Thanks."

Ryan was looking at me peculiarly. "You got a minute?"

"Sure. What's up?"

"I wanted to ask you about Carrie."

I looked at him with interest.

"Is she into anyone?" he asked.

"*Into* anyone?"

"Yeah. Does she like anyone right now?"

"No," I said. "Why? Is someone interested in her?"

Ryan threw back another gulp of his drink before he looked at me. "Yeah."

"Who? *You?*"

"Yeah," he said diffidently. "Only, I don't know if she'd ever consider going for me. You're her best friend—what do you think? Would I stand a chance?"

"Stand a chance?" I said, amazed by his doubt. "Ryan, Carrie adores you. She thinks you're a total sweetheart."

"Yeah?"

I nodded. "She told me that the first day I met you."

"It's just that we've been friends for a while now, and... I don't know if she could ever see me as anything more than that. If you think it might make her uncomfortable or mess things up, then I'm over it. I'd rather just be friends if it's gonna ruin things."

"Well, it doesn't hurt to ask."

"I've been thinking about it, but... I ..." His attention shifted to the floor as he searched for words. A moment later, he met my eyes. "I don't know what she'll say."

"Do you want me to feel it out for you first?" I asked.

He looked up at me, relieved. "Would you?"

"Of course. I'd be happy to help."

"Thanks," he said. "There's something else I've been meaning to talk to you about."

"What is it?"

"It's about Brandon." His voice sounded troubled. "I'm telling you because I know—I've *accepted*—that you'll never see me as anything more than a friend, Kris. I thought I'd let you know... just in case you're interested. I get the feeling that Brandon isn't quite as enamored with Nick as Nick is with him."

"I thought things were going well between them."

"I didn't say things were bad; it's just... I'm beginning to think Brandon's interests lie elsewhere."

"Did he tell you that?"

"No. But he doesn't have to. I know him well enough."

"Is he concentrating more on his surfing?" I asked. I knew he had a series of contests coming up shortly.

"No. I mean, of course he's still surfing like mad, but what I'm talking about has to do with you. I'm kinda worried about him, Kris. This whole Daemon thing... I think it has him more keyed up than you realize. He's been acting really strange. He hasn't been himself lately."

"And you think this has something to do with me?"

He nodded. "He doesn't love Nick."

"Of course he doesn't. Brandon doesn't do love," I said.

"Yeah, he's also full of shit. Kris, one thing you've gotta know about Brandon—when it comes to people, if he stands to lose anything by caring for them, then he'll insist he couldn't care less. Other than surfing, I've never known Brandon to be big on taking risks. He won't knowingly walk into anything where he won't end up on his feet. As far as Nick goes, sure, he cares about him, but Brandon needs space—and lots of it. Nick doesn't give him much. I'm wondering how long it's going to last."

"And this is all your supposition?"

"I know what I'm talking about." Ryan's eyes were completely serious. "Brandon *likes* you, Kris. I see it. I know what you're thinking, but..." He shook his head. "If you weren't so head over heels for Daemon, I think he'd want to ask you out."

"We go out together all the time."

"As friends, not as a couple."

I fought the urge to laugh. "You mean he'd ask me on a *date* or something?"

"I'm almost positive he would."

I took a deep breath. It didn't seem likely.

Ryan shrugged. "Just thought I'd share my two cents with you."

"Thanks, Ryan. I'll think about it." *Just not right now.* I looked at the empty bottle he held and reached for it. He handed it to me. "Want another?" I asked.

"Nah, I'm good, thanks."

I heard a door close down the hallway, and then Josh walked into the kitchen.

"Hey, sorry 'bout that," he said to Ryan through a crooked smile. "You ready to go again?"

"Just waitin' on your ass," Ryan quipped, pushing away from the counter.

Josh gave him a cocky grin. "Let's go."

Ryan turned back to me. "We'll talk later?"

I nodded. As they both walked back onto the lawn to pick up where they'd left off, I headed for my bedroom, prepared to play telephone-cupid.

Just as I sat on my bed, getting ready to call Carrie, the phone startled me with a ring.

I grabbed it. "Hello?"

"I kept my word—I promised I'd call."

The sound of Brandon's voice made me smile. I leaned back against my pillow. "Amazing."

"Don't tell me you gave up on me already? Can't a guy get a few days to regroup?"

I chuckled. "If this call is the result of you regrouping... by all means."

"It's good to hear your voice, Kris."

35

Brandon emerged from his bedroom after making his usual after school wardrobe change. He looked fresh and comfortable in a pair of black slacks and a fine, camel-colored shirt. I was instantly aware of its snug fit — or more accurately, the way his perfectly toned body looked modeling micro-fiber in short sleeves.

"Are you into cruel and unusual punishment, or what?" I asked.

"What?" He looked convincingly unaware of his obvious appeal. Yeah, right. Daemon, maybe. Brandon, no way.

"Don't give me that. You know damn well you look hot right now."

He laughed. "What are you talking about? I thought I *always* looked hot."

"Screw you. You did it on purpose."

He smiled. "Truthfully, no. But, had I known it would create such a stir in you ... Maybe I should buy one in every color."

"Don't." I shook my head. "I'm supposed to be studying."

"Who's stopping you? I'm here to help."

I had to laugh at that. "Sure you are."

We sat on the floor of Brandon's living room using the couch as a backrest, books spread out on the coffee table.

"So, I hear you're playing matchmaker," Brandon said a moment later. "Ryan expressed interest in Carrie?"

"He brought it up the other day. I told him I'd do what I could to help. He tell you?"

"No. Actually, Carrie did. I think I'm going to talk to him about it tonight. If he moves too fast, it'll only freak her out."

I nodded. "You're right. But...you don't have to tell him everything, do you? Carrie'd die if she knew we opened our mouths."

"About Jalen?"

I nodded.

"Don't worry; I know what to say without breaking our word."

"You think she'll tell Ryan?" I asked.

"I doubt it. She won't face the truth herself. Until she does," he shook his head, "nothing's going to change."

I sighed deeply, hearing the truth in his statement. "You're right."

He shook his head quickly. "Anyway," he said, pushing beyond that topic, "where were you yesterday? I missed the pleasure of your company." He smiled warmly at me.

"Oh, yeah...yesterday," I said. "Yesterday, I went over to Aeleise's early, and Daemon took me flying before the group met."

His voice raised an octave at that. "Did he? And how was that?"

"Oh Brandon, it was *incredible*. You should've *seen* the colors of the sky," I said, seeing the dreamscape in my mind. "It reminded me of pineapple rainbow sherbet. It was the most beautiful thing I've ever seen." I shook my head. "We had the most amazing time."

Brandon sat there silently. Finally he said, "Well, it sounds like things are back on track, then. Yes?"

"Yeah. It seems like it."

"And how *is* Daemon these days?"

"He's doing great," I said. "You should see all the new things he's gotten for his room. The other day, he found some of the coolest decorations at some secondhand store that sells antiques." What was I doing? Ryan's words came back to me. I couldn't believe I was so insensitive and besides which I was endangering my relationship with Brandon.

"So what do you and the incredible church man hunk talk about?"

I shrugged. "Church stuff, mostly. This last time, I checked out the lineup for our upcoming series. Guess what we're discussing next month?"

"I'm sure I couldn't guess."

"Alternative lifestyles."

"I can hardly wait. Which will I get—the customary apology speech, or the ever-popular cold shoulder? Should we just say our goodbyes now?"

"What are you *talking* about?"

"Isn't this where it all unravels? After all, I'm a bad influence; I live an immoral life—aren't you supposed to distance yourself from negative elements?"

"I'd never quit talking to you, Brandon."

"You say that now."

"I can't believe you'd ever think I'd just walk away from you, walk out on our friendship. I—" I stopped.

"You what?"

"Nothing. I'm just not willing to give you up, that's all."

He shrugged and said without emotion, "I guess we'll see."

I wasn't getting much studying done. I reached for the binder that sat on the far edge of the coffee table. It slipped from my grip and went crashing to the floor, scattering papers. I sharply pulled back my hand, cutting myself on the edge of my notebook paper.

"Owww!" I looked at a surprisingly deep paper cut on my finger. "Damn!" I hissed under my breath at the pain, then put my finger in my mouth to stop the blood.

Brandon leaned over over me, gathering up the mess and placing everything back on the table. He stopped at one sheet and, keeping it in his hand, returned to rest against the couch. His face was expressionless as, eyes on the page, he read aloud, "Daemon … Daemon Faust … "

Realizing what he held, I jumped for it, but he was swifter than I was—he turned his back, continuing to read aloud.

"*Krista Faust … Kristina Faust …* hearts … flowers … "

"Don't read that!" I wailed in a panic.

Ignoring me, he continued. "Love … Daemon … *Daemon and Krista.* More hearts … *I love Daemon.* Daemon … Daemon … and … Daemon. Well." He shook his head. "Such devotion, and yet you can't spell his name."

He swiveled around and I snatched the paper away easily. Turning my back to him, I crumpled it into a ball and stuffed it in my pocket.

I was mad at myself for forgetting the daydream doodles that remained in my binder. I should have thrown them away long ago. Feeling the heat that signaled pink cheeks, I slowly faced the table again. "Jerk," I said, my voice low.

He was fiddling with his elaborate Swiss Army knife, exploring what looked like its fifty options. He had a small knife pulled open. Without warning, he ran his finger down the length of the blade. My eyes went wide and I looked at him then. He hadn't flinched; in fact, he'd displayed no reaction at all.

"It doesn't always hurt," he said, voice distant, as he looked with mild curiosity at the crimson life blooming rapidly on his finger. "Not always."

Had he spoken in Yiddish, I couldn't have been more surprised. This new voice of his was disturbing.

His elbow rested on the table so his hand was raised before his face; he watched with unaffected wonder as the liquid, ruby ribbon ran down his finger, spread at his palm, then left behind a bloody trail from wrist to forearm. He had grown utterly still.

"Brandon! What are you doing?"

He gazed at his hand with the calm of a porcelain figurine—blank, expressionless eyes remained still, as if he felt no pain. "It will heal," he said.

I stared at him—speechless. I finally found my voice. "Don't ever do that again," I said, voice barely audible.

"Is that an order?" he asked.

I kept my eyes and tone level. "Yes Brandon, that's an order. Hand me the knife, please."

He snatched it from the table and closed it in his palm. He tried to return it to his pocket.

I deftly grabbed his wrist. "Brandon, please...let go of it."

He tightened his grip around the weapon. I struggled to pry it from his hand.

"I said I won't do it again."

"I know you won't; that's why you're going to let me hold the knife for the time being. I'll give it back to you, Brandon—when you're thinking straight and acting like yourself—but I'm not about to take any chances with your safety. Now, will you please take the death grip off the knife?" I implored, "Please, Brandon."

His reluctance to relinquish the weapon only heightened my concern, but I knew I'd never get it from him unless he chose to release it.

"Brandon, look at me," I demanded.

He slowly gave me his eyes.

"I don't want to fight with you, Brandon … please."

Something spoke to him as we were locked eye to eye. Though hesitant at first, he loosened his grip and allowed me to take the knife from him.

I breathed a sigh of relief. "Thank you. I promise I'll keep it safe for you, okay?"

He said nothing as I tucked it into my pants. *Sweet Jesus.* Completely rocked, I sat there almost afraid to take my eyes off him.

Then I saw the blood.

I moved to get up.

He stopped me, holding his unharmed hand firmly on top of mine. "Don't," he said. "I'm a big boy. I can take care of myself."

He got up and walked to the bathroom; I slumped against the couch.

Brandon confused me. I couldn't guess what would upset him, or set him off entirely. He was as unpredictable as the California weather. One minute he'd be bright and full of fervor; the next, despondent and dull; often, he was restless and volatile as a breaking storm. Sometimes his eyes would mist with tears, but the moment he turned cold, his demeanor was as biting as the snow.

He emerged from the bathroom while I was deep in thought. He appeared perfectly normal, as if nothing out of the ordinary had occurred mere moments ago. The large Band-Aid he'd wrapped around his finger was already showing a deep maroon stain.

"Are you okay?" I asked.

"I'm fine."

"What I just saw didn't look like fine to me. What was that all about?"

He shrugged, took his time to answer. "A tolerance test, perhaps." He sat down beside me.

I looked at him. "A tolerance test." I waited for him to continue, but he wouldn't speak.

"I want to know what's really going on with you, Brandon."

He remained quiet.

"Tell me this isn't something new you're into; tell me anything but that." *Dear God.* I insisted on a response. "Brandon..."

"No, Kris. It was merely a momentary distraction."

"What could you possibly need distraction from so badly?"

"Kris, you needn't worry about my safety with sharp instruments. Though perhaps in the future, it would be best to censor your thoughts of Daemon around me. I assure you—your regard for him cuts deeper than any blade."

I replayed what I remembered of the conversation we'd just had. I desperately wanted to understand so I wouldn't make the same mistake twice. "What did I say that was wrong?"

"Nothing, Krista. There's no wrong in telling the truth."

I sure felt like I'd said something wrong.

———

The following day at school, I waited in line behind three girls in the washroom, five minutes before third period. I skimmed over faces I recognized but didn't know, as they passed me on their way out. When the last stall opened, I noticed the amused and subtle double-take from the girl who was exiting. I ignored her sideways glance as she breezed by me. I closed the door and as I took my purse from my shoulder to hang it on the door, I froze. In bright red marker, *Josh McKinley* was scrawled across the bathroom door. Horrified, I read the slander, saw our phone number. I turned inside the stall. I was surrounded; every side had something more horrendous to say.

The bell shrilled above me. I was already late to class. I dug through my purse, grabbed a pen, and frantically tried to scribble the graffiti out. It was no use. I ripped tissue from the dispenser, spat on it, and rubbed with every ounce of energy I had. It was permanent ink; it wasn't going anywhere.

My fist hit the stall. I let the wadded tissue fall to the floor. Palms and forehead pressed against the cool surface of the door, I fought tears and anger as I considered what to do.

Josh and I often argued, and he could be a never-ending source of pain, but I couldn't pretend the graffiti didn't bother me. My mind raced through the list of girls he knew: girls he'd dated, girls who wanted to date him. Julie? But that was ages ago; she was already seeing someone else. A flashback hit me. Jessa's birthday party; her knowledge of Josh and Julie's afternoon together, her blatant come-on. His rejection. My mind settled firmly on Jessa. If it was the last thing I did, I would get even with her.

I phoned Brandon that night and shared what I'd discovered in the girls' bathroom. His opinion was a carbon of mine—he believed Jessa was behind it. He already disliked Jessa for mysterious reasons of his own, but this just anchored it.

"It'll get handled, Kris. That's a promise," he said.

The sight of Brandon talking to Jessa in the center of the sophomore quad irked me.

She stood close to him, and he let her. *That* I didn't understand. She talked against his ear, placed her hand on his arm; it remained there as she continued to whisper. Brandon grinned broadly. The sight of them together made me shake.

Once she left for class, I approached him, clutching my books against my chest. "Why are you messing around with her?" I demanded.

"I'm helping you out," he said.

"You playing kissy-face with Jessa is not helping me out—it's ticking me off."

He placed his hands on my arms. "Relax, Kris. I'm only leading her on. I thought you wanted vengeance on Josh's behalf—or have you changed your mind?"

"How does using your charms on Jessa help Josh?"

"Why don't you leave that to me?" he said. "Don't worry. I haven't forgotten last night's discussion."

I was still shaking.

"Go on, get to class. I'll catch up with you later, okay?"

I didn't see Brandon later that day, and he wasn't around after school. *I suppose he's off surfing,* I rationalized. I called him that night and he apologized for not meeting up with me.

"I had to take care of some things that couldn't wait," he said.

I waited for Brandon on the bench just outside the library entrance, taking shelter beneath the shade of a tree.

Nearby, in the quad, Josh and Meagan leaned against the wall that encircled the statue of our school mascot. It was a rare moment—Josh engaged in a public display of affection. Meagan was wrapped in his arms, her back against his chest. She smiled, head cocked slightly, as Josh spoke to her. Her smile lit up her face.

I had to admit, I liked Meagan. She was sweet and intelligent, not some skank that Josh had got in the habit of bringing home. Some of those girls still tried to get in his pants.

One of them approached them this very minute, and with apparent purpose.

Jessa.

I had to fight the urge to snap and go wild at her. I noticed Brandon following her at a safe distance, hawking her every movement.

Jessa stopped in front of Josh and Meagan.

Her voice carried. "She's a little prudish for you, Josh. How long do you think you can go without getting laid? I give it two days, tops." Her eyes flashed to Meagan. "Don't worry, Meagan, Josh knows how to get what he wants. Maybe not from *you* ... but he gets what he wants."

People started gathering around the commotion. Josh's arms tightened around Meagan, and he whispered something in her ear. I felt sorry for Meagan; I knew she couldn't rattle off the kind of verbal blows needed to ward off Jessa, and Josh had decided long ago he wouldn't give Jessa the satisfaction of his attention.

That Josh ignored her pissed Jessa off more. "Better keep your eye on that one, Meagan. There's a long list of girls waiting in line behind you, and they're all plenty ready to please him if you don't."

"Yeah, and you'd know *all* about pleasing the guys, wouldn't you, Jessa?" came Brandon's voice. "I mean, it's not like you were praying when you dropped to your knees in the front seat of my car."

Shocked, she whirled to see where the unexpected comment had come from. Her face twisted with the ferocity of a witch at the sight of Brandon. "I never!"

He laughed heartily. "Oh, I do believe you did. Yesterday, as a matter of fact, directly after school." He was grinning, full of himself as always, but his eyes were most serious, and then thoughtful. "I forgot to tell you how pretty I found that purple angora puff holding back your hair. Nice touch. I thoroughly enjoyed myself, by the way." His tone made me think he'd just used a toothpick to clean his teeth after enjoying a satisfying meal.

My throat tightened; I could hardly breathe. I started to feel sick. My pulse began to race. They didn't get together...did they? *God, please, don't let it be true—anything but that!*

He slipped his hands into his trouser pockets. "I appreciated your offer for more, but personally..." he shook his head, "I just couldn't bring myself to do it. Though I can vouch you give incredible head. And you're such an eager performer, too."

Everyone within earshot had stopped to listen. Curious faces stared, laughed, snickered at Jessa as she stood there like some trapped animal, burning in her state of humiliation.

"You're a fucking prick, Brandon!" she spat out, her face glowing with rage and embarrassment.

Brandon, ever calm and unaffected, simply said, "And you're just a bitch that's pissed because I wouldn't give you mine." The onlookers gasped. He shook his head. "Take your shit somewhere else." He blew her a kiss with his middle finger. "See ya, Jessa. It was real." He walked away, and she bolted through the snickering crowd.

Josh looked stunned. Meagan was smiling. I was shaking. Everyone was hollering and whistling—the crowd loved it. I didn't.

I felt wretched. I strained to keep myself together, strove to regain some measure of self-control. Brandon headed my way. I hadn't realized that I was already standing, but here I was, trembling on my feet. A look of concern washed over his face. I was highly aware of my breathing and the staccato beat of my heart. He stood squarely in front of me, put his hands on my shoulders so he could look me straight in the eyes.

Just having him touch me made everything all the more intense, and I lost some of the control I was fighting to retain. I felt the ache in my throat as I attempted to speak, and from that point on, everything started to crumble. The tears came. I wasn't crying... yet I was. The stares of admiration followed Brandon like iron filings to a magnet, which would've been fine, except that he was standing next to me. He took hold of my arm and led me to a place behind the library where people rarely went.

"Talk to me, Kris. What is it?"

It came out in a flood. "How could you let her touch you? I can't believe you let her—" My voice squeaked out in a cry. I couldn't finish the sentence, couldn't say what intimacies he'd allowed her to perform. The thought made me nauseous all over again.

"Kris—oh, God. Don't cry, please. It's not what you're thinking."

"You mean she wasn't with you yesterday?"

"Yes, she was, but—"

I quickly cut him off, shaking my head. "That was why you didn't meet me yesterday? Because you were with *her?*"

"Nothing happened, Kris. I swear. Nothing got that far."

That didn't help the tears any. Not that far? 'Not that far' clearly indicated to me that something had happened. "But you did screw around with her?"

His eyes were pleading. "Please. Will you give me a chance to explain?"

Fine. I wiped my eyes with the back of my hand.

"She tried, Kris—and I didn't let her. I swear to you. I took it as an opportunity to have her seen leaving with me so my story would hold some credibility—nothing more. I had to make it seem like we were leaving school together. I only did it to get back at her for what she did to Josh."

"You mean she didn't..."

"*No.*"

"Did you kiss her?" I asked, looking him straight in the eyes.

His gaze dropped immediately. He shifted his weight to his other foot. It was uncomfortably quiet. I knew then that he had. I hid my face behind my hands, covering the tears. I hurt—more than I could ever have imagined.

At least he owned up to it. "Yeah," he said, his voice low. "I did. But Kris, it didn't mean anything."

I couldn't look at him, didn't want to.

"I feel like shit now," he said, and I believed him, but it didn't matter. "Maybe it wasn't worth it."

I'd say not. I hoped Josh appreciated it. The bell was about to ring, signaling the end of lunch, and my face felt completely swollen and blotchy.

"I gotta go," I said, and turned away.

"Wait—Kris," he said, holding onto my arm. "Don't leave. Let's get out of here—right now."

"I can't just leave school like you can. I actually have to attend."

"Everyone is going to be asking you a million questions. Are you really going to get anything done?"

"I don't see how leaving with you is going to make me feel any better. You're the reason I feel like shit right now," I said angrily.

"I'm sorry, Kris. I fucked up. I never meant to hurt you."

I knew he meant what he said, and I suppose that was worth something. "I know, Brandon," I said in a tired voice.

"What class do you have next? I'll walk you there."

"I'm not going to class," I said.

"You've changed your mind? You're going to accompany me, then?"

"No," I said. "I'm just going to go."

"Where?"

"I don't know yet. Somewhere away from here."

"I'll take you wherever you want to go, Kris. Please."

I thought about that. I wanted him to hurt. "You mean that?"

He nodded.

"Fine," I said. "Take me to Daemon's."

He looked like he'd been socked in the chest. He took a deep breath. "All right," he said quietly, the pain evident in those words. "I suppose I had that coming. Come on, then."

I followed him in silence to his car. Neither of us shared a word the entire drive. When we turned onto Daemon's street, he slowed down before reaching his house and stopped at the neighboring house. Then he turned to me. His huge, copper eyes looked beaten.

"I don't want you to go in there," he said, and I had never heard his voice so worried. "I don't want to leave you here alone with him."

I studied him, considering. My tears had yet to dry. I was exhausted and empty, and although I had no right to, I still felt somehow betrayed. "Brandon," I said lightly to reassure him, "You have no reason to worry—not that you would. We both know Daemon and I won't be holding any kissing sessions."

He averted his eyes. "But you *want* to be kissing him," he said.

I shrugged. "Thanks for the lift."

"I'll wait to make sure you get inside," he said.

"I'm going around the back. He's usually back there, and if not, I have a key."

He seemed unsettled by my lie, but was quick to mask it. He waited to see me off anyway, and I walked around the side of the house and ducked into the alcove. He slowly drove off. I waited until the sound of Brandon's car had faded around the corner. Once I thought he was gone, I began my walk home.

At home, I didn't want to think about it. I reached into my art desk, withdrew a stack of coloring books, and dragged them down to the floor with me. The simplicity of fat crayons and recycled paper was comforting.

I was still coloring, lying on my stomach on my bedroom floor, my feet scissoring back and forth in the air, when my bedroom door flew open.

Josh.

"Kris, I've never seen you turn so blue in the face in a matter of seconds. You heard his little speech about Jessa blowing him and you came *unglued*. So it was Brandon you slept with—that fills in the missing piece.

Blood surged to my cheeks in one hot wave. I had *almost* gotten it out of my mind. "Josh, Brandon's dating Nick."

"I believe you," he said. "But now I know the rest of the story—you slept with him."

I just looked at him.

"He shook his head. "It's messed up, how the two of you screwed over Ryan like that. Even *I'm* in favor of Ryan."

"Great for you, Josh. Why don't you date him? Ryan is my friend—nothing more."

"I'm beginning to get into this soap opera life of yours," he said. "So, does Nick know you're doing his boyfriend?"

"Get out of my room."

Marc arrived home early, bringing happiness through the door in the form of a German chocolate cake. He didn't need to announce that twice; within seconds, Josh and I were at the kitchen table, hovering over the dessert like a couple of vultures.

"Just leave a piece for Kaelie, will you?" Marc said. "She's coming over later tonight for a while."

I frowned. "That means you're not going to practice chess with me."

"I'm sorry. Another night, Kris. How about tomorrow?"

I shrugged and muttered, "Fine, I guess. But that doesn't do me any good for tonight." I looked at Josh, considering. Not much of a challenge, not much of a game. It would be an unsatisfying win.

Josh shook his head. "*Uh-uh*. Don't look at me. Why don't you invite your *boyfriend* over? I'm sure he'd play with you." He grinned like a punk.

"I don't have a boyfriend," I said. *Pray, don't let him drag this out onto the floor now—not in front of Marc.*

"Sure you do. You're sleeping with Twinkle Toes, aren't you?"

I glared at him, biting down on my teeth.

"I'm just kidding; I have to say Brandon's all right. I still can't get over that show he put on. Meagan's his biggest fan now."

I gave him huge eyes.

Marc said, "What?"

Through an icy glare directed at Josh, I said, "I'm not sleeping with Brandon, Josh."

"Save it. Once was enough, huh? Bored already?"

Marc turned to me, pausing as it sunk in, then finally asked, "Is that true?"

I didn't say anything.

Josh continued. "So *that's* the reason Ryan left here all pissed off that day. He just found out the two of you had been hittin' it."

Marc worked to remain calm. "Correct me if I'm wrong, but Brandon *is* gay, is he not?"

"Yes," I said, "he is."

"Did you sleep with him, Krista?"

Lying was pointless. *Damn* Josh. I *so* didn't want to have this discussion. Marc was still waiting for my answer. I met his eyes. We faced off for an interminable time.

Marc broke the silence. "I thought you were going to come to me when you made that decision," he said. I could tell he was disappointed. "Did you use protection, I hope?"

Josh threw in his unnecessary two cents. "Yeah, she took off with mine."

Marc hadn't taken his eyes off me. "You haven't said a word yet," he said.

"What do you want me to say?"

"Are you sleeping with him?" he asked again. When I didn't answer, he lightly shook his head again. "Bring him by the house more often."

"Why?" I asked.

"Because I'd like to know more about him. I thought he had a boyfriend."

"He does," I said.

"Then what is he doing sleeping with you?"

Wasn't that the million dollar question?

"He's not," I said.

Josh said, "You mean, not anymore."

I glared at Josh. "I don't need your help, Josh, so why don't you shut up."

Marc was beginning to look tired. "All right, enough. Kris, just bring him by."

"I'm not bringing him over so you can interrogate him."

"No one said anything about *interrogating* him. I'd just like to get a feel for him."

"*If* and when he happens to come over, fine. But if either of you says anything about this to him, we're leaving."

Marc said, "Fair enough."

Josh agreed grudgingly. "I guess I kinda gotta be cool to him after today." He shoveled his last forkful of cake into his mouth. "I'm takin' off to Todd's. If Meagan calls, tell her I'll call her tonight."

Marc nodded, and Josh took off out the door.

Marc turned to face me again. "So…when did all this take place?"

"You were busy. You were tied up for two days with an emergency."

He sighed. "There *is* such a thing as a telephone, and I left you the number where I could be reached. I would've made time." He spread his palms out in front of him. "Kris, I'm willing to be open-minded about this—*if* I know I can count on you to let me know what's going on. Will you make my life easier so I know I don't have to worry about you? That's all I'm asking."

"All right," I said. "I promise I'll do my best to keep you posted from now on—as long as *I* know what's going on. And Marc…I don't *always* know what's going on."

"I know; but just as long as I know you're seriously making the effort, I'll be satisfied. I'll take what I can get."

Brandon called me just as I was getting into bed.

"If I told you I've been moping and miserable since I dropped you off, would it matter?"

I lay tucked beneath my sheets, head on my pillow, staring at the ceiling as we talked. "Moping? I'm sorry, I thought I was talking to someone named Brandon."

"I'm glad to see your sense of humor has returned. So, are you willing to accept my apology, or are you going to ride my guilt until I break?"

I heard undecipherable rustling in the background.

"Brandon VanAulstine, *break?* I didn't know that was possible."

The noise that followed sounded like the faint release of a zipper. "Are you trying to find out?" he asked.

Part of me *did* want to ride it out. I sighed. "No, not really. I just didn't anticipate feeling so ... *adversely* affected by—" I didn't complete that thought—at least, not aloud. "My anger just overwhelmed me."

"Yes, I clearly recall. Kris, I apologize—I should've come up with a different plan."

"Let's just forget about it. You've accomplished your goal, haven't you?"

I heard more movement in the background.

"What are you doing?" I asked.

"Undressing for bed."

I paused on that. I heard the gurgling waves of his waterbed as he slipped between sheets. Did he realize that ridiculously simple, everyday things weren't entirely innocent anymore? In the past, I wouldn't have paid it any mind.

It finally hit me then. *Nothing* between us would ever be the same.

"Am I banned from your top three list?" he asked.

I heard him shifting, making himself comfortable in bed.

"You're not completely ruled out," I replied, and then, giving in far too quickly, added, "Somehow, you always have a way of finding my soft spot."

He released a deep breath. "Thank God for that. I needed to hear it."

———

I did bring Brandon home with me shortly thereafter. Was it pride? Satisfaction? A silent acknowledgement? A fear I was insisting I push through? Maybe a smidge of each all rolled into one? I didn't want to feel like I was hiding or sneaking around if I had him over. It shouldn't be any big deal; it had never been an issue before.

I hadn't said word one to Brandon about Marc's and Josh's assumptions.

I hadn't said the actual words, *"Yes, Brandon and I slept together."* Let Marc and Josh see I wasn't intimidated. But deep down, I really was scared. I didn't know if Marc would treat me differently, or watch Brandon and I like a hawk, forever suspicious we were going to drop right there and go for it in my bedroom. I just didn't know. And that worried me.

Marc was home when we arrived; he was busy cooking in the kitchen. The air was rich with the scent of oregano and garlic; he was making homemade spaghetti sauce, and it smelled as delicious as mom's. As we came in, he was adding something to the large silver pot. He looked over his shoulder from the stove. "Hey, Kris. Hi, Brandon. How's it goin'?"

I was immediately on the lookout for warning signs or strange vibes. Nothing so far.

"Great, and yourself?" Brandon replied.

Marc nodded with a small, self-satisfied smile. "Can't say it's been all that bad." He wiped his hands on the dish towel on the counter. "Carrie left a message for you on the machine, Kris. She'd like Ryan's number."

"Okay," I said quickly. "We'll be in my room if you need me."

"Pasta will be ready in about an hour or so." He looked at Brandon. "Would you like to stay for dinner?"

I tensed. We never had guests over for dinner.

"I would love to stay for dinner, if Krista doesn't have any objections."

Brandon looked at me. My lips barely moved; a voice that I wasn't sure was mine said, "I'd love for you to stay."

"Great," Marc said. "I'll let you know when it's ready."

I led Brandon into my bedroom, closed the door.

"He knows," I said.

"He knows what?"

"About us. That we slept together. Josh figured it out and told him."

"Well...he obviously doesn't have a problem with it, so why should we?"

"I feel weird. Like it's so 'in your face.' At least the way I handled it, there was a *slight* element of ambiguity—at least I could still look him in the eye. Now it's like...sitting right there in front of us."

"I thought you two were so close," he said, taking a seat on my bed.

"We *are*, but..."

"Are you uncomfortable because it's *me*, or just with the concept of him knowing you're no longer a virgin?"

"It's not about you," I said. "I guess it's the latter."

"Well, all I can say is, the cat's out of the bag, so we'll all have to deal with it."

"Is it really any of his business, though? Does he have any right to ask questions?"

"Mmm...yes. He does. And I plan to answer whatever questions he asks, truthfully."

I stared at my plate, absently pushing around long, thin strings of angel-hair pasta with my fork, making a separate section for my spaghetti sauce. I'd been picking at my meal since my plate had been placed in front of me, unable to adapt comfortably to our momentous dining event.

Marc said, "Kris tells me you're really into surfing."

"The ocean is like my second home."

"I caught your surf video," Marc said. "Impressive."

"My sponsors like to see what they're paying for. I'm surprised you've seen it."

Marc laughed, and said as he lifted his glass, "*Oh,* I caught it one of the *umpteenth* times Krista was watching it. You'd think she's the new surfing critic, the way she stares at that video."

"*Marc!*"

"What?" he asked innocently. "I'm just trying to figure out what it is you're studying when you're wearing out the pause and rewind buttons."

Brandon politely covered his mouth with his napkin in an effort to hide his smile. He looked at me. "I forgot you had that. You actually sat through the entire thing?"

"Sorry," I said, keeping my eyes on the pasta as I continued to twirl spaghetti around my fork. "I'll give it back to you tonight."

"Not a problem. I'm glad you enjoyed it."

Silence reigned for what seemed like five minutes. Then we made more torturous small talk. Finally I got up from the dining room table and took my dishes into the kitchen.

I could hear them talking. They weren't whispering, but they were, without question, keeping their voices low. I listened closely, and caught Marc's voice.

"You interested in hearing my opinion?" he asked.

"Please."

"I think she's manifested a desperate crush on Daemon because she fears she can't have you."

"What makes you think that?"

"You ever see her sketchbook?" he began.

Okay. Time to curtail this conversation. I coughed before I walked back into the dining room. "Marc," I said, and even managed to smile, "could you tell me how to make coffee, please?"

"*Coffee?* Since when did you start drinking coffee?"

"You haven't been paying attention. I've developed a taste for coffee."

"Within the last ten minutes?"

I gave him a stare.

"Sure. I'd be happy to help you."

After dinner Brandon followed me into my room. I closed the door behind him. "Don't you think you should leave your door open?" he asked.

"Don't worry about it." I moved to the bed and sat on the edge. "Nick seems upset lately," I began. "He's been kind of weird at practice—really withdrawn and quiet again. Not like he talks to me *anyway*, but ..." I shrugged. "I've noticed a change."

"Yes, well ... I've told Nick that we need to spend more time pursuing our own interests. We were spending too much time together. I think his attachment was becoming unhealthy."

I let my surprise show. "That would certainly explain his melancholy," I said. "He must've taken it really hard. Have you talked to him since?"

"No. I've made it a point to establish a fair amount of distance between us. I spend more time at the beach now."

"Is that *possible?*" I asked.

He laughed. "I find ways."

"So, how are you doing with it?" I asked. "I mean, you guys spent so much time together."

Brandon joined me on the bed. "I've had easier days, but I still think I made the right decision. I won't lie—I miss him—but he cuts himself off from everything else just so he can spend time with me. It may be flattering, but it's not really fair to him."

"Since when have you ever been concerned with fairness?"

He paused, as if disappointed with the truth in my statement. "I don't know... maybe I just feel like giving a shit for a change. This whole thing kinda sucks because I'm the first guy he's ever been with. That hasn't made separating any easier. But I *am* trying to keep that in mind — something I've never done before."

This new regard for others impressed me — no small achievement for Brandon. "Well, it's kind of you to handle it gently. He's like... *lost* without you, Brandon."

Brandon sighed. "Today, at the beach... I'm waiting out in the water for the next set to roll in, when I look toward the shore to check out the time on that huge clock — you know, the one that's above Jack's surf shop."

I nodded.

"I just happened to glance over by the pier, and lo and behold, there he was, standing by himself, watching me surf. I don't even know how long he'd been out there. I decided I'd take the next wave that came, ride it in to shore. Only when I got out of the water, I looked up, and he wasn't there. I felt like shit, Kris. I really did."

"I'm sorry, Brandon. I wish I knew what to say."

He gave me a weak smile. "Me too — especially since it was my bright decision."

"Why *did* you make that decision?"

He paused for a moment and then gave me his eyes. "Because he told me he loved me."

"What did *you* say?"

He rubbed his hands over his face, and his eyes met mine with pained seriousness. "I said, 'I gotta go.'"

An echo of guilt lingered in his words when he said, "Hey, I have an idea — let's drop the subject of Nick."

I nodded. "All right."

He quickly shifted the conversation in a new direction. "Hey... I want to see what you've done in art class. I've never seen any of your work."

"Oh... we don't bring our projects home from class; they stay in the art room."

"But you once told me you keep a sketch pad at home to practice in. I thought you had to have at least twenty drawings or sketches to turn in every quarter."

"Oh, *that,*" I said, trying to play it down. "You know, I don't know where I put it." I offered a lighthearted smile. "I'll have to show it to you another time." *Like as soon as I get a new sketchbook and fill it with drawings of fruit and flowers.*

The look he directed at me was full of skepticism. He pointed to the floor beside my closet door. "What's that?" he asked, getting up. "Even I know what a sketch pad looks like. He pulled the sketchbook out from between my history and math books. "I was right, see?" He held it up to my view, and returned to the bed.

I saw all too well. My pulse raced and my palms began to sweat.

He sat down beside me, held the tablet on his lap. I tried to snatch it from his hands. Brandon must've anticipated my move and he clung to it tightly. So did I. We were in the midst of a tug-o-war.

"I can't look at your drawings?" he asked, as if disappointed.

"These aren't my best pieces. It's just for practice," I explained anxiously.

"I understand, but I'd still like to see them."

"I never let anyone look at my unfinished work."

"Come on, Kris. I share *everything* with you. There's no reason to stress."

Hmph. Little did he know—but he was about to discover. When it was clear he wouldn't let up about it, I took a deep breath, said a silent prayer, and slowly released my hold. I stood and went over to my vanity.

"Where are you going?" he said. I pretended to busy myself by looking through my jewelry box. "Get back here. I want you to look at them with me. That way you can explain if I have questions."

Lord. I dragged my body to the corner of the bed, and sat down on the edge with a bounce.

"You can't see anything from over there; come sit beside me."

I took another deep breath. My skin already itched at our proximity. I was uncomfortable enough without having to sit beside him. I moved closer as he'd requested.

The five inches still separating us were too much distance for his liking. "Will you *please* come sit next to me?" His eyes were beseeching, and I grudgingly moved closer to him. "Thank you," he said, almost exasperated.

He lifted the cover to reveal a sketch of a butterfly. He smiled. "I believe this is the butterfly that perched itself on your head not long ago. This is really good, Kris."

He turned the page. The next one contained a half-finished drawing of an imaginary land, complete with faerie residents.

"You just conjure these up from your imagination?" he asked.

"Sometimes. Depends on my mood. Sometimes I'll draw from life, or a picture I like."

He nodded. "It's interesting to see through your mind's eye. I imagine it's difficult to translate dreams onto paper," he said, still studying my work. "Well, you're certainly skilled with pencil and paper, aren't you? This is really good, Kris," he said again. "I didn't know you were so talented."

I simply shrugged.

He gave me a silly look. "I don't know why you didn't want me to see them. As usual—worrying needlessly."

I wondered if he'd retract his statement once he turned the page.

He gave me an encouraging smile, and then—he advanced to the next illustration. A vacuum claimed all air in the room at that moment; only the billowing sound of the paper as it flipped smoothly to the opposite side broke the silence. Anxiously, I watched his expression. He stared at the page, his melting expression leaving him with slack, slightly parted lips. My heart had become a lump in my throat. Perhaps now he understood my reluctance to share. He was staring at his own likeness, a portrait I had started long ago.

"When did you do this?" he asked in a quiet voice.

I shrugged. "I don't know."

He hadn't taken his eyes from the page. "Shit," he said quietly, appearing awed, speechless. "You never told me you did a drawing of me."

"I didn't think about it." A lie.

He looked bewildered. "It looks just like me."

"You think so?"

He nodded, eyes still on the sketch. "Yeah." He turned the page. Another drawing of him. In a dream, I'd seen him relaxing on the beach between surf sessions, his surfboard beside him, and that's what I put to paper. He seemed transfixed by the image. He didn't move. "You even have my sponsors' logos on my board," he said, tone soft, amazed. "I didn't know you paid that close attention."

I didn't know how to respond to that, so I didn't. He turned the page and saw himself at Homecoming; turned another and he was sleeping in his ocean bed; in the next, he enjoyed a coffee at the Java Hut. The one following that displayed a three-quarter view of Brandon hugging a smiling Nick from behind, his cheek pressed lightly to his. I had never shaded the figure of Nick; he was nothing more than an outline.

Brandon turned the page and found the next one blank—-as all the subsequent pages were.

"I can't believe you drew all these," he said in a reverent tone, almost reluctantly closing the drawing tablet.

I shrugged, feeling foolish. "I just had some extra time on my hands."

He paid no heed to my dishonesty. He hadn't looked at me once since he'd unveiled the drawings of him. Still holding onto the sketchbook that lay closed on his lap, he turned his face to me. "Can I ask you something?"

"Sure."

"Why are they all unfinished?"

"I don't know; I don't know *what* it is, exactly, but…I have a really hard time drawing you. I'll get to a certain point and then suddenly I'll decide it doesn't look like you at all—and I become completely frustrated because I can't get it perfect." I frowned. "I've struggled with it forever, it seems."

He gestured with the pad. "They all look good to me," he said.

"I don't know," I said. "Something's missing; I only wish I knew what."

"Will you do me a favor?"

"Hmm?"

"Will you finish one of these drawings … please?"

"Mm-hmm."

He drew closer, contouring his body tighter against mine. "Thanks."

36

The phone rang while I was reading in my room. I leaned across my bed and grabbed the receiver. "Hello?"

"Krista, hi—it's Daemon."

"Hi," I said, wondering why he would call me, even a little nervous about it, though I was always happy to hear his voice. I looked at my alarm clock. Saturday morning, 10:00 A.M.

"Are you doing anything important at the moment, or can I steal you away for a while?"

"I was just relaxing with a book—I'd much rather talk to you."

"Is it all right if I swing by and pick you up?"

"Sure. Do you want me to bring my study things?"

"No, just yourself."

No study things? "I'll be waiting."

"Sounds good. See you in fifteen."

I hung up the phone. Just myself?

I got up from my bed and got ready. I wore my hair in one simple, fat braid down my back. I tossed on a fresh lilac shirt under white coveralls.

When Daemon arrived, I ran out the door before he had a chance to get out of his car. I slid into the passenger seat of his sleek silver vehicle. "Hi," I said with a smile.

Daemon looked beautiful, as always. He wore a V-neck sweater made of fine, tightly woven fabric—black, of course—and black slacks with faint pinstripes. His car smelled like coconuts. The stereo played music I didn't recognize: an instrumental piece with a deep bass pulse in an energetic, rhythmic beat that was almost hypnotic.

He turned the corner, then reached out and lowered the stereo's volume. "I wanted to let you know that I spoke with Aeleise," he said.

Things hadn't been exactly smooth between Aeleise and me lately. Even time spent at Bible studies had become strained. She still resented me for being in Daemon's bed, innocent as it was.

He said, "Things should calm down now. We discussed everything."

"Everything?" I prayed he'd edited out some of the details.

"Everything I could say without causing her more distress.

I breathed a sigh of relief. "Thanks."

He nodded. "You're welcome."

We pulled into his driveway a moment later; Aeleise's car was gone. We entered the house and he headed straight for the kitchen.

"Make yourself comfortable in the living room; I'm just grabbing us both something to drink."

He came in with a couple of sodas and took a seat beside me on the couch.

I looked at him, not opening my can yet. Something about his manner made me believe I was here for something serious. It felt unusual. Daemon was cool, and I always looked forward to being around him, but I knew he wouldn't call me up just to hang out. I didn't say anything.

"I guess you're probably wondering why I asked you to come over."

"The thought had crossed my mind, yeah."

"All right... I'm going to be straight with you," he said, and I recognized the seriousness beneath his gentle tone. "I did ask you here for a reason. Please don't be upset; I can't help being concerned, Kris. I'm sorry if you feel I'm interfering—I guess I am. But, as the only adult who knows about all that's gone on, I feel it's my responsibility to make sure you're okay. Please, don't be offended, but... did you bother to talk to Brandon about STDs? Do you even know if he's ever been tested for HIV?"

"*Whoa*—wait a minute," I said, unprepared for this.

"*Whoa* is right, Kris. Had Brandon been a virgin at the time, there would be less cause to worry—but he wasn't. I understand it was your first time, but you knew that it wasn't his. How do you know the reason he used a condom with you that night wasn't solely out of the fear of getting you pregnant? He doesn't have to worry about that risk in his relationships with *men,* now, does he?

"Does he practice safe sex with his other partners?" Daemon pressed. "Are you even aware that Brandon falls into one of the highest risk categories as far as sexually transmitted diseases, including HIV? Do you *know* if you've been exposed to anything? Were you even aware that he was still sexually active with other people during the time you two were together—you being the *only* girl?"

How did Daemon suddenly know so much about Brandon's sex life?

"How would *you* know if he's sleeping with anyone else?" I asked defensively.

"I asked Aeleise," he said matter-of-factly. "Apparently he has *quite* the reputation. I know he's dating Nick now, and I know he's slept with plenty of guys—and that's just what I *do* know. I'm sure there's plenty more of which I'm unaware."

I felt slammed. I'd never given it much—*hell,* who was I kidding?—I'd never given it *any* consideration.

"Well..." I paused, unsure of the right thing to say. "You are not the only adult who knows, not that it is any of your business. We did use protection, so I guess that means I'm safe from those things too... right?" My voice became weaker; it sounded more uncertain than I wanted. He was asking questions that Marc had either not thought about or did not know.

He took a deep breath, eyes weary, and said gently, "Well, if you can look me in the eye and tell me that that was the *only* thing that went on between the two of you, then maybe. But I hope you know there are other ways to contract a sexually transmitted disease. You don't necessarily have to have intercourse, Kris."

"What do you mean?"

"Kris..." He pushed through his discomfort. "I don't mean to sound presumptuous, but I'm assuming more than intercourse went on between you and Brandon; it would be uncommon if it hadn't. But maybe in this case I'm wrong. You tell me."

"I don't know what you're talking about."

Unbelieving eyes looked into mine. "No?"

My chest grew tighter. "No," I said nervously. "And what would you know about sex, anyway? I have more experience than you do."

"And are you proud of that?"

I couldn't stand it when his voice dropped to that tone. It always robbed me of my ability to speak.

"It's not my desire or intention to embarrass you." He sat serenely on the couch; calm, intense, black eyes trapped mine, held me captive as I sat tense beside him. We stared at each other. "I'm asking you to consider whether you may have unknowingly put yourself at risk. If you have, then I think it would be wise to check up on the matter with a professional, don't you?"

This conversation scared me. Had Brandon and I done something risky?

"You're being awfully quiet, Kris."

"You look confused," he said.

"I guess I am," I admitted.

"About what?"

"What you're saying. I don't know what counts—what puts me at risk. I don't know if I should be worried. I skipped that chapter."

He took a deep breath and let it out slowly. "Kris, did you and Brandon do anything other than have intercourse?"

I felt the heat slowly rise to my cheeks as my heart rate quickened. That question encompassed a lot. "Like kissing?" I asked nervously.

"Among other things."

His answer left me uneasy. My anxiety grew.

He tensely raked one hand through his hair. "Did you have oral sex with him?"

It took me a moment to recover from the shock.

"Kris…"

I didn't want Daemon to know what happened between Brandon and me. If he knew those intimate details, then he could picture me in the act. That was too much. But now, by my reaction alone, he assumed that we had.

"I didn't ask the question because I want to pry or embarrass you. You act as though I'll be shocked, or think you've done something horrible; that's just not true.

"Krista." He put his hand on my shoulder.

"Don't touch me." I shrugged his touch away. He didn't push that. "Sometimes you make me want to *hate* you," I said.

"I'm sorry to hear that," he said. I'd hurt his feelings, and he didn't pretend he was unaffected. "Krista, I don't think anything bad about you; I just want to make sure that you haven't been exposed to anything you hadn't planned on. He's sleeping with other people. I'm not sure you realize what you've stepped into. Can you blame me for being concerned?"

I had wanted Daemon to care about me, but once again, this wasn't what I'd had in mind. I'd been dealt a bogus hand of cards—Daemon always had a way of popping up like the Joker.

"Can you talk to him about this? Can you ask him if he's been tested?"

I shook my head. I probably could—Brandon was always cool about things—but it seemed insulting to ask. Now Daemon had me wondering.

"Then for your sake, will you at least let me take you to see someone who can make sure you've left this experience with a clean bill of health?"

I didn't like the idea, but he'd managed to instill worry in me. I silently agreed.

37

I needed to make amends with Nick. The silent treatment at practice had been going on far too long, and my follow-up apology was long overdue. I called his pager and left a message on his voice mail, asking him to call me.

"You paged?"

"Nick, it's Krista."

"Yes, I recognized the number." His voice sounded stiff, matter-of-fact.

"Are you someplace where you can talk, or did I call at a bad time?"

"No, it's fine; I'm in my room. I can talk." I heard him close the door. "What is it?"

"We haven't talked in a while, Nick, and I know you're still angry with me...Nick, I'm sorry. I really am. I never meant to come between you and Brandon. I don't know what to do to make things right between us. I just hope you can forgive me."

He was silent for so long that I began to think he wasn't going to respond, but then he sighed. "You aren't the only one I've been mad at. Brandon's decision didn't make me any happier. I guess it just pissed me off that he was willing with you when he's barely receptive to me." He was quiet for a moment, then said, "I've had some time to cool off, and he and I've talked. Thanks for the apology, Kris."

"What do you mean?" I asked, slightly confused by what he'd just shared.

"Well, it's just..."

I waited patiently for him to finish.

"The day the four of us stayed the night at his sister's beach house, Brandon and I ... we almost got together."

"I thought you *did* get together."

He sounded surprised. "What made you think that?"

I didn't want to embarrass him by telling him everything I saw. "You were kissing ..."

"Well, yeah—that happened." I could tell that my witnessing a simple kiss between them embarrassed him. I was glad I hadn't shared more.

"Wait, Nick. Define what *getting together* means to you."

His voice became unsure, self-conscious. "Well ... what does it mean to you?"

At this rate, we could be here forever, debating what first through home base was, as we'd done in elementary school. I decided to get straight to the point. "Well, did you sleep with him?"

"No."

"*No?*" I didn't bother to mask my shock. "Did you just say that you *haven't* slept with Brandon?"

"Yeah."

"Wait, wait, wait—You mean to tell me that you guys have *never* been together? *Ever?*"

"Well, I mean ... he stayed at my house that week. We slept in the same bed together, but ... I'm still a virgin, if that's what you mean. I don't know ..." I could almost see his confusion on the other end of the line, it was so heavy in his voice. "He wanted to stop every time it was about to happen. I don't know what I did wrong."

I was floored. "That doesn't make any sense."

"What doesn't make sense?"

There was a moment of silence.

"Is something wrong?"

"No ... no—it's nothing."

I tried putting the puzzle pieces together; it was a strange fit. I couldn't make sense of it. I now had two very different impressions to consider.

"Maybe he's just taking things slow because your relationship is new." I was fishing and I knew it. Brandon wasn't one to wait for sex—especially when his boyfriend was willing and eager.

"It's not *that* new," he said.

I couldn't exactly argue that.

Something was amiss in the world of Brandon. I didn't play by the same rules as Brandon did, but I had been around him enough to know how his rulebook read, and this new disclosure made me suspect a bad play.

———

After school the next day, I decided to hunt for Brandon. I didn't care if I was late to practice—screw it. Brandon had given me the distinct impression that he and Nick *had* slept together. Why did he lie?

I walked over to the sophomore court, where I knew I'd likely find him. Sure enough, he was putting something away in his locker. The sun left golden highlights in his thick, honey-colored hair.

I walked up behind him and deliberately cleared my throat to request his attention. He turned to face me. The dark purple, cable-knit sweater he wore accentuated the brilliance of his amber eyes.

"You lied to me, Brandon. You *lied*. Why?"

He frowned. "What?"

"You and Nick—you said it happened. You said you slept with him. Why would you lie to me about that, Brandon?"

He went instantly cool and turned back to his locker.

He wasn't getting out of this that easily.

"Answer me."

"How did this subject come up?" he asked in an acid tone. "By you probing him, or his voluntary admission?"

"What does it matter? It did and I know."

He said in a low and neutral voice, "I never said we had sex. You drew that conclusion on your own."

I considered that. "But you made it seem like you did—you didn't correct me."

"I didn't realize it was that important to you."

"*Of course* it's important."

"Why?"

"Just because … it is."

He slammed the locker shut and leaned back against it.

"'Just because' is not a reason, Kris."

"I don't know why it matters to me—but it does."

He studied me, his gaze intense. "So, when he told you we hadn't slept together, how did you feel? Relieved … happy … shocked … disappointed—*anything?*"

He had been dishonest, whether by omission or otherwise. That hurt. Brandon and I didn't have secrets from one another—or so I'd thought. "I—I don't know," I said.

"*Now* who's lying?"

"Brandon, just tell me why it didn't happen."

He looked at me again. "He was still dating Aeleise."

I shook my head. "Try again. We both know you never gave a damn about his relationship with Aeleise."

"No good?" He frowned, quick and thoughtful, and then replaced it with a dry, bored expression. "How about, he was drunk."

I hadn't thought of that. We *had* been drinking.

"I wasn't about to take advantage of him. We didn't do anything that night that we hadn't already done. Even I have rules, Krista."

"That doesn't explain the rest of the time," I said. "You had a million opportunities to be with him, and nothing happened? He couldn't have been drunk the entire time."

"I don't want to discuss this, Kris."

"Well, I *do.*"

"What did or didn't happen between Nick and me is between us."

"So that's how it is."

"Would you have me tell him everything that's happened between us? Shall I make him privy to the details?"

I didn't answer him.

"I didn't think so."

"I wasn't asking for details, Brandon. I just don't understand."

He sounded irritated. "Then maybe you're not supposed to."

"He told me that *you* stopped him."

"I'm allowed to say no, too."

"I'm sorry; I know you are. It's just...suddenly you're so secretive."

"I have my reasons."

"You're just not going to share them."

"Maybe you're asking the wrong question. Maybe the question should be, why does it matter to *you* whom *I'm* sleeping with? Hit me up again when you have your answer."

"I hate it when you get like this."

"Then just let it go. It'll make things easier if you do."

"Easier? For *who?*"

"I don't know. Just shine it, Kris. I gotta go."

38

My mother called Tuesday evening to say she would be returning next month. The three of us were relieved. There had been enough adventure.

Marc pulled me aside after dinner.

"Come on; I want to show you something," he said, and I followed him into his bedroom and took a seat on his bed.

He appeared nervous and excited at once. "Remember when I told you about my plans for Kaelie?"

I nodded.

"Well, I've given it a lot of thought, and ... I'm going to do it. I'm going to ask her to marry me."

"When ... do you plan to ask her?" I said, feeling my throat constrict.

He smiled at the question. "On New Year's Eve. What do you think?"

"Does she have any idea the question's coming?"

He shook his head. "No. I wanted to get your input on something first."

My brows rose. "Mine?"

"Yeah." He fumbled in his jacket pocket and pulled out a baby blue Tiffany's box. Inside it was another box, this one black velvet. He handed it to me. "Open it. It's the ring I got her. I want your opinion; do you think she'll like it?"

I opened the box and let out a gasp. "*My God*, Marc!"

There, boldly perched like a bird upon a band of white gold, was a single, gleaming diamond.

"You like it?" he asked when he saw my reaction.

"It must have cost a fortune!"

"About as much as Brandon's BMW. I was looking at those, too."

My sight shifted to Marc. Brandon drove a $40,000 car. Marc was giving Kaelie a gem that expensive ... to wear on her *finger?* I hoped he knew what he was doing.

I looked back down at the diamond; it shimmered brilliantly, bouncing rainbows in the light. I couldn't think of a thing to say other than, "I'm sure she'll be speechless."

He grinned. "I may not be Brandon when it comes to fashion, but I guess I can pick out a ring all right," he said proudly.

My eyes widened in agreement. I carefully closed the box and handed it back to him. "Yeah, I'd say so." As a joke, I asked him if he couldn't have found anything bigger.

"Well, now that you've seen it and given your approval, I guess it's safe to ask her."

I was surprised when I actually detected a hint of worry in his voice. I knew it was tradition to ask, but would he have spent that kind of money on a ring while having doubts? "Are you worried about her answer?"

"She could always say no, but I have a fifty-fifty chance, right?"

I studied his face and saw genuine nervousness despite his casual words. *God,* I prayed, *please make her say yes. Please let her love my brother as much as he loves her.* I couldn't stand the thought of Marc's dreams crushed.

She's the one, I thought. And for once, I wasn't jealous. Seeing the depth of my brother's happiness, I could finally accept his decision with a smile of my own.

"If you know her at all, Marc, you know she'll say yes."

39

Brandon and I had decided to exchange Christmas gifts early, at the start of winter recess. Actually, Brandon had made the request. He said he had his reasons. Christmas was in five days.

We entered his room and he walked over to feed the trio of looming Morays cruising the tank. I noticed a fishbowl sitting on his stereo cabinet.

The fishbowl?

A single fish fluttered through water. As I peered inside. The maroon inhabitant swam fervently, darting in response to my proximity.

"You have a new addition. Is this the infamous fishbowl that was once beneath your bed?"

"The same."

"And its earlier contents?"

"I think I proved my point."

I nodded, surprised but pleased.

"Well," I said, smiling at the fish, "I like your new roommate."

"I was hoping you would. He's yours. I wanted you to have him."

I wasn't sure what to say, but my smile widened.

"Marc already said it was okay."

I looked at him.

"If you want him ..."

I nodded vigorously, impressed that he'd taken the initiative to ask Marc's permission.

The thought of my brother reminded me I wanted to share his latest news. "He plans to marry Kaelie."

"Be happy for him, Kris. Marc's a great guy. He deserves to be happy."

"I know, it's just hard. Everything is changing so fast."

"It's changing for the better—you'll see."

I sighed. I hoped I'd come to share his view. My attention returned to the fish.

"You gonna name him?" he asked.

I thought for a moment as I stared at the fish, watching it come up to the glass, its fins waving to me in rhythm before it swam away and then returned to water dance once more. I grinned. "I think I'll call him Flirt."

Brandon chuckled. "He is spirited. I like it." He looked at the fish. "Well, Flirt, I'm sure you'll love living with Krista. But you aren't the only reason that we're here." He looked up at me. "I have something else for you," he said, and walked over to his desk, withdrawing from it a small drawstring bag. He handed it to me. "I didn't want to give it to you in front of everyone."

"Do I open it now?"

"Go ahead."

His eyes were warm. "I hope you like it." I loosened the drawstring and carefully turned the bag over in my hand. A ring fell out. It was set with four stones.

"It's our birthstones—yours, mine, Carrie's, and Ryan's. I gave one to Carrie, too. After all, we are the Fierce Foursome." He smiled.

I grinned. "A fitting reminder of our friendship. Thank you, Brandon." I gave him a hug, and part of me wanted to hold on forever.

The scent of fresh pine greeted us the moment we entered my house. The tree in the living room had undergone its first transformation; it was newly dressed in lights. A single ornament hung from the tree. Curious, I went over to inspect it. It was Josh's homemade decoration from grade school.

"Where is our lovely brother, anyway?" I asked Marc, who was on hands and knees, weeding through countless strings of Christmas lights.

"He took off with Meagan to help out at her house."

Even though Josh was a monumental pain, I was still disappointed that he'd ditched out on our tradition—on us. "He'd never get away with this if mom were here," I said.

"And you wouldn't get away with a few things that come to mind either." He looked at Brandon as he tested a string of outdoor lights. A kaleidoscope of colors came to life, shining in a bright row. "Brandon, you're welcome to join us, if you'd like."

"I'll help; just point me in the right direction."

"All that's left to do is hanging the ornaments." Marc nodded to a huge plastic storage box. "They're in there."

Brandon stared at the box. "Gee, have enough ornaments? You think these are all going to fit?"

Marc laughed. "We *make* them fit."

The corner of Brandon's mouth twitched in amusement. "You're the boss."

We began unwrapping ornaments from their tissue paper one at a time.

"Well, I'm going outside and see if I can't make these things work," Marc said, hauling an armload of lights up with him as he rose to his feet.

"Happy hanging," I said.

Brandon and I started decorating the tree. I hung a delicate snowflake on the tip of one branch, and then reached for another decoration. Brandon touched an ornament, paused over it. I came up beside him to see what he was looking at.

I smiled. "That was Josh in the first grade. He was a cutie, wasn't he?" I shook my head. "What happened?"

Brandon ran his finger over the worn green yarn and construction paper surrounding the picture.

I looked at him curiously. "What are you thinking about?"

"I was just remembering ... I made something like this once, for my mother. I haven't seen it since." His voice trailed off and he turned to me with a manufactured smile. "What's next—candy canes? Tinsel?"

"Icicles," I said.

We carefully hung the crystal tears on branches. "Are you going to Aeleise's party?" I asked as I reached for another glistening shard.

"You plan on going, I assume."

"I'd like to. You should come with me."

He shrugged. "I suppose it wouldn't kill me, though the prospect of seeing Daemon doesn't exactly bring Christmas cheer." He arched a branch down so he could dress it. "It'll be strange, having Carrie gone over the holidays."

"What do you think of her decision to meet her dad? Do you think he'll actually show this time?"

"If he doesn't, he's even more of a bastard than I imagined. The last thing she needs is another disappointment."

"Ever since she told me, I've been praying about it," I said quietly.

He sighed. "For once, I'd like to believe in prayer. You pray, I'll keep my fingers crossed."

"So how do you spend Christmas? With your mom or with your dad?"

"I'm spending Christmas Eve with my dad and his girlfriend. Christmas morning I'll be with my mom, but it's quick; I'm usually the first one in the water on Christmas day. My present to myself."

"Speaking of presents, I still haven't given you yours yet," I said. "Come with me."

Brandon hung the last icicle, and then followed me into my bedroom. I opened my closet and withdrew his gift. "I couldn't think of anything to get the 'boy who has everything,'" I said as I handed it to him. "Not from a store, anyway."

"Well, it's bigger than a breadbox. Shall I guess?"

"It'll be too easy. Just open it."

He knelt on the floor, the rectangular package before him. "It would be impolite of me to hope..." he began with a grin. He tore away the paper surrounding the frame. He looked at the completed drawing. "But I'm glad I did." His smile was broad. "I wanted this so much."

"I know."

He looked at all the others I'd done. "Thank you for finishing them, Kris. It... really means a lot to me. They came out beautifully."

"As long as you think so," I said. "But it doesn't compare to the real thing."

He rose to give me a hug.

⸺

Brandon decided to attend Aeleise's party after all. I was pleased; I had a feeling that this would be the closest thing to true holiday festivity that he'd experience. When we arrived, there were already an impressive number of guests at the house. Aeleise greeted us at the door.

She quickly recovered her expression, after the initial shock of seeing Brandon. It was an awkward moment, but Aeleise conducted herself graciously. "Krista...Brandon. I'm so glad the two of you could make it. Please, come in." She opened the door wider.

"Thank you for the invitation, Aeleise," Brandon said as we stepped inside.

"Of course. Merry Christmas." It had to take effort for her to hug him as warmly as she did.

We spotted Chloe and Joy talking to Sean and his friend over by the living room. Aeleise directed us toward them. "Make yourself at home. Everyone's wandering about. I'll catch up with you soon."

Brandon and I surveyed the crowd. Daemon was chatting it up with an acquaintance I had never seen before. I had never met many of Daemon's friends, and there seemed to be quite a few in attendance. It never occurred to me that Daemon's social life was broader than the confines of the church. A few of them looked like loners, as if unaccustomed to social events. Some of them were obviously couples, while a few others looked as if they were hoping to find that special Christmas sweetheart. A quiet girl with long burgundy hair eyed Daemon frequently. He seemed oblivious to it. I was glad.

"Would you like to say hello to him? Or is staring your pleasure?"

"Not now; he's talking to someone. I'll say hi later." I turned away from Daemon.

"Well, I'll be damned. Look who just arrived," Brandon said. I followed his gaze to the front door.

There stood Carrie and Ryan.

Brandon and I hadn't expected either of them to attend Aeleise's party, so when they entered hand-in-hand through the foyer, the surprise flooded me with warmth. There seemed to be a deeper bond between them now, a spark of affection that hadn't been there at Homecoming, obvious in the subtle way their arms brushed against each other, and their intimate glances. I couldn't remember the last time I'd seen Carrie look so comfortable, with herself and her surroundings. Even Ryan seemed to display a quiet self-assurance. They were content, happy — with themselves and with each other. I couldn't have been more pleased for either of them.

Carrie smiled when she saw Brandon and me across the room. She and Ryan approached. I hugged her tightly. "I thought you had plans to meet your dad," I said.

"I did. But Ryan invited me to be his date for Christmas and I knew he wouldn't leave me hanging."

I turned to Ryan. "Thank you."

He grinned. "It wasn't exactly a sacrifice."

Brandon and Carrie hugged. When she released him, I noticed her new jewelry and smiled. "Like your ring," I said.

"Yeah — Brandon's all right."

"So, am I looking at the latest couple?" Brandon asked them with a smile of his own.

"If I'm lucky," Ryan said, "but I'm not calling the shots."

Carrie giggled and squeezed Ryan affectionately.

"Care to join us on the dance floor?" Brandon asked.

"Sure," Carrie said.

"I'm forewarning you, I have two left feet," Ryan said.

Carrie grinned, and pulled him toward the floor. "I promise not to notice."

The four of us joined the small group of people dancing to the light classical holiday tunes. I looked over Brandon's shoulder as we danced. Daemon now sat alone near the punch bowl. We made eye contact and he smiled at me. I wondered what he was thinking. At the end of the song, Brandon and I headed toward the table for drinks.

Daemon handed me a freshly poured glass of punch.

"Daemon, you know Brandon," I said, presenting him without hesitation.

I felt the energy exchange between them.

Daemon extended his hand. "I believe we met once before."

They locked eyes, and for a moment, I feared Brandon would refuse him; I was relieved when he accepted the gesture. Their unexpressed animosity was covered with a handshake.

"You're no stranger to me," Brandon said.

It was clear Brandon would be civil, but nothing more. I prayed the tension between them would break. It seemed their handshake stretched on forever, and I was eager for it to end. It did, with Brandon looking away first. I suppose there are firsts for everything.

I couldn't contain my excitement when they played one of my favorite slow songs.

Daemon escorted me onto the floor and we glided slowly to the music. Brandon stood patiently against the wall, drinking from his glass of punch.

Daemon pulled me closer. "He's in love with you, Krista."

"Brandon?"

"Among others."

I looked over at Brandon and he quickly looked away. He appeared uncharacteristically humble to me, as he faked concern over the fit of his watch.

"He's unhappy that we're dancing together," he said. Then Daemon pulled back to look at me. "Kris, will you come upstairs with me for a minute? There's something that I want to give you."

I nodded, and he took my hand and led me off the floor in midsong. When I looked back, I made eye contact with Brandon, who was watching us leave hand in hand to go upstairs. I tried to ignore his hurt and angry expression.

Once inside his room, Daemon closed the door. He walked over to the nightstand. I was almost worried.

I waited anxiously by the bed as he returned with a scarlet velvet box tied with a matching satin ribbon. He handed it to me with a subdued smile. "Merry Christmas." He sat on the edge of the bed.

I tugged at the ribbon that held the box together, and let it fall to the bed. I lifted the lid to reveal a beautiful necklace—a cross. Its ten diamonds sparkled and glittered brilliantly against the light.

"Shit!" I gasped. It just slipped out. "Daemon, I—" Overwhelmed, I couldn't think of a thing to say.

He smiled. "You like it."

"I *love* it!"

"Good."

I stared at it, then at him, awestruck by both.

"Do you want to put it on?"

"Yes." It was all I could say.

He motioned me closer to him. I handed him the box and he carefully withdrew the necklace. I watched it catch the light as Daemon unfastened the clasp.

"Lift your hair," he said. I did, and he draped it gently around my neck. It came to rest just above my breasts. I touched it gingerly, and then turned to face him.

He looked at me, smiling. "It looks beautiful on you."

I hugged him like a little girl. "Thank you, Daemon."

He hesitated, then leaned toward me, his hand resting gently on my cheek. Lips, soft and warm, kissed me. An electrifying sensation began at my toes and traveled throughout my body. The kiss was close-lipped, but not quite innocent. He pulled back, leaving me breathless. I opened my eyes after a moment.

He blushed through an embarrassed smile. We clasped hands and I led the way downstairs.

When I lifted my eyes, Brandon stood waiting at the bottom of the stairs. I hesitated when I saw the look in his eyes. Daemon squeezed my hand and I looked back. He gave me a small smile and let go of my hand. I held his glance, hating that it all seemed so final. He slid his hands in his pockets and leaned against the wall, waiting for me to continue my descent; it was done. I went to Brandon, who held out his hand to me, and we rejoined the party.

Daemon never came back down. I wondered how long he stood leaning against that wall.

Brandon steered me out the door toward the gardens. We walked past the pool and out toward the center of the grounds, where a gazebo sat surrounded by a trellised garden. A thin sheet of clouds hung like a glaze over the sky, dimming the stars glittering behind it and shrouding the moon's silver glow so there was barely enough light to guide us.

Brandon ascended the first of four steps that led to the gazebo platform and handed me up, then joined me. We stood under the white sculptured dome, illuminated by pale lighting like strings of stars wound around the delicate white frame.

He sat on the gazebo's railing, pulling me with him. I stood facing him. The night was silent, and so were we. He'd been acting strange all night, and I wondered why we were out here.

"I wanted to be alone with you," he said. "I've wanted to leave that house from the moment we arrived."

"Has it been that bad?"

"Seeing you disappear up those stairs with Daemon..."

I bit my lip. "It was rude of me to leave. I'm sorry."

He shook his head. "No apologies—not tonight." His eyes fell to the diamond-studded pendant around my neck. "I see Daemon expressed his feelings after all."

My fingers found the cross, covering it almost guiltily. "He didn't say anything."

He shook his head with a disdainful sniff and looked away. "As if that doesn't say it all."

He remained quiet, looking at the floorboards, thinking. I took a step closer until I stood between his knees. His hair had fallen forward; I brushed it back, letting my fingers run through his hair, and then I found myself lightly touching his face.

He looked up at me. There were things I hadn't told him, things I wanted to tell him but had been holding back. I suppose fear had kept me silent. I suddenly wanted to say it aloud, even if I never said it again. I wanted once to speak the truth I'd kept to myself out of reason, common sense, and self-protection.

When I tried to speak, my voice shook. "I've wan—"

He held his finger to my lips, forbidding me to say more.

"I know what you're about to say. Please don't use those words unless they're true. I won't know what to do with them."

"How do you know what I'm going to say?"

"You're smarter than that, Kris. You don't need to ask how."

"I can't tell you that I love you?" I said, ignoring his request.

His eyes found the floorboards again, and then he looked up at me. "I already know that you do, and you should know that I love you as well—but there's a difference between that and being in love, isn't there? Besides, you aren't ready to do anything about it."

Since when did Brandon care about love? Since when did he believe in it?

He looked into the distance, not seeing the gardens in front of him. "You love Daemon. I don't doubt that you do."

I remained quiet, waiting to see where he was going with this.

"I'm not interested in winning your love by default, Kris. I have no desire to be your consolation prize."

"Who said anything about default?"

"Until you can clearly recognize the difference between what you feel for Daemon and what you share with me, that's what I'd call it. Yet if I were to tell you how I feel about you, those wouldn't be the words I'd choose."

"Then tell me what you have to say."

He made no move to speak. I slowly sat on the railing beside him.

"Brandon, please... do tell me how you feel."

He seemed frustrated. "Daemon has made you blind to all that's been around you the entire time. And you've been searching so hard." He met my eyes again. "Maybe you aren't looking in the right places."

"Meaning?"

"I'm in love with you, Krista."

I was unprepared to hear those words coming from his lips. Brandon simply didn't say things like that.

"I don't believe you." In my shock, it was easy to say.

"No? Well, it's the truth. You tell me—how do I say it so that you'll believe me?"

It was one thing for me to realize my true feelings for him, but entirely another to hear that possibility reciprocated. My mind retreated, unbelieving. "I don't know." I shook my head. "You couldn't possibly be."

He tried again, more emphatically. "Krista, *I'm in love with you.*"

Even with the change in inflection, I still would not allow myself to believe him. "That's not it," I told him.

"Okay then, how about you deliver the line and I'll mimic it?"

"I don't think so."

"I'm trying to be serious here."

"I'm unconvinced."

"I can lie to you if you want me to, but I'd rather tell you the truth. Do you want me to say that I'm cool with it? 'Cause I'm not."

"Then why tell me?"

"Because you need to hear it. I understand that you can't risk accepting that my words are honest, but Kris, whether you're ready to admit it or not, I think we both know how we feel about each other. Maybe you're afraid to hope for that."

I didn't comment on that because I feared it was true. Although Ryan had tipped me off about Brandon's possible change of heart, I'd been hesitant to believe him. Now that Brandon had verbalized it, I recognized just how hard I had been working to ignore what I secretly hoped for.

"What brought you to this conclusion all of a sudden?" I asked.

"All of a sudden? It's never been all of a sudden, Kris."

I stared at him.

"Kris, you gave me your virginity. Curious or not, don't think I don't know how that's going to affect you; damn—it affected me. I could see how much it hurt you when you learned I was spending all my time with Nick. Can you honestly tell me you weren't jealous of him, of what he and I might have been doing when we were alone? Whether you try to conceal them or not, you wear your emotions on your sleeve. I didn't have to be a member of Mensa to figure out how you felt."

"You've slept with plenty of people, Brandon, and love never reared its head on any of those occasions, so why should I believe I'm any different?"

"Kris, I told you my most *appalling* secret. Drunk or not, I knew what I was doing. I trust you that much. Unfortunate circumstances or not, incest isn't something easy to look past ... but I *needed* you to know — everything, even the worst. Even though I was scared you might walk away."

He shifted against the railing as he looked again at the floorboards. "You may not understand where I'm coming from, but it mattered to me in ways you can't fathom. You could've rejected me — my own *father* did at the truth; to this day, he'll barely look me in the eye. I needed to see if you could still accept me after knowing all that had happened." He looked at me then. "Yet, you're still here; you trusted me enough to share in something that I've never shared with anyone. For once, I wasn't just going through the motions, Kris. I cared — and in many ways, I consider that my first time, too. Don't you think I have feelings for you — feelings about that night? You never even asked me how I felt, other than to ask if I regretted it."

I looked across the lawn and the manicured gardens from our perch on the railing beneath the gazebo. The hazy cloud cover had lifted; the night sky now offered us a wealth of twinkling jewels to see by and, uncovered, the moon became one huge, glowing pearl. Flowers slept peacefully all about us; jasmine perfumed the air with its sweet fragrance.

I looked at the house and realized for the first time that we were in direct view of Daemon's bedroom. I looked up at the faint amber glow in his window and saw his silhouette standing there.

Brandon followed the direction of my gaze. In one swift movement, the curtains fell closed and the light went out.

I turned to Brandon, saw the disappointment in his eyes. I didn't know what I was supposed to do, what I was supposed to say. "What is it that you want from me? I guess that's what I don't understand."

I had never seen Brandon like this before, with the strain of his emotions undisguised on his face.

"Kris, I never told you this, but the night we were together ... that was the only time I remember ever making a choice to have sex. It wasn't something forced on me; I wasn't doing it to try to fit in; it didn't happen just because I was out of my head on drugs. Hell—I've never even called a single person from my number stash. Yeah—when I was using, my sex life was crazy. Now I'm sober, but people just assume I'm the same." He looked at me again. "But *you* gave me a choice; you asked me because you trusted me, and you have no idea how much that means to me. Even though I was scared, I wanted to, Kris. I wanted to be with you."

I was moved, and still surprised. "I didn't realize, Brandon."

"I didn't want you to. I'll be the first to admit I tried to destroy what we have in every way possible, but it just didn't work."

"Why would you try to destroy our closeness?"

"Because I'm scared as hell, Kris! I'm not playing one of my notorious games with you. For once, something is beyond my control. You may not want to come to terms with it, but I can't ignore it. I've tried, and each time I do, the fact forces itself on me stronger than before. I'm so jealous of Daemon it makes me sick. I see the way you look at him. I'd give anything to have you look at me that way."

"But you had Nick," I was quick to remind him.

"And why do you think I was so upset to find you knew that we hadn't slept together?"

"I've been asking myself that same question for a while now."

"You know what, Kris? Ryan said some fucked up things that night when we were all together, but he hit the nail on the head with one thing, and at the time I wasn't ready to hear it. It made me realize something, though. Maybe it's not about boy or girl. I'm beginning to think it's about the person, and if that means that I'm bisexual, then I'm bisexual. I would never lie to you and deny I'm attracted to guys—whether it's Nick or someone else. But it takes a lot more than good looks to hold my interest, and that's where my attraction to him pales, next to my feelings for you—by a landslide."

He hesitated, as if he were having difficulty finding the correct words. "I knew Carrie painted a colorful picture of my sex life; I didn't want you to think that anything had changed. I wanted you to believe that I'd been with Nick, the way I'd been with all the rest. But now I have to be straight about it with you so you'll believe me. I'm not sleeping with Nick because I'm in love with *you.*"

This was all so extreme, so unexpected.

"Kris, please," he begged. "*I love you*—I'm *in* love with you. I can't say it any clearer. *Please,* believe me."

"Brandon—" I began to protest, but as soon as I did, he closed the distance between us.

"If you don't want me to kiss you, you'd better back away now," he said.

Stunned, I stood there, not wanting to move, because although this was all a whirlwind in my mind, I knew one thing—I *wanted* his kiss. And before I had time to blink, he had me in his arms, and was kissing me as I had never been kissed before.

1-23-14